THE

Empress

THE

Empress

A Novel

LAURA MARTÍNEZ-BELLI

Translated from the Spanish by Simon Bruni

AMAZON **CROSSING**

Text copyright © 2017 by Laura Martínez-Belli
Translation copyright © 2020 by Simon Bruni
All rights reserved.

Previously published as *Carlota* by Editorial Planeta Mexicana, S.A. de C.V. in Mexico in 2017. Translated from Spanish by Simon Bruni. First published in English by Amazon Crossing in 2020.

Published by Amazon Crossing, Seattle

www.apub.com

Amazon, the Amazon logo, and Amazon Crossing are trademarks of Amazon.com, Inc., or its affiliates.

ISBN-13: 9781542004800
ISBN-10: 1542004802

Cover design by Faceout Studio, Tim Green

Printed in the United States of America

For the countries of my life.
And for those who, when they crossed the sea,
changed not only the sky they were under
but also their spirit.

Cast of Characters

Charlotte / Carlota—Belgian princess who is married to Maximilian of Habsburg; later becomes Carlota, empress of Mexico.

Maximilian—Austrian archduke Ferdinand Maximilian Joseph of Habsburg; later becomes Maximilian, emperor of Mexico.

Charles-René de Bombelles—Maximilian's best friend.

Sebastian Schertzenlechner—Maximilian's valet and another close friend.

Auguste Goffinet—Lawyer of Leopold II. He has a twin brother, also a lawyer.

Manuelita del Barrio—Carlota's lady of honor in Mexico, a conservative, religious woman.

Mathilde Döblinger—Carlota's lady of honor.

Constanza Murrieta—Eldest daughter of a prominent Conservative Mexican family.

Clotilde Murrieta—Constanza's sister; a Conservative.

Refugio de Murrieta—Constanza's mother; a Liberal.

Don Vicente Murrieta—Constanza's father, a leading Conservative; one of the people who orchestrate the Mexican Empire and invite a European prince to take the crown.

Salvador Murrieta—Constanza's brother; a Liberal sympathizer.

Agustín Murrieta—Constanza's brother, destined for priesthood.

Joaquín Murrieta—Constanza's eldest brother, the image of his father, conservative, traditional, and loyal to his father's ideals.

Modesto García—Adopted ward of Juárez's predecessor, Ignacio Comonfort (president of Mexico in 1855, after Santa Anna was overthrown).

Benito Juárez—President of Mexico, leader of the resistance against the empire.

Philippe Petit—Belgian carpenter who becomes a soldier.

Lieutenant Colonel Baron Alfred van der Smissen—Commander of the Belgian army in Mexico.

Leopold I—Carlota's beloved father.

Leopold II—King of the Belgians, Carlota's eldest brother.

Count Philippe—Carlota's other brother.

María Ana Leguizamo / Concepción Sedano—An indigenous Mexican woman.

Marie Henriette—Leopold II's wife, queen of Belgium; Carlota's sister-in-law.

Marie Moreau—Carlota's lady-in-waiting in Laeken.

Victor Hugo—Famous French writer, author of *Les Misérables*, about the French Revolution. Sympathetic to the Republicans / Liberales.

Antonio López de Santa Anna—President of Mexico, Santa Anna was an enigmatic, patriotic, and controversial figure who had great power in Mexico during a turbulent forty-year career. He led as a general at crucial points and served twelve nonconsecutive presidential terms over twenty-two years. He was perceived as a hero by his troops, as he sought glory for himself and his army and independence for Mexico.

Places

Miramare—A beautiful castle on the Gulf of Trieste in northeastern Italy. It was built in 1860 for Austrian archduke Ferdinand Maximilian Joseph and his wife, Charlotte of Belgium, later Emperor Maximilian and Empress Carlota of Mexico.

Chapultepec Castle—Located on top of Chapultepec Hill, the name comes from the Nahuatl word *chapoltepēc*, meaning "at the grasshopper's hill." The castle is known for its magnificent views, said to be unsurpassed in beauty anywhere in the world. It became the official residence of Emperor Maximilian and his consort Empress Carlota during the Second Mexican Empire (1864–1867).

Cuernavaca—The capital and largest city of the state of Morelos in Mexico. The city is approximately a ninety-minute drive south of Mexico City and has long been a favorite escape for Mexico City residents and foreign visitors because of its warm, stable climate and abundant vegetation.

Querétaro, Las Campanas Hill—The hill on which the emperor, who had been trapped in the besieged city of Querétaro for several months, surrendered to General Mariano Escobedo in May of 1867, officially ending the Second Mexican Empire.

Tervuren—A municipality in the province of Flemish Brabant, in Flanders, Belgium. One of the wealthiest municipalities, it is linked to Brussels by a large processional avenue built by King Leopold II for the Universal Exhibition of 1897.

Laeken—The Royal Castle of Laeken, official home of the Belgian royal family, is situated here. The castle was built in 1784 by Charles de Wailly. It has been the royal residence since the accession to the throne of King Leopold I in 1831.

Bouchout Castle—A castle in the Flemish town of Meise, Belgium. After Maximilian's death, Charlotte led a secluded life at Bouchout Castle until her death in 1927. Since 1939, the Bouchout Domain was incorporated into the National Botanical Garden of Belgium, and since being renovated in 1989 it has been used as a meeting and exhibition hall.

Lokrum—A small island in the Adriatic Sea off the coast of Dubrovnik, Croatia, where the archduke Ferdinand Maximilian Joseph of Habsburg built a house and magnificent gardens.

In 1855, a group of Mexican liberals led by Benito Juárez and Ignacio Comonfort overthrew Conservative president Antonio López de Santa Anna. With Comonfort as the new president, the Mexican "Liberales" enacted a new constitution that brought in massive reforms for the common folk. In theory, it represented the will of all the people—but the Conservative Party strongly opposed the reforms, which chipped away at some of the institutionalized privilege associated with the Church. Mexican society became instantly and viciously polarized.

Then, in July of 1861, Benito Juárez's government declared a debt moratorium, alarming Mexico's international creditors—Spain, Britain, and France—who swiftly mobilized a military expedition to demand the fulfillment of its obligations. The unpaid debt totaled eighty-two million pesos: seventy were owed to Britain, nine to Spain, and three to France. An expedition of almost ten thousand soldiers disembarked in Veracruz in December of that same year. Juárez's government promised to pay the debt, and the Convention of La Soledad was signed. The Spanish and English troops withdrew immediately, but the French commandants rejected the agreement and remained in Veracruz.

Mexico was on the verge of celebrating its fortieth anniversary as a republic, and its story so far was disastrous: three federal and two centralist regimes; three constitutions; 240 coup attempts, rebellions, and uprisings that in turn led to sixty changes of presidency; half the national territory lost;

the Church's assets disposed of; schools, universities, hospitals, and shelters gone; and now a new intervention of foreign forces.

In this turbulent time in the nation's history, the Conservatives—heirs to what was once the Mexican aristocracy—allowed themselves the luxury of imagining. They imagined a Mexico with a European Catholic prince who would embody the grandeur and sovereignty of an opulent and majestic people. They imagined the Second Empire . . .

Beginning

His hands. Those hands, accustomed to brandishing a sword, glide over her back. Her whole body is a bristling cat. She trembles. And yet she knows this place is the only place in the world. For now, that's all he does: he brushes his fingers against her, he unfastens the buttons down her back. No more and no less. But she anticipates the surge from the wave that approaches. He touches her, slowly, as if afraid his hands might break her. But he knows what he's doing. He has done it many times before, though with less smooth flesh. Less noble. Her breathing, hurried. Her energy, pulsing in places unknown before now. She moistens. She feels the urge to open her legs but she doesn't. She controls herself with supernatural force. She is afraid. But she wants it. She wants to feel. At last. She feels at last. Her skin speaks to her, it begs her to keep feeling. To let the hands keep going, let them search. Let them find her. She tilts her head back, and then he kisses her. He kisses her neck. She tastes not of nobility, but of woman. With one hand he holds the small of her back, and with the other he strokes her collarbone. His mouth. That mouth, which has spoken to her so many times in the closeness of silence, begins to explore her. Under her ears. The center of her neck. And she can't hold back any longer and searches for his lips. He responds. She feels a strong, firm tongue against hers. She moves urgently and then he says, "Slowly, relax, let me." Embarrassed, she stops. But he looks at her. He looks at her with those eyes that tell her there is no other moment, there is no present other than the one they are experiencing, loving each other, touching each other, feeling each other. They are two people for the first time. With no names or titles. A man and a woman. Nothing more. Then she opens her lips and lets him in. She needs to prolong the moment. She lets him discover her. She feels that she is going to explode. But no, not yet. She cannot even remotely imagine what is still to come. He lays her down. He keeps kissing her as he undresses her. She trembles and covers her face with her hands. She doesn't want to see. She does not want to. All she wants is to feel those hands, that mouth exploring her. She fears the nudity. She doesn't want to see him. But then he positions himself over her. He whispers in her ear. He looks into her eyes as he penetrates her. She receives him, juicy as a ripe mango. She wants to let out a moan but contains herself. The part of her that was missing is now complete, she feels. He moves. And she feels that she wants to move to his rhythm, to rock with him. She closes her eyes and a prayer slips out. But then he covers her mouth. "Quiet," he orders her. And he looks at her. She obeys. "Kiss me," she pleads. And he kisses her while they rock together, disintegrating with pleasure.

Part One

1

Not once in the last two years had the idea of fleeing her own empire crossed her mind. Two years and two months in Mexico. That was all it had been. A massive and naïve adventure. An imperial dream in foreign lands. Two years of borrowed and illusory glory. Seven hundred and ninety days, each with its night. A very short period of time, and yet too long. Enough time to believe that, if she stretched enough, she could touch the stars with her fingertips. And now here she was, escaping in a coach under torrential rain back to the Europe that had spat in their faces. She knew it. She knew it with the sadness of someone irreversibly giving up her life's work. She had to return.

Carlota looked out the window. Through the drops of water blurring everything, she could just make out a vast landscape of trees being battered by the angry wind with biblical force. Sorrow twisted her eyebrows and mouth. A fitting goodbye. She was no different than those trees being beaten by destiny. The landscape filled her with grief, and with a pull she closed the green velvet curtain embroidered with the imperial eagle. Had she not been an empress, had she been just a simple Mexican, she would have cried. From inside the coach, they could hear the horses' frightened whinnies and the thundering sky. They had warned her. The roads were dangerous at that time of year; nobody in their right mind would travel to the port of Veracruz through the mist of the Acultzingo peaks in the season of rains and yellow fever. But as soon as she learned her emissaries had failed and Napoleon III's refusal to withdraw his troops remained firm, Carlota—who'd always been strong and foolish in equal measure—gave orders to leave immediately so she could intervene in person. To her great regret, she knew that waiting for the rains to abate was one luxury she could not afford. She could not. Everything was crumbling before her eyes. The empire. Maximilian. Herself. Everything. She had to stop it. It wouldn't be the first time that Napoleon III—*Louis*, as those close to him knew him—had listened to her, however hard it would be to go down on her knees and beg.

The badly pocked road jostled her like a marble in a shoebox. In an attempt to still herself, she shifted, and, after a moment's hesitation, she clung to herself, seeking refuge. She was tempted to stroke her belly, when suddenly the coach tipped onto two wheels as it swerved to avoid an enormous stone, forcing her to clutch one of the doors. Her lady-in-waiting, Manuelita del Barrio, went white, terrified they would overturn, and stifled a scream that became almost embarrassed under the severe gaze of the empress, whose emphatic silence struck her with the same force as the storm. Carlota was accustomed to repressing fear with the determination of a martyr being burned over green firewood, and that wouldn't change now just because torrential rain was turning the ground to mud as they drove along the edge of a precipice. That was how her life had been for as long as she could remember: a life on the edge of the abyss. And controlling any sign of weakness was a skill that Carlota had perfected. In any case, worrying about the safety of the road was trivial compared to her ocean of preoccupations. Best leave that in the hands of God. Her God would not allow her to die tossed off a cliff. He wouldn't abandon them to their fate in a ravine. Her God would guide her to the gates of the Vatican to meet Pius IX and intercede on behalf of a barely nascent empire. The empire must not be lost. Maximilian had to hold on.

Abdication was tantamount to a death sentence. She had seen it in her grandfather, who upon abdicating the French throne had only brought dishonor and discredit to the dynasty. Abdicating the Mexican throne would catapult them in the direction of Miramare, to looks of pity. Abdicating was not the act of a thirty-four-year-old prince, but of the elderly, infirm, lacking in spirit. There was no property more sacred in the world than sovereignty. One does not abandon a throne like a person fleeing a rally dispersed by the police. They did not have the right to abandon a nation that had called on them. Louis the Great had said it: "Kings must never surrender." Her thought exactly: "The emperor must never surrender." For while there was an emperor in Mexico, there would be an empire, even if it was just six square feet of land. They had arrived as champions of civilization, as regenerators and liberators, and they wouldn't leave with the excuse that there was nothing to liberate or to civilize, nothing to regenerate. She had put it all in writing to Maximilian. "One does not abdicate," she had told him. He had to wait for her. Yes. The dangers of the road to Veracruz were, without doubt, the least of her problems.

Her thoughts suddenly became blurred; everything began to spin around her, as if the carriage had lost its course and her God had abandoned her for a moment. In the distance, through scattered echoes, she heard her lady-in-waiting whisper to her. "Your Highness? Your Majesty? Are you all right?"

Carlota blinked a couple of times before feeling the floor under her feet again. She fixed her eyes on the woman, trying to recognize her.

She spoke again. "Do you need anything, my lady? You look terribly pale."

Eventually, Carlota responded. "No, no, I'm fine . . . a dizzy spell. That's all. I'll have some water."

Manuelita quickly offered her some. "Are you feeling faint, Your Majesty? From all this movement . . . Don't worry, Majesty, it will pass, it will pass."

She took a fan from among her skirts and began to flap it energetically at the empress.

It wouldn't be Carlota's first dizzy spell during the journey back. She would feel faint on many more occasions on the way, all of them attributed to the movement of the sea or land. But Carlota knew it was just a matter of time—nine months—before the reason for her fainting fits would be clear.

It didn't take that long. The rumors had begun to spread that the empress was pregnant long before she set sail for Europe. Under their breath, mindful they weren't being listened to, in the cantinas of the Gulf of Mexico, people sang, "*Adiós*, Carlota, the people rejoice to see you so plump!" in place of the well-known lyrics composed to sing her praises and see her off with the honors she deserved: "*Adiós*, Mamá Carlota, *adiós*, my tender love." But she either never heard it or she pretended that she hadn't. Because, when all was said and done, what was carrying a bastard in her womb compared to the responsibility of saving an empire?

2

July 1857, Belgium

Trying in vain to count along with her heartbeat, Carlota stood spell-bound in front of the mirror. It was the novelty. She had never seen herself so beautiful. Her parents had taught her to be austere, and she rarely dressed in colors other than gray. The sin of vanity, suppressed since childhood in favor of cultivating her intellect, erupted with fury. She couldn't suppress the pleasure she felt seeing herself like this— for the first and perhaps only time—as if her spirit were finally able to express itself in her aspect. She wore a full silk satin dress embroidered with silver and a long Ghent lace veil held in place by a diadem of orange blossom and diamonds. She smoothed down the billowing skirt with both hands, taking care not to crush the crinoline. What would Maximilian think when he saw her like this, a bride brimming with youth and beauty? How would he look? She felt her cheeks flush. She was just seventeen, as fresh as a blanket of green grass, and filled with hope for her life. However, first and foremost, Charlotte of Saxe-Coburg and Orléans, about to marry her prince, was in love.

She took a deep breath and fixed her eyes on the face in the mirror. The face of a girl about to become a woman. Her grandmother, Queen Maria Amalia of Naples and Sicily, had informed her of her marital duties. "You must not be afraid, my child," she had told her in a loving attempt to fill the void that her mother had left, a mother who had taught her, at the age of ten, what it meant to be an orphan all too early. "Do not be afraid. The consummation of marriage is a natural act, like eating or breathing." How far her sweet grandmother was from knowing her soul, she thought, for she felt no fear—far from it. The hours seemed to stretch out forever when she thought about the moment she would become one with her archduke. From the moment they met he'd struck her as gallant, cultured, and exceedingly attractive. She wanted to be with her Max, and thinking about it made her pulse race. She looked at herself one last time to see the woman ready to emerge from the mirror. She lifted her chin. Proud. She had a queen's bearing, and she could almost feel the weight of destiny gazing back at her. She shook her head, and, barely suppressing a smile, she set off to the Royal Palace of Brussels's Blue Room, where Maximilian of Habsburg, in the prime of his youth at twenty-five, wearing a rear admiral's uniform, was waiting nervously.

In her worst moments, Carlota had wished that she could have a wedding like that of Maximilian's sister-in-law, the empress Sissi, who'd married his brother Franz Joseph with great fanfare. But since they weren't firstborns, Maximilian and Carlota would have to make do with a quiet marriage in the palace. When the envy began to eat at her, she shook her head, trying to rid herself of the bad thoughts, and told herself that her life would be as happy or even happier than Sissi's, who, in her darkest thoughts, she detested.

None of the heirs to the royal households of Europe attended the wedding; however, her grandmother, who wouldn't have missed it for anything in the world, witnessed the union. Carlota was the apple of her eye, and she'd raised her with the same love with which she had cared for her own daughters. Despite her apparent severity, she couldn't suppress a tear of joy when she saw her beloved granddaughter walk in on her father's arm. On behalf of Queen Victoria of the United Kingdom, Carlota's cousin on her father's side, her consort Prince Albert was in attendance, and Maximilian's brother, the archduke Karl Ludwig, had traveled from Vienna to be present at the ceremony. Carlota advanced with care, aware that she was heading not just toward love, but glory. She was certain that Maximilian—and therefore she—was destined for great enterprises. The veil prevented her from seeing clearly; even so, she could make out her groom's unmistakable slender figure at the end of the hall. She was trying to look sidelong at the guests and greet them with a slight nod of her head, when suddenly, close to Maximilian in the background, two figures caught her attention: two young men, handsome and very serious, were watching her like lions. Carlota felt uncomfortable and for a moment lowered her gaze. She quickly looked up toward her father, who looked back affectionately and whispered, "Safe passage, flower of my heart."

The two men, she discovered later, were the count Charles de Bombelles and Maximilian's Hungarian valet, Sebastian Schertzenlechner. When she saw them, Carlota's stomach knotted, though she wasn't sure why.

When she reached Maximilian, he flashed a smile of amorous complicity that lingered for a few seconds before fading to absolute indifference. *He must be enraptured, like me,* Carlota thought. Because as soon as she saw him, the infatuation that had already overwhelmed her was only strengthened. Again, he seemed the most elegant man on the face of the earth, his naval officer's demeanor making her legs tremble. But however much she smiled at him, Maximilian, fixed in a cold, ceremonious posture, kept turning his eyes back to the priest. Carlota attributed it to the solemnity of the occasion. What nobleman would allow his passions to betray him in a ceremony as public as a wedding? Her Max was not that banal. There would be time for pleasantries when they were alone together. This was a public occasion, and her father had taught her that duty came before all else. A monarch—he'd told her since she was a child—must never show frailty or weakness, even at the gallows. A Habsburg never showed emotion in public. That was how great her Maximilian was, how noble. And if he thought she looked beautiful, he wouldn't diminish himself by telling her so now. *I'll wait,* she thought to herself. And that was what she did.

She waited all night and the next night and then the next, as her heart saddened and her soul grew distressed. She tried to understand what caused his behavior, but she couldn't. Carlota was left waiting forever for her beloved Maximilian—who bit by bit began to crumble before her eyes—to offer her a sign of affection, let alone lust. Maximilian let her slowly dry out, like a grape in the sun, until nothing remained in her except the shame and sadness of knowing herself utterly unwanted. The woman in the mirror could never emerge, and the seventeen-year-old girl was condemned to the desert of unrequited desire. Maximilian spent each night aboard his ship, while Carlota, filled with anguish, remained in the castle asking herself over and over what she'd done wrong. One day, seized by crushing disappointment while at tea with her brother Philippe, the Count of Flanders, she said, "Oh, brother, this marriage has left me as I was before."

He looked at her with wide eyes, thinking he must have misheard. "What did you say?"

Carlota, suddenly ashamed and aware of what such a statement meant, reconsidered. "Ignore me, Philippe. I'm just tired. Everything is fine."

They fixed their eyes on their cups, trying to elude the terrible specter of doubt that would install itself in their hearts from then thereafter.

3

Two months after the wedding, Leopold I, who had little faith in his son-in-law's talents, asked Franz Joseph to find a good position for the young archduke, and the emperor of Austria, who also had little trust in his brother's political abilities, reluctantly agreed. The couple traveled to the Austrian territory Lombardy-Venetia, to the capital, Milan. At first Carlota thought it would become her home, but she soon realized she had no choice but to learn to be bored gracefully.

They weren't wanted there. The kingdom had Austrian sovereignty but an Italian soul, and the people made it clear they weren't welcome. In the streets they heard shouts of *Non siete nessuno*, "You are nothing," to humiliate them by emphasizing that they held no sway there. *Va', pensiero*, the chorus of a Verdi opera heavy with the composer's immense sorrow of losing his wife and two children, was in fashion. The Italians adopted it as their anthem, an anthem that echoed in their hearts, demanding sovereignty: "Oh, my homeland, so beautiful and lost!" Though Maximilian was open to liberal ideas and was, to some extent, charismatic, he was universally disliked; the Italians saw him as the representative of a foreign occupying force, and the Austrians thought he was too tolerant of nationalist ideas. Carlota could see his face drop every time he received a letter from Franz Joseph. She didn't trouble him with questions to which she already knew the answer. But like a mischievous little girl, when he left her alone in the palace for days, she took the correspondence from his drawer and read it. With a violent hand, the Austrian sovereign, her husband's elder brother, wrote things like "I cannot expect you to agree with my decisions, but our opponents must not be emboldened by the idea that you are on their side." Carlota knew Maximilian didn't care about that. He didn't care if he became separated from a regime that he considered indolent. He didn't care about much other than the restoration of the Royal Villa of Monza, some miles from Milan; Maximilian enjoyed the pomp of courts and wanted to re-create his own in the seventeenth-century style. He amused himself picking out curved swords for the guards and period livery for the footmen. He wanted Moorish pages, and for dinner to be served by black servants while an orchestra played. He boasted he was the only monarch with such exotic servants. Carlota thought that perhaps Maximilian would have been happier with someone like Sissi, beautiful on the outside and empty within, drawn to luxury and power like sailors to a mermaid. These excesses horrified Carlota. From a young age, her mother—and after her death, her father—had taught her the importance of using clothes until they tore, and then to wear the patches with dignity. In the Belgian castle, the austerity of the monarchs and the court was visible in every piece of fabric. Which was why, among other reasons, Carlota couldn't stand her sister-in-law. They spent little time together, but it was enough for ill will to emerge between them. On one occasion, the Austrian empress referred to Carlota as the Belgian Duck. Far from upsetting Carlota, this merely confirmed how far beneath her own intelligence and lineage Elisabeth of Bavaria was. Sissi's mother-in-law, the princess Sophie, did not like her either: she considered Sissi fanciful, spoiled, and foolish, and didn't think her qualified to raise her children in the correct manner. Carlota, though she never said it aloud, thought the same.

But Carlota never allowed herself a moment's doubt. She knew that governing was a burden disguised as a privilege. She didn't expect peace or gratitude; being a monarch meant making difficult decisions.

Above all, she was prepared to not be universally liked. Her father had reminded her every day and night: "Duty, Charlotte, duty." Omnipotent God bestowed this duty on them, and they answered only to Him. "Men err in their judgment, Charlotte; the Almighty does not." So she put on a brave front and bore her cross as Jesus Christ had, writing letters to her grandmother in which the most frequent word was "blessed." How blessed she was! Blessed inside. Blessed to live in such a beautiful country. Blessed for everything that was agreeable to her. Blessed because God had given her everything. But sometimes, while writing, she had a bitter taste in her mouth, aware that for each line of lies, she would have to confess. For blessed she was not. She was not blessed at all. She was married to a man who appeared romantic on the surface but who seemed to grow ever more impotent. Impotent and effeminate. Carlota was beginning to see the libertine look of strange tastes in his eyes, though sometimes, on nights when she longed for a warm body beside hers, she yearned to be the object of his perversions, whatever they were. To make matters worse, when she awoke, she found herself weighed down by their Italian dominions: they were living in a powder keg, a feeling of unease everywhere. The Italians didn't want Austria to become kinder; they wanted it to leave.

To ingratiate himself with the people, Maximilian decided to organize a performance at La Scala, as rulers customarily did. Carlota didn't think it was a good idea, but she was beginning to understand that her husband was motivated more by beauty than by politics. She had not yet seen him truly govern. If she were him, she would have held meetings with the political leaders to see how they could address the matters that most concerned the Italians, to lay certain foundations, and prevent the situation from escalating. Instead, Maximilian organized sumptuous concerts and lunches, always surrounded by twenty or thirty sycophants.

Carlota found him one afternoon choosing the gold envelopes for the invitations he was sending to the foremost members of Lombardian and Venetian society inviting them to the opera. She sighed, disappointed and a little envious. Sometimes, when boredom struck, she wished she could be infected with her husband's enthusiasm at undertaking a project—it would make everything easier. For some time, she'd felt subdued, apathetic, with no interest in anything. Taking a step forward required monumental effort. She looked out the window and wondered how she could be in such a beautiful place and feel so empty, so trapped. There had to be something more. She felt as if the future were waiting for her on the other side of the street, but she didn't dare cross it.

She retraced her steps to Maximilian, who remained engrossed in his guest list, imagining how honored the recipients would all feel when they received the royal envelope sealed with his initials. She came up behind him and was about to kiss his head when suddenly he exclaimed, escaping her embrace, "Mind my wig!"

She froze, petrified inside and out. Finally, she plucked up the courage to speak. "Wig?"

Barely hiding his displeasure, Maximilian replied in the most casual manner he could muster. "It protects me from the cold and from toothache. Anyway, it's very discreet."

Carlota, swallowing, still motionless, replied, "Yes, yes, very discreet."

Days later when they arrived at La Scala, Maximilian almost lost his wig from the shock as they entered the theater: there wasn't a single empty seat. A full house. At first, his vanity swelled like a dove's chest, but then he realized that he didn't recognize any of the seats' occupants; the cream of Milan society wasn't there. To Maximilian's horror, it gradually sank in that he'd been the victim of a gigantic orchestrated snub. None of the guests had deigned to attend. In their places, all of the nobles whose names had been written in gold ink had decided to send their servants. Carlota held Maximilian tightly by the arm and they continued. He wanted to say something but couldn't; she prodded him with her elbow to walk on. From the box, maintaining the dignity that never abandoned her, she raised her hand to greet everyone in attendance with a royal wave. Then, in a low voice, she instructed Maximilian. "Sit down and, by all that's sacred, do not show your displeasure."

He obeyed.

It was the most dramatic opera that they would attend in their lives. That night, as if the universe were conspiring against them, Sissi and Franz Joseph had their first son: a boy who, before he'd even opened his eyes, had kicked Maximilian down to third in line for the throne, while he swallowed ignoble, weak tears, his spirits as threadbare as the hair his wig concealed.

4

Mid 1800s, Mexico City

Across the ocean, Constanza Murrieta had had the misfortune to be born a woman in a world governed by men. Her father had prayed aloud for another boy to succeed him, helping with the conservative military effort he championed, and he never learned to hide his displeasure. She was born on September 14, the day that, to the shame of every Mexican, the Stars and Stripes was hoisted over the National Palace. That was when she entered the world, and there was nothing she could do to avoid being born on that turbulent day. She'd been expected later, but the cannons booming in the heart of Mexico City made her mother give birth prematurely. It was September 1847, an ironically patriotic month, for it was when the nation's independence was usually celebrated, but not this year. This year, the only shouts were horrified screams as people saw the soldiers being massacred by snipers on the roofs. The Mexicans defended their city tooth and nail and, running out of munitions, they even threw flowerpots at the Americans, but in the end, they had no choice but to surrender. Sometimes Constanza thought that the confusion of being born in an occupied territory was what led her to a life of multiple identities, turning her into a Mexican disguised as a foreigner in her own country.

Across the Atlantic, Europe would soon witness the birth of a new world. The old authoritarian regimes were being battered by liberal revolutionary waves—the Spring of Nations, as they were called—and everywhere, from France to Hungary, nationalist protests erupted, supported by the workers' movement. All of the uprisings were crushed by the upper echelons of power. That year, Emily Brontë published *Wuthering Heights* under the pseudonym Ellis Bell; a single time zone was established in Great Britain, a convention that would later be extended to the rest of the planet; and Spain held its first April Fair among the palm trees. It was also the year of the birth of Thomas Alva Edison and Alexander Graham Bell, while General Santa Anna was president of Mexico for his ninth term. In the midst of all of this, the gringos believed for a moment that Mexico belonged to them, and they decided to claim sovereignty, with many deaths on both sides.

The Murrieta Salases were a family of five. The two elder brothers, Joaquín and Salvador, were career soldiers like their father, and from a young age they bore the burden of being Major Vicente's sons. After Salvador came a baby who'd been unable to survive the harsh winter and died a few days later; nobody spoke of her, as if the silence prevented them from suffering. Constanza was the only one to understand that her mother always missed that child; it was her spirit, more than her body, that was broken, but she was young and strong, and somewhere in her soul she must have found the will to conceive a third child. Before the baby was born, Major Vicente decided that, should it be a boy, he would be a priest, and Agustín was born. From a very young age his father guided him toward saintliness, as Vicente liked to say wholeheartedly. They always dressed him in black and taught him Latin; in the shade of a tree in the courtyard, they explained to him that priesthood meant dedicating one's life not just to God but also to power. Perhaps he might even become a bishop. "Can you imagine? You'd be Monsignor Murrieta." Agustín laughed at the idea, and from that moment on he ordered everyone in the house to start calling him Monsi. When the time came, nobody was surprised that Agustín took holy orders as naturally as a river reaches the sea.

A couple of years after Constanza was born, the telegraph arrived in Mexico, and Refugio gave birth to Clotilde, a girl as beautiful as she was frail; the slightest exertion brought on unstoppable coughing fits that sent her mother into a panic, still haunted by the specter of infant death. Each night, her mother prayed with fervor, gripping her rosary hard, asking Our Lady of Guadalupe to take care of her beautiful little girl. For Clotilde really was very lovely—much more so than Constanza. She'd been born with black hair—so black it seemed to sparkle with a blue gleam—and though her eyes were green, they seemed gray in a face that was always fixed in a sad countenance. And somewhere between the boys' stoicism and Clotilde's weakness, there was Constanza.

As a child she was convinced that women were born for two things: to be mothers or nuns. It was all she had ever seen. Everywhere she looked, she saw women taking orders from men, whether they were husbands, fathers, brothers, priests, or soldiers. The natural fate of women of a certain privileged status, like her, was to serve men and support them in their decisions. To accompany them on the path to glory—their glory, of course. In exchange, women were provided with food and a home, and given plenty of children so they could be self-less mothers to more of the same men. It was prescribed in the Holy Scriptures; she knew it because each night after dinner they read the gospels. Once, Constanza started to read Song of Songs, and before she knew what was happening, hypnotized by the poetic eroticism contained in the onionskin paper, her father dealt her a slap. That night while she unknotted her braid, Refugio whispered something in her ear that became branded with hot iron in her memory: "Don't ever marry."

Sometimes, when she saw her mother flipping through *Le Bon Ton, Journal des Modes*, a magazine full of lace scarves, wide-brimmed hats with feathers, and pearl and diamond accessories; or when she saw her deciding which dress to have sent from Paris or London for a reception in the home of some important military officer, she shook her head and thought she must have misheard. Her mother could never have wished such a thing for her.

One February afternoon when she was ten years old, Refugio told her to get ready to go to Mass.

"Just the two of us?"

"Yes, child. Fetch your gloves."

Perhaps it was the way she walked, but Constanza sensed they weren't heading to church. Her pace was quick, nervous, and every now and then her mother turned around to make sure nobody was watching them.

"Mother, what is it?"

"Nothing, child, keep walking."

She obeyed without saying a word the rest of the way, until they reached a carriage parked on the corner a few blocks from their home, awaiting them.

They arrived somewhere completely unknown to Constanza, in the center of the city. There were a large number of tables arranged in rows, and she thought that they were in a school. Refugio passed through to a room where several clerks were interviewing people: whole families, small children, young couples. Almost no elderly. After they waited half an hour, a gentleman offered them a seat. Refugio remained standing.

"Good afternoon."

Refugio replied with a nod.

"Name?"

"María del Refugio Salas López."

"Names of known father and mother?"

"Augusto Salas and Zeneida López."

"Age?"

"Thirty-five."

"Marital status?"

"Married."

"Name of husband?"

"Vicente Murrieta Molina."

"Children?"

"Five."

Constanza listened as her mother gave the man each of her brothers' names, ages, and dates of birth. Bored stiff, she fought to hide her yawns. They'd been there even longer than when she had to go with Clotilde to her piano lessons, and she had to listen to her play the wrong note over and over again. Fed up with the tedium, she wandered off among the desks; everyone there was offering a litany of the names and dates of their lives. She stopped to watch a ladybug fighting to climb out of a glass of water on one of the tables. She looked around but saw no one nearby. She was about to rescue the little creature when suddenly a boy not much older than her came out of nowhere, his cheeks red from the cold and with slight bags under his eyes. Seeing what Constanza was reaching for, he snatched up the glass, reclaiming his possession. To her astonishment he seemed determined to drink a good mouthful. She reached to stop him, but he held the glass out of her grasp—he wasn't going to share his water with anyone, especially this well-dressed girl with white gloves. He knew her kind and didn't hold them in high regard. He was moving the glass toward his lips when Constanza, without knowing how or why, heard herself call out, "Stop!" Then she slapped the boy's hand, and, startled, he dropped the glass and looked as if he wanted to strangle her. Without being able to do anything, Constanza watched the glass fall and smash into pieces on the floor.

"What was that for, you dimwit? That was *my* water!"

"I'm sorry. There was a bug and—"

"You hit me for that? Stupid runt . . ."

"You would've swallowed it if I didn't!"

"You're insane! You almost smashed the glass in my mouth!"

A man with eyebrows bushier than his moustache walked heavily toward them, took the boy by an ear, and led him out of the room, saying, "It's always the same with you! I told you to keep out of trouble, boy!"

He lifted him into the air as easily as Constanza would have removed the ladybug from the glass, given the chance. The boy cried out in pain while he struggled to advance, barely able to balance on the tips of his toes. He didn't look at Constanza.

She looked around for her mother, but she must have moved on to another room, because she wasn't there. Far from being frightened, Constanza was glad that her mother hadn't witnessed the incident—she would've given her a good thrashing. Most other girls would have sought the protection of a parent in case someone was coming to pull her by her ear, but Constanza was made of sterner stuff. Instead, she went in search of the little boy; she shouldn't have behaved so outrageously. Her mother had told her many times: ladies don't shout or make a fuss—let alone slap down glasses while people are drinking. She felt very stupid, rash, and guilty, as if a man had just been sent to the gallows.

She found him in a little courtyard, sitting on a wicker chair, making circles in the earth with his feet.

"Go away, girl. You only bring trouble," he said without looking up.

"I came to apologize. I didn't mean to knock the glass to the floor, or for your papa to give you a scolding."

"He's not my papa."

Constanza was very surprised that someone other than his father had dared treat him like that. In her house, Vicente might take a sandal or even a belt to her brothers, but God help anyone else who dared lay a finger on them.

"So why do you let him treat you like that?"

The boy frowned.

"You're stupider than I thought."

"I'm not stupid."

"Just leave me alone."

"Not until you accept my apology."

23

The boy snorted. "Stupid and silly."

"Don't insult me. I just want to go with a clear conscience."

"That's your problem, not mine."

Constanza frowned now. She really didn't think it should be so hard to obtain his forgiveness. At home that was how everything was resolved: an apology and that was that. She stood in front of him with her arms crossed until, suddenly, for no apparent reason, he looked up at her. Constanza got goose bumps. He was looking at her in a way that made her feel naked. Her discomfort began to outweigh her pride; she was thinking about turning around and getting away from this rude boy, when she heard her mother call her from a window.

"Constanza!"

She turned around, afraid and relieved at the same time. Her mother gestured at her to come right away. Without saying anything more, she turned and left. That was when she heard his voice.

"Goodbye, Constanza . . . I'll see you again."

The hairs on her arms stood on end when she noticed a certain lilt to his voice, something she'd never heard before in anyone. It was not hatred or bravery, it wasn't even mockery: it was malice.

While a stout woman gripped one of her mother's thumbs, dipped it in ink, and pressed it against the page where they had recorded all of the information about the Murrieta Salas family, Refugio asked, "What were you talking to that boy about?"

"Nothing."

"Who is he?"

"I don't know. He didn't tell me his name."

The woman taking fingerprints, eager to break the routine of stamping fingers on documents, said, "Him? He's Comonfort's charge."

Refugio raised her eyebrows. "He is?"

"Yes, well, don't tell anyone I told you—I'll be strung up if they find out. But yes, he was brought in from the streets; he was lost, he hadn't eaten for a few days, poor thing, and they don't know where he came from or who his parents were. Nothing. He was brought here, and Sr. Comonfort, when he came to conduct an inspection one day, took him in."

Constanza had never spoken to a street urchin before. Her life had been sheltered from the poverty and misery of the world; her parents had paid special attention to ensuring it. And, as if by magic, the boy, who minutes before she had wanted to erase from her life forever, suddenly became the most interesting person in the world. Constanza didn't know who Comonfort was or why the boy had been brought to this place, but she paid no attention to such trivial matters. Refugio, however, was listening carefully, nodding at each word from the woman.

"And what is his name?"

"Modesto . . . Modesto García, I believe."

Modesto, thought Constanza. What an inappropriate name.

"Done!" the stout woman said, slamming the register shut.

Refugio gave a slight start in her chair, as if someone had clapped in front of her face to wake her from a trance. After a polite *thank you,* she stood and took Constanza by the arm.

As they left, Refugio took a handkerchief from her bag and—to the complete astonishment of Constanza, who had never seen her mother do anything so vulgar—spat on her handkerchief before scrubbing her finger hard.

"Promise you won't tell your father we came to the registry."

"You want me to lie?"

"Promise me, Constanza."

"I promise," she said seriously. Then she asked, "What's the registry?"

"Didn't you see? It's where all the births, marriages, and deaths must be recorded from now on. It's a new law of President Comonfort's . . . a law I welcome, of course," she muttered, as if speaking to herself.

Comonfort, thought Constanza.

"The one who took in the boy?"

Refugio stopped after seeing that her finger, while reddened, was clean. She looked at her daughter, who seemed to study her eyes; the girl was searching for something in her, too. They both knew they were thinking many things that wouldn't be said.

"The same."

"Mamá . . ."

"Yes, child."

"Why don't you want Father to know? Are we doing something wrong?"

Refugio breathed. She never allowed herself to speak ill of her husband to anyone, and she wouldn't do so now.

"Your father isn't a bad man, Constanza, but he resists change. He's always resisted it."

Refugio adjusted her hat and smoothed her skirt. She took a deep breath, as if she'd just made a declaration of independence with her words.

With an innocence that she was beginning to lose, Constanza asked timidly, "But if you wanted to keep it secret, why did you bring me?"

The woman bent down and looked directly in her eyes.

"Because I want you to see that the world is bigger and more complex than you think, child. Changes are coming and you must know how to recognize them. Don't ever forget that." Then, in a low voice, almost a whisper, suppressing a half smile, she added, "There's another Mexico, Constanza. A freethinking, modern Mexico."

And she believed her. In part because her mother's word was law, in part because the image of Modesto, a boy her age who wandered the streets, appeared to her every time she tried to sleep, and in part because after that day came three years of civil war, pitting conservatives against liberals. Her brothers served on the front, Clotilde had to give up her piano lessons, and Vicente stayed home in the capital to conspire against Juárez's government, which had established its headquarters in Veracruz.

5

In the carriage, Carlota had time to think to the point of torment. Her mind kept returning to her bitter farewell with Maximilian. As if with premonition, she sensed that their parting embrace in Ayotla, five leagues from the capital, would be their last. Carlota hadn't wanted to let him go; for the first time in all their years of marriage he felt close, vulnerable, and it had been an effort to separate herself from the warm body she had missed so many nights, as so much love had gone to waste. With the retinue's eyes on them, she somehow found the strength to slowly pull him from her chest. Then she saw that Maximilian, her Max, the emperor, in front of everyone, was crying.

"Why are you crying? I'm only going for six months," she said with a smile that got stuck halfway.

Maximilian lowered his head, unable to look her in the eyes. She held his face in both hands and lifted his chin. For a moment, she thought he was going to speak, but he clearly didn't know what to say. So Carlota spoke.

"Don't worry, everything will be fine. I'll fix this," she said, and hearing herself, she realized that she was consoling him with a maternal voice, as she so often did. Their nine years of marriage had been long enough for Maximilian to become a kind of child to protect in the hope that, one day, he would spread his wings and fly.

Maximilian's only response was to nod his head. If he'd wanted to say something, he couldn't; he just broke into tears, falling to pieces like a defenseless young boy. Unsure how to react, perplexed at his weakness of character, Carlota kissed him on the lips and climbed into the carriage as quickly as she could. She held herself rigid in her seat, straight as a post, not allowing herself to show a hint of weakness.

"Go! At once!" she called to the coachman.

As soon as the horses broke into a walk, Carlota held her face in her hands and, between prayers and vows, cried the tears she hadn't shed in years. True, the emperor had not been a good husband, but she didn't feel she had the right to judge him. If it was anyone's fault that she'd fallen in love with a man more interested in admiring his uniformed reflection in the mirror than lifting her underskirt, it was hers. But she had been very young then and had known very little about life. She had mistaken fragility for sensitivity. How could she have known her beloved Max was more interested in what trees to plant at Miramare than in governing? That he was more concerned with the exuberant vegetation of Mexico, as novel as it was unspoiled, than he was with satisfying his wife? Their marriage had been an endless shared silence, a sea of complicity in which they both pretended not to know what the other was doing, hiding their sins behind a dense veil of duty. She put on a brave face each time Maximilian laughed with Bombelles, the close childhood friend from whom he was never willingly parted. And she said nothing when his valet, Sebastian Schertzenlechner, a blue-eyed Hungarian tall as a tower, was hired and moved into the palace for the sole purpose of bringing wood for the stoves. Sometimes she watched them. While Maximilian never allowed himself to be careless in her presence, she learned to examine him with the same attention with which her husband looked at his butterfly collection. When Sebastian entered the room to add wood to the fire, Max stopped breathing. Then he coughed. And often, at that precise moment, he would remember he had some unfinished business somewhere else. Sebastian then left the room moments later. Carlota, in her most private thoughts, wished that someone would look at her in the way Maximilian looked at Sebastian. But she and Maximilian had a shared responsibility that they had to fulfill until death. The empire was bigger than them, bigger than their happiness, much bigger than desire. And if martyrdom was the price they had to pay, they would pay it with interest. Together, even if an ocean of betrayal and suspicion separated them. She promised herself she would protect the emperor from everyone.

As they drove off in a cloud of dust, Carlota watched the guards help the emperor into another carriage; Maximilian was weak and sick and no longer bothered to hide his malaise. Carlota hoped he would have a safe journey to Chapultepec, his Miramare in the Valley of Mexico, a peaceful haven with a view of the snowy mountains where he could listen to the mockingbird's song. While she knew she carried Mexico's fate on her shoulders, a pain in the pit of her stomach made her aware of another horror. Failing this mission was not an option. She had to be more Carlota than ever. More empress than ever. She could never allow doubt to cloud her judgment. Before she left, Maximilian had asked her to settle all their overseas business and financial affairs. She had to persuade a military expert to return with her to Mexico, though all the high-ranking officers expressed their desire to remain in France. She had to obtain a concordat with the Vatican, a task at which several emissaries had previously failed. And, as if any more pressure were needed, she had promised herself that she would make Vienna return Moctezuma's headdress to Mexico.

The journey's challenges soon made her forget her emotional struggles; there wasn't time for self-pity. The mountain rain gave her goose bumps, and her ladies-in-waiting were as pale as the embroidery on their dresses. Near Córdoba, one of the carriage wheels broke on an enormous rock. They slowly climbed out of the coach; Carlota was grateful for the forced rest so she could stretch her legs. Her chamber-maid, Mathilde Döblinger, approached and said, "Your Majesty, we must take shelter. We cannot go on in these conditions."

"We cannot stop, Mathilde. If we delay, we'll miss the ship."

"We have no choice, Majesty. We shall have to stay here until the morning, when we can find a replacement carriage."

Carlota looked at the men and women accompanying her; they all seemed strangely relaxed, as if they were in no hurry to live their lives. And then Charles de Bombelles, her husband's friend and her rival for his affection, ventured to say, "You'll see how lovely Córdoba is, Your Majesty."

Carlota exploded with rage.

"Don't speak nonsense, Bombelles!" She yelled so hard her face flushed red. Her hands began to tremble. But Carlota, hearing her own raised voice, no longer cared. "We're not here for sightseeing! Mexico's fate hangs on this journey! The emperor's future, the empire's future! However beautiful it may be, do you think I'm going to stop and admire the scenery?"

Bombelles, blushing, lowered his head.

"Forgive me, Your Majesty, I didn't intend to upset you."

Dr. Bohuslavek, her personal physician, intervened.

"Don't upset yourself, Your Majesty. It's not advisable for you to become agitated in your . . . Please, stay calm."

The doctor held some smelling salts under her nose, but she batted them away.

"Don't you start with the frailties of health. I am perfectly well. A woman has the right to raise her voice when she hears a person talk nonsense!"

Everyone was silent, not daring to say anything that might earn them an earful from the empress. They had never seen her like this. She appeared to have lost her senses.

Carlota observed them with an unfamiliar rage. She suddenly wanted to slap them all: she imagined herself flogging them one by one until their buttocks were raw. She breathed. She tried to calm herself. She looked at the coachman.

"You," she said to him. "I hope you're not trying to delay us so we miss the ship."

"Of course not, Your Majesty. It was an accident. The stone was in the road, there was nothing I could do to avoid it," he said without looking at her.

Then Carlota spoke as if from a pulpit. "Nobody is going to stop me. Do you hear me? Nobody! Tell the spies that were sent to prevent me from reaching France in time that they will never succeed. Never!"

Mathilde plucked up the courage to speak on behalf of everyone. "My lady, rest assured. Nobody wants to stop us. Spies? Here among us? We are your faithful servants. Look at us . . . We are here to serve you, to assist you."

Carlota suddenly seemed calm again after her panic attack. She slowly looked around, seeing their frightened expressions. She felt ashamed.

"Very well," she said. "But I insist that we travel on horseback to Paso del Macho and take the train from there."

Seeing her less agitated, Dr. Bohuslavek approached her again. "That is not advisable, given your . . . given the conditions, Your Majesty. Let us spend the night here. The new carriage will arrive tomorrow at first light. We won't be late and we'll make the ship."

Carlota turned away, holding her hands to her face for a few seconds. She felt exhausted, furious and exhausted. Furious that she'd lost her temper, exhausted from the grueling journey. Finally, she lowered her hands and turned back to the others. "Very well. Let us go to this inn, then. We'll try to rest."

The next day, the replacement carriage arrived, and they set off without incident, but the previous day's episode had cast a pall over the entourage that remained with them for the rest of the journey.

After several days passing along roads that the rain had turned to mud chutes, with landslides and stones blocking the narrowest passes, they finally reached the port of Veracruz, where they would set sail for Saint-Nazaire. They had survived the roads and the vomiting sickness at the worst time of year. Carlota thanked God and crossed herself. She was dirty, she smelled of sweat and tears; a violent stench penetrated her nose and nauseated her. But she attempted to control herself, breathed deeply, and hoped that the salty sea air would cleanse her of the constant feeling of disgust.

The *Empress Eugénie*, a ship of the Compagnie Générale Transatlantique, was waiting to be boarded. They were about to board when Carlota noticed that atop the mast a French flag was blowing in the wind. Her expression darkened and her heart tightened. France had turned her back on them, it had betrayed them from afar, abandoning them to their fate. This treacherous France would not fly its flag over her during the weeks at sea. As soon as she set foot on deck, she addressed Captain Cloue, who'd come to welcome her without much enthusiasm. Before he was able to speak, she made a firm demand.

"You understand, Captain, that I shall not sail on a ship that doesn't fly the Mexican flag."

Surprised, the captain resisted with arguments that, while true, seemed abrupt and tactless.

"Forgive me, Your Majesty, but we were only informed of your arrival yesterday . . . In order to accommodate you, we even had to refuse passengers who'd been waiting a long time."

Carlota could hear the unease in the captain's voice. She knew it would be an uncomfortable voyage: it was clear this man would've been happier transporting a large group of civilians rather than an empress demanding protocol. But Carlota wasn't one to show weakness; God only knew how hard it had been to learn to do a man's work in a woman's skirts. She interrupted the officer midsentence.

"You heard me. I shall not sail aboard a ship that does not recognize the greatness of the empire."

"But time is pressing—"

"Then you had better be quick, Captain." And swallowing her impatience, heavy as a brick, she added, "We shall wait for as long as it takes." Then she turned and addressed Manuelita del Barrio, who had learned to recognize when a response to an order could be delayed for a little longer than it should be and when it couldn't. "I will wait in the command building. Send for me when the captain is ready to depart."

The captain watched her walk away with a firm stride and knew that it would be a very, very long journey.

They set sail two days later. From the port, the people watched the empress leave with her retinue: her ladies-in-waiting headed by Manuelita del Barrio; the foreign minister, the count of Orizaba; the commander of the Chapultepec palatine guard; the treasurer of Miramare and Chapultepec; a chambermaid; a secretary; Carlota's maid, Mathilde Döblinger; and her personal physician, Dr. Bohuslavek. And of course, Charles de Bombelles, whom Maximilian had ordered to watch over the empress on the crossing.

On her sleepless nights, of which there were many, Carlota couldn't stop thinking about how convenient it would be for Bombelles if she suffered some kind of accident. Who would console Maximilian if she died? And then she closed her eyes and saw faithful Charles, so polite, so serene, smiling malevolently in the darkness.

6

Philippe Petit was beginning to grow weary of his ordinary life. He worked as a carpenter in Antwerp under the apprenticeship of Mr. Walton, a man whose only consideration was to provide a roof, a bowl of soup, and a hunk of bread after an endless day polishing wood. Philippe didn't dislike the work. The repetitive sound of gouges against wood soothed him and helped empty his mind of thoughts, because, if he dared to think, he often slipped into imagining a future that might not be better but was certainly different. He preferred to hypnotize himself with the sound of the file rubbing at the rough surfaces until they were as smooth as marble. That was how he'd spent his days since the age of thirteen.

He was the fifth child in a family of six. When his parents died, he and his siblings had been forced to fend for themselves. The landlords didn't hesitate to throw them out when they learned they wouldn't be able to pay the rent. They knew they'd be unable to remain together, since no one in their right mind could take responsibility for six orphans at once; the logical thing was to find homes for them according to their skills and ages. Under the circumstances, the eldest brother, Arthur, promised to care for them all, and one night the six of them fled in the direction of the mountains. They found a cave, where they took shelter. On the first night, Philippe was so afraid and so cold he didn't think he'd be able to stand another night. They huddled together for warmth, but also to ward off the immense feeling of loneliness. In that moment, with no candles and in silence, Philippe discovered the cruelty of the night, but they were together and that was what mattered. On the second night they built a fire. On the third, little Noah began to cough up blood. Arthur knew then that they couldn't escape their fate. He could tolerate many things, but not seeing his little brother die, so he decided to return to the town and place each of them in homes where they could at least grow up without too much hardship. Philippe, as he smoothed the wood, sometimes remembered his brother's words. *I'll be back for you,* he had promised, and that was ten years ago. Every day Philippe tried not to think about the family he'd once had—it hurt too much. He preferred to fill his days working hard and saying little, but lately he'd begun to think that he didn't want to die with a carpenter's hands. Perhaps there were other things he could do, other paths to take. He was twenty-three and, despite his dalliances in the slums of Antwerp, he had no one to come home to at night. In his life there was only Mr. Walton with his soup, his wood, and his frugality. But the most intolerable thing of all was that he was beginning to sense, as sure as the sun rises in the morning, that the next day would be exactly the same as the one before. Routine—that was his own private hell. Philippe went to bed, like he did every night, in the hope that a miracle would change the course of his life.

7

Philippe woke, as he did every day, to the sound of a cock crowing. He couldn't remember what it felt like to open his eyes naturally, when the tiredness had left his body. He got up, washed his face and underarms with a little water from a bowl in his room, put on some loosely laced boots, and went down to the kitchen. As he did every morning, he heated water to make tea, serving himself a cup with a spoon, though he hadn't added milk, for the sheer pleasure of making tiny swirls in the liquid. He took a sip and burned his tongue. "Ah!" he exclaimed as he snapped the cup away from his lips and spilled a bit of tea on the table. "Damn it!" he whispered. He didn't want Mr. Walton to wake up; he liked the solitude of the kitchen at this early hour.

He looked for a cloth to wipe the table. If there was one thing he'd learned in all his years in the trade, it was that water made wood swell, and as the perfectionist he was, he couldn't allow such a blunder. He found an old newspaper and without hesitation laid it on the surface to absorb the spill. He leaned against the table with a hand at either end of the paper, which gradually soaked up the liquid. His eyes fell on an article that was changing color as it became wet, and before the paper was ruined, he lifted it up, completely engrossed. The wood's potential swelling became a secondary concern as Philippe read:

> At the request of Leopold I, king of Belgium, Parliament authorizes the formation of a regiment to guard the Belgian Princess Charlotte, who will travel to Mexico to be empress.
>
> Wherefore, the king calls for two thousand unmarried men, no older than thirty-five, with a medical certificate and a letter of recommendation bearing witness to their good character. Members of the Belgian army who enlist shall be given a military rank immediately above the one they hold, and their years of service in the Belgian legion in Mexico shall be taken into account for their pension. Six years of service shall be required, with one year's leave. Those who, upon retiring from service, wish to return to Belgium may be repatriated and shall receive compensation. Civilian volunteers . . .

Philippe opened his eyes wide. Civilians. *They're recruiting civilians, too,* he thought. He continued reading:

> Civilian volunteers shall be employed for a sum of sixty to a hundred francs and shall be granted a military rank. They shall receive military training so that they may perform their duties. At the end of their six years of service, whether soldiers or officers, those who wish to remain in Mexico shall be granted land.

It couldn't be right. A piece of land; volunteers could have their own land. In Mexico . . . Where was that? What did it matter! And a salary, too. And military rank. Too good to be true.

Philippe laid the paper back on the table and sat in silence for a few minutes. He distantly heard Mr. Walton waking up: he was calling for him to put the kettle on the fire. Leaving the kitchen to head to the workshop, Philippe stopped and retraced his footsteps, tore the damp page from the newspaper, and carefully put it in his trouser pocket.

8

Constanza grew up between two worlds without realizing it, worlds that coexisted naturally despite the gulf between them.

One world was male dominated, full of military men and priests who dreamed aloud about strict authoritarian regimes to control the troublemakers who were upsetting the established order. Presiding over this world like an all-powerful god was her father, Don Vicente, to whom she owed obedience and respect. He had lost a leg in the Battle of Palo Alto, when he still believed that Mexico belonged to the Mexicans. The sound of the walking stick that preceded him always filled Constanza with fear, like the drumroll before an execution by firing squad.

The other world was domestic, and yet, within it, Constanza was able to enjoy the illusion of free will. This world was led by her mother, her Refugio. Her mother taught her to see with different eyes, critical eyes that questioned everything, eyes capable of asking why. Deep down, she saw in her daughter something that she once possessed herself, something from before her marriage, before having children. Something lost to submission and routine.

They lived in a beautiful house that filled Vicente with pride. He was proud, too, that his new and hard-earned family fortune, the result of a great deal of sacrifice and expertise, had opened doors for him. Not everybody could build wealth from nothing, but he was a Murrieta, and, even during the worst turmoil, his good sense and political nose had enabled him to back the winning horse. At least, that was the official version—the true story was that, when she married Vicente, Refugio had brought to the marriage her family's cotton mill in Chalco, which they owned because her grandparents had done good business with the mining families of New Spain. Vicente, meanwhile, brought good breeding, and everyone was satisfied with the arrangement.

Perhaps because he knew himself to be rich for the first time in his life, after the army, building the house became Vicente's great calling. He knew exactly which materials were used in each room; he knew the origin of every tile on the stairs. He'd promised himself that, for the years he had left, the house would be the home of a refined family. He knew he was on the right path when the block became known as the location of the Murrieta house. Sure enough, there was a constant buzz of people at the house: Vicente loved to host dinners and lunches to fête—the euphemism he used for "buying favors"—high-ranking officials in the army and the Church. That was how he was; he liked to think he called the shots. His sons usually joined the gatherings; however, Clotilde and Constanza were sent to their rooms and told to be quiet when there were guests. The visitors never seemed trustworthy to Constanza, though neither did she consider them enemies: they were snakes waiting to shed their skin. They were very serious when they arrived in their impeccable military uniforms, politely introducing themselves before disappearing into the library to discuss political matters. The women waited in the parlor, limiting themselves to the trivial subjects that women converse about, or at least what they pretend to.

The women's days were spent between embroidery and the gospel. The three women of the Murrieta house, immersed in their silent complicity, listened to their father and husband put the country, if not the world, to rights. According to him, Mexico was slowly being brought down by the Liberales; little by little, the country was descending into chaos. The way he saw it, since the Plan of Ayutla, which overthrew President Santa Anna in 1855, political decisions had been one absurdity after another; if they went on like this, they'd end up with Benito Juárez as president. This man, among other aberrations, was drafting laws to eliminate the ecclesiastic and military courts' jurisdiction in civil affairs.

"Who does he think he is to decide anything in this country? The upstart. An Indian as president . . . *Por favor!* What's the world coming to?"

When Vicente began to rant and rave against Comonfort and Juárez, Refugio pricked her finger with her needle and excused herself to go wash the wound.

He wasn't a bad man, but he showed little affection for his children, and his manner was coarse. He had never been very loving; he was never seen to kiss his wife in public, let alone any of his children. He remained so proper that sometimes Constanza wondered how he had won her mother if he didn't even look her in the eyes. Nonetheless, he loved them in his own manner; the way he showed it was to ensure their family name was never the subject of gossip, and that they always had a roof over their heads and a hot plate of food on the table. Beyond that, they didn't expect much affection or understanding from him. Not even when Constanza was a little girl who liked to be held did she have the confidence to climb onto his lap; her father commanded respect and fear in equal measure, and for her they amounted to the same thing. She feared his limp as much as his stick: seeing him advance toward his study dragging his leg, and hearing his wooden support banging on the floor, made her run as fast as she could to her bedroom. He only addressed his daughters to request something to drink or to ask them about their prayers or chores, and often Constanza preferred to save herself the effort of a formal conversation. Even so, under his fierce appearance was a good heart, even if Vicente had spent half his life trying to hide it: since he was a boy, he'd known the pain of war and the death that came with it. A man was born to survive, and nobody would ever persuade him otherwise.

Since his early years in the militia, Vicente had pledged himself to Santa Anna, for whom he was prepared to die if necessary; as the years passed and he rose in rank, he had gradually become a staunch

Santanista. He had sacrificed his best years, his best friends, and his right leg—ruined by shrapnel—for the struggle alongside him. He believed in Antonio López de Santa Anna as much as he believed in the Holy Trinity; he believed in his intelligence and in his idea of Mexico. But, eventually, in Vicente's mind, fame went to the man's head, and Santa Anna was drifting into excesses such as demanding to be addressed as His Most Serene Highness, among other extravagances. The last straw was when he spent only forty days in mourning for his wife before marrying a girl who could have been his daughter—this seemed a serious defect in the moral integrity of a man of noble birth. Constanza thought it was curious that it was a personal and not a political matter that caused her father to turn his back on the figure who for so long had embodied his ideals. On stormy nights, when his rheumatism gave him severe pains in his leg, she heard him fulminate about Santa Anna and curse his ancestors.

Though she didn't agree with it, Refugio allowed him to take his anger out on the Liberales; she understood that her husband was simply a disappointed man, deeply wounded by the pain of having fought for a cause that ended up being bankrupt. From her own trench, Refugio found another way to fight battles. While it was Vicente's voice that reverberated around the house most loudly, everyone knew it was Refugio's softly spoken words to which they must pay attention. Graciously, and with a manner as stiff as the starched garments she wore, she took responsibility for maintaining order. Nobody did anything without her permission, and even when Vicente gave an order that contradicted hers, no servant would lift a finger, even when he raised his voice. Refugio, using who knows what artifices, always managed to make her husband believe that it was he who made the decisions.

She was the perfect wife, the perfect lady of the house. But when night fell, she gave free rein to her most secret dreams. When everyone retired, she went into Constanza's room to give her a kiss and, after tracing the sign of the cross on her forehead, slip her a book that only men were permitted to read. With this simple gesture, she would take her due. Bringing up a freethinking woman would be her way to rebel against an established order that she'd never been able to openly defy. Whenever Constanza asked where she got the books and why she gave them to her, she placed her fingers on her lips and said in a low voice, "Return it before sunrise." That was the only condition. At first, Constanza read slowly, hesitantly, afraid she would be discovered, but the fear disappeared as she quickly became absorbed in the book. The world became infinitely broader, larger, more interesting. She learned about the geopolitics of a Europe that seemed to be crumbling like a cookie, and, without fully understanding it because of her age, she read *The Spirit of Laws*, sensing that she was witness to an important document.

Her clandestine reading became their secret, and in the mornings, when she awoke looking like a raccoon, Refugio covered up the rings around her eyes with makeup. On a few occasions, Constanza almost gave them away with the urge to correct her brothers as they discussed politics at dinner. Refugio would open her eyes wide from across the table, telling her with the severity of her expression to keep her mouth closed. Constanza gathered that Clotilde wasn't interested in reading the prohibited books, because even on occasions when the atmosphere could be cut with a knife, she remained oblivious, coughing delicately into her silk handkerchief. In her most private thoughts, Refugio imagined that the fragility of her youngest daughter's body was a reflection of her mind. To her, Constanza was always the strongest, but she was as afraid as she was proud: she suspected that so much strength would come at a cost.

In the Murrieta household, life went on, far from the wars and the betrayals of politics; the eldest brothers left the home, Clotilde's health improved as quickly as Easter flowers sprout, and Constanza began to understand that, within one territory, there were several Mexicos that were about to collide like trains.

9

1866, on a ship bound for France

For three and a half weeks, Carlota locked herself in her cabin. The sound of the engines was driving her mad, she insisted; it prevented her from sleeping, and she had intense headaches that were becoming increasingly unbearable. She tossed and turned in her bed; the voyage at sea seemed much worse than traveling by carriage. She was dizzy. She was nauseous. She vomited every morning and, contrary to her initial thoughts, the sea air turned her stomach even more.

One day, pale and tired, she spoke to Frau Döblinger.

"Mathilde, I need you to line my entire cabin in mats."

"Excuse me?"

"I need to do something to reduce the noise from the machines; it's as if they're rumbling in my head."

"As you wish."

Mathilde left the cabin puzzled at the empress's request. She wasn't an eccentric woman; she never asked for senseless things and certainly couldn't be considered fussy. In fact, these last few years, she had adjusted to eating tortillas and enjoyed the *cajeta*, she had adapted to the new climate and landscape, and adopted the Mexican customs. A request of the kind she had just made therefore seemed strange. *She really must hate the noise,* Mathilde thought, before instructing the servants to carry out the task.

The cabin's walls were soon lined, but the insulation came at the expense of the temperature, which rose to the levels of an oven. Air no longer flowed through the portholes, and Carlota sweated constantly. Manuelita, overwhelmed by the stuffy room, tried to persuade her to go for walks on deck.

"It will give you some air, my lady. It will do you good."

After a great deal of negotiating, the lady-in-waiting managed to convince Carlota to break her self-imposed imprisonment and go up on deck for a short walk. But even then she was silent, lost in her thoughts, asking herself over and over again how, in a few weeks, she was going to solve what had proved unsolvable in the two years of the empire. She felt the pressure on her at all times, and to combat anxiety, she chewed on handkerchiefs, sometimes ruining them. When her nerves got the better of her, she let go of her lady-in-waiting's arm and, in desperation, said, "I can't allow myself to waste time strolling on the deck like a damsel, Manuelita. I must write pleas, take notes, make calculations. I cannot, I cannot . . ."

"But, my lady, a few minutes won't make any difference . . . France isn't going anywhere."

"Oh, Manuelita! You are so naïve. France has already gone. Don't you see? Minutes, months, years . . . it's all relative."

Suddenly the empress seemed to be lost in the passageways of her mind. Then, abruptly, she turned and rushed back, calling, "I'm retiring to my cabin to work."

"But that place is an oven!" Manuelita answered. "You'll fall ill shutting yourself away with no air. I'm not surprised you feel nauseous stuck in there, Majesty."

Carlota stopped dead. She turned and said, "The nausea will be with me for some time, however much air I have."

Manuelita raised an eyebrow. "Why do you say that, Majesty?"

The empress turned again. "No reason, Manuelita, no reason."

Since they left on this foolish journey, as he called it, Dr. Bohuslavek had monitored her health closely, in part because an effusive Maximilian had entrusted him to do so before leaving, and in part because he was sure that the dizziness and nausea had nothing to do with the state of the roads, the sailing, or the high temperatures. He had observed her closely since they left Orizaba. At first, he feared it could be typhoid, but he soon ruled that out. What Carlota was suffering from, he'd seen many times over the course of his career, and it wasn't a cause for alarm, but for celebration, especially when the subject was a young and healthy sovereign, ready to produce heirs to her throne. Even a blind man could see the empress was pregnant. Three months pregnant, Dr. Bohuslavek estimated—no more. The worst time to travel, without a doubt, which was why he was so watchful. Lately, the empress had been given to extravagant outbursts, hysterics, losing her temper. The doctor didn't like that. When Carlota returned to her cabin, she found him waiting at her door.

"Doctor, what are you doing here?"

"I've come to examine you, Your Majesty. I'm concerned about your dizzy spells."

Carlota gestured at him to enter the oven of a cabin.

"But I'm fine, Doctor. You don't need to examine me every five minutes."

"In your condition, it would be negligent of me not to do so, Your Majesty," he replied.

At first Carlota held her breath, but then she slowly sighed, releasing the tension.

"How long have you known?"

"A few weeks."

"I see."

"How have you been feeling? Apart from the vomiting and discomfort . . ."

"Not well, Doctor, not well. I'm nauseous all the time, and I no longer know whether it's from the child or the worries I have in my head."

"Does the emperor know, Your Majesty?"

Carlota opened her eyes wide before answering. "No. I haven't told him."

"And may I ask why, Empress?"

"I didn't want to tell him anything until I was sure."

"But this heir could change everything. Your Majesty should inform him."

Carlota sat down on a two-seat settee that occupied the center of the space.

"Yes. I know. It's the heir we've waited so long for."

Her voice dragged a protracted groan along with it. She wanted to hold her face in her hands and hide from Bohuslavek's eyes, but she resisted the urge with all her strength and held his gaze.

Dr. Bohuslavek remained standing, silent. Before he could say anything, Carlota spoke.

"Thank you, Doctor, you may leave."

"If Your Majesty needs me, I shall be close by."

The heat that rose in Carlota as he left was different than the one in the room.

She knew she couldn't hide her pregnancy. She could leave, she could flee the rumors, but the pregnancy would pursue her from the inside. It was inevitable—something that can't be hidden. If the baby she was expecting had been Maximilian's, everything would've been different. They'd been given three years to produce an heir, so time had been against them. For a young couple, three years was a prudent and reasonable time in which to have a child, but since Max was unable to consummate the marriage, it proved impossible: only Holy Mary could give birth as a virgin. But the blame had always fallen on her; in the eyes of the world, she was the sterile one. What other reason could there be for their failure to conceive? The rumors of her infertility had spread like wildfire from the moment dear Maximilian had decided to adopt a native boy in Querétaro to make a Habsburg of him. He had him baptized and adopted him without Carlota's knowledge, surprising both her and the Conservatives who'd crossed the sea for a European prince, only to find he'd taken a dark-skinned child as his own. The little prince lived just two days, and, though he'd been baptized as a Christian, he was buried as a native. To quell his fury, Maximilian then tried to adopt a child in keeping with his position; the most obvious was to take in the grandsons of the previous Mexican emperor Iturbide. Agustín, two, and Salvador, almost fifteen, were set to become the heirs to the throne after Maximilian died; in the meantime, they would study in Europe. The plan fell through when the boys' mother, who had initially been persuaded, decided that she preferred to have commoners for children so long as she could be their mother. To Carlota's delight, she took them away. At heart, Carlota hadn't lost hope that she would one day give birth to her own heir, born from her blood and body. How often she had wished she was pregnant . . . She'd prayed for it each night, imploring God the Father to make her conceive. And now there she was, at twenty-six, onboard a ship set for Europe, under pressure from everybody, from her husband, from the empire, to demonstrate that the Mexican adventure had not been an act of folly or some delusion of grandeur, finally pregnant, feeling more alone than ever.

10

Following Mexico's adoption of a new constitution in mid-1857, the Murrieta household was abuzz with men wearing solemn hats and worried faces. More meetings happened there than in the government offices, and the comings and goings of men in formal coats and white gloves had become as routine as Don Vicente's bad mood. The head of household received his guests discreetly, inviting them into his study, where they talked behind closed doors. It was futile, because the heated discussions could be easily heard from the hallway. Constanza listened to their raised voices as they called Juárez a traitor, or said that Ocampo and Juárez were insane, while Vicente tried to call order by banging his cane like a gavel.

Constanza fervently wished that she could take part in these debates. Knowing it was impossible, after a quick reconnaissance to make sure she wouldn't be seen, she held her ear to the door.

"But, Vicente, they're granting tax exemptions for the Isthmus of Tehuantepec and some of the borderlands; it's as if they were a condominium!" one man yelled.

"And what's more," another voice added, "they're giving free passage to the gringos between Guaymas and Rancho Los Nogales, between

Camargo and Matamoros, and wherever they want on the Tamaulipas border."

The voices grew in intensity along with their grievances, passions were inflamed, and Constanza stifled the shock and delight she felt hearing such rude language come from such honorable mouths. La Reforma not only enacted freedom of religion and the nationalization of church assets—matters crying out for a solution for opponents of Juárez—but also established civil marriage, secularized hospitals, removed clerical intervention in cemeteries, and eradicated all religious communities.

"We have to do something," they all agreed.

"But what can we do? Take up arms again?" one of them would ask.

"I can't bear another war, and I don't think Mexico can, either," another would say languidly. "I buried all four of my sons in three years."

"But we can't sit here and do nothing while the country is thrown over a cliff."

"Juárez will be our downfall."

And during each discussion, Vicente's stick thumped the floor, marking its metronomic rhythm while he thought: *We have to do something. Something. But what?*

11

As days, months, and years passed, the reform laws were enacted one by one with everyone watching, sometimes with astonishment, sometimes with disbelief. Mexico was gradually transformed, eliciting despair from some, and fueling the hopes and dreams of others. Refugio marveled at modernity reaching the country. She felt angry that they knew themselves to be an independent nation, in theory, but that they were still governed by the sons of viceroys, criollos born in Mexico of European descent, with a complex because they are from neither here nor there. She'd seen it too much, for too long. She was fed up with Santa Anna and sick to death of His Damned Excellency, as she privately called him. She much preferred Juárez. She admired and respected him, and in the silence of her heart she hoped that the notables who gathered in her parlor remained unable to agree until they learned to flow like stones dragged by the sea.

At night, away from the raised voices, as if the moon brought peace to their politicized souls, Refugio and Vicente spoke calmly. With his wife, he was a different man, unknown to anyone except her. Not even his children knew this side of him: the man who had doubts and needed advice. He didn't always allow this facet to emerge, but when it did, Refugio knew that her husband listened, at least until the moon faded and was replaced by an overbearing sun that allowed no other celestial body to shine.

"Refugio, I've been thinking," he said to her on one of these fleeting nights.

She snuggled behind him so that he could feel but not see her; she knew her husband spoke more freely without having to look her in the eyes. He felt her soft breasts pressed against his back.

"I think I know what we have to do to save the country."

"The country, or yourself, Vicente?"

He pretended not to hear her.

"I think we must become monarchists again . . . we Mexicans, I mean. Don't you think? We should have a king."

Refugio closed her eyes, or at least she thought she had, because, all of a sudden, she could only see darkness.

"What on earth are you saying, Vicente?"

"Yes . . . it's the logical thing to do. Think about it: Mexico was at its peak when it had Aztec emperors."

"Where are we going to find a *tlatoani* now, Vicente?" Refugio asked sarcastically.

"Don't be ridiculous, woman. I'm referring to a European prince."

"A European? Now you're talking nonsense, Chente."

"And why not? Independence brought disaster. Mexicans don't know how to govern themselves. We need a strong ruler, someone born to reign, someone who knows how to lead us in peace."

Refugio couldn't believe the words coming from her husband's mouth. Had he completely lost his mind? Were they all crazy, or just afraid? Couldn't they see the sovereignty that Mexico had won through blood, sweat, and tears? Refugio let go of her husband's back and leaned up on her elbow. She wanted to be upright to say what she was about to say.

"Vicente, Mexico is not a nation of monarchists. Some old fossils—like the ones that visit us so much, in fact—pretend to be because they've lost power or wealth, but there's nothing aristocratic about them."

With some effort, Vicente turned to her.

Refugio went on.

"And even if every man calling himself a monarchist joined forces, they wouldn't be a fraction of the population. The rest, as you well know, would fight the monarchy with everything they had. And a foreigner! What an absurd idea."

Vicente exhaled. He wasn't accustomed to being opposed.

"At first, perhaps, but if we asked for support from Europe . . . If foreign troops came until the situation was stable . . ."

"Are you suggesting a coup? I hear your voice but I don't know who you are, Vicente. Did you forget the humiliation of seeing the gringo flag flying in Chapultepec? Don't you remember you lost a leg fighting those who wanted to invade? You sacrificed your life, your youth; you sacrificed all of us, the children. Me. And now . . . now you want to invite them in?"

"Times change."

"And evidently people change even more."

Silence.

Refugio was burning like a lantern. To stifle the urge to slap him, she grabbed a pillow and pressed it against her chest.

"All I ask is for you to support me in this, Refugio."

"You're asking me to betray everything I believe in, which isn't the same."

"It's what you've always done, my dear."

Silence.

When she swallowed, she tasted bile. Vicente knew exactly what to say to wound her. Really wound her. It was true: she might be liberal minded, but she lived like the most committed Conservative. She had married in church, she had never opposed the demands of her father or husband, she had raised a priest and two soldiers, and she kept her daughters at home sewing, while in the privacy of her thoughts she fought for a different world. Yes, she didn't have the necessary nerve, and Vicente knew it as well as she did. She was guilty by default, for remaining silent out of inertia.

Refugio slowly let out the breath she'd been holding.

"Be honest with me, Chente, is this decision final? Is this what the meetings have been about these last few months?"

"Yes."

Another silence.

"I hope you can live with this burden on your conscience," she finally said.

"My conscience is clear," he answered.

Refugio lay back down. Now it was she who turned her back to her husband; she didn't want him to see that she was on the verge of tears. And just as Vicente thought they'd be immersed in silence again for many days, he heard her pass judgment.

"Whatever poor wretch they send, the day he no longer has the support of Europe, his head will roll."

Vicente lay on his back, staring at the ceiling. His wife's words tormented him until dawn.

12

Another person, leagues from there, also couldn't sleep. In his office, with his glasses on and head bowed, Benito Juárez was reading a letter the American government had sent him. As he had already assumed, they informed him that they couldn't intervene in the event that Mexico went to war with a European power; they were already fighting their own civil war, and men were dropping like flies. However, they offered to pay Mexico's foreign debt. Juárez settled into his seat and, in the comfort of solitude, undid the top button at his neck. As a lawyer, he was well aware that offers always came with strings attached.

Juárez narrowed his already small eyes when he reached the line: *We offer to settle the foreign debt on the condition that Mexico agrees to repay the sum within a period of six years, with interest.*

So far, so good. Juárez didn't expect something for nothing. He continued reading and came to a passage that made him jump up and support his body's weight on his knuckles. There they were: the strings.

Holding the paper closer, he read again: *In exchange, we require as a guarantee the public lands and mines of the territories of Baja California, Chihuahua, Sonora, and Sinaloa, which will be transferred as collateral to the United States when the six years have elapsed.*

Juárez took off his glasses and threw them on the desk.

"The snakes," he said to himself.

He knew without a moment's thought that he wouldn't give in to this extortion. If the Americans expected Mexico to sell them its territory in lots, they would have to wait a very long time. He wiped his forehead with a handkerchief. He knew there was no other way out. He had to make a hard but inevitable decision. Mexico had no choice: wars had impoverished it, wounded it, but it still had its dignity.

"Sovereignty is not something to be traded for a loan," he told himself.

He exhaled sharply. He had no choice but to break the Convention of London and cancel payment of the foreign debt. Mexico would officially declare itself bankrupt. Neither France nor the United Kingdom would see a single peso; not for now, at least. But there was something that concerned him: he was about to pull on the cat's whiskers, and that cat was Napoleon III.

13

The *aventure mexicaine* had begun. The British and Spanish had decided to bring the tripartite alliance to an end. The British because they were waiting for a payment that, while distant, was at least not being refused; and the Spanish, seeing that France intended to invade, decided they'd rather watch the bullfight from behind the barrier. It would be a war between the French and Mexicans. Mexico and France. And nobody else.

Juárez knew it. He had expected it from the outset, not only thanks to his astute political nose, but because he was well aware of the state of their finances, Mexico's strategic position between two oceans, and Napoleon III's colonialist aspirations. He sat at his desk and rested his elbows on the table. The weight of his head fell onto his hands for a few minutes; then he took a pen and paper and drafted a manifesto calling on Mexicans to defend their independence. He ruminated that rebel priest and leader of the Mexican War of Independence movement José María Morelos y Pavón would turn in his grave if he knew that a son of his was betraying the heroes that gave them their sovereignty and freedom not so long ago. Juan Nepomuceno Almonte—Morelos's love child—was dishonoring his father's memory by going to entreat Napoleon III to bring an emperor as foreign as he was blond back to Mexico. The word *traitor* escaped Juárez's gritted teeth. But once he'd regained his concentration, he continued with his manifesto:

I hope that you will prefer any manner of hardship or disaster to the humiliation and dishonor of losing our independence and consenting to foreigners seizing our institutions and interfering in our internal affairs.

Juárez sat back in his chair. He liked using words like that: *humiliation, dishonor.* Who could have imagined when he was tending sheep in his village that he would one day write something like this? How far he'd come, and how high the price he'd paid. Power was terrible in this way: it took with the same intensity with which it gave. He stared blankly for a few seconds. He thought. He thought about so many things. It seemed absurd to him to have to issue such an appeal. He could understand the need to fight for political ideas and systems of governance, but having to ask Mexicans to have faith in the republic, in *his* republic and nation, was the last straw. He grimaced and picked up his pen again.

Let us have faith in the justice of our cause, let us have faith in our efforts, and united we shall save Mexico's independence, bringing victory not only for our country, but also for the principles of respect and the inviolability of future nations' sovereignty.

He carefully read what he had just written. Yes, he thought, it was just right. He signed the document.

Juárez hadn't met Maximilian, nor did he want to. He imagined him to be like any other blond-haired, bearded prince, inflated with power and a lust for conquest. He had some vague ideas, he'd heard rumors that he was a little delicate, and somewhat liberal, too. Something inside was telling him to establish some kind of contact with him, not out of politeness, but for political expedience. The moment the Austrian set foot on Mexican soil, he would have to kill him. An affront such as the one Maximilian was about to commit couldn't be answered in any other way, even if Juárez was a man of the law. The law was his temple, and that included martial law. Always the law. Always in accordance with what was right. That was what had kept him going: the certainty of knowing that a man without laws is a barbarian, a caveman. And since he wasn't, he knew he must act in good faith, without treachery or unfair advantage, that each step he took must represent firm progress toward maintaining sovereignty and justice. *Justice*, that was his favorite word. His second favorite was *Margarita*, the name of the woman who loved him for who he was, for nothing more than what he was when he was naked. It seemed impossible that a statesman like Maximilian couldn't see the absurdity of his enterprise. What sane man, noble or otherwise, decides to cross the ocean to govern a land that doesn't belong to him? Not even animals do that.

He sent for one of his trusted men and ordered him to travel to Miramare to meet the prince in question. The man wasn't pleased with the request. Seeing the look on his face, Juárez explained.

"If the Habsburg still comes here after what you're going to tell him, it won't be on my conscience, but on his."

"And what must I say exactly, Presidente?"

"Show him the other side of the coin, of course. They have the man convinced Mexico will lay out a carpet of roses for him when he sets foot in Veracruz. We must tell him he'll find only disdain and resistance."

"I see . . ."

"We must tell him that the letters of support are a trick."

"But why warn him, Presidente? Why put him on the alert?"

"Because that is what decent men do." Then he added, "And so they can't then say I didn't warn them."

With a marked lack of enthusiasm, Juárez's emissary set off for Trieste, where he was received weeks later by a bemused and incredulous

Maximilian, suspicious of everything he said. Even if there was resistance at first, he was sure that, little by little, Mexico would soften. That was what everyone had told him. Even so, Juárez's courtesy touched his soul, and so, honoring the nobility and benevolence with which he was endowed, Maximilian, with a smile that seemed inordinately stupid to the emissary, said, "Tell Juárez he shall by all means have a place in my cabinet."

14

It was a cold spring. The air still carried winds that made shelter and blankets necessary to keep warm. But Juan Nepomuceno Almonte couldn't have cared less about the freezing nights. He was a man who knew power didn't exist in a vacuum. Since his arrival in Europe, he'd done nothing but conspire to install a Conservative government in Mexico, headed by a Catholic European prince. He was determined to destroy the fool Juárez, along with his republic and his reforms. Almonte incited; he changed sides at his convenience; he stirred up trouble at will. Nobody ever knew what he really thought, because he strung them all along—sometimes in French, sometimes in English, often in Spanish, but always seeming to protect interests. And his interests now hinged on the empire: an empire that, if everything went according to plan, he would do well from. Power. That's what motivated him. He was beginning to feel the glory of being in power. When he spoke, kings listened; they received him in their palaces, they sat him alongside dignitaries and people of noble birth. And he began to imagine he wouldn't spend the rest of his life as he had spent his youth, fighting on the battlefield, plagued with death and grief, but would rule from behind a desk in an office. Governing. That was the dream of his old age. He'd sown seeds in his favor, and expected to be regent of the empire until Maximilian and Carlota arrived in Mexico. *Regent,* he said to himself when he looked in the mirror. And vanity made the base of his neck tingle.

Trusting his judgment, on one cold spring night, a French general came to him to ask him the best way to advance through the country after they left Veracruz and climbed the hazardous peaks of Acultzingo. Almonte offered enthusiastic encouragement.

"You'll have already done the hard part, and your army is the best in the world. All you have to do then is advance toward Mexico City, through Puebla, which will be child's play."

"What makes you say that?"

"Puebla is Conservative and Catholic. It's hostile to Juárez. I'm certain you'll be received with jubilation by the Poblanos. They may even shower you with flowers," said Almonte, flashing a row of white teeth that contrasted with his dark skin.

The French general smiled back at him, like someone infected by another's yawn.

Almonte went on. "At any rate, I've cleared the way for you. As you know, I'm making sure that the French army are welcomed in Mexico."

The general knew that the Mexicans weren't receiving them with open arms; quite the opposite: they were a ferocious and battle-hardened people who, when they exhausted their ammunition, used stones against bayonets. The bucolic image that Almonte was peddling to them of Mexicans throwing flowers from balconies hadn't materialized, not yet at least.

Almonte sensed some suspicion in the Frenchman's eyes. With complete serenity, the Mexican said to him, "You have nothing to worry about, General. *Ne vous inquiétez pas.* Puebla will be a walkover."

15

The walkover became a journey through hell. The French found neither flowers nor cheers when they reached Puebla. The weather didn't welcome them, either: for five hours they had to fight against four thousand men in rain of biblical proportions. It was May 5, 1862, and Almonte, for the first time in years, felt as if the ground under his feet was soft, slippery mud.

In Paris, the rivers of ink reporting on the campaign were comparable only to the rivers of blood spilled on Atlixco. The papers reported that the Mexican informants had sent the French to their deaths, and they were branded spies or backstabbers; with such allies they didn't need enemies. The French had been told that the Mexican army was disorganized, naïve, and inexperienced, but they were beginning to believe their grasp on Mexico was as weak as their knowledge of it. The streets reflected the tension that prevailed in the palace. Eugénie de Montijo bit her cuticles when nobody was watching. Napoleon III was furious; he'd rarely been so furious. They couldn't afford to have lost such a decisive battle, and only four contingents had fought against the French army: it was a humiliation. The court was unhappy, but they hid beneath a veil of tranquility while they sipped tea. Napoleon wandered about in a gloomy state and seemed to be in constant contemplation. Feasts and hunts were canceled. And the entourage, as if infected with the monarch's sorrow, wandered with heads hanging, speaking in low voices. All Napoleon could do was sit at his desk and remove and replace his wedding ring as if it burned.

One afternoon, Almonte, ashamed and afraid, visited Eugénie de Montijo. He was nervous, prepared for a verbal lashing. He had all the answers ready. He'd recriminated himself in silence for his foolishness, but who could have imagined that the Poblanos would stand up to the finest army in the world! Because that was what the French were . . . Or was he wrong? Either way, there was nothing he could do now. He appeared before her calm on the outside but terrified within. He'd invested too much energy, too many years, in the empire project to lose it all because of a few thousand plucky rebels. No sooner did he see the empress than he felt a pounding in his chest. He waited for a long time for her to make a complaint, an indirect one, perhaps, but nothing came. Almonte broke the silence.

"Your Majesty, I understand you are upset at the Battle of Puebla."

To which Eugénie only replied, "These things happen in war."

"I assumed we would easily—"

"Wars aren't won on assumptions, Almonte. I hope you have learned your lesson."

"Of course, Your Majesty."

16

In Miramare, uncertainty and unease were in the air. Carlota paced the room, shocked and anxious. The news from France was disheartening. The army that was meant to pave the way to their imperial throne, the army that guaranteed their investiture, had just suffered a crushing defeat. Carlota didn't know what to think. The Italians resisting them from the shadows tormented her, and she prayed they wouldn't encounter the same situation thousands of leagues away. Not more disdain. Not more. Maximilian must be suffering the same agony, she thought. Agitated and tired of brooding alone, she went to her husband's study: after all, a burden shared weighed less, or at least, she'd heard her grandmother say something like that. She found him reading with keen interest.

"Am I interrupting?"

Maximilian roused from his trance and invited her in.

"Oh! Come in, Charlotte, you must see this," he said.

She went closer to read over his shoulder. She thought he might have been rereading the letters of support, the ones Mexican diplomats sent by the sack load, conveying the goodwill and express desire of the people of Mexico to have an emperor. Those messages filled them with such hope in times of doubt. But no: as she approached, she saw that he was reading a book about Mexico's flora and fauna. Surprised and touched, Carlota wanted to say something, but she wanted to choose her words carefully. He spoke before she did.

"It's fascinating how many animals go to Mexico to complete their reproductive cycles. See?" he said, pointing at an illustration. For an instant, Carlota wished that Mexico's influence, if there were such a thing, would have the same effect on her that it had on animals. Perhaps some Aztec god favored maternity in some miraculous way, beyond human understanding? Was there a scientific reason why nature converged in that part of the world to bless species and their progeny? Perhaps, she dreamed, in Mexico she would become a mother. And then, shaking her head and feeling deep sorrow, she forced herself to forget these heretical thoughts of false gods.

"What a splendid place! Don't you think?" Maximilian went on, oblivious to his wife's thoughts.

"Yes, yes, it is," Carlota murmured.

"Beginning tomorrow, we'll receive lessons in Spanish and Nahuatl. I've already given instructions to a Spanish priest, and—"

"Maximilian," she broke in, "have you heard about the French army's defeat in Puebla?"

"Oh. Yes, they informed me. But don't worry: Napoleon assures me his plans haven't changed."

Carlota took a breath before saying, "Don't you think we're counting our chickens before they've hatched?"

Maximilian gave her a dry look. "Do you no longer desire Mexico's throne for me?"

"It's not a question of desire. We must be certain, because once we've embarked there'll be no turning back."

"Certainty? There is no certainty, Charlotte. You know as well as I do there will be resistance from Juárez, that's to be expected, but in the end the empire will win. You'll see."

"Are you sure you wouldn't prefer to remain in Miramare?"

The question wounded Maximilian's pride.

"I've withdrawn, distancing myself from my brother. I believe he's jealous of me; he envies the freedom of my travels . . . my liberal ideas scandalize him. Since he is sovereign, he's pushed me aside. But I'm not sure I can die in the silence of Lokrum, no matter how glorious the island's gardens are."

Carlota pressed her lips together. Though she'd never admitted it to anyone, she was also horrified by the idea of contemplating the sea until she was seventy.

Maximilian continued. "And now, from nowhere, at my thirty years of age, the Mexican throne appears, giving me the opportunity to free myself once and for all from the snares and the oppression of a life without action, a life without purpose."

Carlota held him by the hands. "Very well, my love," she said. "Let's not lose faith."

Carlota left her husband to delve into his books on animals and lands as exotic as they were unfamiliar, while she devoted herself to reading about matters befitting their rank. She wanted to know about the nation she would be empress of. She immersed herself in volumes as thick as bricks on politics and economics. She drank in everything she found on Mexico's history, from the Spanish conquest to independence. She studied conscientiously, in great detail, until her heart was filled with a profound respect for the Mexican people, and almost without realizing it, she began to feel something akin to love for their culture, their customs, their struggles. And she made her growing admiration for this far-off country occupy the space that Maximilian continued to leave empty in her heart.

17

Exiled on the British island of Guernsey, Victor Hugo was brimming with joy. He was proud, as if Ignacio Zaragoza, the general who led the Mexicans to victory, had been his own son. Any victory over the Second Empire was cause for celebration and hope for humanity. His rejection of Napoleon III exuded from his every pore, and he was in exile because, among other things, he'd baptized the emperor "Napoleon the Little." That was what the monarch represented to him: a tiny being of negligible intelligence. But while there were people like the Poblanos, there was hope, he thought, jubilant. As bold as brass, letting out little exclamations that weren't quite laughter but greatly resembled it, he began to write a letter.

A couple of months later, on one of the many afternoons when clear skies revealed the snowcapped volcanoes in the distance, Constanza's mother handed her a book. Constanza sensed she was tense, trembling even.

"Mother, what is it?"

Refugio held Constanza's gaze. There was emotion in her eyes, and it took her a moment to let go of the volume. Then she said, "Read all of it. And, for the love of God, don't let your father see it." Then she left.

Constanza frowned. *How strange,* she thought. For the first time since she was a child, she felt afraid receiving a prohibited book from her mother; or was it just foresight? They'd been doing this for years, and they'd never been discovered. There was no reason to be afraid now. Or was there? Of course she wouldn't show it to her father! Had she ever slipped up and jeopardized this window to the world she had? Constanza read the title. It was a law book. She let out a breath of air that sent her bangs up for a moment. She turned it around and looked at the back cover. Nothing. At first glance, it was a boring book, but her mother had said *Read all of it.* She settled back against her cushion and opened it: a crumpled letter—a well-traveled letter—fell out. It was a letter that had been read many times by many people; this was evident because it had been handled, hugged, kissed, and it wasn't a love letter. Constanza picked it up carefully and began to read.

> *People of Puebla,*
> *You are right to believe that I am with you.*
> *It is not France that wages war on you. It is the empire.*
> *I am with you; you and I are fighting against the empire. You in your country, I in exile. Fight, battle, be terrible, and, if you believe that my name may serve you, make use of it. Aim bullets of freedom at that man's head. Brave men of Mexico, resist.*
> *Victor Hugo*

Who could have told Refugio that, just a year after Constanza read that letter, French troops would lay siege to Puebla? The French counterattack was to be expected, but nobody could have imagined its ferocity. It was a while before Refugio came to terms with the fact that Joaquín, her firstborn, would be on the front line when it happened. A siege. The worst experience in a war, but among the most effective strategies. A military blockade to the death. This time, to avoid over-confidence again, the invading troops numbered thirty-five thousand men, and they were joined by the Mexican Conservatives. The city couldn't have been more desolate: there was no way in or out of Puebla. It became a coffin from which nothing escaped alive. It was surrounded by 176 cannons, a wall of death that smelled of gunpowder. General Zaragoza, who had fought bravely the previous May, was gone, and it wasn't combat that killed him, but typhoid fever. An undignified death for such a valiant man. Others took his place, but despite their willingness, there was nothing anyone could do in the face of such an overwhelming force. If every man in Zacapoaxtla had fought, they still wouldn't have been able to stop the French. As Puebla became a war zone, it wasn't the bullets that claimed most lives. For sixty-two days, every living creature inside the city experienced the horror of a siege. There was no food, no water. People died of hunger and thirst. The bodies, piled on top of one another, carpeted the streets, and the survivors learned to avert their eyes, in an attempt to make their hearts believe they would live to bury them when it was all over. Starving, they began eating any animal they could find, even domestic ones, and before long there wasn't a single pet left because, sensing their fate, they ran away if someone came near them. The military commanders had to accept that it wasn't the French they were losing to, but hunger. With no other solution, the only way to survive was to surrender.

One by one, the French captured the generals, who handed themselves over with their arms in the air. Despite the defeat, the men made an enormous effort to preserve their dignity before a haughty, clear-eyed French marshal; had he been Mexican, they would have considered him a man to follow, but he was the Frenchest of Frenchmen. His name was Achille Bazaine, and nobody had yet found his weak spot.

"Name?" he asked.

"General Porfirio Díaz," the prisoner replied.

They held each other's gaze. Díaz, not caring whether the Frenchman understood him, said, "Hunger finished us off."

Bazaine looked closely at him. Something told him he must remember this man, defeated and surrendering. Pretending he didn't understand, he continued.

"Name?" he asked the next man.

"Mariano Escobedo," the man replied.

Thus, one by one, man by man, victory for one side and defeat for the other were decided. *One battle does not a war make,* they told themselves, disheartened. Puebla could resist no longer and surrendered.

Juárez withdrew, knowing that twelve thousand could not succeed against the invading army.

"We fall back because of the strength of the enemy, not because we are going to make any kind of compromise," he said on the gallop.

His men had anguish in their eyes, and so without stopping, Juárez, to fill them—and himself—with hope, yelled, *"Justice is on our side. Walk on!"*

His wife, Margarita, pregnant, also undertook the retreat. They moved slowly to the north, where, for the next three years, they established a temporary presidency while they waited for a more favorable moment.

"Favorable for what?" Margarita asked him one night.

"Why, for revenge, of course."

18

They finally reached the port of Saint-Nazaire on August 8, 1866. Carlota had expected to be received by a court befitting of her rank. Instead, there were just two people waiting for the ship. Carlota took a deep breath and, hiding the immense disappointment that threatened to make her lose her footing, she slowly descended. To her surprise, she saw that the flag flying to welcome her was not green, white, and red, but red, white, and red. Apparently, a member of the port's citizens' council had recently traveled to Peru and bought a flag there, and in the absence of a Mexican flag, the port authority had hoisted it as an alternative. *They'll never notice the difference,* they thought, unaware of Carlota's patriotic soul and pride.

As soon as she saw it, the empress cried out. "What despicable act is this!" she yelled.

The mayor, who had arrived at the disembarkation, began to stammer nervously. "Forgive us, Your Majesty, our town is barely born. But we will endeavor to serve you as you deserve."

Carlota was unable to hide her indignation. "Mr. Mayor, I am grateful to you, but how is it that the prefect isn't here to welcome us? The troops have not presented arms, and so the Mexican court will pass through your city unescorted. Take us immediately to the train."

Juan Nepomuceno Almonte and his wife, the only members of the foreign service who'd come to welcome the empress, alarmed at her unceremonious fury, interceded in a low voice. "Forgive us, Your Majesty . . . It appears they don't know the diplomatic protocol."

"Outrageous! Outrageous!" And then, looking at the Peruvian flag, she murmured, "I know more about China than these people know about Mexico."

Carlota calmed herself, certain that God was testing her. *Humility, Charlotte, humility.* She looked around, with a mixture of rage and sorrow, for the other members of the welcome party: nobody except a couple of imperialists had come to receive her. She was alone. It appeared that would be the constant in her life. Though she was always surrounded by people, she was beginning to recognize the worst loneliness of all: the one felt in company. She had only herself. There was no one else.

She was in Europe and, nonetheless, she didn't feel at home. Since her arrival in Mexico, she'd known she would die in those warm lands full of vegetation and the sounds of wildlife. She had Mexico under her skin, in her heart, and for the first time in her life, she thought she'd found somewhere not just to arrive, but also to return to. Mexico was far away now. Very far away. But she would return. Soon.

"We'll depart for Paris as soon as possible," she said to Almonte.

On the train, Carlota learned from Almonte that Austria had just lost the Battle of Königgrätz. The defeat was terrible not only for Austria but also for France, for now a war with Prussia seemed closer.

"How many dead?" asked Carlota.

"Thirty-five thousand, Your Majesty."

Thirty-five thousand, she repeated silently to herself. As many as they had sent to Mexico. After a few seconds of reflection, the empress spoke. "Napoleon is going to need all his troops back. This is going to be harder than I thought, and I already knew it would be hard."

"Indeed, Your Majesty. What's more, you should know that Napoleon's health has deteriorated. Just a few days ago, he returned from his treatment at the thermal waters of Vichy. He goes there often."

"I wasn't aware of his delicate health."

"And not only that: the atmosphere at the Tuileries is tense. People are blaming Empress Eugénie for making France go to war, Your Majesty."

Carlota nodded. Eugénie de Montijo was an ambitious woman who'd always known how to whisper in her husband's ear to inflame his imperialist instincts. Carlota could feel it in her bones. It had been Eugénie who'd suggested Maximilian of Habsburg, archduke of Austria, as a possible emperor of Mexico when the Assembly of Notables turned to France in search of a European prince; Napoleon had sworn then that he would always be by their side, supporting them. Not even three years had passed since this ultimately unfulfilled promise had been made.

"Don Juan, send a telegram to the French emperor informing him that I shall arrive in Paris tomorrow and that I've been entrusted with a special mission by Emperor Maximilian. I request an urgent audience."

"I will do that, Your Majesty."

Receiving the telegram, Eugénie de Montijo ran to her husband's bedchamber.

"Charlotte is in Paris."

"Charlotte of Belgium?"

"Of course. Who else?"

"I suppose they tired of sending emissaries who never make it past the waiting room."

"I told you, Louis. Now you'll have to receive her. She's an empress."

Napoleon lay back on his canopy bed. He looked ill and seemed to have aged.

"How can I avoid receiving her? We're on the verge of collapse, and the last thing I need is a battle with a hysterical woman demanding help that anyone can see I can't give."

Eugénie, who always supported her husband, gave him an idea. "Send her a telegram telling her you're indisposed."

Napoleon reflected for a moment. Then he ordered, "Do it."

Carlota received the telegram with the refusal the next day. Unfolding the piece of paper, she read:

> *Just received telegram from Your Majesty. I have returned from Vichy unwell and must remain in bed, impossible for me to receive you. If Your Majesty goes to Belgium first, it will give me time to recover.*
> *Napoleon*

Carlota crumpled the paper into a ball as she grunted in disgust.

"Belgium! I have no intention of going there. What for? To visit Leopold and Philippe, when Mexico hangs by a thread?"

Carlota was speaking to herself aloud so that she could hear her own voice. She needed to reassert herself.

"In any case, what have my brothers done for me now that France has turned its back on us? Nothing! I shall not move from here!"

Almonte had reserved an entire floor for them at the Grand Hotel to distract the empress from the fact that she wouldn't be received at the Tuileries. Carlota installed herself in a large, comfortable room that smelled of flowers and summer. A general and a count came to pay their respects.

"I hope you are comfortable in the room, Your Majesty."

Carlota attempted a smile in response to the courtesy. The men, faced with her silence, added, "Empress Eugénie will call on you when you are ready to receive her."

Something in Carlota's heart darkened. She understood the language of protocol; she had grown up hearing it. These words could only mean that Napoleon was refusing to meet her in person. She knew when her intelligence had been insulted.

"I shall receive the empress immediately, so you may summon her."

The men, uncomfortable, agreed to her request with a nod.

"And tell her that I intend to remain in the city until I have completed the mission entrusted to me. Not a day longer. I have no family here, and nobody who cares about Mexico."

When she was left alone, Carlota burst into tears. She didn't allow any of her attendants to enter her bedchamber, despite their attempts to console her, for her sobs could be heard through the door.

19

While Europe marveled at *Les Misérables*—Victor Hugo's novel that, they said, was an authentic portrayal of French society—on the other side of the ocean, Vicente Murrieta was struggling with his own ideas on law, politics, justice, and religion, deciding which pawn to move first in his particular game of chess. His hand was unsteady. And it wasn't a trivial matter, for the piece he was about to move was one of his own sons.

Since he and the other Conservatives had begun to execute the plan to install a European monarch in Mexico, not a moment passed in which he wasn't pondering the issue. The way the negotiations were going in Vienna, it appeared it would be the brother of Franz Joseph of Austria, Maximilian of Habsburg. The Murrietas had to be present at a historic moment like this: one of his eldest sons, Joaquín or Salvador, must be among the Mexicans who would travel to Europe in search of the prince. Neither Joaquín nor Salvador would be surprised, for they were also present in the meetings behind closed doors, and from a young age they'd been instructed in military and diplomatic arts. Being part of an imperial army excited them; it was what they had been prepared for, and they would be ready when the moment came. They had been ready for a long time. But Vicente had more ambitious plans.

He wanted one of them to be considered for the Assembly of Notables, which would not only travel to Europe, but also speak to the future emperor in person.

He knew he couldn't send both sons on this assignment. He had to choose one. Like in chess, he couldn't move a single piece without establishing why and what for. A bad decision could lead to ruin. Each move, as insignificant as it might seem, must lead toward an objective that might only become clear several moves later. Who would he send? Why? What for? His sons, though both well prepared and highly intelligent, were very different. Each had his talents, but sometimes, under certain circumstances, virtues could become defects. Joaquín was the firstborn and therefore first in the decision-making line. In his father's absence, Joaquín would be head of the household; that had been instilled in him since he was a child. At some point in the—God willing—distant future, he would take up the role of patriarch. He would be responsible for his mother and sisters in the event that his father—may God preserve him for many years—left this world before his sisters had found husbands. Joaquín had carried this responsibility since his head appeared between his mother's legs and he emerged as the first male child. He'd been brought up in the image of Vicente, for better or worse. Everything he knew, he'd learned from his father, from the way he gave orders to the servants, to the manner in which he joked over a drink; he was his replica without the walking stick. Reaching adulthood, he even seemed to speak with the same tone of voice. He had been a good student, a good son, and a good soldier. He was, Refugio might say, the son that every mother would like to have, and perhaps it was the combination of Vicente's toughness and her humanity that resulted in such a fine man, a mixture of severity and kindness in equal measure. As a child, he never acted out, never answered back, and always fulfilled his obligations and duties willingly. Later, he became a handsome young man, athletic and devout, affectionate with his sisters, and disinterested in women. As a man, before going into combat, he wrote tender letters to his family giving them courage in the event that they lost him and hope that he would return, and when it came to it, he fought the enemy with conviction and bravery, with a great love of life and without fear of death.

Salvador, on the other hand, was very unlike his father. He was sensitive, and from a young age they scolded him for talking to himself for hours on end, discussing all manner of subjects. He too was a good son but, for his father's taste, he was too much like Refugio. He didn't have the sense of responsibility that seemed to exude from Joaquín's every pore. He only spoke when he was directly asked something, not out of shyness but because he preferred thinking to himself. He never missed a detail, but others didn't seem aware of his quick wit. They thought, perhaps, he had his head in the clouds, dreaming impossible dreams, forever waiting for a distant future. Like his brother, he also received military training. That was the family custom, and he never showed any interest in doing anything else. Had they asked him, he might have said he wanted to be an architect, an engineer, or an artist, because to him, happiness consisted of building; anyone could destroy. He proved to be a good soldier with little inclination to show off. Medals did not excite him as they did Joaquín, whose uniform was covered in them. On occasion, Salvador had seen a tear in his brother's eyes while he polished them. For him, the only decorations that were worth anything were ones made of flesh: he treasured scars, whether he made them or they were the ones that marked him. He struggled to see an enemy in the young men who fought against him. Being a soldier was the most difficult exercise in discipline he faced each day. He believed the best battle was one that remained unfought. He would sooner negotiate peace than win a war, and yet, every morning, he put on his uniform, commended himself to the Virgin, and prayed he wouldn't have to kill anyone this day or the next. Still, he brandished his bayonet mercilessly, like a gladiator in the Roman circus. To kill or to die, that was his struggle. He never admitted it. Never. It was something he kept to himself.

Nevertheless, Vicente knew it. He knew them both perfectly. He had watched them grow up; he had seen them ripen until they fell from the tree. He knew their hearts and their fears with the skill of a psychic. He had seen them suffer, and though he had wished he could intervene to ease their burden, he had never allowed himself to do so. His way of being a good father was to teach his sons to accept failure as well as victory, to overcome the intoxication of success, allowing them to cry in peace. He kept his distance, watching them discreetly, taking pride in their triumphs as well as their defeats, because he knew in his flesh—in his own leg—the immense value of falls that force one to stand back up again. He never hugged them or showed affection, but sometimes gave them a pat on the back and a lesson in life in the hope that he had said something that would stay with them forever. Yes, he knew them well, though they thought he didn't understand them at all.

He knew who to send, why, and what for.

He summoned them to his study, closed the door, and gave them the news.

There were reproaches. Questions. Accusations. Tempers flared, and the brothers began to air the dirty laundry they had kept locked up until that moment. Vicente, fed up with the foolishness, thumped his stick against the floor so hard the ivory handle almost came off.

"I do not have to explain my decision. It will be obeyed, and that's that!"

Joaquín left the study certain his father had just made a terrible mistake.

Salvador would go to Miramare.

20

1863, Belgium

Getting the letter of recommendation from Mr. Walton proved to be more than a headache for Philippe. It hadn't been easy to persuade the man that he truly wanted to join the empress's regiment in Mexico. When he brought it up, Mr. Walton thought the boy was joking and laughed so hard he had a coughing fit. Philippe offered him a glass of water. As soon as he could speak, the first thing Mr. Walton said was "Good one! The carpenter's apprentice turned soldier. A soldier for the empress, no less! Lad, if you're trying to kill me with laughter, you're doing a good job . . ."

Philippe was accustomed to his master's rude remarks, but this was a whole new humiliation. Mr. Walton had yelled at him, and scolded him, but he'd never laughed in his face because of a request made in all seriousness.

"I'm being serious," said Philippe. "I need you to write me a letter of recommendation. I'll take care of everything else."

"What're you talking about, lad? Have you completely lost your mind? Open your eyes. Why do you think this offer is so good? Land, wages, military rank . . . They don't care if they're sending a trained soldier or a beggar. They need cannon fodder, lad . . ."

But Philippe wasn't listening. From the moment he'd read the advertisement, his heart had dreamed of adventure. He imagined what it would be like to live so far away from everything he'd known until now. In fact, he'd never really emerged from the damp cave that terrified him so much as a child. If he'd been waiting for a turning point, this was it; this was his moment to let go of doubt and free himself. This was his opportunity to find out what he was made of, and nothing would please him more than dying in the attempt.

Mr. Walton continued his argument. "Plague, fever, vomiting . . . Civilization hasn't reached there yet, lad. Let these delusions of colonial grandeur go and get to work; it's getting late."

Philippe realized the letter would be harder to get than he'd first thought. He hadn't imagined that Mr. Walton wouldn't let him leave. Since he'd moved there, he had always felt like a burden, a nuisance. When Arthur found homes for his siblings, scattering them like seeds on a field, Philippe was the last one settled. He didn't feel comfortable anywhere, and fled each house, until one day he arrived at Walton's carpentry workshop. He marveled at the things he saw there. The workshop's specialty was figureheads, so when he walked in, he immediately encountered a mermaid's bare breasts right in front of him, her hair blowing in the wind. Philippe stood spellbound when he suddenly heard a mammoth's footsteps. A fat man emerged from the room at the back, swaying from side to side as he walked, so corpulent that he reminded Philippe of the strong man on the circus posters: his thick moustache joined up with his sideburns, and his hands could have destroyed an apple with a single squeeze. He brayed when he breathed, no doubt because of the gigantic belly that prevented him from seeing his feet. When he approached, Philippe unconsciously retreated.

"Open your mouth," the man ordered without even asking his name.

"Why?" Philippe asked.

"You open it, lad, unless you want me to open it with this!" He gestured at some kind of pincers on the table.

Philippe timidly opened his mouth. Walton squeezed his cheeks together with fingers like sausages and inspected his teeth.

"Good," he finally said. "You can stay."

That was it. A superficial inspection of his teeth, and nothing else. Not even a *welcome*, or a formal introduction, or a pat on the back. That was how, amid teeth and varnish, Walton entered his life.

He grew up under the guidance of this man of few words, something Philippe was grateful for at first. The silence gradually made them accomplices in its own way. They carved together from morning until night and, after a job well done, Walton contemplated the piece with satisfaction for a while. He said nothing and never praised Philippe; his way of doing so was to entrust him with new pieces and better wood. They learned to understand each other without crossing the boundary that would lead to friendship: Walton erected a barrier between them that he never took down, and Philippe never did anything to overcome it. It was their status quo. Little by little, they grew accustomed to one another's presence. Over time, Walton taught Philippe marquetry, carving, turning, and inlay, and he started to feel at home creating wonders from pieces of wood. Despite the silence and bad manners, it was a refuge where Philippe grew up without fear of the cold winters, and learned to embrace the solitude of his trade. When he created something, he felt less lonely, though he sometimes wished he could talk to someone about hopes and dreams that extended beyond the workshop's four walls. But this was his life and this was how he'd learned to live it.

After his proposal to leave for Mexico was met with mockery, he carried on working without saying a word. Mr. Walton didn't realize that in that sea of silence there was anything but calm. Philippe's mind churned: if Walton was the only obstacle between him and his future, he'd have to do something about it. He started plotting. He needed to find his master's weak point. *Don't we all have one?* he thought. Something that would enable him to torment Walton, if necessary, until he extracted the damned letter from him. For the first time he recognized that he knew nothing about the man. He wondered whether he'd ever been in love, why he lived alone, and, most of all, why he'd taken Philippe into the mausoleum of his solitude.

Walton didn't allow Philippe into the room at the back under any circumstances, not even to clean or get materials. Sometimes, when he ran out of paint, Philippe had been forced to contrive a way to color some varnish in order to finish painting a figurehead's Phrygian hat, because Mr. Walton wouldn't give him the key to the storeroom. He rationed all the materials. Whenever Philippe asked for something, Walton replied, *What do you need it for?* He had to justify every last drop used in a job. And God forbid the accounts didn't balance one day; he would be made to pay for it with extra hours or missing dinner. So it was clear Walton was hiding something in there. Philippe had to find out what.

For a month, he saved every cent Walton gave him. He reduced his consumption of food so much that he lost a few pounds. But he needed as much money as possible: he had to be able to afford the most extravagant of nights for his master. After a great deal of effort and sacrifice, it was finally time. Philippe woke at the crack of dawn, as ever, went down to the kitchen to make tea, as ever, and waited, as ever, for Mr. Walton to yell from upstairs to put the kettle on. But when Walton came down, he didn't find himself alone as he usually did: Philippe was waiting for him.

"Good morning," he said politely.

Walton frowned and, puzzled, he sniffed hard.

"What're you doing here gawping, lad? Get to work, it's getting late."

"Yes, right away, sir. It's just, I was wondering . . . do you know what day it is today?"

"Today? Today's Wednesday, lad."

"Yes, yes, Wednesday. But do you know what we're celebrating today?"

Walton put his hands on his hips. The conversation was beginning to make him feel uncomfortable.

"The only thing we're going to celebrate is me giving you a couple of slaps if you don't get to work!"

"It's ten years today since you took me in, sir."

Walton sighed. He seemed to be counting.

"And?"

"Well, I was wondering if I could buy you a beer after work."

Walton crossed his arms.

"A beer?"

"If I may, sir, as a token of my appreciation."

"Hmmm. Maybe. Finish your work. Then we'll see."

And that was the end of the most intimate conversation they had had in a long time. Philippe had tossed the coin into the air; now all he had to do was see if it was heads or tails. And it landed on the right side. After work, Walton, who seemed to have been reflecting all afternoon, stood and gestured at him, and then Philippe knew it was only a matter of how much beer the man could hold, which judging by his size could be a lot.

The biggest problem Philippe had that night was carrying Mr. Walton's dead weight up the stairs. The man weighed more than a sea lion, and the poor lad had to drag him by the feet to his bed. It took him several hours to transport the immense body, unconscious from drink, from the tavern to the house, and on the way, Walton took several bumps to the head.

He's going to kill me when he wakes up, thought Philippe.

But everything had gone according to plan. For a moment, he'd been worried the alcohol would never take effect. And Walton drank as if he had a hollow leg! But just when Philippe thought he was going to have to spend another month saving even more, Walton broke down in tears and began telling him that he loved him like a son.

Job done, thought Philippe, and then he let the situation unravel by itself.

By the time he got the man into bed, Philippe was soaked in sweat. He sat on the steps to catch his breath and held his hand to his jacket pocket, feeling for the object inside. In the background he could hear Walton snoring.

"Poor man," Philippe said. "Tomorrow he'll have a headache the size of a cathedral."

He didn't want to tempt fate, and, after regaining his breath, he ran to the back room of the workshop and searched the closely guarded drawers in Walton's desk.

It turned out that his master was as solitary a man inside as he was on the outside: Philippe found no clues about his past. What he did find was something interesting about his present; Walton, as cantankerous and stingy as he was, had two sets of accounts. Two ledgers. He paid no taxes.

"Well, well . . . ," Philippe said through gritted teeth. "So that's it." Walton was boring even when it came to the secrets he kept.

And to think he kept Philippe almost on bread and water while he hoarded every penny! He was grateful he'd not grown up unprotected and that he'd learned a trade, but Philippe suddenly felt furious. He'd given his life to a miserly man who would be buried with a heap of coins, who couldn't even show affection to the person who had made him tea every morning for the last ten years. Any remorse, any doubt that remained in his heart, vanished.

He took the ledgers and shut himself in his room.

Walton's bellows the next morning preceded the cock's crow: he woke feeling as if an army of elephants were marching in his head. With difficulty, he went down to the kitchen and sat in one of the chairs, resting the weight of his head on his forearms. Philippe was waiting for him in the half-light.

"I'm going," the young man told him.

"Yes, go, go. Get to work, it's getting late."

"No. I'm leaving. Forever."

With some effort, Walton looked up. He narrowed his eyes. "What did you say, lad?"

"I'm going. I'm going to volunteer for the Belgian regiment in Mexico."

Walton let his head drop again. "Don't be a fool, lad. You can't go."

Philippe's only answer was to slide a letter of recommendation that he had written himself across the table, attesting to his excellent character.

"Sign it and I'm gone."

"I'm not signing anything!" Walton yelled, thumping the table with his fist.

"Sign it or I'll tell them about your books."

"What books?"

"These ones!" It was then Walton saw that Philippe was holding two large red ledgers.

Defying the pain in his body, Walton stood and lunged, but Philippe, with quick reflexes, backed out of the way. The long table separated them. Walton began to cough.

"Let me go. Sign the letter, and I'll leave forever. No one will ever find out about your fraud."

"How do I know you won't blabber?"

"Look . . . all I want is to get out of here. Go far away. I don't care what you do with your life or your money. Just sign the letter and you'll never hear from me again."

Walton slumped back into his chair, which strained under the sudden weight. All at once, his tone softened. "What're you going there for, lad? You'll probably die on the way."

"And what do you care?"

Walton looked up. He wanted to say, *I do care,* but he didn't know how. He reflected that he had never really known how to love someone.

"Help me," Philippe pleaded.

Walton held the letter. He read it, picked up the pen, and reluctantly signed it.

"You're out of your mind, lad."

21

In mid-1863, Salvador Murrieta set off for Trieste with a group of Conservatives. The delegation was made up of ten men, one of them a priest—nicknamed the Doctor for his wisdom—representing the Catholic Church, and the rest staunch Conservatives of the finest stock, all with political legacies or heroic deeds under their belts. Several were graduates of the Chapultepec Military School; some, ironically, had defended the homeland from the invading United States forces alongside Los Niños Héroes in 1847. Sitting in the front row, Almonte occupied the position of honor, flanked by a pair of renowned diplomats, accustomed to the pomp of the European courts and well versed both in languages and etiquette. Also present were a French-born general naturalized as a Mexican, a banker, the editor of a monarchist newspaper, the director of the School of Mining, a landowner, the grandson of a judge, and, representing the highborn families of Mexico, Salvador Murrieta. There they were, on the other side of the ocean from Mexico, making a final attempt to rescue an idea of the nation that had been lost. Salvador was trying to look older than he was, dressed in a suit and a black bow tie, but alongside the men with white hair and moustaches, the truth was he stood out more because of his youth than his attire. He didn't mind being beardless, not anymore, at least. There was a time when he would have felt uncomfortable to be the only man without whiskers at a table like this one. Once, he had tried to let his moustache grow.

For weeks, he looked on in desperation as his face, for all his daubing it with oil and shaving with a razor blade, barely produced a soft fuzz. He decided then, more out of resignation than acceptance, that his jaw looked better hairless, and from that moment on he promised himself he'd never envy another man's beard again. The drawback to his youthful appearance was the condescension with which the other notables treated him, thinking of him as a mere bystander without a voice or a vote, an ornament like the four-armed candelabras on the mosaic table. Behind his back, some said they were uncomfortable with the young Murrieta being imposed on them, but it was unwise for them to argue with Don Vicente if they wanted to keep receiving cheap loans. Salvador pretended he didn't care, because he didn't mind remaining silent, provided he had nothing relevant to say, which was the case in Miramare. He knew his father had sent him precisely to keep quiet and watch: he didn't trust even his own shadow, and had sent him, his youngest son, not to speak his opinion, but to return with a detailed report on everything that happened on the other side of the ocean. As much as Salvador regretted the delegation's indifference, he'd been sent there as a listener and nothing else.

Miramare was the final destination on a journey in search of a monarch that had begun a long time ago: years of searching had led them there, because the archduke Maximilian's name had not been first on the short list. They were in Trieste thanks to the diplomatic work of some—those who had been whispering in the Spanish ears of Empress Eugénie de Montijo—and to the high ambitions of others. All the princes who'd been offered the empire declined. All except one: a man whose imagination was captured by the idea of being useful again, to himself, to his family. To Austria. A man ready to sacrifice himself, like Christ among the thieves on the cross. A man groomed to be a replacement for a throne that wouldn't come to him by line of descent. A man naïve enough to believe that the hundreds of letters the Mexican notables delivered represented the sentiment of a people, a people publicly recognizing its inability to govern itself, a people out of their senses to the point of absurdity. They needed such a man, and Eugénie knew exactly who that man was.

Leaving Mexico opened Salvador's eyes. Being the astute observer he was, as soon as he set foot on foreign soil, he began to see things from a new perspective. Unlike the others, Salvador never missed an opportunity to get out and read newspapers and hear the views of ordinary people. That was how he learned that the Mexican delegation were known as *Napoleon's puppets*; that the French people called their emperor *the Little* to differentiate him from the other, *the Great*, the true and genuine Napoleon that France had known. They said it was a habit of the Napoleons to make gifts of crowns. The throne that Maximilian was going to take up would be supported by French bayonets, but not the will of the majority of Mexicans. The Mexican Republic was being violated in one of the most bizarre historical events of the century, Salvador read to his shame. In his heart he knew—however much he had been instructed to the contrary—that what they wanted made no sense. He didn't know whether any of the notables harbored the same doubts, for none of them could abide criticism, and it was unthinkable to cast doubt on the mission. Nobody spoke unless it was to rejoice at the anticipated empire: they dreamed of a noble, monarchical Mexico that would relive the past glories of great temples now converted into modern castles. Mexico would be Europeanized to come out from the shadow of the gringos, who were threatening to swallow them whole. The glories would return, and the sorrows would disappear. Culture, modernity, equality, the rule of law, and fraternity would embrace the eagle atop the prickly pear. Mexico's greatness would be even greater in the empire; it was all for Mexico. And if at any time the tiniest shadow of doubt passed through the mind of any of these men, it quickly vanished with cries of *Long live Mexico, long live the emperor!*

The notables weren't the only ones deaf to criticism. Eugénie de Montijo, with tenacity and stubbornness, championed the idea of a Mexican empire more than any Conservative. She had adopted the idea when a Mexican diplomat remarked as if in passing at a bullfight in Bayonne how good it would be for Mexico to have a European monarch. From that moment on, she'd nurtured the thought that she could expand her dominions not only as empress but also as wife. Napoleon III was having an affair with an Italian, and Eugénie knew about these infidelities, but for each infraction, she took from her husband a part of his power, and this time it would be Mexico. Her intentions were commented on in the corridors of the Tuileries, not always in a complimentary way. That the French intervention had riled a few people on the American continent was evident; Abraham Lincoln himself turned his attention from the Civil War to write a warning to Napoleon:

> *A foreign monarch installed on Mexican soil, in the presence of naval and military forces, is an insult to the republican form of governance, which is the most widespread on the American continent. The United States will offer support to its sister republic and in favor of the continent's liberation from all European control, the defining characteristic of American history in the last century.*

Napoleon ignored Lincoln's letter.

One afternoon, while Eugénie was having tea with the United States ambassador in Paris, the American told her that the archduke would meet a tragic end.

"As soon as the North wins the Civil War, the French will have to leave Mexican soil, and that is a fact."

Eugénie paused in the midst of taking a sip and held the cup away from her mouth. "*Monsieur*, I assure you that if Mexico weren't so far away and my son were not so young, I would put him in charge of the

French army so that he could write one of the most beautiful pages of history."

In a mocking voice, the ambassador added, "Then you can give thanks to God for both things, Your Majesty: that Mexico is so far away and that your son is still a child."

They didn't part company on good terms, and it was the last time the ambassador was received at the Tuileries.

22

Philippe joined the first group of volunteers in the main square of the small city of Oudenaarde in the north of Belgium, between Brussels and Ghent. Of six hundred men, only forty were soldiers. Almost none had fought in a war, and they were unaccustomed to any kind of discipline. But Philippe, for the first time in his life, felt in control of his own destiny; until now it had always been someone else making decisions for him. Being responsible for his own actions frightened him a little, but his fear of making a mistake was overshadowed by the immense feeling of freedom.

Suddenly, the few soldiers who were there fell in to show their respect for the man who was approaching on horseback. Seeing him appear at a trot made everyone fall silent. A fresh-faced youth who had introduced himself to Philippe as Albert from Brussels said out loud, "It's King Leopold!" and a soldier to his left slapped him on the back of the neck.

"Idiot! That's your commander."

They looked at the soldier with a puzzled expression as the commander stood staring at them in disbelief.

"Let's hope we never have to enter into combat," Van der Smissen muttered to himself, realizing he was surrounded by fools.

Someone was bold enough to ask, "Who is he?"

"It's Lieutenant Colonel Baron Alfred van der Smissen. You'd be wise not to forget," someone behind him replied.

As Van der Smissen dismounted, a military march began to play, and Philippe was filled with a patriotic, soldierly feeling. Everyone seemed to be infected with a sense of pride unknown to them before now. The lieutenant colonel began his inspection. He examined them one by one, and now and again exchanged a few words with them. The entire detachment was impeccably uniformed. There were all kinds of specimens. Van der Smissen's expression was stern and—Philippe thought—also worried. He recognized the look. He'd seen it twice before: when Arthur left him forever at the carpenter's workshop, and when Walton knew his secret had been discovered. Sure enough, Van der Smissen was a career soldier decorated for his achievements on the battlefield, and he'd never seen a battalion as ill prepared as this one. To make matters worse, their mission was on the other side of the world. He asked them what their trades were, and it confirmed his worst suspicions: his battalion, which Leopold I was sending to guard his beloved daughter, was made up of farmhands, tailors, barbers, carpenters, gardeners, a few students, a composer, two scribes, and a beggar.

Trying to hide his displeasure, Van der Smissen issued his first order: "Board the boxcars; we leave for Angers."

Philippe was beside himself with joy. He'd always wanted to see the Loire region.

Several hours after beginning the journey, his initial excitement waned. October wasn't a warm month by any means, but unaccustomed to the stiff uniform, he could barely breathe. He would've given anything to be able to just take off his hat, but no one, not even the beggar, dared do so. Night was falling by the time they finally reached their destination, and all the discomforts of the journey were forgotten thanks to the welcome they received. People with Belgian flags and the coat of arms of Mexico were everywhere; Maximilian had arranged for them to be sent.

A couple of days later, they set sail for Veracruz from the port of Saint-Nazaire. As he boarded the ship, Philippe thought, like many of them did, that the hardest part was over: they'd been traveling for three days, and the men, undisciplined and inexperienced, were beginning to grow weary. How wrong they were; adversity and inclemency began to crush the spirits of even the bravest. Within a few weeks they were attacked by privateers. Those who survived the attack succumbed to typhus, and those who managed to escape the sickness were robbed in Martinique. While some of them held their hands on their heads and cursed the day they embarked on such an adventure, Philippe just marveled at the novelty of it all. With no wood to carve, he wrote. He traded his chisels for a pen and recorded everything that happened on board the *Louisiana*, the French steamship that transported them. They were also traveling with a French captain, a German prince, some creoles from the Caribbean, and a couple of Mexican families. Arriving at Cuba was a revelation for Philippe: he marveled at the smells of sugarcane, coffee, tobacco, and the copper that emerged in the form of red mountains among the foliage, defying nature. They'd been at sea for almost a month. They were close to their destination: Mexico. To the empress Charlotte. As night took over from day, Philippe closed his eyes to feel the wind on his suntanned skin, and he knew then, with the certainty with which faith emerges, that when he disembarked, it wouldn't just be another country that he arrived at but a new beginning.

Part Two

23

1862, Miramare Castle

"Your brother can't demand this of you," Carlota said to Maximilian with a shocked expression.

Maximilian said nothing and handed her the note that had arrived in the latest post, a clipping from an Austrian newspaper excerpting the speech the emperor, his brother Franz Joseph, had given at the opening of the Reichsrat. Impatient, anxious, Carlota skimmed over it: acceptance of the Mexican throne was subject to a family pact.

"What family pact?" Carlota asked, fearing the worst.

"Franz Joseph wants me to formally renounce all my privileges as a Habsburg."

"Even your dynastic rights?"

"All of them, Charlotte."

"That's unacceptable!"

"It is. But I must sign the pact if I want to be emperor of Mexico."

There was a long silence. They both struggled with their thoughts, pacing the room. Carlota reread the clipping while Maximilian's eyes wandered. After a few minutes, Carlota spoke.

"You realize what that means, Max? They're forcing you to burn your ships, like Cortés."

"You think I don't know that?"

There was another pause.

"You must show it to the court jurists. I'm sure it will be ruled invalid."

"That doesn't matter."

"It doesn't?" Carlota asked, puzzled.

"Franz Joseph wants to ruin me. He's always wanted to, and this proves it. We have no future in Austria. They'll never allow me to govern, as insignificant as the territory may be. I'll rot in silence and oblivion. I might as well shut myself in my rooms and forget everything."

Carlota bowed her head. How could she have fallen in love with a man with so little character? Where was his courage? His desire to conquer the world? Had they ever been there, or had she imagined them? She tried to remember what had attracted her to this man. Perhaps it had been the disdain they both had for everyday life, their aspirations to reach the top. Spending their youth without doing anything had never been part of the plan. No matter how heavy the cross was, she'd always believed Maximilian would bear it. Why not confront Franz Joseph? If only she were a man . . . Given the chance, she would command a navy.

Then, invested with the pride she possessed beneath her ample skirts, her voice broke through the uncertainty.

"You will have an empire. That's what Franz Joseph can't bear. Sign it, Maximilian. Let us burn our ships."

Carlota sensed some sorrow and a slight air of disdain in her husband's look, but she said nothing. She tried to put her arms around him, but he pushed her away, gently, without much fuss. He simply withdrew, taking a step back. With no one to receive her affection, Carlota hugged herself, crossing her arms over her chest.

"How could you say such a thing? You want me to give up my homeland, the country of my first joys? Leave my golden cradle and break the sacred bond that ties me to it?" Maximilian said.

"The truth of it is you're afraid to learn that you only know how to dream, and not to actually govern. You don't have the strength to fulfill the task that has been entrusted to you."

He stood gaping; she remained serene, with contempt in her eyes.

Maximilian swallowed whatever he was going to say in disgust and left the room.

Carlota remained pensive, tense, sad, and furious at the man she had married and who, much to her dismay, she was finally beginning to know.

Maximilian withdrew to the summer house on the pretext of feeling unwell, and shut himself away there for three days.

That was his way: when he disliked something, he walked away. He preferred to bury his head in the sand. It no longer surprised Carlota. She'd known it since Madeira, since the honeymoon that turned sour. She still felt the pain of it in her soul. It was when she finally understood. At first, she'd refused to admit the unthinkable, but little by little she had no choice but to accept the evidence, just as Joseph accepted Mary's virginity. They hadn't been married long, just a couple of years, and Carlota was still waiting for the magic to happen. Then, as if her prayers had been answered, Maximilian mentioned his desire to cross the Atlantic.

"We'll go to Brazil," he said.

With the excitement of the nineteen-year-old that she was, Carlota began to make preparations. They would set in at the beautiful port of Málaga, and from there they would sail for Algeciras, before heading to Gibraltar, and then Madeira. Carlota harbored fantasies of all kinds of marital complicities: conversations on deck, afternoon walks, exploring each other's bodies in the evening. She knew that state marriages lacked romance, but not hers: hers had been a union between a prince and princess in love. They'd married two years ago, and the political intrigues and tense atmosphere to which they had been subjected had kept them apart, but this voyage would set things straight. Her woman's body was ready to love. It had been for a long time.

But Madeira tossed everything over a cliff. When they reached the island, it was as if Maximilian's heart had dried up like a raisin. Carlota would approach him, and he would brush her aside. *I can't see you,* he would say, leaving her heartbroken. Carlota had to ask among the court whether anyone knew what was happening. No one dared say anything, but she watched Maximilian sink into a deep depression until, one day, succumbing to her pressuring, a servant told her.

"The archduke grieves for his first love."

"His first love?" asked Carlota.

"The young Maria Amélia of Braganza, my lady. She died here, on Madeira."

"The daughter of Brazil's late emperor?"

"That's right, my lady. The archduke was secretly betrothed to her for a year, but then she died of tuberculosis."

"When was this?" Carlota managed to ask.

"Five years ago, my lady."

Carlota ordered him to leave. She needed to be alone.

For the rest of the afternoon, she sat contemplating the scenery through the window, waiting for Maximilian to find her. Night fell again and she went to him. His eyes were red.

"Why didn't you tell me about her?" she asked.

Maximilian didn't have the courage to look his wife in the eyes, so he spoke to his shoes.

"I thought I'd forgotten her. Stupid me."

Having to compete with a dead woman was all she needed. Carlota thought that perhaps this explained her husband's lack of interest in her. She had to know.

"Did you love her?"

"I thought her life would bring tranquility and happiness to mine."

Carlota swallowed. Was that not what she was doing now? He went on.

"She was a perfect creature who left this harsh world like an angel of pure light to return to heaven, her true home."

Carlota recognized the tone from the letters he wrote to her before they married. It was the voice of a romantic. The voice in which she had thought she recognized love. Poetry. Now, she realized it was the voice of a man only capable of loving muses, in love with unconsummated love; a man incapable of loving flesh and bone. At least, not her flesh, or her bones. Carlota observed him while he spoke. Maximilian was turning a locket ring she'd never noticed before around on his finger.

"What ring is that?"

"Oh. This," he said, clearly trying to hide his agitation. "It's *her* ring."

"May I see it?" Carlota asked, ignoring the bitterness in her mouth.

He took it off, doubtful; she opened it. Carlota almost fainted when she saw that he kept hair there. Some of *her* hair.

They looked at each other without speaking. She returned the ring to him feeling somewhat repulsed and, speechless, she watched him put it back on like a loving widower.

"Would you visit her house with me?" he suddenly asked.

Carlota opened her eyes wide.

"Would you like me to?"

Maximilian nodded.

Carlota agreed, thinking it might be a way for him to face his demon; perhaps it would allow him to bury her once and for all.

The next day, Carlota visited the house and watched Maximilian fall to pieces in front of her, as fragile as a baby. She felt neither tenderness nor pity for this man: such behavior didn't befit an archduke, or a Habsburg. And for a brief moment, she saw him with the same eyes as Franz Joseph.

Carlota slept alone again that night, without the hopes and dreams of a woman in love. A piece of her love had turned to hard, dry stone. It didn't disappear; it remained there, in her, but dead. Without blood to warm it or desire to set it alight.

The next day she searched for Maximilian but was unable to find him until, finally, she learned from her ladies-in-waiting that her husband had continued the journey without her. *It's not possible,* she thought. But it was. Maximilian's cruelty came to light in the most abrupt fashion. How could such a wretch harbor so much romanticism and sentimentality? On what was supposed to be a honeymoon, he abandoned his wife on an island, but he didn't give her free rein. Before she had recovered from the shock, a count and a baron arrived whom Maximilian had instructed to remain with Carlota until his return. She fired a barrage of questions at them.

"How could he just go? To Brazil! How long has he gone for?"

"We don't know, my lady. The archduke didn't tell us."

"But how could he have embarked on the voyage alone?"

The men looked at each other for an instant before one spoke.

"That's not entirely accurate . . . He left in the company of his friends, my lady."

Carlota turned pale.

"What friends?"

The count cleared his throat before replying.

"Charles de Bombelles accompanies him, my lady."

Carlota felt a stab of pain in her stomach; the look the baron tried to hide by looking at the ground didn't go unnoticed.

"Who else?" asked Carlota.

The men were silent.

"Who else?" she yelled, already knowing the answer.

"Sebastian Schertzenlechner."

He was always there, like a shadow. From the moment the Hungarian arrived to be the prince's fencing teacher, Max had been bewitched by him. Franz Joseph warned Max that it was inappropriate to become close to servants, but he didn't care, or at least not when it came to Sebastian. He took him to Lombardy. He took him to Miramare. And now he was taking him to Brazil. Like water that manages to bore a hole through rock, he'd wormed his way in little by little, slowly, almost imperceptibly. The familiarity infuriated Franz Joseph, but Max used it as the ace up his sleeve in a child's game in which he made it clear that, even if the emperor ordered it, he wouldn't hold back on his eccentricities, including the company he kept. He enjoyed provoking his brother, and at any rate Sebastian's smile hypnotized him. Carlota was as repulsed as he was attracted by this character who'd seeped into their lives like dampness on walls. His friendship with Max always aroused a feeling of suspicion that she couldn't fully comprehend. And now, all of a sudden, everything was clear. She felt like someone confessing in the open air, someone vulnerable. She finally understood why she felt such profound sorrow when she looked at him, a sadness so dense it prevented her from breathing. Maria Amélia of Braganza was a ghost; Schertzenlechner was real.

Aware of the implications of the news they'd just conveyed, the men requested permission to leave. Carlota, lips pressed together, nodded.

She waited on that island for Maximilian for three months. Three long months in which she learned how to be alone. A hundred days was enough to give her an idea of the kind of marriage she had. She frequently wanted to cry, but wouldn't let herself. She held in every last tear. Much like when her mother died, grief made a prisoner of her, but she swore to herself she wouldn't cry. Never again, not a single drop. A princess, she told herself, cried without tears.

24

It was 1863, and at Miramare, Carlota spent every day preparing for the mission she was about to undertake: in a few months' time, she would be empress. She became active, she went riding to refine her figure, she bathed in the sea, and she went for long walks. The ladies of the court, tired from trying to keep up with her, sometimes asked, "Didn't you tell us it's better to cultivate the mind, Majesty?"

She answered with a smile, "Without energy, you turn to fluff."

Though she would never dare say it in the confessional to Father Deschamps, she wanted to stay strong and firm in case Maximilian decided to lift her skirts one day.

At court, everyone talked about the Mexicans who'd visited Miramare to anoint the archduke as emperor of Mexico. The atmosphere was one of cautious joy in the corridors of the castle.

However, Carlota's grandmother Queen Maria Amalia didn't share their caution or their joy. In fact, she was very worried: Carlota was the apple of her eye, her most beloved grandchild. Since the death of Carlota's mother, Queen Louise, whom Maria Amalia always called *my angelic Louise*, she had been devoted to her youngest grandchild, whom she considered fragile because she was a girl.

How the little one had missed her mother, and what a good queen her mother had been: both in Wallonia and Flanders, there wasn't a single railway station, hospital, or restaurant that didn't have her portrait on its walls. The Belgians called her the Good Queen, and that was exactly what she'd also been for Maria Amalia. Losing her so young was a tragedy: for the Belgians, for Leopold, and for Carlota. The void she left couldn't be filled. Maria Amalia thought that was when Carlota discovered the loneliness of the soul. A void that could never be filled. She'd kept in touch with her granddaughter with letters: they had a postal relationship that was abundant, strong, and affectionate, which gave them both moments of peace and was based on a sincerity that meant they could discuss anything. However, this sincerity had faded since Carlota's marriage to Maximilian. Queen Maria Amalia could feel it, she sensed that Carlota's character had changed. She was more distant, in spite of her affection; more sorrowful, in spite of her smile; more alone, in spite of the company. And from the moment she received news of the Mexican throne, there'd been a knot in the Queen Mother's stomach. In her view, it was a ridiculous thing to do, an act of folly, an eccentricity that only a fool would consider. She was shocked that her Charlotte, so upright and so educated, could have stumbled over such an enormous absurdity. However much she tried to dissuade her granddaughter, she always came up against a wall of justifications. The child, she knew, was very clever; even so, the queen decided she would use any means possible to make her see reason.

"Oh, child," she said warmly. "I don't understand where this longing for a crown comes from now, when you turned down the chance to depose Peter of Portugal because you didn't want a throne."

Carlota stood straight as she listened, like a tin soldier.

"True, but it's one thing to seek a throne and another to refuse one."

"I hoped for a better future for you, child."

"But, Grandmother, Mexico is a beautiful country . . . and I feel we have a calling to reign. It's like a religious calling."

"The beauty of the country isn't important, child, what matters is how stable its foundations are."

"All thrones are unstable, Grandmother."

Maria Amalia then tried a more personal angle.

"And the senselessness of giving up your dynastic rights?"

"Max hasn't given up any of his succession rights. He is still third in line. All he's done is given himself an occupation. Can you imagine the life we'd have if we stayed here? Building another house, designing another garden, and occasionally him going off on a long journey while I stay here . . ."

Maria Amalia could sense both anguish and reproach; she went to her and took her hand maternally. Carlota continued in a low voice.

"I've seen little of life, Grandmother, but I want something to love. I need a broader horizon than I have now."

"So. It's not for Maximilian. It's for you."

"All I want is to lead an active, useful life, to do something good in the world. I want to love in greater circles."

"But you can do that here, at Miramare."

"Life at Miramare couldn't be more boring," she said without blinking.

"You're only twenty-three . . . you don't have to live your life in such a hurry. You haven't missed anything in Mexico. There's nothing for you to do there."

"I'm aware of the dangers of this enterprise, believe me I am. But I also believe I have the strength to endure them, Grandmother."

"Wouldn't you be happier in Greece?"

"Are you suggesting Maximilian should take that throne instead of Mexico's?"

Maria Amalia knew that Leopold I, her son, was worried about the course Carlota and Maximilian were taking and had been discussing with Franz Joseph the possibility of offering them the Greek throne. The Greek revolution the previous year had sent the royal couple into exile.

Carlota pressed her hands together in a pleading gesture.

"For the love of God, Grandmother, Maximilian would never accept King Otto's crown knowing it had been offered to a dozen princes before him."

"Mexico's was also offered to others, my dear. The Infante Juan de Borbón y Braganza of Spain turned it down, as did his uncle Antonio."

Carlota swallowed bitter saliva.

"But it's not the same. In any case, Maximilian believes the Greek people to be wicked and deceitful. Mexicans are more noble."

"You wouldn't be succumbing to ambition, would you, child?"

"It's not ambition, Grandmother. If a throne allows one to love the people one governs, then I must love thrones. But if this pleasure could be obtained with the most modest title, that would satisfy me."

The queen leaned back in her chair with sadness, thinking to herself that intelligence was, sure enough, the cousin of pride.

While Carlota tried to hold back the tide with a broom, Maximilian dwelled on much more puerile matters. Under very little pressure, brilliant projects evaporated, leaving only a sediment made of fantasies. In his heart, he truly believed that governing a powder keg would happen by divine grace. Other matters excited him more: he imagined himself as a Roman emperor whose court would be remembered in years to come like Nero's: for luxury, good taste, ostentation. He imagined himself appearing in the center of gigantic paintings hanging on the best walls in palaces on both sides of the ocean. When he closed his eyes, he thought about whom he would commission to paint his portrait, and he fell asleep thinking about what he would wear for the occasion. When he woke, he would draw sketches of possible coats of arms for his empire on white sheets of paper: crowned eagles on prickly pears, or plumes like the ones the ancient Aztec monarchs wore; the imperial cloaks; the green, white, and red tricolors. He went over and over the motto that would round off the coat of arms, until he finally decided it would be *Religion, independence, and unity*. Yes . . . that was it. And a scepter. He would need an imperial scepter. He searched for fabrics with which to upholster the imperial chairs. When he had finished coming up with decorative ideas, he took up pen and paper to set out the rules of protocol and etiquette, as well as the new medals and decorations that would be awarded on his arrival in Mexico. And his palatine guard! He mustn't forget the royal guard. He wanted one like the pope's, a sort of Swiss Guard, extravagant and well organized. How great his empire would be! How great.

And on one of many such afternoons, under pressure from his brother and the grandeur of his aspirations, he signed the family pact: he closed the doors on Europe in order to open them on Mexico, and he felt that this would suffice.

In Trieste, the emperor and empress were given a hero's send-off. There were tears and good wishes amid the cheers while, waving, Carlota and Maximilian boarded the fifty-gun *Novara*, a three-mast frigate that hadn't been designed for long voyages. A small craft loaded with coal escorted them in case the winds failed. There, confined by the sea, Maximilian had time to draw up the rules for the court's honorary and ceremonial service. To Carlota, who questioned why he devoted so much time to trivial matters, he said, "What a stupid question! Mexican society is unaccustomed to the ceremonial protocol of a court. This document will be very useful."

"It would be more useful if you wrote to Benito Juárez," she retorted.

Maximilian tensed. He didn't like hearing that name. Nonetheless, he nodded.

"Yes, undoubtedly. Undoubtedly."

"We'd better prepare for the worst and hope for the best," she said, before leaving him alone again, in his paper empire.

25

Leagues away, Juan Nepomuceno Almonte waited. Acting as imperial regent, he had already announced in the press that, on the arrival of the monarchs, titles would be conferred. There would be Mexican barons, dukes, counts, and marquises. *Good day, Marquise,* women said to themselves in the mirror. *If I may, Countess,* others imagined. And like schoolgirls writing their would-be married names in their diary, they blushed at the sound of their names preceded with a title. In the Murrieta house, the servants rushed back and forth, searching closets for medals that for so long had been nothing more than things to dust. Vicente, thrilled at the idea of being named a noble, told Refugio to organize a welcome dance for their distinguished guests. One day, some grandiose ladies, stuffed into their dresses in the French way—at least according to them—came to ask for Refugio's help and connections to organize a collection.

"We want to give the empress a solid silver dressing table," they explained.

"What a wonderful idea!" Clotilde exclaimed before being overcome by a coughing fit.

Refugio smiled at them, sensing Constanza's inquisitive gaze through the parlor. When the women left, Constanza recriminated.

"It's one thing feigning ignorance, Mother, and quite another to go along with such idiocy."

"I know, darling, I know. It makes my blood boil! But what else can I do?"

Constanza wanted to shake her. "Stop receiving them! Tell them you're indisposed! Refuse!"

"I can't do that, darling."

"Then don't come to me every night talking about how the Juaristas are right, when we eat, drink, and breathe empire in this house."

Constanza couldn't understand why her mother refused to stand up for her beliefs; she thought to herself that if she had ever known how to, she'd forgotten.

"Constanza, I have to tell you something. Sit down," she said, patting the armchair to indicate she should join her. Constanza obeyed. "Your father wants you to join the imperial court."

"What did you say, Mamá?"

"You heard."

"But that's . . . No, Mamá, don't do this to me. I couldn't. It would be obvious immediately that I didn't want to be there. Don't ask me to do this."

Refugio took her daughter's hands, but Constanza snatched them away. If anyone had been watching, Refugio would've had to slap her to keep up appearances. But they were alone, so she allowed her daughter to rebel in this way. It was what she'd wanted to do when Vicente had told her. Deep down, Refugio felt as if she were sending her children to be sacrificed, as if time were an imperfect machine and, imbued with the spirit of ancient beliefs, it was throwing her best offspring into the lava of a volcano.

"Send Clotilde," Constanza begged. "She's docile, she'll fit in perfectly in that absurd court."

"She can't go, Constanza. Her health is fragile, and they don't want sickly people in the court."

"I'd sooner enter a convent."

"That's not for you, Constanza. You know it as well as I do."

"What difference is there between cloistering myself and fanning myself until I die of boredom?"

Refugio, glancing around the room, took a chance and whispered in her ear.

"For appearances that's what you'll do, yes, but your work will be much more than that. They need you, Constanza. They need you more than you know."

"Who does?" Constanza asked with disgust.

Refugio spoke softly, her eyes fixed on her daughter's. Constanza had to bring her ear closer to her mother's mouth.

"The Juaristas, darling."

Constanza didn't understand.

"Yes, darling, the Juaristas need you: they need someone in the court, and no one would suspect a Murrieta. No one will suspect you."

"They want me to be a spy?"

"An informant. Someone to share reliable information about what happens in the palace. What you see. What you hear. What people say."

"And to whom will I be passing on this information?"

"When the time comes, you'll be told."

Constanza fell silent. Neither of them spoke for a while. Then Constanza held her mother's hands.

"But, Mother, how do you know this? How . . . ?"

Refugio took a deep breath. "A woman wears many disguises, dear, to defend an idea. To survive. Mine is that of a self-sacrificing wife. There are nuns, there are prostitutes, but we all choose what we want to be under the mask."

"Are you telling me, Mother, that you're a . . . Republican?"

"One of the truest," she replied.

26

1866, Paris

Carlota's black dress contrasted sharply with the pale gown Eugénie de Montijo wore when she visited that summer morning. Carlota was still in mourning for her grandmother, and even if she wasn't obliged, black seemed the most appropriate color given the circumstances of her mission.

She couldn't suppress her surprise when Eugénie arrived at the Grand Hotel escorted by two women dressed in pastels wearing wildflowers in their hair.

"What a pleasure to see you, dear. Allow me to introduce the Countess of Montebello and my good friend Madame Carette."

"Enchantée," they said in unison.

Carlota, ignoring protocol, said, "It seems inappropriate to me that you should arrive with friends as if I'd invited you to spend the day in the countryside, when you know that my visit is official state business."

The atmosphere could've been cut with a knife. The women had never been treated with such directness. Eugénie de Montijo drew upon all her considerable diplomatic experience to defuse the situation.

"Of course, dear. Please don't be upset. You see, I had hoped that you'd have that conversation with Napoleon in person."

"That is what I hoped, too."

The Countess of Montebello, feeling deeply uncomfortable, decided to withdraw.

"I see it would be better to take tea another time," she said, turning to leave. But Eugénie stopped her with a severe look.

"Not at all, Countess. Sit down, please."

The women looked at each other and then reluctantly sat down under the force of Eugénie's severity.

Carlota decided to play by the same rules. If they wanted a fight, a fight is what they'd have.

"We need the French troops to stay in Mexico," she said point-blank.

Eugénie, who also knew how to play the game, evaded the issue.

"We can see about that later. Now, how was the journey? I hope you're comfortable in the hotel, this place is marvelous. I heard there was a small altercation at your reception in Saint-Nazaire . . ."

"Maximilian is still emperor, and he will not abdicate, if that is what you'd hoped. We need France to tell us where it stands."

"All in good time, dear, all in good time. How is the food there? I'm sure you'll be delighted to have a proper vol-au-vent."

"Don't insult my intelligence with banality. I demand to see Napoleon no later than tomorrow."

"I'm afraid that won't be possible, dear. You know Napoleon is indisposed."

Carlota stood and did what she'd been wanting to do since Eugénie walked through the door; she was an empress, too, after all, and she demanded respect. At the top of her voice, she yelled, "If the emperor refuses to see me, I shall force my way in!"

The three women left the room in utter shock; they'd never had to suffer such rude behavior. A lady—not to mention a princess, the granddaughter of a king and queen, and cousin of the queen of England—never raised her voice, let alone issued threats.

"That woman has completely lost her mind, Highness," Madame Carette said to Eugénie.

And the Countess of Montebello added, "She seemed unbalanced to me from the first moment. Did you see what she was wearing? I thought I'd suffocate just looking at her! In black from head to toe, as if in a convent, and in this August heat!"

Eugénie listened in silence. It was true: the Carlota who received them was a woman with her nerves in tatters. Eugénie knew what it was like to be under pressure, what it was like to have a nation turn against her; all of France had branded her ambitious and manipulative, and they considered her the cause of all of Napoleon's ills. However, she'd learned to keep her emotions in check. She would never allow herself to shout as Carlota had just done.

"Leave it," she said. "She'll dig her own grave."

Alone now, Carlota knew she had gone too far, but it was too late. She didn't know what in God's name was happening, why she was losing her temper so easily. Was it a symptom of the pregnancy? Why didn't anyone understand her anguish? She wanted what was best for Mexico. France and Belgium were distant cousins to her now. Only two years had passed, but the country that flowed through her veins was on the other side of the ocean. She'd learned to love it, to understand it. She felt Mexican. She needed to return with good news, and instead everyone seemed to treat her as if she were hysterical, volatile, ambitious, and self-centered.

To add insult to injury, she was carrying a bastard child and didn't know how to hide it. How easy it would be to say the child was Max's. How easy it would be to announce that the Mexican throne had an heir. Why not? Better an heir with half-royal blood than no heir at all. Perhaps she should say it was Max's child and be done with it. Her head was spinning. She was exhausted, she needed to rest. She lay on the bed and let her drowsiness take away all the pain and anguish for a few hours.

The next day, Carlota went to see the emperor; ill-mannered or not, Napoleon had agreed to receive her. Though the news pleased her, she cursed the fact that she couldn't postpone the visit. That morning, she'd awoken feeling extraordinarily unwell. She'd barely slept because of the dizziness and nausea; she woke up vomiting. Every smell disgusted her. The chambermaid came to clean the room and found the empress curled up on the floor, vomiting into her chamber pot. It was a pitiful sight. Frau Döblinger came as soon as she was informed. Mathilde was a source of great comfort and support. She spoke in a soft, unhurried voice; hearing her, Carlota often recalled her mother: had she been alive, this was how she would've spoken to her. In private—only ever in private—Mathilde spoke warm words, such as *Don't worry, my child; you'll feel better soon, my child.* During the first trimester, she gave her lemons to suck to ward off the sickness. Carlota allowed herself to be cocooned by her.

"Oh, Mathilde, what would I do without you!"

"You'd be just as brave, my child," she said while stroking her hair. "Now enough crying, you'll upset the little one."

Carlota looked at her with sad eyes.

"Nobody must know of my condition, Mathilde. Not yet. This child couldn't have arrived at a worse time."

"I shall be as silent as the grave, my child."

And then, gently, she helped her dress.

In the carriage, Carlota was a bundle of nerves. She wrung her mantilla between her fingers, not caring if she ruined it. She was frightened to death. She had to appear before Napoleon exhibiting the dignity of the rank that had been invested in her just two years ago, but inside she was trembling like a crème caramel. She wound the mantilla around a finger until it stopped the blood flow; when the digit felt numb, she unwound the fabric and began to bite it. As they approached the château, Carlota noticed that, for the first time since her return, she would be received as the empress that she was. A guard of honor flanked her path.

After a formal welcome, they led the empress to Napoleon III's study. It was on the ground floor, and to Carlota it seemed a gloomy, cheerless place. She had to contain her shock when she saw the emperor looking much older than she'd imagined. By all accounts, Napoleon the Little was very unwell.

"Don't allow my appearance to deceive you, Charlotte. I still have the strength to refute any argument," he said.

"Your Highness, I'm sorry to see you suffering," she said. And then, perhaps thinking of her Maximilian, who'd also been afflicted by delicate health, she added, "We've all suffered a great deal."

"Yes, well, you haven't traveled all this way to discuss my health, have you?"

"No, Your Highness, as I'm sure you're aware."

"With great regret, I can do nothing for your empire. I must do what's best for France."

"But you swore to support us to the end. It was only two years ago you signed the Peace of Vienna. You had plans to build a nation; we can still save it."

"It is unsustainable, Charlotte. War with Prussia could be on the horizon; we need all our troops on the continent."

"If you withdraw the troops, Mexico will descend into anarchy. God knows what will become of us. We have paid you for them."

Carlota then showed him a series of letters setting out the financial and military details. She knew them by heart: she'd studied them backward and forward during the crossing. And in any case, even if she hadn't done so, she was acquainted with every detail, every decision. While Maximilian explored the hidden corners of his empire, Carlota was left in charge, conducting the country's affairs from Chapultepec. While Maximilian devoted himself to writing political theory, she governed. Until her subjects, tired of being told what to do by a woman, even if she was an empress, asked Maximilian to give her tasks more in keeping with her sex, such as charitable work. But no: Carlota knew what governing was. *If only I had been a man,* she thought. *If only . . .*

Napoleon III started to talk about Mexico as if he knew it. Carlota listened in astonishment, aware that this man, for all his reasoning and arguments, didn't have the first idea what Mexico was. For him, Mexico was a place on a map, nothing more. As the conversation became heated, Napoleon seemed subdued. He was weak, tired, physically spent. And while, in her pettiest moments, Carlota was glad to know that this traitor would die in pain, soaked in his own urine, she couldn't help but feel some sorrow at the inexorable passing of time.

Napoleon, weary, his eyes watering, raised his voice.

"Understand, there's nothing I can do!"

Carlota felt her cheeks burn.

"How could you claim such a thing! What do you mean *nothing*? As the head of an empire of thirty million souls with supremacy in Europe, you have vast resources, you enjoy the most generous credit in the world, with victorious armies always at the ready. Can Your Majesty not do anything for the Mexican Empire?"

They were behind closed doors, but outside, alternating voices could be heard, interrupting each other in an unintelligible echo. Carlota waved the letters he'd signed when he feared Maximilian wouldn't accept the Mexican throne, letters full of promises now broken.

"What happened to the word of the man who wrote these letters? Maximilian accepted the throne because it was your will."

Napoleon, agitated, back against the wall, ventured to say, "Lady Charlotte, you would be advised to stop insisting, or I shall be forced to make you stop."

Carlota went wide-eyed.

"Are you threatening me?"

"I would be incapable of such an act," he said in his defense. "All I'm saying is that it would be a great shame if you had to abandon the Mexican cause for which you fight so hard because of some setback. It has come to my attention that you are not in the best health. What's more, you're a long way from your empire."

For the first time since she walked into the room, Carlota hesitated. She didn't know how to interpret his words. Were they a threat? Did he know of her condition? What did he mean by a *setback*? They both fell silent.

All at once, a footman burst in with a pitcher of orange juice.

"Ah, at last!" said the emperor. "I've been waiting some time."

"Forgive me, Your Majesty," the footman replied with his head bowed.

The interruption unsettled Carlota. She disliked being distracted in the middle of an argument. It was a tactic she'd seen a thousand times in the palace: when someone wanted to change the subject or make an adversary lose the thread of an argument, a servant always interrupted with refreshments. It was a classic ploy, and Napoleon was using it against her now. The heat was stifling, and drops of condensation slid down the icy glass pitcher.

"Drink a little, it will do you good," Napoleon invited her.

Carlota watched the emperor himself, having dismissed the footman, pour her a glass. He did not pour a second.

"Drink."

It wasn't a request. It was an order. Carlota swallowed dry saliva and shook her head.

"No, thank you."

Napoleon frowned.

"Drink. It will do you good."

"Thank you, I am not thirsty," she lied; her throat was raw from talking. The cool drink tempted her like the devil tempted Christ in the desert, but something in Napoleon's manner made her suspicious. Why was he so insistent that she should drink while he did not? Something froze inside Carlota. *He's trying to poison me.* Doubtful, Carlota picked up the glass. Napoleon seemed on edge. She held the glass to her mouth but didn't let a drop pass her lips. It couldn't be true. *Poison? Me?* The thought that they might try to assassinate her made her furious, but it wouldn't be unusual: she wouldn't have been the first nor the last noble to be poisoned for political reasons. As a child, she'd seen that her father wouldn't touch his meals until they'd been approved by a taster. It was a trick older than time. Gathering her composure, she returned to the reason for her visit.

"Let us resume the matter at hand, Your Highness."

"You are the most foolish woman I know, Charlotte."

She took it as a compliment. Napoleon, exhausted and aching, put an end to the conversation.

"I shall consult my ministers again before giving you a final answer. That's all I can promise you."

"My thanks, Your Highness." She put the glass down on the silver tray.

Carlota walked to her carriage as quickly as she could; she wanted to run but knew it would be unseemly. The heat and her fury had flushed her cheeks as red as ripe tomatoes, and her glazed eyes suggested an imminent cascade of tears. She climbed into the carriage; inside, two ladies-in-waiting looked at her with sorrowful expressions.

"Well, Majesty?" they asked when they saw her.

Carlota, frustrated, confused, frightened, exhausted, threw herself into the arms of one of them and began to sob inconsolably.

"I did everything humanly possible; I did everything humanly possible . . . ," she said over and over again.

27

1864, Veracruz

When Philippe arrived, his first thought was that Mexico was a country of great contrasts. The Pico de Orizaba greeted him from the distance, covered in mist and snow. He'd never seen such mountains in Belgium, he thought to himself. The view played tricks on the senses, because though the mountains were snowcapped, it was hot and humid. It was like being trapped between two worlds. Mexico was exactly that: two worlds coexisting in a single land. One could go from paradise to hell within a league's distance. Within a single day, one could experience the four seasons: it could pour in the morning and suffocate with the heat of an oven in the afternoon. They walked through a desert, and then, passing through a valley, they suddenly found themselves amid verdant landscapes covered in flowers and trees abundant with exotic fruits. Aridness and luxuriance coexisted like angels with demons.

Philippe hadn't seen much of the world, but as they approached Veracruz, he heard someone say it resembled the Holy Land. A bald, gray-eyed man corrected the speaker.

"Don't be an idiot! In the Orient the buildings have domes and minarets, and here the houses have flat roofs."

Looking up, Philippe saw hundreds of strange black-headed birds gliding above them menacingly; some of the men seemed alarmed by this animal they'd never seen before.

"They're *zopilotes*," said one of the sons of the Mexican family traveling with them. "Vultures. Scavengers."

One of the soldiers picked up a stone and aimed at the bird flying over his head. The boy called out to him.

"Don't! The fine for killing a *zopilote* is twenty-five pesos."

"A fine for killing a scavenger bird?" the soldier asked in disbelief.

"They clean the garbage from the streets," the boy replied with a smile.

It was as though everyone had been given new eyes. They opened them wide, engrossed and amazed. They were going to spend six years here, and to some of them it suddenly seemed like an eternity.

Philippe, despite his excitement, went carefully. Walton's words still echoed in his memory, warning of diseases and other dangers. And though he marveled at the nature, he was aware that they weren't safe, at least they wouldn't be until they reached the city. The port was unsanitary, the air carried the scent of rotting waste, and the *zopilotes* seemed to be everywhere in anticipation of death. Within a few days, Philippe confirmed that he'd been right to be afraid: a dozen men fell sick with yellow fever, others began to vomit blood. Within a couple of weeks, he watched young men die with fevers and in pain; like him, they'd traveled in search of adventure, but for them it had come to a tragic end.

Philippe promised himself that he would follow all the hygiene measures they'd been taught onboard the ship, and which, with the insolence of youth, he had previously decided to ignore. They mustn't overuse their *strength of mind*, which, in the words of the physician, was *always weak in tropical climates*. They had to avoid *physical love, muscular exertion, and excesses of the voice*. Philippe scowled: he missed physical love, but having seen the working women in the port, that guideline wouldn't be too hard to follow, at least for the time being. Of all the instructions, the one he liked most—though he wasn't sure how it would help him avoid yellow fever—was taking an afternoon nap.

His favorite time was the night. He liked it more than the day. He could feel the cool wind bringing the scent of the sea to flush the stench from the coast. But he mostly loved it because he'd never in his life seen so many stars in the sky. He sat on a bench in the square and, lulled by the darkness, listened to the waves breaking against the city walls. The darker the night, the more beautiful the stars, and that, somehow, kept alive his hope.

Like many others, Albert from Brussels, who'd become if not a friend then a traveling companion, imagined the worst dangers at night: whenever he closed his eyes, he thought snakes would slither over his body or a horde of natives with machetes would leap out to murder them as they slept.

"These people are peaceful, Albert; they wouldn't harm a fly."

"I wouldn't be so sure. Have you seen how they look at us?"

"The same as we look at them."

"They're strange. What race is it they say they are?"

"*Totonacas, tonatacas*, something like that."

"Their singing gives me the shivers. It's so mournful."

"That's because we can't understand what they're saying."

After a pause, in a low voice, Albert said, "I think death visits this country often."

Philippe laughed at the lad's absurd ideas. He was beginning to grow fond of this young adventurer, as frightened as he was; he piqued Philippe's interest. He must've had a very good reason to travel halfway around the world when he was such a coward. Perhaps, Philippe thought, one day he would find out. And after joking with each other for a while from their respective hammocks, Philippe would say to him, "Come on, brave man. The sun will be up soon."

On the way to Mexico City they passed through Córdoba.

"It smells of oranges!" Albert exclaimed, recognizing smells from other lands.

Sure enough, it smelled of orange and lemon trees and coffee, and they saw missions all over the place. The soldiers observed the various fruits that the landscape revealed to them. Though the doctor warned them against eating too much in hot lands, they'd decided they would only pay attention to him if they got sick, so they freely picked the oranges they found along the way, and they were juicy and sweet. Philippe and Albert reached an expansive area with trees that bore fruit resembling elongated yellow potatoes.

"What's this?" they asked the young Mexican who was still with them.

"Bananas. You don't know bananas?" And the boy, astonished at the soldiers' ignorance, showed them how they were eaten.

They reached a convent, where they were lodged, while families sympathetic to the empire billeted the officers in their houses. Benito Juárez, Mexico's president, had issued a decree: anyone helping the invaders would be shot for betraying their country; even remaining in the occupied territories and acting in any capacity to assist the enemy would be considered high treason. However, there were still those who truly believed that the French and Belgians were coming to help, and since Bazaine had cornered Juárez in El Paso del Norte, his threats seemed remote, so they opened their doors as hospitably as they could.

There the soldiers lived for a bit alongside the locals. The houses were humble, without the comforts of most European inns. Language was the biggest barrier that divided them, but with interpreters and some Mexicans who'd studied French, they set about boring holes in the walls of the Tower of Babel.

Philippe and Albert observed everything closely. Their attention was drawn to the way in which the natives showed consideration for their animals: they didn't even throw the dogs out of the churches, which outraged the senior officers. The natives displayed a special fondness for roosters. On one occasion, the Belgians observed two local men greeting each other; instead of asking after his family, one said to the other, "And your rooster, how is he?"

Albert looked at Philippe.

"What strange folk," he said.

To which Philippe replied, "I think it's wonderful."

In the evening, the troops requested permission to frequent the establishments that sold a kind of alcohol.

"What do you call this?" asked one of the soldiers, gesturing at a cloth-covered cask.

"Pulque," replied a dark-skinned man with jet-black hair.

"And is it good?"

"*Very* good, señor. They say it's almost as nourishing as meat. We drink it for bellyache, loss of appetite, weakness . . . new mamas even drink it to bring their milk on."

The Belgians didn't understand much, but didn't need any translation to understand that this liquid as thick as chocolate could be dangerous. They began drinking with caution, but as the night wore on, there was laughter and wailing in equal measure; some because the pulque had loosened their homesickness, and others because it had loosened their sphincters. The days passed with the men in this state, both the body and the soul deteriorating, until without realizing it, Philippe and his companions reached Puebla, where their compatriots of the Belgian legion welcomed them with their homeland's national anthem. One by one, each note erased the pains and fears of the journey through Veracruz.

Mexico City was ever closer. Philippe had never felt farther from home. It was only a few months since they left Saint-Nazaire, but it felt like years. They all seemed to have aged, even Philippe. A blond beard had grown in, and the sun had tanned his face, wrinkling his eyes at the corners. Even Albert's moustache was beginning to grow. They'd lost weight from the diarrhea they suffered from eating food to which they were unaccustomed. Sometimes, when they reached a victualing point half starved, they were received with tortillas and maguey worms. Famished, they ate the so-called worms with disgust at first, but in the end they developed a taste for what were in fact the caterpillars found clustered at the roots of the maguey plant. The road to the capital was arduous. The land, in comparison with what they had left behind, was barren. Wherever he looked, Philippe saw magueys, prickly pears, and endless cacti. They were told that in the rainy season the vegetation exploded with greenery, but seeing this arid landscape, it was hard to imagine it any other color than brown. They crossed several lakes, the largest ones with dikes that prevented Lake Texcoco, which was very close to the city, from flooding. Philippe noted with horror that if any of the dikes burst, the capital would be submerged, but the people didn't seem to notice, or if they did, they preferred to live without worrying about things that hadn't happened yet. In time, he would also learn to live in the present.

28

When the *Novara* docked in Veracruz, not a single soul came out to welcome the emperor and empress: Juárez's threats, which included the promise to execute anyone who offered them water or helped them unload the ship, were etched into the memories of every inhabitant of the port. The laughter that would've been heard on the streets days before had subsided as the ship approached the coast; those on the wharf hid as soon as they saw the vessel. Nothing moved. The port was utterly desolate, no sign of life. Nobody came to meet them. A cat knocked over a bucket of waste when it shot off in a panic. Carlota, though full of anxiety, managed to draw a comparison:

"It looks like Cádiz, if a little more oriental."

The court nodded with serious expressions, not daring to comment. Maximilian remained serene, though Carlota knew his restraint masked a layer of sarcasm that could erupt at any moment.

Without the protocol or the etiquette that Maximilian had so carefully planned, they set off on the torturous journey to Mexico City over impossible roads, mud, and torrential rain that seemed to be telling them to turn around and go back. They traveled in mule-drawn carriages that allowed them to see only the impenetrable foliage. The caravan was vulnerable to attack, and the enemy was scattered throughout the territory, hidden in the shadows. The retinue's spirits verged on desolation. Nobody dared break the tension, and they merely allowed themselves to be rocked by swaying stagecoaches, which creaked as if they might fall apart at any moment. Maximilian fixed his eyes out the window, contemplating the land of which he was lord, while Carlota tried to remain calm in anticipation of whatever might happen.

"I wouldn't be surprised if Juárez himself attacked us on the road," she suddenly said, exhausted and uncomfortable from the conditions.

"Don't invoke the devil, Charlotte."

Their spirits needed a respite, some vision that would make them feel at home. And that finally appeared in Orizaba, where they were to spend the night because Almonte, imperial regent in the absence of the emperor, was waiting for them there. As if the heavens had shone on them, everything was different there. Carlota peered out through the window, and, marveling at the scenery, she broke into a smile. She looked at Maximilian, searching for her husband's complicity. He, too, was openmouthed. They were greeted by a snow-topped volcano surrounded by coffee plantations.

From that moment, hope found a place in both of their silent thoughts. As they progressed, they encountered cedar and fir forests, haciendas with vast crops of sugarcane, maize, coffee, and cocoa, and orchards full of orange trees whose aroma was carried in the wind. The fruit colored the landscape brightly; pomegranates, bananas, and palm trees seemed to dance. Carlota forgot her grievances and began to reconcile herself with her new land. As they traveled farther inland, the threat from Juárez seemed to fade, and there were spontaneous manifestations of joy, with onlookers leaning out of windows to see the monarchs and throw flowers at them. A number of barefooted people dressed in calico elbowed their way through the crowds to greet the young sovereigns. From her seat, Carlota observed them closely.

"Who are those unfortunates?"

"Natives, Your Majesty. They work the land."

"They work their land?"

"No, Your Majesty, the land does not belong to them."

Carlota frowned. She took the notebook she always carried with her and, in poor handwriting due to the movement of the carriage, she wrote, *Protect the needy.*

They finally reached their destination. Exhausted and somewhat bedraggled, they arrived in Mexico City. Carlota sensed that the capital was like a piece of Europe in America. Before long, triumphal arches appeared with the inscription *Eternal thanks to Napoleon III*, marking the entrance to the Chalco Valley. People waving large hats cheered for the sovereigns. A kind of delirium had seized thousands of Mexican gentry; some cried with emotion as the imperial carriage passed by, parents hugged their children, and many hearts were filled with confidence, including those of the emperor and empress.

Carlota thought it was wonderful. She rejoiced at the affection the people showed them and the love from those she already called *her people*, even if some balcony doors slammed shut as the entourage passed. It had been a year since the French army took the capital, forcing Benito Juárez out.

"It will go well here so long as the French support us," Carlota said to Max through her smile while she waved at her subjects with the palm of her right hand open.

29

From the moment Carlota and Maximilian set eyes on Chapultepec Castle, they decided it would be their official residence. It was an architectural wonder, facing the two volcanoes that guarded the valley like holy beings; the snow on one took the form of a sleeping woman, and beside her, a warrior in love rose up to guard her.

"It will be my Miravalles," Maximilian said, and with that he cured his nostalgia for Miramare.

The National Palace hadn't been what they'd hoped for an emperor's residence. The one night they spent there became a nightmarish memory: the cold and bedbugs forced the emperor to lay his regal body on a billiard table, while Carlota tried to sleep in an armchair. After that, they decided they would only use it for official functions. But Chapultepec Castle . . . ah! That was something else. It also needed some maintenance and improvements, but that was trivial for an emperor. He would make the castle his very own Schönbrunn. He quickly employed two hundred builders to refurbish the place at top speed under his instruction, and when the work had progressed sufficiently, Maximilian was thrilled to take charge of the decoration. He decided where to put the tapestries, furniture, and chandeliers that had been sent from Europe; the Sèvres vases, Boulle commodes, and two pianos that Napoleon III had generously gifted took pride of place. The castle was embellished a little more each day thanks to the sovereign, who didn't allow his wife to participate in the decorating; he and Schertzenlechner alone assumed this role. In his view, his wife didn't have good taste, and he entrusted nothing to her: she liked gray, austerity, sobriety. Carlota didn't complain and, since the emperor's mood depended on his love of art, poetry, and literature, she decided, as always, to channel her energy into politics.

Carlota did take responsibility for choosing the ladies of her court. Constanza had been living in Chapultepec for a week, after reluctantly moving there with her mother's blessing and mission and to her father's pride. Three of his children now, in one way or another, were present in the upper echelons of power. And not just any power, but royal power. Power invested by God the Father.

"You must earn yourself a place among the ladies of honor," Vicente had reminded her.

"Yes, Father, you already told me. The *petit service*."

"That's right, *petit service*, not the *grand service*, Constanza. Anyone can be a lady of the court, but not a lady of honor. Don't forget."

"No, Father," she replied laconically.

"And don't look like that, girl; being part of an empress's court is a great privilege. Several friends of mine had been hoping their wives would be called upon."

"And others preferred to avoid the trouble," Refugio blurted out from behind. "Did you hear what Don Pedro from Puebla said when they summoned his wife to be a lady of the court?"

"What did he say?" Constanza asked, her interest suddenly aroused.

"That his wife couldn't go, because she who is a queen in her own home can't be a servant in anyone else's."

The women burst out laughing.

"Don Pedro speaks nonsense," Vicente added seriously. "They almost got themselves sent into exile!" he protested to interrupt his daughter and wife's laughter. "He's all bark and no bite. His wife is at Chapultepec now, as it should be."

Refugio resumed. "And, you know, they named Josefa Varela a lady of the palace? They say she's a direct descendant of Netzahualcóyotl . . ."

Now Vicente laughed.

"She's certainly the right color!" he replied sardonically, referring to her dark-bronze skin.

The ladies of the palace had in fact been carefully selected, and only the wives and daughters of important Conservatives and influential politicians were invited, endeavoring not to offend anyone, which was inevitable for those who were left out.

And so, amid the laughter, Constanza gathered her courage and turned up at the castle, certain her life was about to be turned upside down.

Carlota's inspection was like an officer mustering a battalion: she lined the ladies up in a row, and as she passed, each of them curtsied. The empress looked them up and down, asked them to introduce themselves, and then made them take a step forward. Constanza sensed that the empress was in no way weak or delicate; quite the opposite. The smile she gave was anything but sweet. She was serious, dry, and to all appearances hadn't laughed for a long time.

"Tell me your name," she ordered a lady in the row.

"Manuelita Gutiérrez del Barrio," the woman promptly replied. "At God's and at your service, Your Majesty."

Carlota felt pride reemerge somewhere in her soul. She liked the way this woman, a complete stranger, had known how to address her; Mexican women, she thought, were by no means out of touch.

"You shall be a lady of honor, Doña Manuelita," Carlota said in a Spanish that allowed a suppressed French accent to come through.

Manuelita bowed her head again. The empress asked the next, "What is your name?"

"Guadalupe Blanco," the woman said unceremoniously.

"And tell me, under which viceroy was the School of Mining built?"

The room went still. The woman seemed petrified. Test questions? Nobody had been expecting that. Nobody dared break the silence. At last she replied with an almost imperceptible "I don't know."

Carlota looked her in the eyes and said, "Return to the line, please."

The woman retreated, bearing the weight of her ignorance on her shoulders.

She asked each of the women in front of her a question: *How old is the cathedral? Who designed the Sagrario's façade? When was the National Palace built?* And to each of the questions, the women, ashamed, replied with an *I don't know*. When it was Constanza's turn, she took a step forward, smiling.

"Name?"

"Constanza Murrieta, Your Majesty."

"And could you tell me, Constanza, what the name of the most distinguished Mexican of this century is?"

Constanza opened her eyes wide. She hesitated for a second before answering.

"Would Your Majesty like a diplomatic reply or the truth?"

Now Carlota's eyes grew wide.

"Honesty will always be appreciated in this court."

Constanza swallowed. She was about to say *Benito Juárez*, but feared such a response would have her banished or, worse still, ruin the plan to become a spy, a scheme that suddenly seemed exquisite. A spy inside the court. She was becoming increasingly attracted to the idea. And so, shrewdly, and thinking on her feet, Constanza lied out loud in the middle of the imperial hall, saying, "His Most Serene Highness Antonio López de Santa Anna, Your Majesty."

30

1866, Paris

Carlota walked with a firm step, escorted by her finance minister, to her second meeting with Napoleon. Racked with worry, she hadn't slept for several nights, and when she had finally managed to fall asleep, Napoleon appeared before her like the devil himself. She had received a few letters from Maximilian, and the situation in her beloved Mexico couldn't have been worse. It was all or nothing, and she wouldn't accept nothing.

Walking in, Carlota introduced the minister, saying *He knows Mexico's finances backward and forward*, and they sat at a marquetry table. Despite her fragile appearance, it was as if Carlota had an artillery squad hiding in her skirts. Once again, she put Napoleon up against the wall. Once again, she took him into legal territory, with arguments that made Napoleon uncomfortable. Carlota demanded. Napoleon apologized. And the more pressure she applied, the more intimidated he felt. She reminded him of his promises, all of them broken.

"What would you think of me if Your Majesty were in Mexico, and all of a sudden I told you I could not fulfill the terms of our agreement?"

"Circumstances have changed. War is war."

"And agreements are agreements, Your Majesty. You promised us we would always have your support."

"There's nothing I can do."

"We can't leave the Mexicans at the mercy of the United States."

The emperor fidgeted uncomfortably in his chair.

"France will lose everything it has invested in Mexico if we leave. Mexico possesses great riches," said Carlota. "We are pacifying the country, and that takes time. Mexico is a powder keg of constant civil wars, that's why they turned to us. Mexicans want peace."

Napoleon stood and paced nervously around the room. How small he was compared to the greatness of Bonaparte. Beside him, Napoleon III was a minnow, a coward, a man whose word was worthless.

To Carlota's surprise, the emperor suddenly broke down in tears.

Eugénie de Montijo, who had been listening through the door, entered the room. She was furious: she'd warned Napoleon that, whatever happened, he must not crack. *Men,* she thought with scorn.

"Let's continue this conversation in my study," Eugénie ordered. "We'll give the emperor a few minutes to regain his composure."

Carlota, stunned, stood and followed Eugénie. Entering her study, she found the French minister of war and minister of finance waiting for them.

The two women sat down to negotiate. Eugénie was a tougher nut to crack; she defended her husband's decision with a coldness that drove Carlota to despair. There was no argument that could make Eugénie see that withdrawing the troops from Mexico would be suicide. Carlota felt as if her nerves were about to betray her; her throat was dry and she could feel her temple palpitating at great speed.

"It is not France's fault that you have been unable to spread out your resources," said Eugénie.

"But it's the French bankers who are appropriating the loans that should be going to Mexico!" said Carlota, raising her voice.

"You insult us. If anyone is dishonest and ungrateful, it's the Mexicans," one of the ministers said.

"Mind your manners, if you please. You don't know the valor of the Mexicans!"

With Carlota hyperventilating due to her tight corset, Eugénie urged calm.

"You are in breach of the Treaty of Miramare!" Carlota yelled. And to everyone's surprise, she recited some paragraphs from memory.

The room was filled with shouting; Carlota insulted Bazaine by saying he was an informant for Napoleon, a spy in her own house.

"Bazaine is one of the best soldiers we have, he's too devoted to France's honor to compromise it," Eugénie argued.

The minister of war, riled, responded with a series of allegations against Maximilian.

"I demand respect for the emperor!" said Carlota.

"The man isn't even capable of coming in person; instead he sends his wife."

Carlota pressed her lips together.

"Enough, for the love of God," Eugénie pleaded. "I think I'm going to faint."

"For heaven's sake, Eugénie, stop playing the damsel in distress; we're discussing politics!"

And so, with her insults and truths, Carlota signed her own sentence. The next day, Napoleon ordered the immediate, permanent, and irrevocable evacuation of the expeditionary troops. Carlota's failure had been colossal.

Despite everything, Carlota kept faith; she thought she could still do something to persuade Napoleon. The Mexican minister gave her the terrible news in person. Unperturbed, unblinking, she listened to him in complete denial, knowing that until she heard it from the mouth of the emperor himself, the battle wasn't over. Eugénie had also sent her baskets of flowers and fruit that Carlota intended to let rot. With her requests going unanswered, she began to hate Napoleon with all her might. She wanted to slap him, call him a liar, a coward, an imbecile. In a final effort, she informed the French ministers that their war bonds would be worthless if she left without obtaining help.

On August 19, 1866, in the late afternoon, Napoleon III, the source of all her misery, arrived at the Grand Hotel to speak to Carlota. The decision had been made.

She asked for clemency. "If Your Majesty authorizes a loan of ninety million francs for Mexico, the empire will be able to save itself. We would return it in monthly installments."

Napoleon was moved by the woman's strength. Breathing her last breath, she still fought. *What a great monarch she would have been,* he thought. He got up from the armchair with difficulty due to his arthritis, approached her, took her hand, and kissed it with great tenderness and profound respect. A single silent tear slid down Carlota's cheek. Then, without saying a word, he left the room.

The formal refusal of her requests took a few more days to arrive. Carlota then sent a telegram to Maximilian. The message contained three words written in Spanish. Three words that seemed to encapsulate all the sorrow in her heart and the erosion of her spirit. *Todo es inútil,* it said. It's all useless.

31

Carlota left Paris on the imperial train, heading for Rome to intercede for the empire with Pope Pius IX. She barely spoke; she had weakened, and dark rings circled her eyes. Though Manuelita and Frau Döblinger tried to get her to eat, she hardly touched a bite. Asleep, she was tormented by nightmares in which she was being slowly poisoned, and she feared her dreams were a premonition. Dr. Bohuslavek was concerned about her, especially given her condition, and he worried that if she didn't take care of herself and continued to be burdened with so many worries, she would end up having a miscarriage. Sometimes he wondered if that was what the empress wanted. Regardless, the young doctor tried every means at his disposal to dissuade her from visiting the pope in her condition. Luck was on his side, however, when halfway there they were informed that northern Italy was in the grips of a cholera outbreak, forcing them to take a different route.

"We should rest at Miramare," her attendants said to her. And Carlota, who was mentally and physically exhausted, didn't protest.

The road was tortuous. She vomited constantly from the nausea, and Dr. Bohuslavek decided to administer tranquilizers to make the journey more comfortable. But when they reached Italian soil, Carlota seemed reborn. When she lived here, she'd still thought that she was on the verge of finding happiness. She remembered the excitement of falling in love, thinking that if she was loved by her archduke, nothing in life could be bad. She thought about the time that had passed since then, and a shiver ran down the back of her neck as she realized that it wasn't even a decade. Time . . . it was so relative, so inexorable. One of many afternoons when she was moved by her memories, she wrote to Maximilian:

> *Beloved Max,*
>
> *From this country of so many happy memories, where we enjoyed the best years of our lives, my thoughts turn constantly to you. Everything here makes me think of you: your Lake Como, which you loved so much, is in front of me, tranquil and blue. It's all here. Only you are missing, so far away, and almost ten years have passed! Even so, it's as if it were yesterday, and the nature here speaks to me only of immutable happiness, not of difficulties and disappointments. All the names, all the events are emerging again from forgotten corners of my mind, and I am living again in our Lombardy, as if I had never left it. I'm reliving two years that were so dear to us. I only wish I could see you here.*
>
> *Carlota*

Perhaps it was the calm that the setting brought her, or the knowledge that she'd done everything Maximilian had entrusted to her, but Carlota's health began to show signs of improvement. Perhaps she started to forgive herself. She reached Miramare just in time for September 16, Mexico's Independence Day. In an act of patriotism and liberalism—and because his was a liberal soul trapped in the body of a Conservative—Maximilian had adopted the custom of celebrating the occasion by imitating the insurrectionists' cry of independence. To mark the occasion, Carlota ordered the Austrian fleet to fire a twenty-one-gun salute at six o'clock in the morning, wore an imperial cloak and diamond diadem, and fêted her people with a lunch. She had the table dressed in the colors of the Mexican flag, she drank a toast, and, after raising the Mexican flag in the garden, she intoned a *Viva México!* with her eyes full of emotion. She missed it all. She missed Chapultepec, the view from her window of the immense valley. She missed the sound of the markets, the smells of the fruit. She missed the women's braids, the hot sauces. She missed the people's affection and the innocence of their voices. She missed speaking Spanish, and she missed loving Maximilian.

Strolling through Miramare's gardens soothed her. Manuelita usually accompanied her on her walks through the artificial forest that Max, little by little, plant by plant, had slowly created. The castle was just a mass of stones compared to the splendor of that garden. *If only Maximilian could see it,* she thought. Walking among the trees made her feel at peace. She listened to the birdsong and liked to think the wind that caressed her was the same wind that blew on the other side of the ocean.

Charles de Bombelles always followed her at a cautious distance. Since their arrival in Paris, they had hardly crossed paths. With so many thoughts in her head, with so much at stake, she had barely noticed the presence of the man who managed to arouse immeasurable jealousy in her. And suddenly, at Miramare, Bombelles emerged in all his splendor. He didn't give her a moment's peace: when she went out to stroll with Manuelita, there he was, right behind her, walking the same route. When she sat down to write letters, Bombelles would be a few yards away, reading in an armchair; when Dr. Bohuslavek attended to her, Bombelles waited at the door. But what worried Carlota most was seeing Bombelles in the kitchen, inspecting all of the food that was prepared for her. She began to feel watched. She couldn't take a step without Bombelles taking one, too, and far from reassuring her, it began to unnerve her. One day, seized by panic, she confessed to Mathilde.

"Mathilde, I think Bombelles is Napoleon's spy."

"What do you mean, my child? He's the archduke's right-hand man."

"I think he's a traitor," Carlota argued.

"Oh, don't say that, child! Charles is here to watch over you."

"I'm afraid, Mathilde."

The chambermaid enveloped her in an embrace that both comforted and immobilized her with equal force.

"No, child, don't be afraid. Everything will be fine, child. Everything will be fine."

But Carlota knew that the fear she felt would neither be allayed with motherly words nor disintegrate in the wind like clouds in the sky.

32

1864, Chapultepec Castle, Mexico City

Chapultepec was a Tower of Babel. Voices in German, French, and Spanish could be heard in the corridors at all times. Austrians, Belgians, French, Hungarians, and Mexicans struggled to avoid becoming lost in the mosaic of languages and customs that coexisted in the palace. Sometimes they had to use interpreters who suppressed words at their own discretion or convenience, depending on how sympathetic they were to a speaker. The work of some was hindered by the work of others, and it wasn't long before quarrels, grudges, and intrigues began to emerge, and courtiers needed to keep out of these disputes if they were to ensure their advancement. Mexico's future was of little importance to many of them so long as they could look the part and ensure the well-being of their families for several generations.

However, there was a single issue, just one, on which they all agreed. They were united in viewing Sebastian Schertzenlechner as a malign and harmful presence, always lurking, whether in the shadows or broad daylight. The emperor's office was in his clutches. Nothing went in or out of the royal study without him knowing, and everyone, including Carlota, knew he had the emperor's ear. Everyone wondered what his credentials were, and some even suggested it was his blue eyes for which the emperor held him in such high regard. But the reality was that, for good or ill, Maximilian listened to him and, worse, paid attention to him. It had been Sebastian's idea to demote Almonte and his team, giving him a purely ornamental role after having been the imperial regent. Maximilian dispensed with his services in his cabinet overnight. When the emperor was asked about this decision, he merely said that Almonte was miserly, cold, and vindictive, and that he didn't justify the use of funds. Everyone knew the real reason was that one afternoon in an argument with Sebastian, Almonte had called him *effeminate*.

Constanza, meanwhile, didn't miss a detail. She was alert to everything, taking in every look, every insinuation, every gesture. The slightest sign of doubt aroused her suspicion. She wanted to be very sure who could be trusted in that nest of vipers. How many ladies of the court would be there out of conviction, and how many, like her, were acting as Trojan horses? She understood from the moment she set foot in the castle that she couldn't retreat into her shell. She needed to make friends, mix with the court, get close to the servants who made the monarchs' beds, changed the chamber pots, and prepared the food. It was the only way she felt she had some control. She had to watch and remain silent. Like when her mother slipped books to her at night, and the next morning she would feign stupidity in front of the men of the house, to whom she was just a docile woman who was prettier when she was silent.

It was undoubtedly an inconvenience not knowing all the languages. All of a sudden, she felt cut off, unable to understand entire conversations right in front of her. The empress tended to speak to them in Spanish, but if someone addressed her in German, Italian, or French, she switched languages with incredible speed. Far from upsetting Constanza, it made her envious. She wanted to learn all the languages the empress knew, though she knew such privileges were bestowed only on kings and queens. The empress was fluent in six languages. Her native tongue was French, and she acquired German from her father, which she also used to communicate with her husband. She had mastered English, and the years in Lombardy-Venetia had enabled her to learn Italian. Before coming to Mexico, she had learned Spanish and also took lessons in Nahuatl. Such learning wasn't for common folk. But Constanza had a good ear and a love of books, something that Carlota discovered after a couple of conversations with her. She soon placed her among the small number of ladies of honor with whom she could discuss more elevated matters, which also gave Constanza access to the castle library. There she found translations of books that she, secretly, already knew. And though it was a huge effort, Constanza managed to learn a few words of French. Even so, she knew that in order to be successful in her mission, the issue of language was something she urgently needed to resolve.

One morning while Constanza was walking with Carlota after Mass, a hummingbird hovering to drink nectar from a nearby flower caught the empress's attention.

"What a beautiful creature!"

"It's a hummingbird, Your Majesty."

"I'd heard of them, but never seen one."

"According to a Nahuatl legend, they are warriors who died in combat, Your Majesty."

Carlota, Constanza thought, was delighted. A smile even appeared on her lips. The two of them stood watching the little bird suspended in the air.

"Maximilian would have loved to see it. Mexico is full of beauty," Carlota finally said.

"Your Majesty," Constanza said timidly, "I wanted to ask you a favor."

The hummingbird flew off when Carlota turned around. Constanza, curtsying, went on.

"I'd like to learn French, Your Majesty. I've realized that I would be more useful to you if I had a better command of the language."

Carlota scrutinized her without blinking.

"Then learn, Constanza. Learn. You don't need my consent for that."

"Yes, but is there someone in the court who would teach me?"

"*Ma chérie*, the court is full of Frenchmen."

And without another word, they set off. Constanza thought to herself that she knew nothing about the woman in front of her. She had to be cautious and very astute. Who could she practice French with without losing sight of the empress? She would search with a careful eye until she found the right teacher.

33

Without knowing exactly why, Philippe felt at home at last in the Valley of Mexico. Perhaps it was because the city's Belgian merchants welcomed them with a banquet complete with wine and champagne, or because wherever he looked he saw French soldiers in their medaled uniforms. But most likely it was that, for the first time in his life, Philippe felt that he was part of something important.

He couldn't say that Mexico City was the most beautiful city he'd ever seen. The streets were chaotic and dirty, and there were stalls everywhere selling everything from hot food to ointments for rheumatism, but the bustle made him feel alive; the city was like a great being that never slept. Again, Mexico with its contrasts. Its greatest riches existed side by side on the streets with barefooted natives. Reaching the center, Philippe—along with the rest of the soldiers—fell silent. There were churches, parks, beautiful buildings. Had it not been for the fact that they'd crossed seas and mountains to reach it, he would have sworn he was in a European city.

A cloud of dust approached them. To everyone's surprise, including Van der Smissen's, the sovereigns had come to welcome them. Maximilian was on horseback, followed by the French marshal Bazaine, and a short distance behind, the empress Charlotte rode in an open calash. The emperor began his welcome speech, but Philippe couldn't take his eyes off the empress behind him. He hadn't imagined her like this: she seemed so young, beautiful in an austere way, without the gaudiness of some Belgian women he'd seen. She seemed greatly moved; Philippe could see it. Drums suddenly began to beat. The officers saluted with their swords, the troops presented arms, and after the cheers they yelled, "Long live the emperor! Long live the empress!"

Carlota was touched. She hugged herself, and then with a gesture she sent the embrace to her loyal soldiers.

Behind the empress, Manuelita del Barrio and Constanza rode in a smaller calash; the former was visibly excited, as if the regiment of Belgian volunteers had arrived to protect her; the latter, astonished to see the number of foreigners willing to cross the ocean and risk their lives for this endeavor. Never in her life, thought Constanza, had she seen so many fools in one place. She was absorbed in her thoughts when a boy ran toward her.

"The empress sends you this," he said, handing her a piece of paper. Constanza read a sentence in the empress's hand:

Parlez-vous français?

"What does it say, *niña?*" Manuelita asked anxiously.

"I think the empress wants us to practice our French . . . with the Belgians."

"What? Let me see."

Manuelita read it, too, and they looked at each other without understanding the sovereign's instruction. They looked out to one side and saw a crowd of men who needed a good bath.

"If I have to speak French, I'll do so at the reception this evening, not now . . . Look at the faces on those soldiers!"

Constanza observed the scene.

"Fools," she now said out loud. "A bunch of crazy fools."

Manuelita scolded her.

"Hush, *niña*. You're going to get us exiled."

The carriage started moving again. Constanza looked at the crowd of men as they passed. Many of them had the same look of bewilderment she had. Then, for no apparent reason, her eyes fixed on one of them. Many years later, when fate turned against her, she had time to reproach herself for noticing him and no one else. But it wasn't just anyone: it was him. And once she saw him in the middle of the crowd, she couldn't look anywhere else. She watched him for a long time, hypnotized, memorizing his face as if she knew that the man she was looking at would change her destiny. He must have felt the force of her gaze, because he made eye contact with her. They looked at each other for an instant, no longer. But Constanza quickly looked away, embarrassed.

"Why, *niña* . . . you've gone bright red!"

Constanza held her hands to her cheeks. She was burning.

"Seems to me you just fell in love."

"Ay, Manuelita, the things you say."

For the rest of the journey she didn't interrupt Manuelita once, who, incapable of being quiet, gave her opinion on everything she saw. But Constanza wasn't listening: she wanted to examine the new feeling, something between nervousness and impatience, that fluttered in her soul. She needed to see him again. To see that soldier again.

In the evening, clean and wearing their dress uniforms, the French soldiers in Mexico fêted Carlota's Belgians, as they'd begun to call them, with a reception held at the Palacio de Minería. Constanza knew she would see *her* soldier, so she went to great lengths with her appearance. The other ladies of the court noticed her new enthusiasm.

"You can stop primping yourself now, *niña*, or you'll outshine the empress."

"Ladies!" she replied jovially, aware that, sure enough, there was little she could do to look better.

She felt ridiculous. The chances she would speak to him were negligible. She didn't even know his name, and if she did, it would be of little use. Still, something pulsed inside her, a new hope. Before going to the reception, she took a deep breath and pinched her cheeks.

When the men arrived at the Palacio de Minería, not a single soldier or officer didn't marvel at it. Many of them had thought they would find only Aztec temples, but they were received in a building whose stairways were on a par with those of any royal hall in Bruges. The central courtyard appeared dignified amid the flowers and ostentation of the royal ceremony. Many of the soldiers had never seen such a building before; most of them were strangers to wealth, and before embarking, their only concern had been to put food on the table. All of a sudden, here they were amid royalty in an elegant reception, admiring the grandeur that they'd only ever heard about in conversation.

Albert from Brussels was one such soldier. His father was a butcher, and for as long as he could remember, his life had consisted of slitting throats and dismembering cows. He knew how to use a knife, but he'd never driven one into any being with fewer than four legs. He preferred animals to people, especially when he felt out of place, as he did that evening. Philippe could sense his discomfort from the other side of the courtyard. He approached him and, handing him a glass of punch, said, "Hold it together, lad. It's not just about who you are, but also who you appear to be."

Albert took the glass, grateful.

"Appear?"

"Being worthy of the uniform, lad. It doesn't matter where you come from; what matters is where you go."

Before he had a chance to respond, the sovereigns appeared with their retinue. Constanza scanned the crowd from a prudent distance.

From the moment he'd seen the empress, Philippe couldn't take his eyes off her. *She* was the reason for his journey, not the emperor, or

Van der Smissen, or Bazaine. Her. He watched her closely, as if anticipating her movements. Even knowing she would never notice a poor carpenter from Antwerp, he felt drawn to this woman. He observed every detail. Her skin was pale, almost translucent; Philippe could've sworn the sunlight had never touched it. She wore white silk embroidered with gold, and a crimson velvet cloak, also embroidered in gold, protected her from the cold of the night. Her slender neck sparkled with a necklace of diamonds and two strings of pearls that—Philippe thought—were a little distracting, and on her head, she wore an imperial diadem. Accustomed to the noble simplicity of wood, Philippe realized the only adornments he knew were varnish and oil. How distant he was from her. How remote, and yet, they were united by the invisible bonds of fate.

Constanza spent the entire evening searching for her soldier's face, but with all of them dressed in the same uniform and their hair waxed, she didn't recognize him. *Where are you? Where are you?* she said to herself as she searched for him. Her mood began to darken when, as the night wore on, she still hadn't seen him. And Manuelita didn't leave her alone for a second, chattering like a cockatoo. She was in her element, mixing with the cream of Mexican high society, who suddenly acted as if they'd worn a crown from the cradle. Many of them spoke other languages and, out of courtesy to the newcomers, Spanish was rarely heard.

"Practice your French, *niña*. Empress's orders."

Constanza gave her a forced smile and, after wasting some time with a *merci* here and an *enchantée* there, she carried on her search. She greeted people politely as she escorted Carlota, putting on a façade like when, as a young girl, she'd said rosaries with Clotilde, while really, she was thinking of Baudelaire poetry she'd read the night before.

The evening came to an end. It was late, and everyone returned to their lodgings. At Chapultepec, Constanza removed her makeup with disappointment in her heart and fury in her head. That's what she got for being a dreamer, she told herself, and she promised that from then on, while at the palace, she would stop distracting herself with matters unrelated to the mission her mother had entrusted to her: nothing less than to spy on the empress. While she unknotted the braids gathered at the back of her head, she chided herself for being so foolish and missing what was in front of her because she was searching for a rankless soldier. She was rubbing shoulders with the grandees who'd come to usurp Mexico's sovereignty. Who had the empress been with? Who was the Belgian colonel she'd spoken with for so long? Who was the blue-eyed man, wide as a wardrobe, who hadn't left the empress's side for one second?

You stupid, stupid girl, she said to herself as she removed the red from her lips roughly.

In the center of the city, the soldiers were divided into groups of a hundred. Without sufficient barracks, some were lodged in houses. Hearing this, some welcomed the news: they preferred the comfort of a house, modest as it might be, to the coldness of military accommodation. However, they soon discovered there was little difference between the two. The large building Philippe's group was assigned was an enormous hall with high ceilings in which pigeons had found the perfect refuge; the floor underneath was covered in a thick layer of white and green. There was no furniture or beds; it was a dovecote.

"Where will we sleep?" Albert asked.

"We'll have to lie on those planks," Philippe replied.

Albert made a face.

"It's that or the floor," Philippe said as he grabbed one.

"How is it you never lose heart?"

"I've slept in worse places," Philippe replied. "Now shut up and go to sleep."

Albert obeyed, unaware that his words had stirred up memories of caves, fear, and loneliness.

The next morning, most of the men awoke covered in mosquito bites, so many they feared they might be infected with some strange disease. The lumps were the size of five-centavo coins and strawberry red. While the mosquitoes seemed to have ignored Philippe, Albert woke up inflamed from the itching.

"I'm going to die, I'm going to die because of these infernal bugs!" he said while he scratched.

"You're not going to die, Albert. It's just a few bites."

"Easy for you to say. Look at you! Why didn't they bite you?"

"Let me see," said Philippe, taking a closer look. Sure enough, the allergic reaction had left Albert with burning arms.

"Damned sweet blood . . . My father always said that. But the mosquitoes here don't just bite; they feast! Is it serious? Do I have a fever?"

"Will you calm down? You haven't come this far to die from a mosquito bite, you hear?"

And Albert nodded like a small child, distressed at the prospect of dying, however it happened.

He wasn't the only one unhappy with the situation. There were complaints all around: *They're going to starve us to death. We can't sleep on the floor. If I'd known how bad it was, I'd have stayed in Belgium.* Their plaintive voices made the atmosphere ever hotter. The officers struggled to maintain order among so many novice soldiers. Philippe, who was a man of few words, except for the occasional conversations he had with Albert, preferred to just listen. He dressed and, waiting for instructions that didn't seem forthcoming through all the cursing, took an apple and went out for some air. He was surprised to find himself looking at a figure on horseback accompanied by an imperial carriage: without warning, the empress had decided to visit her men. He didn't know it then, but Carlota went riding every morning; she was an excellent horsewoman. And though she preferred to go alone, in Mexico she was always escorted; for her safety, they told her. Philippe held his breath, not daring to move a muscle. Unlike the night before, she was wearing neither a diadem nor gold-embroidered dress. Philippe thought she looked better this way. When he saw her move toward him, he stood to attention.

"What's your name?" she asked as if she had found a frightened child.

"Philippe, Your Majesty. Philippe Petit."

Carlota smiled. "Well, Philippe, you're not so *petit.*"

He kept a straight face. He was unsure if he should smile.

"Where are you from?"

"From Antwerp, Your Majesty."

"And how was your night?"

Philippe hesitated. Carlota, with her usual intelligence, anticipated his response.

"You may speak freely."

"Well . . . truth be told, not so good, Your Majesty. We lack supplies, we have no mattresses, and there are many insects."

Carlota remembered her own first night in Mexico City: it hadn't been very promising. She remembered Maximilian sleeping on a billiard table to escape the bedbugs in the mattress. If that was what it had been like for them, she could only imagine what it was like for these poor soldiers.

"Thank you for your honesty, Philippe Petit. I'll see to it that your needs are met as soon as possible."

And then she rode off, urging her horse into a trot with the carriage following. Those men had volunteered of their own free will to accompany her halfway around the world. And she felt close to them, as if all of them, including her, were suffering the same affliction. She remembered her own arrival clearly. Reaching Mexico City had been torture: the journey through the wooded mountain passes had been harrowing, and on more than one occasion she'd hit her head on the carriage ceiling. The nobles who greeted them ran out of excuses for the poor state of the route.

"Apologies, Your Majesties; there has been much rain and the roads have broken up. Apologies . . ."

A pothole. *Apologies.* Another pothole. *Apologies.* More potholes. If the empress had been older, she could have ended up with a broken rib. But Carlota still had her hopes and dreams intact; she loved everything about Mexico, it all seemed wonderful to her. And despite everyone's contrite expressions, the poor state of the roads wasn't enough to ruin their welcome. The streets, squares, and public buildings were decked out in green, white, red, and with all the flowers in bloom everywhere, Carlota felt as if she were in an immense garden. At night, the balconies of the houses were decorated with little colored lanterns and lights, turning Mexico City into a stretch of sky on earth. Mexico. Glory. Recognition. The chance to transcend history. Nobody knew then that, in Mexico, glory and failure were two sides of the same coin that turned perilously.

Philippe watched her ride away. Standing there, he waited for her silhouette to disappear like a ship sailing over the horizon. He watched her go and found himself wishing from the depths of his soul that she would turn and look back at him. But it wasn't she who turned around. A short distance away, holding her breath like Philippe, Constanza watched in a state of paralysis from the carriage that escorted the empress. The soldier. The man whose eyes took her breath away more even than the corset she wore. *Her* soldier had spoken to the empress.

34

That morning, Carlota ran her hands slowly over the cloth that covered her, then sighed. While the dresses she wore were loose, the bulge at her belly was increasingly obvious. If she wanted to see the pope, she had to do it soon; it was a race against time, and she couldn't lose. She feared for her safety and was suspicious of everyone. Bombelles's constant surveillance made her nervous, as did Bohuslavek's drops diluted in liquids he made her take. Of course, it was to be expected that Napoleon would keep watch on her. It's what she would do in his place: the enemy must always be watched; it had been thus since Brutus stabbed Caesar. While she was on European soil, her presence was a threat. France was on the cusp of war, and Europe was a powder keg. No doubt Napoleon had found more than one person with a price to make them his spy. She had to hurry.

The day after the Independence Day celebrations, she decided to set off for Rome overland. During the journey, Mathilde was her refuge, a haven of peace. In her company, her fears disappeared, and she could relax in the simplicity of being a normal person. With her, she didn't talk about politics, treaties, or agreements. It was only with her that Carlota forgot about her call to reign. But when she was alone, her mind couldn't stop agonizing over it all. If her audience with Napoleon had been torturous, she could only imagine what it was going to be like pleading with Pius IX. Maximilian had trod on many of the Church's toes: only a fool would ignore the fact he was a child of the Revolutions of 1848. On arriving in Mexico, more liberal than the Conservatives who'd summoned him to govern, Max had stripped the Church of its assets and prerogatives. He was sympathetic to the reform laws enacted by Juárez, and to add insult to injury, he had decreed freedom of worship. On top of that, his personal physicians and advisers were Jews. Carlota knew that persuading the Holy Father would be no walk in the park.

When they finally reached Rome, Carlota alighted from the train at the station amid crowds of people gathered on the platform. It was a spectacle; people pushed to see her descend surrounded by a retinue of servants dressed as charros. Cardinals, ministers, and representatives of Italian high society were there to welcome her, and Carlota, while satisfied with the welcome, felt harried by all the people. They struggled to advance through the mass of onlookers who'd come to see the empress pass. Finally they reached the hotel on Via del Corso where they would stay. The entire second floor was hers. In the peace of her room, Carlota opened the balcony doors and smiled. It had been a long time; the view was magnificent. San Carlo alle Quattro Fontane, for no obvious reason, reminded her of Puebla's cathedral. She closed her eyes and breathed in deeply. In spite of everything, Mexico was always there, latent, in the smells and colors of the old continent.

A few days later, Pius IX received her at the Vatican. The Holy Father was dressed all in white, and he seemed to shine brightly amid the golds and reds of the papal throne. Carlota threw herself at his feet to kiss his sandals. The pope, with remarkable speed for his seventy-four years, quickly stopped her.

"Stand up, child," he ordered as he held out a hand for her to kiss his ring.

Carlota looked up; she wanted to find something in the old man's eyes to give her confidence. With all her anxieties, she wanted to find a crack through which hope could appear. They spoke for a long time. She set out her proposals for a concordat, telling heartfelt stories of her far-off land that nobody seemed to care about.

"Napoleon has abandoned us," she said, and, mentioning his name, a terrible feeling of dread stirred inside her. She hesitated before speaking the next sentence, but she was in a safe place.

"I suspect he wants to poison me, Your Holiness."

The pope tilted his head to one side.

"He wants to poison you, child?"

"He does. Everyone does. He's turned everyone against me. I no longer trust anybody."

"Napoleon? What makes you say this, child?"

"They put white powders in my water. I've seen it. The doctor thinks I'm not aware of it, but I am."

Pius IX remained silent. Carlota went on.

"If they must kill me, let them get it over with, without the sadism of doing it slowly."

"But that's impossible, child. Why would they kill you?"

"Why not? Right now, I'm a hindrance. All my lifelines have died: my father, my grandmother, my mother. Who would miss me if I died all these leagues away?"

The pope heard the weight of desperation in the young woman's voice.

"Help me, Your Holiness, don't leave me at the mercy of these men. They want to drive me out of my mind."

Hearing this, the pope thought she must be delirious. To soothe her, he offered her some words of comfort; they came naturally, without thought. He consoled people instinctively. Everyone came to him with requests, sick children, serious cases, seeking miracles. He spent the day hearing requests, one after the other, and all he could do for any of those souls was pray.

"Fear not, child. Nobody gets poisoned in Rome."

Then they spoke of other matters. They said goodbye with the pope promising to examine the concordat document. Carlota didn't know what to expect. Three days later, dressed and ready at eight o'clock in the morning, she woke Sra. Del Barrio.

"Get dressed, Manuelita. We're going to the Vatican."

Sra. Del Barrio blinked a couple of times at the torrent of light that had flooded into the room. Startled, it took her a few seconds to react.

"They summoned you already? So soon?"

To which Carlota replied, "I'm not going to sit here with my arms crossed while Mexico's future hangs in the balance. If I was a man, they would've already received me."

Sra. Del Barrio looked at the empress's clothes. She was wearing an everyday dress, clearly not appropriate for an audience with the pope. She delicately brought it to the attention of Carlota, who was pacing around the room.

"Forgive me, Majesty, but do you think you should wear something more suited to a visit to the pope?"

Carlota stopped. She hesitated for a second, then said with pride, "You forget, Manuelita, it is we monarchs who make the rules of etiquette. We are exempt from them."

As they passed the Trevi Fountain, Carlota suddenly ordered the coachman to halt. The carriage stopped dead, and the women had to grab the armrests to steady themselves.

"What is it?" Sra. Del Barrio asked, hoping the empress had changed her mind and decided to change her clothes.

But Carlota just said, "I'm dying of thirst."

Sra. Del Barrio watched in disbelief as the empress climbed down from the carriage with a small silver cup she'd never seen before.

"Where did you get that cup, Majesty?"

"I borrowed it from the Vatican."

Sra. Del Barrio quickly crossed herself, hoping the ritual would cancel out the sin of theft.

Carlota walked toward the fountain like a bride walking to the altar, stretched out her arm, and, allowing the water to splash her dress, filled the cup and drank it all down. Sra. Del Barrio, with astonishment all over her face, watched her return to the carriage with a big smile; she sat watching the empress in silence, as if she'd just seen her butcher an animal. Sitting down, Carlota broke the silence.

"At least I won't be poisoned here."

They reached the Vatican early enough that they found the pope having breakfast. The Holy Father, who wasn't accustomed to unexpected visits, was glad that, for once, someone had skipped the protocol.

"Let her in," he said. "She can share the sacred food."

When Carlota walked in, the first thing she noticed was the exquisite smell of bread and hot chocolate floating in the air among the tapestries. Her stomach rumbled with such force that she thought everyone must have heard it. She'd been hungry for days, sometimes because her nerves took away her appetite, and more often because she didn't trust the food she was served. She approached the table. The pope spoke a few words to her, but she wasn't listening: she was fixated on the steaming cup of thick chocolate in which His Holiness was dipping bread. She heard voices, but didn't understand a word. She began to feel dizzy. A high-pitched sound went off in her ears, like sailors' whistles. *That's it,* she thought, *I'm going to faint.* She tried to pull herself together, taking a deep breath. The pope was speaking. He was looking at her with concern. She noticed His Holiness stand up, and Sra. Del Barrio held her around the waist. She had a thousand thoughts in two seconds. *If I faint, they'll discover I'm pregnant.* No, she couldn't. Not here. Not now. And just as she felt her legs buckling, she lurched into the table and without a second's hesitation stuck her fingers in the papal cup.

If they had been able to hear it, they would have heard the devil bellow with laughter at the two deadly sins he'd managed to smuggle into those sacred rooms for the first time: with gluttony and lust, Carlota, empress of Mexico, sucked her fingers.

35

Carlota knew a man's love was a privilege she would never have. By now she was well aware of this. Nobility and duty were oblique to falling in love. Sex, perhaps; but love . . . that was a horse of a different color. She had thought—in her naivety—that she would find love with the archduke, but one by one she'd cut loose those moorings until the ship disappeared over the horizon.

Philippe, on the other hand, never gave up on love. When he was a child, despite the hardship and the hunger, despite the struggles and disappointments that marked him forever, he always maintained an opening in his heart for love. He never dared admit it even to himself, but now and then, when the moon disappeared from the sky and the night turned darker than usual, a treacherous part of his soul dreamed. One day he would have children. One day he would have a family with which to regain the innocence he lost in that freezing cave. One day he would sleep in the arms of a woman who would keep him safe in the curve of her flesh. When he reached adolescence, his dreams of love and family evaporated to make way for pleasures that were no less gratifying. Loving wasn't always satisfactory: the first women he visited terrified him. They were much older, with plenty of experience. Some felt tenderness toward the young man, others didn't hide their boredom at being tutors in the amorous arts; teaching an adolescent took longer and was therefore less profitable. Some more sympathetic women allowed their maternal side to emerge and spoke to him as if he were a small child: *Come to your mama, baby.* When that happened, Philippe tensed, unable to combine two different beings in a single person: he was either with a mother or a whore. He tried to banish the few memories he had of his own mother from his mind, but broke down in tears because he missed her, and ran out of the room. He would rather pleasure himself; it was free and he could imagine whatever he wanted. He did so and then, having calmed himself, felt more alone than ever. He became a rock battered by the force of the tide, immersed in a solitude as vast as an ocean. He lay his head on a pillow and waited for the new moon to spirit in dreams of future loves.

And then he met Famke.

She wasn't like the others. Seeing her dark eyes, Philippe felt as if he were looking into a black night where anything was possible, an imperturbable sea of tar. She couldn't have been much older than him, a few years, perhaps. Her mother had been one of the best prostitutes in Brussels, and though at first she'd resisted sending her daughter into the same profession, she realized that if she could guide her to the right lovers, the girl would end up with wealth and power, or at least that was the excuse she told herself when she was overcome with guilt. Then she shook off her remorse, telling herself that Famke, as well as giving and receiving pleasure, would learn history, languages, and music. What she didn't predict was that Famke would turn out to be even more successful than her; little by little she developed a repertoire of looks that made the men she lay with feel as if there were no other men on earth. That each of Famke's kisses were the first she had given. More than one of them promised to take her away from that sinful, carnal world in which they so often and so pleasurably sinned. She smiled, lowered her head, and allowed herself to be kissed on the forehead, knowing she would never see them again. Because Famke's mother had ignored something that proved to be her most beneficial virtue in such a profession: Famke didn't possess one speck of innocence. She knew that marriage was a tombstone of financial and mental dependence under which she did not wish to lie. There was no inferno that could compare to the life of submission and subjection to which talentless women were condemned. It wasn't easy. At first she cried a lot. But in time, she learned to embrace her profession, discovering that, in fact, men not only listened to her but also heeded her advice and opinions. And she was in charge of her own finances. Once she had sampled freedom and independence, there was no human power that could have persuaded her to turn to a life in the kitchen.

Philippe, a young man whose beard had barely begun to grow, also fell into her clutches. He met her by chance one night when, leaving Mr. Walton's workshop, he found her lost, or pretending to be, in the dark streets. She had come out of a bourgeois merchant's house and was returning to the tavern where her mother was waiting for her. Philippe offered to accompany her. That was all it took. At first he observed her reservation, keeping a distance, until he found himself thinking that he'd never seen such a perfect creature. Her golden hair hanging down to her tiny waist, breasts that bounced with each step, and a smile the heavens could fit in. From her conversation, he could tell she was different from the other girls. She knew Latin. And the more she spoke, the more Philippe was silent. Famke asked him all kinds of questions, but when he asked one, she evaded it with lightning-fast reactions. Finally, they reached the tavern.

"Thank you," she said. "You made my night."

Philippe bowed his head.

And then something unexpected, almost magical, happened, taking him by surprise: Famke took his hand, led him to an alleyway where there was a cat purring, and kissed him on the lips. Without saying a word, she guided Philippe in each movement of their tongues, each touch. Then she began to speak to him quietly. *Slowly. Not like that.*

Open your mouth, but not too much. And so, without rushing and without resting, she waited for the young man to ripen. Suddenly she lifted her skirt and invited him to enter. Philippe learned many things that night, protected by the secrecy of darkness in that dead-end alleyway.

"Consider it a birthday gift," she said.

"But it's not my birthday."

"It is now," said Famke. And then she left.

They never saw each other again, but he tried—to no avail—to find her in every woman he met. Sometimes, when alcohol numbed his senses enough for him to love without losing consciousness, he thought he saw her dark eyes again, looking back at him. He closed his own eyes to be able to see her clearly, and then he would become the best of lovers. In time, Philippe's fame spread among the brothels of Ghent, until there was a proliferation of people claiming to be him in order to get a discount. They were all found out, because if there was one thing the women of the bawdy houses could recognize, it was a man in love with an illusion.

Since his arrival in Mexico, Philippe hadn't thought about her again. For many years, he believed Famke had been a dream, but nothing lasts forever, and Famke faded like any memory given long enough; it was an open wound that scarred badly. And Philippe embarked for Mexico. The army and the possibility of adventure beckoned. And one day, having turned twenty-four, he found himself dreaming a new dream, one as fragile and as elusive as water slipping through fingers. This new dream was named Carlota, and it was, by some margin, the stupidest of all his dreams. Unlike Famke, she wasn't some fantasy in an alleyway: Carlota was tangible. Carlota was there, every day. She had a voice. She had a body. Carlota was on the banners, on the medals, on the carriages. Carlota. Always Carlota. The empress.

He struggled to admit it. At first, he thought the interest that she aroused in him came from simple curiosity from meeting a member of royalty. Carlota had a lot of time for *her Belgians*, as she called them, and every morning she ensured they got a cup of hot chocolate and a tortilla. Philippe disliked the tortilla—he much preferred the crusty bread from bakeries back home, whose smell could make even the dying hungry— but he ate it without a word of complaint. He watched her go with a slight smile on her lips, a rare occasion in which she seemed happy, at least for an instant. Her smile was nothing like Famke's. Carlota didn't seduce him in the same way, and that made her more interesting. Carlota seemed completely defenseless to him. Despite the pomp that surrounded her, for someone as empty as him it wasn't hard to see the void in her. He knew there was an ocean between them; he wasn't stupid, and he knew, as he did with Famke, that he would have to learn to see her vanish. Even so, though he was aware of the chasm between them, he couldn't help thinking they were similar, as if Carlota was waiting for dawn in a cave like the one from his childhood. Watching her had become an obsession, so much so that whenever he had the chance, Philippe volunteered for her personal escort. He did it to be near her, but once he'd overcome his awe, he realized that it wasn't just a privilege to be at her side but also a tremendous lesson in political ability. Carlota thought a lot and said little, yet she issued orders left and right. The emperor was forever absent, but Philippe thought that it was an advantage, because it fell to her to attend to matters. Philippe sensed that this was Carlota's natural state, and she seemed to rise to the challenge with all the majesty of the orchids in summer. She rose at five to contemplate the sunrise lighting up the volcano Iztaccíhuatl, and starting at six she received ministers and heard all kinds of requests. Her primary concern was with the terrible treatment of the native population. In that, she was identical to Juárez, but Philippe would never dare say so. He saw her act with firmness, with an assuredness expected in men but not women. For Philippe, her education made her seductive without showing an inch of flesh. She governed with courage, energy, and intelligence. The way in which she carried herself, the way she firmly held a pen to sign a document, the way she was always one step ahead of ministers in their discussions, leaving them bewildered; all this captivated him.

One time, Philippe overheard a couple of ministers who, after showing respect for her in the absence of Maximilian, complained bitterly as they left her office.

"It's unheard of to be ordered around by a woman who should be opening gardens, visiting the sick, and decorating the palace."

The other replied, "But the emperor is more interested in choosing curtains for Chapultepec than watching over Bazaine's actions! Wanting to make the castle his Schönbrunn, whatever that means . . ."

General Bazaine, in his reports to France, took the view that the empress possessed such a gift for governance that, were the power left totally in her hands, she would lead the empire better than her faint-hearted husband. Philippe thought the same.

During sleepless nights, Philippe gave thanks for Colonel Van der Smissen's belligerence, which had brought him to the doors to Carlota's rooms.

He knew little of Van der Smissen; he'd only seen him when they left Belgium and on their arrival in Mexico. He flitted among the rows of men with the austere look of a Christ Pantocrator. While his manners were French, his mien when giving orders was that of a German through and through. Philippe could recognize his colonel from a distance, not just because he had sharp eyes, but because Van der Smissen stood out in a crowd. He was tall and well built, with a back so broad that, had he not been a soldier, he might well have worked on Antwerp's docks unloading goods. He was imposing not just because of his physical appearance but owing to his hard gaze. He was a man of strict judgments and uncompromising punishments, which was why his heart sank when he inspected his soldiers: he knew himself to be in command of a bunch of bandits, former mule drivers, or bakers who had become soldiers overnight. One of his best men had been a curtain-maker's assistant twelve years ago, and had just been arrested for stealing handkerchiefs in the center of Mexico City. Many of the imperial "soldiers" had been sent there by force: recruited at bayonet point, which meant they could desert if they were so much as allowed near a sugarcane plantation. The enemy was within, and Van der Smissen knew it; the Belgians who had arrived were not of the best stock. *The day the French army leaves,* he thought, *the empire will fall like a house of cards in the wind.* Nonetheless, he'd joined the army to serve his king, Leopold I, and to climb the ranks; he was a career soldier, and he knew that medals were earned on the battlefield. He was responsible for turning these wretches into warriors prepared to die for a cause. He was responsible.

He formed them into rows and then, puffing out his chest, he spoke in a loud voice as if motivating them to go into battle.

"Soldiers!"

The echo of his voice reverberated among the Montezuma cypresses behind them.

"I know you have come here to protect the empress, and that you are eager to face the enemy. Believe me when I tell you, that is what we shall do in order to fight for the noble cause that brought us here! A man demonstrates his courage in war; in battle he shows what he is made of. I know that many of you have not been trained for combat, but you will not fight alone: we will fight *together*! For the empire, for the empress, and for Mexico!"

Guarding the empress had begun to seem more banal than glorious, and among themselves they joked about whether they were ladies of the court or Van der Smissen's soldiers. So every morning, Van der Smissen mustered them and gave rousing speeches that filled them with pride and motivated them in equal measure. And it wasn't long before they, too, were infected with the enthusiasm of the officers, who with each word from the colonel gradually regained the dignity lost amid the typhoid, rancid food, and infested barracks. Little by little the soldiers began to think that perhaps there was a purpose to their anonymous lives, and that was what war would give them. They hadn't embarked on their journey to die, but neither did they live a dream life. Dying in combat, even if it wasn't their war, would bring them honor and greatness. Their small egos began to swell with the promise of a worthy death or an honorable life. Yes, Van der Smissen's words fertilized a soil that had been left fallow for many years. The colonel's plan bore fruit when the order came one day to leave the empress and go on campaign. The Republican army had taken Oaxaca, Saltillo, and Monterrey, and all hands were needed to halt their advance. Against Van der Smissen's wishes, they were divided into two battalions: the Empress's Battalion, and the King of the Belgians', consisting of artillerymen. They would depart for Michoacán, where, according to Bazaine, they would have an opportunity to prove themselves against the Republicans, given that it was a controlled situation: maintaining the province within the empire would require only a small force. They all set off with high hopes and their heads filled with dreams of victory. Before leaving, Van der Smissen chose six to stay and guard the empress. Five were recruited against their will, unhappy to lose the opportunity of their lives in order to act as nannies. But there was one, just one, who stepped forward when Van der Smissen requested volunteers to stay. His name was Philippe Petit, and there was only one battle he wanted to fight: the one against his empty heart, the heart that quivered when he learned he would be beside Carlota from dawn until the sun went down behind the snowy peaks.

It wouldn't be the only quivering heart in the palace. Constanza believed that a force stronger than destiny was pushing him straight toward her.

36

"She's gone mad," Bombelles said to Philippe, the Count of Flanders and Carlota's brother, whom he'd summoned to Rome.

Philippe paced the room, dubious.

"What do you mean she's gone mad? It could be just a nervous breakdown."

"Excuse my frankness, but she's utterly lost her mind. She thinks we're all spies, that we want to poison her; she refuses food, she eats only walnuts and oranges because she peels them herself; she drinks water from the fountains . . ."

"It can't be," Philippe said, frowning. "Carlota's a brilliant woman and has always been in full control of her faculties. She never showed any signs of derangement."

"See for yourself, if you wish."

"Has Maximilian been informed?"

"Dr. Bohuslavek is heading to Mexico right now to give him the news."

"He's traveling all that way just for that?"

"Well, sir, there is something else."

With a troubled expression, Philippe joined his hands behind his neck.

Bombelles went on. "You see, the empress is expecting."

Philippe let his arms drop.

"She's pregnant?" There was a very short silence that the count quickly broke. "Then let's not waste any more time. Take me to her."

Philippe doubted everything Bombelles had told him when he saw his sister. He had expected to find her in bed, sweating, with damp handkerchiefs on her forehead, but Carlota was beautiful when she received him. She was clean, tidy, well dressed—in black, as she had liked to dress since her beloved grandmother Maria Amalia died, but presentable and in good spirits. Seeing each other, they hugged.

"Philippe, how I have missed you!"

"Me too, dear Charlotte, me too."

"Sit down, please."

The siblings took a seat. For a few seconds, Philippe tried to detect some sign of confusion. Nothing. Then he noticed there was nothing to drink.

"Will you not offer some tea to your brother?"

Carlota's smile vanished. She looked from side to side to check that they were alone.

"Philippe, they're trying to poison me. And you too, no doubt."

Philippe leaned on his elbows.

Seeing his look of disbelief, Carlota persisted.

"It's true. They think I'm mad, but I'm not. I swear. I'm as sane as you are. They want to kill me."

Philippe began to worry.

"What are you saying? Why do you think that? Have you felt unwell? Are you sick?"

"All the time. Since I set sail for Saint-Nazaire. They're weakening me. I know they are."

"And couldn't there be another reason for your discomfort?" Philippe gestured at her bulging belly.

Carlota stood up.

"You know?"

"It seems a lot of people do."

Carlota hugged herself.

"Who knows? I told only Mathilde and Bohuslavek, for obvious reasons."

"And Max?"

Carlota raised her eyebrows, concerned.

"Oh, Philippe. I haven't told Max."

"Why not?"

Carlota swallowed with difficulty.

"Because he would know it cannot be his."

Philippe sat back in his chair; Carlota huddled next to him.

Then, remembering her other brother, she requested, "Don't tell Leopold."

Philippe said nothing.

That night he couldn't sleep. Carlota didn't seem insane, or incoherent. The idea that she was being poisoned was undoubtedly an eccentricity, but it might have been the result of what she'd endured in recent months. More than months . . . years! Going to Mexico had been foolish, as good as her intentions may have been. They'd been tricked, manipulated by Napoleon and Eugénie de Montijo, and his idiot of a brother-in-law had believed the Mexicans really wanted an emperor. The Mexicans had had emperors, Aztec ones. If anyone was mad here, it was Maximilian. Philippe's poor sister was a woman in love with a weakling, nothing more. He mulled it over. And the child? What should they do with it? Without doubt, they should pass it off as a Habsburg. It had been done in every royal house since time immemorial; there was no reason to change now. He made a decision: he would give Frau Döblinger a couple of days off so he could observe Carlota up close. He needed to assess her true mental state.

He spent two nights with Carlota, two nights in which he listened to her speak about many things. About Mexico, about Maximilian, and about the fear she felt.

"God wants to punish me," she said.

The last straw was when Frau Döblinger returned from her break with a live chicken that she killed in Carlota's room so she could eat it with confidence.

He didn't know what to think, or what to do.

Just before leaving, Philippe saw a note that Carlota had received from the Holy Father; enclosed was the concordat that Carlota had presented to him in Rome, unsigned. Curious, Philippe opened the note.

> *Your Majesty,*
> *I return to you the document you presented to me, and it would give me pleasure if you would keep the cup. In my prayers I beseech God to restore peace to your mind and free you of the suspicion that is causing you such unhappiness. I bless you with all my heart.*
> *Pius IX*

Philippe folded the letter, put it back in its place, and unaware that the decision he was about to make would end his sister's life, he decided to tell his elder brother. Despite everything, he was Leopold II, patriarch of the Belgians; he would know what to do.

Leopold squirmed with pleasure. While Philippe, distressed, told him about their sister's situation, he kneaded his hands, stroking the knuckles.

"This is exactly what we needed; don't you see?"

"What do you mean?"

"Charlotte is incapable of administrating her funds, which, as we know, are considerable."

Philippe frowned so hard his eyebrows met.

"What are you suggesting?"

"From now on, we'll control Charlotte's money. There's no reason a woman should manage such sums. You know I sent a draft law to the chambers to exclude women from inheritances; Charlotte will be granted a life annuity that may be canceled should she behave badly."

Philippe listened in horror as it became clear that all his brother cared about was appropriating Charlotte's fortune.

Leopold smiled openly as he calculated how immensely rich his sister's madness had just made him. At last he would be able to seize the Congo.

"In relation to her health . . . ," Philippe intervened.

Returning to the conversation, Leopold II said with absolute finality, "The insane are locked up, Philippe."

37

1864, Mexico

Constanza only had eyes for him. She watched him guarding Carlota day and night, and his seriousness captivated her. He wasn't like the other inhabitants of the palace, obsessed with standing out and intent on making sure that everyone, from the chambermaid to the cook, knew their names. He seemed to prefer anonymity. She tried to do the same, but she was a dreadful actress. Despite her attempts to act natural, to appear disinterested, her thoughts always seemed to be in dissonance with her body. She said no when she wanted to say yes, smiled when she wanted to remain inscrutable, and her eyes moistened when she wanted to show indifference. Philippe drove her mad even though they'd spoken no more than the minimum required to bid each other a good morning or good night.

Life in the palace swung between receptions and banquets. In the midst of the merrymaking, with all the patience with which she made bobbin lace, Constanza managed to obtain information from the lieutenants and senior officers on how the battles were being won and lost, and how Juárez's guerrillas were advancing or retreating, or attacking carriages and roads. Nobody was safe from the *bandoleros*, they told her. They danced, they ate, and they slept only to be woken the next morning by the sound of cannons. That was how life had been for as long as they could remember, under the constant threat of cannon fire and foreign invasions. She was beginning to wonder whether she would live long enough to know a Mexico at peace, silent, a Mexico that included everyone, though Comonfort had tried before Juárez, and had been sent into exile in the United States. Mexico didn't know how to reach a consensus, and with this certainty, Constanza was as accustomed to the rumble of guns as she was the sound of thunder. Chapultepec Castle was watched over day and night by Van der Smissen's men and by Frenchmen who regarded the Belgian colonel with distrust; he seemed arrogant and self-satisfied to them, but above all they knew he was surrounded by novices. Not even Mars himself could help him among so many incompetents. For all that, Constanza couldn't get used to the fear palpable outside the palace. Though the city was only a short ride away, nobody dared travel without an escort. Inside, however, as if a spell protected them from reality, the fear vanished: Chapultepec became a medieval fortress surrounded by an enormous fairy-tale moat, where royalty reigned and enjoyed the approval of their subjects. Food and drink flowed, and the musicians played melodies that would have delighted the palaces of Vienna, like a magic music box that for a moment made everyone believe the empire was here to stay.

Each week, dances were held with European sumptuousness. Before the dance began, the ladies gathered on one side of the great hall, and the gentlemen assembled on the other. If Constanza had met Elizabeth Bennet herself on one of those evenings, she wouldn't have been in the least surprised: everyone there harbored pride and prejudice in equal measure, some because they felt part of the powerful elite, and the rest because of the endless judgments they made about the others. Constanza, since she spent most of her time assisting the empress in the preparations for each event, always made her appearance shortly before the monarchs, at around eight o'clock in the evening. The guests puffed out their chests pretentiously when they saw them descend the stairs, as if treading the same ground suddenly made them less provincial and more cosmopolitan. The Europe that had dazzled them with the beads they traded for gold blinded them once more with its splendor. Carlota would cross the great hall and position herself on the gentlemen's side, while Maximilian did the same on the ladies' side. Constanza knew that he would gladly have traded places with her. What she did have to admire was the talent the emperor had for speaking in public. There were things that nature had denied him, but not the gift of poise and being an extraordinary master of ceremonies. There were cheers, applause, appreciation, and bows. Then, each gentleman offered his arm to the lady in front of him, and each pair followed the court, like the rats following the piper of Hamelin; the music started and the celebration got underway. Manuelita had instructed the ladies well on the protocol: after two or three dances, they had to introduce their family members and husband, if they had one, and with the utmost courtesy and a natural manner, add, *My house is at your disposal.* The French were especially receptive to this offer, or least Constanza thought so from the way they smiled. All the women dressed in the Parisian style, and all of them, to some extent, spoke French. Many believed it was the official language of the court because Bazaine's army had spread throughout the country's streets imposing it, but in truth Maximilian was grateful when he was addressed in German. Constanza felt uncomfortable when everyone around her struck up rapid-fire conversations in which she barely understood the occasional *oui* or *merci.* She could speak a little, but not with the speed or ease with which these ladies—all of them Mexican through and through—seemed to transform into foreigners as soon as they saw a coat of arms. In her mind, the French were the ones who should have been speaking Spanish, and not the other way around.

Still, perhaps she could take advantage of her lack of language. Constanza had noticed that, on such occasions, Carlota's Belgians, as the volunteer soldiers were now known, hid behind the pillars, watching. Some, to break the routine they'd been subjected to since their arrival in Mexico—a routine with scarce pleasures, as if they had enjoyed many before—even made use of their uniforms to mix with the guests and sneak a glass of champagne. They did it deliberately, hoping their lack of discipline would have them sent to the battlefield, to war, to the action they longed for instead of playing tin soldiers. However, the only one who aroused Constanza's interest was *her* soldier. She had to find a way to speak to him. She was unaware that, keeping a distance, he was observing her, too, and how could he not. The woman walked by him under any pretext. He was familiar with this behavior: it wasn't the first time a woman had tried to attract his attention; he'd seen it in taverns on both sides of the ocean. In Europe because his eyes were as tender as they were lustful; here because they were blue and adventurous. What surprised him was that it was a woman of the court encased in crinoline; he hadn't found a way with them until now. And what was more, it wasn't just any lady. This lady was one of the closest to the empress. Unsurprisingly, since he watched the empress like a hawk, he'd noticed how they took walks together and how much Carlota seemed to enjoy her company. This being so, he remained as stiff as a post, not daring to move a muscle. Any man knew when a woman was forbidden to him; he wasn't prepared to get himself into such a mire. Nonetheless, that day, the lady looked different, beautiful. He wondered whether knowing she was prohibited was what was making her desirable; the fact was, she walked with a different confidence. Famke's shadow slapped him in the face.

While they were all dancing to "La Paloma," Constanza left the group she was with and, after advancing with some difficulty through the middle of the hall, she reached the pillar where he was stationed.

"*Bonjour,*" she said, putting on her best French accent.

Astonished, he lowered his head.

"Do you speak Spanish?" she said, slightly embarrassed.

"A little," he replied, indicating how much with his fingers.

"*Bien . . . Je veux apprendre le français. J'ai besoin d'un enseignant.*"

"A teacher?" Philippe remarked, pronouncing the *r* with his throat.

"*Oui.* Yes. *S'il vous plait.* Please."

They were silent for a second. His mind was a flurry of thoughts as he tried to guess her intentions.

"I'm a fast learner," she said helpfully.

So was that what it was? She needed someone to help her practice her French. For a moment, Philippe was suspicious. Something inside him told him he was a mouse, she was the cheese, and this castle was a gigantic mousetrap. At the same time, it wasn't an unpleasant job, nothing unusual. He could also practice Spanish, and God knows he needed it.

"*L'Impératrice avait autorisé cela?*"

"*Oui. Elle m'a donné la permission.*"

"You already speak quite well," he said.

She smiled, saying, "Come find me. *Je m'appelle Constanza. Et vous?*"

"Philippe, mademoiselle. Philippe Petit."

"*Enchantée,*" Constanza said. For the first time since she'd been in the palace, she said it with complete and total sincerity.

While she climbed the imperial stairs, she thought about how ridiculous she must have seemed, but the fact was she struggled to contain herself so that she didn't turn around and, from the last step, yell to him, *My house is at your disposal.*

38

They decided to take her to Miramare. Carlota was becoming increasingly fearful and paranoid. She was convinced everyone was conspiring against her. They locked her in her bedroom for hours. From outside, they could hear her screams asking to be freed, until, exhausted, she cried and cursed.

"God damn you, Napoleon! God damn all of you who dance to his tune. Don't you see he wants to ruin me?"

With Dr. Bohuslavek departed for Mexico, they entrusted her health to Dr. Riedel, a specialist in mental derangement and director of Vienna's lunatic asylum. The first thing he did was to confine her to a small house in the garden. The windows were barred, the main door sealed, and the only exit led to the servants' room, which had to be crossed to reach the parlor and dining room.

"It's for your safety," Dr. Riedel told her.

Prince Philippe didn't agree with the extreme measures they were subjecting his sister to.

"Carlota's no danger to herself," he said. "She's just tired, overwhelmed by recent events."

"It's likely, yes. The trigger for her insanity was probably the pressure of the journey to Paris and Rome."

"Forgive me, Doctor, but don't you think those causes too feeble to make a healthy twenty-six-year-old woman lose her mind?"

"You'd be surprised, Count. Women are especially prone to madness; all that's needed is for the right trigger to be pulled."

Riedel was the kind of physician who preferred to amputate rather than clean the wound. He imposed discipline more suited to a prisoner. Carlota, who was perfectly aware of everything, said to him one day, "I shut myself in here because it's what Max wants. Not because of you."

She woke at seven o'clock in the morning and went to sleep at nine o'clock at night, like an infant. She had bread and butter for breakfast with a white coffee. They gave her very little to eat, almost starving her, to see whether extreme hunger would stop her fear of being poisoned. She wasn't permitted to read. She was allowed to write letters, paint, play the piano, and stroll a little in the afternoon, always escorted by Bombelles. She was also forced to take long baths in warm water to relax her.

Philippe, exasperated, saw how her imprisonment, far from making her better, plunged Carlota into a state of utter desperation. One day, consumed with guilt, he took it up with Bombelles.

"There's no doubt that her husband's impotence has impacted my sister's health."

Bombelles, halfway through pouring himself a glass of cognac, froze.

"I'm afraid I don't understand, Count."

Philippe stood directly in front of him. He didn't want to give him the opportunity to evade his gaze.

"You understand very well, Charles. Maximilian has never touched her."

Bombelles ran one of his hands through his bangs.

"Idle talk from ill-meaning people, my lord. I know on good authority that the emperor is perfectly capable."

Philippe scrutinized him.

"What do you mean?"

"Well, my lord, the emperor has been with Mexican women. And, well, it seems he even has a son, a bastard."

The Count of Flanders served himself a drink.

"And where is this boy?"

"Apparently the emperor entrusted him to a family in Orizaba."

Philippe was speechless. If it was true, why in hell's name hadn't Maximilian procreated with his sister? She wasn't infertile, as people said; that was clear now.

Bombelles, taking advantage of the situation, ventured to ask, "Forgive my forwardness, but why the doubt? If not Maximilian, to whom does the child that the empress is expecting belong?"

Philippe remained silent for a moment, as did Bombelles. Then the count spoke.

"That is precisely the doubt that plagues me. Carlota won't dare say. You, on the other hand, seem to watch her very closely."

"Are you asking me to betray her?"

"I'm asking you to help her."

Bombelles held his glass to his lips and took a good swig. Then he added, "I'll do what I can, my lord."

Philippe stayed with her for a few days, but for some time now Carlota's behavior toward him had been different. She was hard and cold. As much as he tried to behave normally, the truth was he had to make an enormous effort to endure Carlota's gaze, scrutinizing him from the other side of the table. He tried to talk about banal things, and she tormented him.

"You must be happy, having locked me in here to turn me into a puppet you can move at will," she said to him in all seriousness.

"You've barely eaten a thing," Philippe said, changing the subject.

"Are you worried I won't ingest all the poison?"

Philippe despaired.

"For the love of God, Carlota. Nobody's trying to poison you!"

And unperturbed, she replied, "I know exactly what Leopold and you intend to do with me. You want to drive me out of my mind. What have I done to deserve your resentment? Is it my money?"

Every day they had the same conversation. Sometimes Philippe was hopeful that the paranoia wouldn't manifest as they were having a normal meal together; then suddenly, something happened, and Carlota began to accuse him, to tell him to leave her in peace, to free her, that she wanted to return to Mexico to die by Maximilian's side.

On occasion, Philippe wondered whether Carlota was right, and everyone was mad except her. He was constantly plagued by doubt: he'd seen what Leopold intended to do to her and thought that, if he were in her shoes, perhaps he would see things, too. One afternoon, anxious and tormented, he kissed Carlota on the forehead, embraced her for a long time, not saying a word in case he woke her demons, and then, almost breaking down in tears, he left and never returned.

Carlota never imagined that Leopold II, her Machiavellian brother, was plotting meticulously to declare her marriage void on suspicion of failing to consummate; that way, Carlota's entire fortune, in the event of mental derangement, would go to her brothers and not her husband. Everything would remain in the house. The marital bond had to be broken urgently. Under these circumstances, a child couldn't come into the world: nobody could witness Carlota becoming a mother.

One by one, the members of the Mexican delegation were sent away from Miramare. At first they believed the dismissal was due to some passing malaise; they'd followed her all the way from Mexico, and they weren't going to turn their backs on her now. But weeks passed, and whenever someone asked to see the empress, the door was closed in their face. Manuelita del Barrio insisted in every way possible on seeing her sovereign. With her requests denied, she stayed with her husband in a village near Trieste, in case her presence was required.

"It's very strange," Manuelita said to her husband. "Why won't they let us see her? Why won't she write?" Her anguish grew. "Do you really think she's mad?"

"I don't know," her husband replied. "You saw her in Rome. She was erratic, absent-minded."

"Yes, a little," she said. "But mad? No one thought she had any kind of problem with her mind before. And what if . . . ?"

"What if what?"

"What if they really are conspiring against her? Doesn't it seem strange that they won't let us see her? A few days ago, nobody cared whether she stayed or returned to Mexico, and now they're suddenly keeping her under guard, hiding her from us. Why?"

The Barrios waited longer than others. A few returned to Mexico, anxious about the uncertainty into which the empire had been plunged. But the Barrios knew that, if they went back, they would be signing their death sentence. Without the French troops, the road would be clear for Benito Juárez, and there was only one possible punishment for those who had collaborated with the foreign enemy.

"We can't return," Manuelita said to her husband one day. "They'll execute us, and we can't stay here and wait forever."

"Spain," her husband suggested.

With anguish and uncertainty in their hearts, they packed their shattered dreams and left for the Iberian Peninsula. No Mexican saw the empress again after Rome. Carlota disappeared as if by magic, imprisoned in the little garden house like a fairy-tale princess. Only Charles de Bombelles, Dr. Riedel, Mathilde Döblinger, and a chambermaid named Amalia Stöger remained with her. Until one day, months later, the empress gave birth in isolation from the world.

39

Since her arrival in Mexico, one of the matters that concerned Carlota most was the condition of the natives. They weren't slaves, but they were tied to the haciendas with chains as strong as those of the blacks in the United States. The empress thought the reports must have been exaggerated by impassioned minds, but when all the French emissaries she sent to the haciendas returned with the same stories, her heart, accustomed to severity, trembled with rage. They told her that the men were flogged until they bled, the wounds so deep that fingers could be inserted in them, just as Saint Thomas did with the wound in Christ's side. They told her entire families died of starvation, and that they were subjected to forced labor until they dropped—or died—from exhaustion. And once dead, they weren't given Christian burials, but cast into holes in the ground like stray dogs. They wore rags because they bought the cloth at extortionate prices from the landowners. As if that weren't enough, they were forced to buy food at higher-than-market prices.

"How much did you say they are paid?"

"For fourteen hours' work, they receive less than a peso, Your Majesty."

"And there's no priest who protects these people from this treatment?"

"They're made to pay exorbitant prices for the sacraments, Your Majesty. Only the landowner can afford to pay for them."

"But that is outrageous!"

"The priests exploit the natives' superstitious credulity, my lady."

"This won't be tolerated. Not in the empire," said Carlota.

And she set to work. In August 1865, taking advantage of one of Maximilian's many periods of absence, Carlota sought the approval of the ministers on the matter. The men were faced with a determined woman with much less patience than the emperor. At first, they believed it would be easy to persuade her: the Conservatives weren't interested in changing a situation that benefited them. Why change something that worked well? Someone had to work the land; they needed labor, whatever the cost. Maximilian would assemble his ministers, make them set out the pros and cons of every proposal one by one, and the meetings were endless. They went over the matter until agreements were reached, often more out of exhaustion than persuasion. The ministers thought that Carlota would be the same. A pushover.

Carlota asked Constanza and Manuelita, her most trusted ladies of the court, to remain at the back of the room in case they were needed. Finally, Constanza thought, finally the moment she'd been waiting for had arrived. Carlota was beginning to let her in. Manuelita, on the other hand, complained.

"I don't see why we have to be present for matters of state."

"Ay, Doña Manuelita, this is the first time I've seen you unhappy with an instruction from the empress," Constanza said to her.

"And why wouldn't I be! These are men's things. They're nothing to do with us. This is not what ladies are for."

For a moment, Constanza was reminded of her brother Joaquín; she was used to hearing men look down on women in matters outside the domestic sphere, but to hear a woman putting herself down was something else, and she didn't like it. Still, she tried to act natural.

"Cheer up, Doña Manuelita. We'll have some hot chocolate afterward."

"And we shall need it! The empress has summoned us for six in the morning! Let's pray she doesn't make it a habit, or it'll take years off me!"

"I hope she doesn't make us stand behind her," Constanza said to needle her, and Manuelita crossed herself to ward off the demon of aching legs.

Carlota appeared before the council of ministers the next morning at six sharp, bringing all the relevant documents that she'd already studied. She had archives, maps, statutes . . . everything necessary, learned in detail with the help of the people in the palace she considered most competent. Constanza sharpened her senses so she wouldn't miss a detail. She even memorized the outfit the empress had chosen, a dark, sober dress that made the ladies feel ashamed of their own bright and ostentatious dresses. She memorized the names of the ministers and tried to record each of their faces: the one with the white moustache, the one with thick sideburns, the one with round spectacles. She checked the time when the meeting began and registered what was on the table. Everything. Anything she could use later to give a detailed account of what would be said there.

"Gentlemen, this is what we're going to do," the empress said without even saying *good morning*. "We're going to sign a decree to improve the natives' working conditions."

The men were astounded at the empress's determination, which gave no occasion for objections. Some of them adjusted their shirt collars, as if suddenly feeling stifled. She went on.

"To prevent the workers from falling into debt, landowners won't be permitted to lend more than thirty francs."

"Your Majesty—"

"I haven't finished, Minister. Children will be freed from their parents' debts."

"Your Majesty, if you will allow me—"

"I haven't finished, Minister. A decent wage will be guaranteed."

"But, Your Majesty—"

"The next person to interrupt me will be relieved of his duties," Carlota said in all seriousness.

The room was silent.

Constanza also held her breath. She'd never seen a woman, not even her mother, speak with such authority. For a moment, she forgot her hostility toward the empire and thought that, had she not already been on her feet, she would have stood to applaud her.

Carlota continued.

"Working hours will be reduced, and, under penalty of imprisonment, corporal punishment will be prohibited."

The silence that gripped the room for a few seconds was thicker than jelly. Carlota observed her ministers one at a time. Some looked down, unable to endure the severity of her gaze. Others thought they were facing some kind of witch capable of reading their minds, and fought to keep out any impure or scornful thoughts.

Then, the empress said, "After close examination, I believe we must bring these provisions into law. What do you say?"

The most senior minister ventured to speak.

"Perhaps we should wait for the emperor to return to address an issue of such magnitude."

Carlota burned inside, but on the outside it did not show.

"Delaying will not help; either the provisions are viable, or they are not."

"Your Majesty, what you're proposing is impossible."

"'The word *impossible* is not French,' Napoleon used to say."

"Perhaps we could try another way, negotiate with the land-owners . . ."

"I will not countenance that. If we can't fit something through the door, we will certainly not force it through the window."

Nobody dared contradict her and, after a moment's hesitation, they began to nod their heads with some enthusiasm.

To Manuelita's delight, the meeting didn't take even fifteen minutes, and she thought she would soon be able to drink the hot chocolate she'd been thinking about since she opened her eyes. She was sorely mistaken, for that was just one of the matters Carlota intended to deal with that morning.

Constanza, on the other hand, would have liked to prolong each minute. Something stirred inside her. What had just happened? What could the empress know about the suffering of the native Mexicans, bled dry for so many years? The empress was deciding matters that didn't belong to her, without knowing, without being acquainted with the reality of Mexico, and it was with this conviction that Constanza was there, to help from the little trench she could dig for herself inside Chapultepec. In fact, the night before, she had barely slept, devising ways to get the information she obtained out of the palace. She couldn't write letters, because if they were intercepted for any reason, it would be the end of her. She remained unsure how to do it, and was awaiting instructions from the Liberales, while she wove a shroud that she undid each night like Penelope. And then suddenly this: what she'd just witnessed had left her on tenterhooks. No Liberal could have done it better.

Weren't the Conservatives there to maintain the status quo? Weren't Catholics, apostolic and Roman? But Carlota, who was steering the ship, was neither fragile nor tractable in the slightest. Could her father be right that what Mexico needed was to be governed by a foreign monarch? But Carlota wasn't the emperor: she was the empress consort, though she was clear thinking and had courage in her heart. Betrayed by these thoughts, Constanza suddenly felt something resembling pride. And without knowing for certain what to expect, she decided to observe Carlota from a different angle.

When Carlota reigned, she took an interest in all matters of government. A commander had to provide her with a daily report, and she could summon him if she considered it necessary. She was convinced that strict administrative efficiency was needed to govern Mexico, and she would use all the tools she had: the symbolism of her position, as well as contact with her subjects.

Constanza looked on in astonishment as laws were adopted that scandalized many people, including Doña Manuelita, who prayed in secret for the emperor to return before everything got out of hand. Carlota legalized prostitution because, she said, it was a public health issue. She created the San Juan de Dios Hospital, where women who sold their bodies underwent periodic medical examinations. Constanza accompanied her there and was surprised to see the empress sit and talk with the prostitutes. She cared about them, about the dangers of their profession. Listening carefully, Constanza saw that Carlota treated them all with dignity, paying no heed to their rank or their sins. The empress calmly explained that to practice, they had to have a photograph taken, which would be placed on an identity card with their name, age, previous occupation, address, and whether they worked in a brothel or were self-employed. Constanza recalled the day she went with her mother to the civil registry. *There are two Mexicos, Constanza,* she had said.

"The other Mexico," she repeated through clenched teeth.

She returned to the palace with her mind spinning after spending the day visiting hospices, schools—for which a decree had been issued making primary education free and compulsory—and music academies. Every evening she had to endure Manuelita's volley of complaints. She was beginning to grow weary of the woman's two faces: she agreed to everything in front of the empress, but once her back was turned, she criticized even the clothes she wore.

"Can you believe how many young girls there were at that hospital for fallen women? The shamelessness! The empress shouldn't lower herself to helping those girls. It's a disgrace. A member of the royalty shouldn't assist women in that condition. She will undermine the empire's cause. The empress is too obliging. Shameful, it's shameful having to set foot in those places, to talk to those women. What a disgrace!"

"The empress is dealing with a reality. Hiding problems won't make them disappear, Doña Manuelita."

"Then send people of lower rank to attend to those *inconveniences*. An empress has no place there."

"And where is her place, then?"

"Other, more elevated places, girl. She belongs to another social class. What stupid questions, Constanza. Get some rest and let's hope the emperor returns soon."

"Where did he go? Do you know?"

"They say he went to Querétaro, on reconnaissance."

"And did he go with that man who always accompanies him?"

"It's Baron Schertzenlechner, girl. You'd better start learning names."

Like the rest of the court, each time his name was mentioned, Constanza sensed something sinister. She closed her eyes and settled into her pillow. Before falling asleep, she hoped the emperor wouldn't return soon.

Just as the serpent seduced Eve by offering her knowledge, almost without realizing it, Constanza gradually fell in love with the apple that Carlota represented. Perhaps she could sink her teeth into it without being expelled from the earthly paradise; perhaps she could take a bite without betraying her mother's trust. Perhaps . . . And so, giving herself the benefit of the doubt, every day, she learned from the empress's energy, reasoning, and charm. She began to realize that Carlota did govern, or tried to, for the good of all and for the country. Could it be possible that red blood flowed through her royal veins? She was active, she disliked stagnation, and Constanza noticed how it exasperated her that Maximilian lived the contemplative life of a prince.

One day, driven by the desire she had always had to speak to a woman with responsibilities and ambitions, Constanza ventured to say more than protocol permitted.

"Your Majesty, I hope you'll forgive me, but I wanted to say, with the utmost respect, that I admire the way you conduct yourself in the emperor's absence."

Carlota took a few seconds to grasp the compliment.

"It's my duty, Constanza."

"Yes, but, if I may, you enjoy your duty, Majesty."

"I would command a navy if necessary."

"Do you really think a woman could command an army, Majesty?"

"I could," Carlota replied without embarrassment. "I have experience in war, seeing the one waged in this country."

Constanza marveled at the confidence with which she spoke; there were no limits to her. Carlota recognized something in her lady's face that she knew very well: a woman sick of being told what she could and couldn't do.

"Do you think you might be able to negotiate with Juárez one day, Majesty?"

Carlota thought for a moment.

"Juárez and his people were born here and they're democrats, but they will never be the founders of a Mexican power and a state that governs without partisan injustices." After a pause, she added, "Mexico's tragedy, Constanza, is that respect can only be gained through fear. And the emperor is impossible to fear."

They both fell silent, one digesting what she'd just heard, the other wondering whether she'd said too much. However, buoyed by the pleasure of being able to speak honestly for the first time in months, Carlota continued. From the moment she'd met her, she'd known this young woman was different, that she thought differently. Constanza reminded her of her governess, the Countess of Hulst, not in age, but because of the confidence she inspired in her. It was nice to be able to say out loud what she only told her grandmother in letters.

"Your Majesty, if I may be so bold, are you not concerned you'll be said to be overambitious?"

"Men aren't ready to recognize a powerful woman. It frightens them and they'll do everything necessary to prevent it. But know one thing: women do what is necessary when it matters."

"Even a peasant woman?"

"Even in the fields, women contribute to the cultivation."

Constanza had the impression the empress was thinking. And it was true, because suddenly she said, "In any case, with no children and nothing better to do, I don't see why I shouldn't be occupied with something useful. Like I said, it's my duty."

"And when you have children, Majesty?"

"When I have children . . ."

Constanza heard the empress's voice crack. The conversation had hit a wall.

". . . it will be up to God," said Carlota, before asking Constanza to please leave her alone.

40

Carlota let out a cry from deep inside. After several hours, the empress finally gave birth to a seven-pound boy. Not being robust, she had a hard time delivering the child, but Mathilde didn't move from her bedside for one moment. She was tired, too: her flushed and sweaty face beside the empress's made plain the great effort involved in bringing the baby into the world.

"What is it, Mathilde?"

"A boy, Your Majesty."

"Thank heavens it's not a girl," said Carlota.

The chambermaid placed the child on the empress's belly. She observed it through tired eyes. A newborn. A baby born from her body, engendered by her. A son. Not an heir: a beautiful, healthy bastard who seemed to contain all the force of those nine months of madness. A survivor. Carlota had just kissed him on the forehead when Charles de Bombelles entered the room.

Without explanation, he snatched the boy from her arms, wrapped him in a cloak, and left with the same coldness with which he had entered.

Mathilde looked at the empress; Carlota looked at Mathilde. They both wore the same look of grief. Horror. Fear. They could each see it in the other woman's eyes and feel it in their hearts. Carlota screamed through her tears.

"Where are you taking him?"

But Bombelles didn't stop or even turn. Carlota's jaw began to tremble.

"They're going to kill him. They're going to kill him. Mathilde! Mathilde, do something!"

Mathilde wanted to soothe the empress, but the truth was she, too, feared for the newborn. She ran after Bombelles and found him in the corridor, with the child still in his arms. *Thank God,* she thought. Then she found the voice she had quelled during all the months of imprisonment to confront this man.

"Give me the child."

"I can't. I have instructions."

"From whom?"

"That doesn't concern you."

Mathilde could see the baby's wrinkled little feet poking out from between Charles's arms; he was crying like a kitten. *Some start in the world,* she thought. *Torn from his mother's arms at birth.*

"Give the baby to me. He needs to feed."

Bombelles looked at the chambermaid. The baby's crying was beginning to set him on edge. He'd never held a newborn; that was for midwives. His coat was bloodstained.

"I can't," he repeated.

"Have you no heart?"

"It's for the good of Austria."

"What're you talking about? Look, I'm nobody, I don't know anything about political intrigues. Just let me see to the child. He's cold. Can't you see him trembling?"

"You're right . . . ," Bombelles said.

Mathilde stifled a sigh. And as she held out her arms to receive the little boy, Charles said, "You're nobody." And turning, he walked off with the child.

Mathilde implored him at the top of her voice:

"Don't hurt him! I beg you! Don't hurt him! Please!"

Bombelles didn't answer.

Mathilde returned to the empress's bed. She wasn't crying, but her glazed eyes were threatening to overflow with tears. Seeing her walk in, Carlota knew she would never see her son again. Mathilde wrapped her enormous arms around the empress's fragile body, telling her something that Carlota, deep down, was telling herself: "This, too, shall pass, it will pass, my child."

"Oh, Mathilde . . . why? Why do they torture me like this?"

Carlota dissolved into tears with a long and heart-rending moan. Mathilde knew the pain would last forever, and she allowed her to cry until, exhausted, she fell asleep. Something in Mathilde Döblinger's soul died, too, that day.

When the empress was finally asleep, after making sure she didn't have a fever and was out of danger after the birth, Mathilde headed to the kitchen. Amalia was waiting for her with a dish of hot soup.

"Eat, Mathilde," she said. "You're about to faint."

So tired she'd lost her appetite, Mathilde rested, almost sleeping, against the kitchen table. Amalia, taking pity on her, picked up a spoon and began to feed her, spoonful by spoonful.

During the night, Mathilde started getting stabs of pain in her stomach; she could barely sleep, writhing from the sharp pain that burned her insides. At first, she thought it must have been due to the stress of the situation. Too many emotions torn to shreds in her stomach. Too much anguish. Too much disgust at the baseness of human beings. Disbelief at what men were capable of doing. Her child, her Carlota, exploited by sinister minds. Her child, her Carlota, in the hands of people prepared to use her like a puppet. There was no doubt,

Mathilde told herself, that evil made no exceptions for thrones or cradles. The perversity hidden in the walls of the Gartenhaus. And the boy. Good God, where was the child? Where? What had they done with him? The reigning silence was broken by the empress's unbearable wails. The house seemed to be bewitched, for the walls sobbed, and not even Amalia Stöger, who normally shook the sheets and dusted with impetuous violence, dared tread heavily, for fear of awakening more misfortune.

The next morning, Mathilde headed with difficulty to the empress's bedroom. Each step was an entire world of pain and anguish. But she knew she had to get there. She found Carlota pale, with purple lips and blue rings around her eyes. The poor woman was trembling in an endless shiver. Mathilde sat beside her on the bed. It wasn't an empress lying there, but an abused woman. A woman from whom everything had been taken. There, in that bed, there was nothing. Breaking all the rules of protocol, Frau Döblinger lay beside her, in part because she wanted the empress to know she wasn't alone, and in part because she couldn't hold herself up. She heard Carlota whisper:

"I couldn't even give him a name. Maybe it's for the best."

Mathilde wanted to offer encouragement, but when she opened her mouth, she could only groan with pain. Carlota seemed to come out of her trance for a moment.

"What is it, Mathilde?"

"Oh, I don't feel well, my child."

Carlota found strength where there was none to lift herself up on her elbows.

"Mathilde, look at me . . ."

Carlota examined her closely: she recognized the drab, greenish color, and then horror broke out in her soul.

"Mathilde, what've you eaten?"

"Same as always, child; what they give me in the kitchen."

Carlota held her hands to her mouth.

"You must vomit, Mathilde. You must vomit! Don't you see? They've poisoned you."

Mathilde opened her eyes wide. *No, for the love of God, not the paranoia, not now,* she thought. Of all the alternatives she'd considered, poison had never occurred to her. But she felt so dreadful that, for a moment, a very brief moment, Frau Döblinger wondered.

"It can't be, child. Who'd want to poison me?"

But the empress was talking to herself now.

"I know it. I know it. They're going to kill us all. They're going to kill us."

Carlota began to yell at the top of her voice. A few seconds ago, she'd resembled a dying woman more than a madwoman, but paranoia had struck again like lightning. Carlota was frantic. She screamed. She kicked in her bed. Mathilde was afraid. She had given birth the day before, she could tear her innards, she told her, but Carlota didn't listen. Charles de Bombelles burst into the room in the company of Dr. Riedel. They tied her to the bed and, with Carlota screaming incessantly, Charles slapped her.

"Get out! You're upsetting the empress!" he yelled at Mathilde.

Frau Döblinger stood to leave the room. Everything was spinning; she was breathless. She looked at Carlota, held down by the men, and felt an immense urge to cry. She took two steps toward the door, then another two toward her chamber. She covered her eyes because she couldn't bear to hear the screams. She felt lightheaded. Everything turned upside down. She was hot, very hot; hell was in her belly. With great effort, she reached her room, but as soon as she did, her legs failed and she fell to the floor. Mathilde didn't have time to say goodbye to Carlota or anybody else, nor did she have time to write anything; she didn't even have time to fear God. All she could do was call to Amalia Stöger a couple of times for help. Then, with terrible spasms, death struck her like a thunderbolt in the middle of a storm. Amalia Stöger, at the other end of the corridor, never heard Mathilde's screams.

She couldn't: in the privacy of her rooms she was hanging from her nightdress.

It was done.

There were no witnesses to the birth. There were no witnesses to anything. There was no one left.

Days later, as Carlota called for Mathilde at all hours, they gave her the terrible news. One didn't have to be very perceptive to realize what was happening. Carlota, with the strength of a martyr hearing her sentence, accepted that she was next on the list. It was the end. She had, in any case, no reason to continue living. Death was preferable to the void into which they had cast her. She had no one left. The loves of her life were dead: her father, her mother, her grandmother, and now Mathilde. And her Max? Maximilian was far away and, with the French troops in retreat, he would probably die, too. She might as well wait for him on the other side.

So on that day, Carlota became lost in the dense darkness of utter despair. She preferred to keep her eyes closed, for when she opened them, she could only contemplate the void. She preferred to lose herself in an imaginary world where pain was bearable because it was imagined and where absences became presences at will.

Madness kissed her on the lips with its moist tongue.

41

Everyone in court knew the emperor and empress didn't sleep together, whether in Puebla or in Chapultepec Castle. Constanza knew it firsthand.

It was not difficult to see. Each morning the chambermaids went in to dress the empress, and they could see that she'd spent the night like a vestal. And while descendants were essential in order to guarantee the continuation of the empire, the sovereigns, despite their youth and their seven years of marriage, had no children. The chamber pots were changed every day, and those doing so saw that the empress menstruated on time each month. Constanza, ever on the alert, observed how Juana, the youngest servant, would sneak out of the bedchamber. Taking care not to be seen, after walking around the fireplaces a couple of times, she would approach the laundry room, where a member of the Austrian or, who knows, maybe the French court would be waiting for her. Constanza narrowed her eyes and pricked up her ears, but the conversation was always the same.

"Any news?"

"No, sir. She's still not expecting."

"Thank you, Juana. See you next month."

And after a slight curtsy, the young girl headed back to her work.

Every month it was the same. The empress's condition was no longer an intimate matter but a matter of state. A great deal was at stake, many economic and political commitments, and Constanza wondered how the miracle would be worked if the emperor never visited Carlota's room, and she never visited his, for that matter.

Monarchs were taught to put up with infidelities with the elegance with which they lifted a teacup. Everyone knew that the most passionate love affairs never took place in the royal bedchambers, and romantic adventures in one chamber or another—whether a secret room, a side room or a back room—were far from infrequent. Sharing a bed and room was therefore a tremendous inconvenience, as well as an unnecessary chore. It was better if the burden of duty borne with stoicism during the day was lifted at night, allowing the married couple to writhe in peace with whomever they pleased. To some extent, everyone had let their hair down with a member of the court; naked, they were all the same. Carlota hadn't expected that, no matter what she tried, Maximilian wouldn't touch her. In her most private desires, she sometimes found herself wanting to learn that her husband had a lover, anyone that had a nest like her own between her legs, a honeypot he wished to drink from. But no: not even under a decree that obliged them to produce an heir within three years did Maximilian make the effort. Why wouldn't he meet his political obligations and ensure the succession to the throne? Did she repulse him so much?

Carlota couldn't find an explanation for it. In his letters he called her *angel of my heart, star of my life, lady of my desire*. She was neither his lady nor did she arouse his desire. It turned Carlota's stomach. His words weren't worth the paper they were written on. Lies. Like when she wrote to her grandmother about how happy she was, how blessed she had been, as fortunate as anyone on the face of the earth. A mountain of lies repeated a thousand times not to deceive everyone else but to persuade oneself. Because instead of saying three Lord's Prayers and consummating the marriage, Maximilian would sooner do anything else. He'd take any opportunity that presented itself to do something foolish rather than stick his cock in his wife.

Constanza listened in astonishment one day when she found Carlota, the empress, curled up in a ball on the floor of her bedchamber, pulling her hair and beating her chest. That was when she understood that she wasn't a fortunate woman, quite the contrary. While Constanza stroked her hair as if she were a baby, sobbing, humiliated, Carlota told her that, on his return from Querétaro, Maximilian had encountered a woodcutter from Huimilpan carrying something in his arms with a worried look on his face. Seeing him, the emperor stopped the caravan to speak to him.

"Are you all right, good man?"

The man, after a moment's hesitation, showed him the bundle he was carrying. Maximilian peered down into the face of a newborn, pale in spite of his indigenous features, and breathing quite fast.

The man spoke.

"He's just born."

Maximilian opened his eyes wide, surprised.

"And where are you taking him, so far from his mother?"

"He was born in the hills. His mama cannot support or baptize him; she gave him to me to look after."

"Dear me!" said Maximilian, crossing himself.

Then he asked the man if he could hold the child. He handed him over without hesitation. Maximilian felt compassion and tenderness for the newborn, but once the feeling faded, he thought that perhaps it had been an auspicious encounter: the problem of succession that had overshadowed the court could be resolved.

"I will adopt him," he said. "Summon a wet nurse immediately, the best in the region," he ordered. And with a look of astonishment, seeing that the emperor did not mean it in a figurative sense and was deadly serious, a footman went in search of one. "I will see to it that he's baptized. His name will be Ferdinand Maximilian Charles Joseph; he shall be a prince."

The woodcutter looked around with suspicion; he thought that he was dreaming or it was a joke. If the emperor wanted to help, he could just send money each month to cover the cost of the child, there was no need to adopt him. But Maximilian seemed to grow more enthusiastic as he warmed to the idea.

"You will care for him until he's weaned, then you will bring him to the capital."

"Yes, master," the peasant replied, stunned by what had just happened.

Maximilian resumed the journey feeling content, having become the father of an indigenous child. A boy darker than Benito Juárez, but who would wear a crown like Napoleon's.

Providence didn't cooperate: two days later, the child died. A catafalque was covered with a purple velvet pall with a heraldic symbol in gold leaf on it. It was decorated with white candles that hid the black mourning ribbons, and the emperor was sent a telegram that said, *The Indian prince has died. Send funds for the burial.*

Maximilian screwed the paper up and threw it in the trash. How fleeting his delight had been; the boy was no use to him dead, so he declared that, though he would've been baptized as a prince, he would be buried as a commoner. The boy was interred like an ephemeral plant in soil that quickly forgot his grandiose name.

He didn't tell Carlota about the incident. In his mind, the dead should be left to rest in peace. At any rate, there was no longer anything to tell, and he kept the story, along with many others, in his chest of unspeakable secrets.

But secrets are there to be told, and rumors soon began to spread, both in the squares and through the corridors of the imperial palace. At the market, on the avenues, in the stores, people whispered that Carlota was infertile and that, instead of disowning her, in his infinite mercy poor Maximilian was adopting little Indians. What started as a rumor was then confirmed by the press, and Carlota was again forced to learn to swallow the dishonor and shame.

Constanza was present when the empress read the story in a newspaper. She ran after her through the corridors.

"My lady!" she yelled, trying to stop her.

"Leave it, Constanza, leave me alone!"

She slammed the door behind her and shut herself in her bedchamber. But Constanza stayed at the door and listened to the usually demure empress kick the furniture, sob as she threw cushions, and pull on the curtains in rage, screaming for someone to do a favor for the empire, for her, and for the imbecile Maximilian, and have the courage to come and deflower her.

"I'll show them who's sterile here! I'll show them!"

When Carlota had finished fighting with her ghosts, Constanza knocked on the door. Without waiting for an answer, she went in and found Carlota on the floor, curled up and staring blankly. She sat next to her, and the empress, as if she were ten years old again and had just been told that her mother was dead, allowed the weight of her head to fall into Constanza's lap. The two of them remained there, in silence, until her heart stopped hurting. At least for the moment.

42

Just as Constanza was beginning to have doubts about her mission as a spy, the unexpected happened. She'd been waiting for months for someone to contact her. At first she'd been anxious, excited to be pushing the boundaries of the prohibited. She expected to have to encounter a stranger behind the bushes in the palace grounds, in the darkness of night, to pass on key information. But days passed, and the stranger never materialized in any form. Nothing. Weeks passed without anyone indicating to her through their actions or absence thereof that they were there for any reason other than to accompany and serve a foreign empress, to serve the country like a lamb to the slaughter. So much silence began to gnaw at her, doubt hung over her like a shadow, and she began to think it had been a ploy of her mother's to coax her into the palace. At the same time, in the secret depths of her soul, she hoped that nobody would come forward to ask her for information on an empire that was beguiling her. As the intervention forces gained territory, pushing back Juárez's troops to the north, slowly, Constanza's loyalty also began its withdrawal. Perhaps, she told herself, her father was right, and Mexico needed the emperor and empress; Carlota was without doubt the woman she wanted to be, or at least part of her. But life put Constanza's convictions to the test, and just at that moment, a Liberal appeared in the court, with such an effective disguise that even she, who was always on the alert, never suspected him. To her surprise, the person wasn't a complete stranger. One day, her brother Salvador turned up at the palace in his best clothes, his charming beardless smile, and liberal ideals. Constanza received him as if there were nothing to it, without imagining for one instant that his visit was about to cast her into an abyss.

As Vicente had predicted, Salvador had been known and well received at Chapultepec as part of the group of notables that traveled to Miramare in search of the emperor. He had played an active role in the meetings, and despite his youth, he was beginning to earn the confidence of the foreigners in the court thanks to his command of French and German. Constanza often encountered him in the corridors as he was on his way to his meetings, and she was accompanying Carlota to hers, though they rarely had the chance to be together when the empress was dealing with matters of state. One Empress's Monday, they finally found themselves together. It was one of the customs that Carlota, imitating Eugénie de Montijo, established in Mexico: one day a week, the palace was opened to her subjects, though not just anyone. Members of conservative Mexican society coveted these invitations and did everything possible to be taken into consideration. To Vicente's great pride, the Murrietas were always on the list. They listened to music, they were fêted with hors d'oeuvres, and they could admire the view from the hall with spectacular views of the Valley of Mexico. Contemplating the view during such visits to the palace, José Zorrilla, a Spanish writer who'd been living in Mexico for a decade, said, *He who has not seen Mexico from Chapultepec has not seen the earth from a balcony in paradise.* That was enough for Maximilian to appoint him as director of the Grand Imperial Theater and reader of the court.

The most fortunate were invited to one of the plays performed within the National Palace, for the emperor was a staunch advocate of the need to nourish the mind with art. Salvador and Constanza sometimes met at these performances and, in spite of all the preconceptions they had, they enjoyed them. Constanza was usually unable to see the end of the ones she liked most, because the emperor always retired to sleep at nine o'clock, and the play was interrupted.

"We shall finish another day," the monarch would say, excusing himself because his functions began at five o'clock in the morning.

One night, tired of being left in suspense, Constanza ran and, almost at the Zócalo, caught up with the director.

"Sr. Zorrilla!" she yelled shamelessly.

The man turned around.

Embarrassed, she said, "If I may be so bold, it's just I can't wait another day to know how your play ends."

The man smiled with pleasure.

"You like my *Don Juan* that much?"

"I adored it! I am eager to know the ending."

"You will see it"—he bent toward her ear to give her the revelation—"as soon as the emperor doesn't fall asleep before it is over!"

Then he winked at her.

In the dances, the Murrieta siblings spent some time in each other's company, and even danced a song or two together, but Constanza always had the feeling that attending these functions made her brother uncomfortable; in that, he reminded her of Philippe. Unlike her eldest brother, Joaquín, who always tried to make his presence known in the court, Salvador kept a low profile, trying to be as unnoticed as possible, though this only increased the interest he aroused among the women. Salvador Murrieta's name was on the lips of every lady in the court, who remarked how young, how intelligent, and how formal he seemed. Since he proved to be an impenetrable wall, they went out of their way to ask Constanza about him, and she endeavored to make excuses for him, telling them not to waste their energy, because his interests lay not in court but in armed conflict. And she believed it unquestioningly. Ever since they were young, her two elder brothers had been trained for the army, not for politics, and she'd never known them to court women. So, when he suddenly requested to have tea alone with her, it was unusual. Perhaps one of the ladies had managed to bore through his stone façade, and he was coming to see Constanza to pour his heart out to her. However, after consideration, this seemed puerile, and she let the idea go. Then she grew afraid that something might have happened to Clotilde or their parents. After that she felt guilty for not sparing a thought for Joaquín, knowing he was helping the Army of Intervention, fighting alongside the French. The idea that something bad could happen to Joaquín had never occurred to her: since she was a girl, she'd seen him as a demigod, one of those men whom bullets brushed past but who were never wounded, and now she had no interest in persuading herself otherwise.

Salvador turned up punctually to the appointment with his sister. She received him at the door to her rooms.

"I had to see you," he said after kissing her on the cheek.

Constanza saw that Philippe was watching them from the end of the long corridor. She kissed her brother's cheek and tried to discern the Belgian soldier's reaction. She couldn't see it, but when they went in and were alone, Philippe found himself frowning and experiencing a strange feeling.

"What is it?" Constanza said to her brother with a worried expression. "Is everyone all right at home?"

"Yes, yes, fine."

Constanza breathed, easing the weight of her conscience.

"Even Clotilde?"

"Yes, as far as I know. She's gone all winter without suffering a relapse."

"Thank God. You frightened me with all the urgency to see me."

Salvador stood, went to the door, and made sure nobody was lurking.

Then he asked her point-blank.

"Have you discovered anything that may be of use?"

Constanza bent her head, like a dog hearing a whistle.

"What did you say?"

Salvador approached and sat right in front of her. He fixed his dark eyes on his sister's.

"It's me, Constanza. I'm the messenger for the Liberales."

She was struck by a mixture of emotions. On the one hand, she was relieved that the person she'd been waiting for was someone she already trusted, and on the other, she was terrified. It was true, she was there to spy. She'd promised to do something, and now she had to look the devil in the eyes. But it couldn't be . . . Salvador? It had to be a joke. Disguising herself behind the discretion she'd learned over so many years, she chose her words carefully.

"I don't know what you're talking about."

"You know perfectly well."

They held each other's gaze. Salvador had never seen her like this: it was as if she were made of glass and he could see right through her. Suddenly she felt defenseless. It was hopeless: she couldn't lie to Salvador. Though she had been able to operate for months without being discovered, she'd never deceived anybody.

"But . . . how do you know? How?"

"I asked Mamá to involve you. It was my idea."

"It was you? How? Since when?"

"Since my return from Miramare. After I arrived back in Mexico, I approached the Liberales to offer my help. They accepted."

Constanza stood up. The wolf had just taken off the sheep's clothing, and she still didn't believe it. Salvador was an upright man, incapable of lying; his father had entrusted him with momentous tasks, he'd placed all his trust in him, how was it possible that, all of a sudden, he was double-crossing him?

"Who else is involved in this?"

"Just you and me. If Joaquín finds out, he'll have us both shot, believe me, and let's not even mention our father."

Hearing this, Constanza came out in goose bumps, as if she had dived into icy water. A gelid sensation ran down her back.

"And Clotilde?"

Salvador shook his head.

"She doesn't know anything. Nor should she ever."

Constanza approached the door nervously. Now it was she who assured herself that there was no one listening. He waited. Constanza rubbed her hands together as if trying to polish them while she paced the room. She thought. She was beginning to understand that she was playing with fire. She sipped some water and sat down again. He held her hands and sat close to her to speak in a low voice.

"The first time's the hardest . . . you'll get used to it. But I have something to tell you: if you're afraid, don't do it."

Constanza took a deep breath. She felt a slight surge of pride.

"I'm not afraid."

"Good," he said, and he began questioning her in a whisper. "So tell me, what've you found out?"

"Well . . . the empress and emperor don't sleep together."

"Everyone knows that. Tell me about strategies."

Constanza thought quickly.

"It seems the emperor wants to build a railway."

"From where to where?"

"From Veracruz to the capital, with a branch line to Puebla. The other day I heard the empress say they wanted to create the Imperial Mexican Railway Company with the help of a British company. The idea is to connect the north to the south."

"Hmm . . ." murmured Salvador. "That would complicate things, but it would take time." Then he asked, "Do you know anything about Van der Smissen?"

Constanza was surprised.

"The colonel?"

"Yes."

"Not much. It appears he doesn't get on well with Bazaine, but he's very discreet. Sometimes he walks with the empress in the gardens. When they're together, she cries."

"Cries?"

"She sheds a tear or two. I think it's homesickness."

Salvador appeared deep in thought.

"Interesting. You must get close to that colonel."

"And how can I do that?"

"That's your business, little sister."

Constanza reflected. Why of all the people in court was her brother interested in Colonel Van der Smissen? Was she missing something? True, she'd observed some complicity between the colonel and the empress, but she attributed that to the fact that they both spoke the same language, that they were Belgians, and that he was there under the instructions of Leopold I, Carlota's father. She wouldn't dare suggest they were friends, but undoubtedly Carlota didn't trust many people in that court of sharks. She trusted Constanza.

Salvador pulled her from her thoughts.

"We have to be very careful. I didn't come sooner to allow you to familiarize yourself with the court, but this is serious, Constanza. Our lives and Mexico's future are at stake. Take great care."

She nodded.

"We won't be able to see each other like this again. You'll have to find another way to get information to me."

They parted with an embrace that united them in collusion and in a sense of apprehension they had never shared until then. When he said goodbye, Salvador gave her one piece of advice:

"Watch out for Bombelles," he said.

43

Auguste Goffinet walked full speed through the Castle of Laeken's corridors. The king of the Belgians had summoned him with urgency; it was something important. He'd been the minister plenipotentiary of the Belgian Crown for years, and he'd become Leopold's right-hand man. The honor of being his left-hand man fell, no less, to his identical twin brother, Baron Constant Goffinet. When the Goffinet brothers' machinery was set in motion, it shook the foundations. Leopold II never had more-devoted servants: they liked money as much as the king, but they liked power even more. They enjoyed the privilege of having the king's ear, and everything that Leopold wanted, they translated perfectly into the necessary legal or financial arguments.

Before reaching the king's office, Goffinet sent a footman to announce him, and he was allowed to enter immediately. Leopold II was waiting for him with an anxious smile.

"My dear Auguste," he said.

"Your Majesty," Goffinet replied, clicking his heels together in a military fashion.

"Listen, Auguste, we have a problem that, with your help, I trust we can turn into an opportunity."

"Tell me, Majesty."

Leopold, who never beat around the bush, went straight to the heart of the matter.

"As you well know, when my poor sister Carlota married Maximilian of Habsburg, her fortune amounted to one million eight hundred thousand guilders."

Goffinet began to make calculations.

"And as you know, Maximilian went to great lengths to ensure my father granted him a vast dowry."

"It's no secret, Majesty."

And no, it was no secret. In his negotiations with Leopold I prior to the marriage, Maximilian had stretched him almost to the breaking point. He wanted no less than three million francs to marry his beloved daughter, and the king emphatically refused. But in addition to being king, Leopold was a father, and, softened by the pleas of his only daughter, smitten with the archduke, he finally agreed. Goffinet knew—because he had ears everywhere—that Maximilian had written to his brother Charles Louis boasting that he'd finally managed to extract, in his words, *some of the gold that's so dear to the old miser.* Yes, Goffinet knew that and other things, too, but he was prudent and knew when to keep quiet; that was one of the many virtues that Leopold II valued in him.

The king of the Belgians went on.

"You also know that, in the early years of their marriage, half the ownership of Miramare and half the island of Lokrum were given over to my poor sister." And seeing Goffinet nod, he asked him, "Who will be personally liable for repaying the loan that Maximilian requested from the Royal House of Habsburg for the construction of Miramare Castle on the Bay of Grignano?"

Goffinet was silent for a moment, in case the monarch was asking a rhetorical question. Seeing that he was waiting for an answer, Goffinet replied, "Your esteemed sister Charlotte, Majesty."

"My poor sister, yes, financing that aberration of a building. What do you think of Miramare, Auguste?"

Though he knew when to be quiet, Goffinet also knew when to respond honestly; that was one of the virtues Leopold II respected in him. And, as if more endearing qualities were needed, he'd never contradicted him.

"In my humble opinion, Majesty, Miramare is an uninhabitable chocolate box. I've looked around the castle, and around the gardens twice, and one of the two is superfluous."

Leopold nodded, raising his eyebrows and pursing lips that were already invisible behind his enormous beard. He liked confirmation of how right he was. Sure enough, he considered Miramare an appalling place as a permanent residence. He stood up and began to pace the office; when his mind was performing calculations, he always walked in circles.

He continued.

"And though I tried to bar women from inheriting, so that princesses would depend on the male heirs, as is only natural, the fact is that my sister has inherited an immense fortune. Immense," he repeated as if to make sure he was understood.

"Indeed, Majesty."

"But"—and saying this, Leopold broke into a half smile—"as I'm sure you've heard, my poor sister has lost her sanity."

There was silence.

Goffinet knew what his king was about to ask him to do. He knew him well; he knew him all too well. Leopold waited. After a few seconds, Goffinet offered a solution.

"Perhaps, with Your Majesty's consent, we should notify the banks and the administrators of her fortune that, owing to her incapacity, it shall be you who controls her finances, Your Highness."

"I expected nothing less of you, Goffinet."

"Consider it done, Majesty."

"There is another matter."

"Anything you say, Majesty."

"I want to recover the absurd dowry that my father, blinded by his weakness at the time, granted to the Habsburgs: they shall not enrich themselves at the expense of the Saxe-Coburg fortune. The only person who should profit from the family wealth is the sovereign of the Belgians; that is to say, me," Leopold remarked in all seriousness.

Goffinet hesitated. This, by all accounts, was much more difficult. It wasn't surprising that the sovereign should wish to increase his wealth—he'd known of his avarice for years—but recovering a dowry was another thing altogether.

"Don't look so worried, Auguste. If there's one thing you've learned under my rule, it's that there are no impossible roads, only long ones."

"Whatever you say, Majesty."

"There are rumors that Maximilian never consummated the marriage with my poor sister."

Goffinet hid his astonishment.

"You must confirm these rumors, Auguste. If they're true, Charlotte's dowry will return to Belgium. Send word when you have news."

Clapping his hands, he brought the conversation to a close.

Auguste Goffinet left the royal office as hastily as he'd arrived. He would have to send out his scouts, buy favors, uncover secrets. He had to begin operations immediately.

Before long, the Goffinets confirmed what seemed to be an open secret in Mexico. Everyone was saying it. Nobody denied it. The empress hadn't been happy with her husband. The emperor had never been alone with her. There were ladies of the court who ventured to say that they doubted they'd ever had relations. They never slept together, whether in Europe or in Mexico. Sovereigns sleeping in separate rooms was nothing new among royalty; it was common knowledge that their chambers were usually connected by secret doors so that marital visits could take place in privacy. But what struck Auguste most was a comment from one of the emperor's private secretaries, who said that Maximilian would sooner sleep on a filthy camp bed than share a bed of silk with Carlota.

It was said that the emperor was a man of dubious habits. He had become close to a vulgar servant, in spite of the concern it aroused among the rest of the court. They nicknamed this man the Great Moo for being as bestial as a cow, but his name was Sebastian Schertzenlechner. Maximilian met him when he was a rankless soldier, and he soon became a servant at Hofburg, where he swept chimneys. He went with Maximilian to Lombardy-Venetia, and then, when he was named emperor, he accompanied him to Mexico. There Maximilian decorated him and made him an imperial adviser. When Maximilian traveled, exploring his dominions, Carlota remained in Chapultepec while Schertzenlechner accompanied him, *for matters of duty*, the emperor hastened to explain. Goffinet, astounded, uncovered documents that proved that the Great Moo had been blackmailing Maximilian, and Schertzenlechner had been expelled from the empire for treason. Someone close to Maximilian had leaked to a newspaper details of the family pact that Maximilian had been forced to sign before accepting the Mexican throne. Maximilian, for all intents and purposes, had renounced his dynastic rights in Austria, and someone in his circle had released this information. All fingers pointed at Schertzenlechner, who ended up confessing. The betrayal was punishable with imprisonment, but Maximilian, in his infinite mercy, had commuted his sentence, returning him to Lokrum and paying him the salary that corresponded to a state adviser: the not inconsiderable sum of a thousand florins. *A good deal for a traitor*, thought Auguste Goffinet. But Schertzenlechner didn't waste time once he got to Europe: he began telling everyone he was the emperor of Mexico's lover.

Auguste sat back in his chair and handed a pile of papers to his brother, Constant.

"What's this?"

"It's this Schertzenlechner's memoirs; the contemptible swine deposited them with a European notary and is threatening to go public with them if anything happens to him or he's forced to return to Austria."

Constant didn't ask how his brother had obtained them: Auguste was an expert in acquiring secret documents. They had hundreds of incriminating pages in their possession, which was why they burned any written communication between them, and always preferred to speak face-to-face. The things people confessed in writing! They had to be either naïve or very stupid. Either way, it suited the Goffinet twins fine. Hundreds upon hundreds of letters revealing affairs, betrayals, jealousies: it had made them powerful from the shadows. The twins no longer asked each other how they managed to acquire the information. They never asked questions to which they didn't want to know the answer.

One of them—it mattered not which, for they were two peas in a pod—removed his spectacles and rubbed the mark the frame had left on his nose. The failure to consummate the marriage couldn't be verified, but as they say, there's no smoke without fire.

After many long discussions with the Habsburgs, held with the utmost discretion—for the Goffinet brothers were masters of secrecy—Leopold succeeded. With shame and humiliation, the Habsburgs, unable to refute the evidence, declared the marriage between Maximilian and Carlota to be void; the alliance had been doomed from the start. The Belgians could keep Carlota, filthy rich; she was all theirs.

Before he'd even shaken the twins' hands, Leopold had bought shares, made deposits and investments overseas, acquired promissory notes in England, transferred properties to his name, and taken possession of Carlota's art and jewelry collection, including the gifts that Franz Joseph, her brother-in-law, had given her on the occasion of their wedding, to the value of three hundred thousand florins. These included the Bleeding Heart: a priceless heart-shaped diamond encircled by rubies, a symbol of the misfortune that had befallen them from the moment the couple looked at one another, condemning each other to a life of misery.

44

1864, Mexico

Constanza had aroused Philippe's interest. For the last few weeks, he'd
found her more serene, less impetuous, more interesting even. It wasn't
that Constanza stood out for her beauty; it was more like some sort of
spell had kept certain qualities hidden until now. He met with her for a
couple of hours each day to teach her French, when the empress retired
to write letters. At first the lessons had been tedious. Though Constanza
did her best to make progress—which she undoubtedly did, for she was
clever, and as she'd told him herself, a fast learner—they were always
watching the clock in anticipation of having to return to serve Carlota.
Being away from the empress made him anxious, like a dog whose
owner has gone away. But since Constanza's brother had visited her
(thanks to a couple of inquiries, Philippe now knew who the regular
visitor to the palace was), some instinct had put him on alert. He didn't
know why, but it gave him shivers down his spine. He knew that feeling: it was the one he'd felt when he had looked through Mr. Walton's
accounts. But it wasn't just that; there was something else. After that
day, Constanza became more distant, more silent, more cautious. Put
simply, the young woman had suddenly grown, like in a story by Hans
Christian Andersen, the writer to whom the emperor had just awarded
a medal. Philippe wondered how he could decorate a man for writing a

story in which an emperor walks around naked because people are too afraid to tell him. Even an idiot could see the criticism hidden in that children's tale. Like the magic beans that grew until they touched the sky, Constanza had changed. Since Famke wounded him with unfulfilled love in that alleyway, he'd distrusted any woman who was an easy catch, and until now Constanza had been a little mouse waiting for the cheese. Not anymore. She used to melt into a smile whenever he bounced his tongue against his palate to pronounce rumbling consonants. Not anymore. He used to feel her tremble each time he held her hand to help her write a word. Not anymore. And that, paradoxically, had made her irresistible. Constanza changed overnight. And it wasn't just her attitude toward Philippe, but also toward the rest of the court.

Sure enough, a veil of caution covered her from dawn until she retired to sleep, and even then, the slightest movement of the curtain woke her. Discovering that her brother was an accomplice of the Liberales had sharpened her senses. If he was on the other side, anyone could be a double agent. Constanza began to distrust everyone. They all seemed like imposters: Juana, the housemaid who faithfully took some of the empress's monthly menstruation to show the French; the cooks; Manuelita del Barrio, who with her shrewd maneuvering gained ground every day; Mathilde Döblinger, who acted as matron from the shadows; Bombelles, the emperor's stalwart . . . All of them and yet none of them. She even struggled to look in the mirror, because in it she recognized her own duplicity.

One day, gathering her braid in a bun, she began to fear for the empress's safety. How convenient it would be if she suffered an accident. If both of them, she and the emperor, suffered one. Removing them would solve a lot of problems at once, leaving the Mexicans to continue killing one another without interference. Were they expecting *her* to assassinate Carlota? She shook her head, forcing herself to banish the monsters in her imagination. She couldn't do that. She was fond of the empress, who was just a few years older than her, but had the burden of so many lives on her shoulders. She felt close to her. She had never been near such a powerful woman. In her world, women didn't give orders but obeyed, and being shoulder to shoulder with one who exuded so much power had captivated her, amazed her. Carlota filled her with hope. Perhaps one day women would be able to lead governments, command armies, take part in the decision-making, and no longer be condemned to accepting their oppression. But it wasn't simply a matter of gender. If Carlota had been a man, Constanza would have followed him, too. She had only one defect, a gigantic and obvious one. Charlotte of Belgium, archduchess of Austria and empress of Mexico, was not and would never be a Mexican. However much good she did, she would never be one of them. She was an intruder, an uninvited guest. She had usurped the throne, and not as governor but as consort.

Constanza then thought about herself. She told herself that, as ambitious as she aspired to be, she could never marry for convenience. The thought of ending up like Carlota horrified her: married to a man disparagingly nicknamed the Austrian Pulque. And that was the kinder term, because more than once, anonymous hands had graffitied the walls, alluding to his tastes. Constanza knew of one such sentence that the palace servants had had to quickly cover with gallons of paint: *You came as Maximilian, but you leave as Max the Small; for everyone knows, how you cast off your clothes, and offered your anus to all.*

An ignominious rhyme someone had scrawled in large black letters in the middle of the night. They didn't want him; he, too, had the same massive defect Carlota had. Their arrival hadn't stopped blood being spilled; it had only exacerbated it. Because of them, Mexico continued to bleed, and however much affinity she felt for the empress, Constanza couldn't allow that. She *was* Mexican. She had to act according to her beliefs and remain cold-blooded.

She took a deep breath and put on her best disguise, the one she'd always used: that of a woman satisfied with the life she'd been given. She pinched her cheeks and gave them a couple of slaps.

It wasn't hard to make out the colonel. Alfred van der Smissen was tall, dark-haired, blue-eyed, and imposing, not so much for his appearance as for his gaze: he never looked happy, he could only look severe. Even when he congratulated his men, he did so with such rigidity that the lucky recipients only wanted the moment to end. Still, he was an upright man, and his promises were as unbreakable as the steel of his sword. Nothing intimidated him; he spoke little and observed everything. Maximilian listened to his opinion, for he considered him a man of reason and a believer in the empire, and his military expertise was renowned. However, the colonel had little patience for the Mexicans; in his mind they lacked discipline, and it wasn't uncommon to hear his booming voice shouting throughout the palace. All of these qualities were a gift, as far as Carlota was concerned. If she'd been born to reign, Alfred had been born to command. Nature had equipped him with forbearance, loyalty, and intelligence, virtues that she recognized and valued in those closest to her. She knew that Alfred van der Smissen was the kind of man who would sooner turn a gun on himself than betray the empire, Leopold I, or her.

Constanza knew it, too, so she would have to be diligent if she was to gather any kind of information. To get close to Van der Smissen, she would need help, and she knew exactly who could give it to her. She needed a Trojan horse, and that horse's name was Philippe. *Time to get to work,* she told herself. And that's what she did.

45

Juárez, arms crossed over his desk, was speaking to a young man in his twenties. They were talking with the intimacy with which a mentor speaks to his student. Juárez, insignificant only in appearance, looked even smaller in his presence. The young man's expression was hard and dry; he had jet-black eyes with the malice of a cat in them, and his bronze complexion seemed polished smooth, like a rock tumbled by the tide. His general demeanor was of indifference, which made him tremendously dangerous for anyone trying to guess his thoughts.

"Are you sure?" the president asked him.

"As sure as I know my own name," the young man replied.

Despite the intention behind the phrase, which was meant to be a guarantee of authenticity, Juárez was suspicious for a moment. He knew that the young man had been orphaned almost at birth. And Juárez knew what it meant to be orphaned at the age of three. His guarantee, therefore, seemed more romantic than disingenuous: Who knew what his real surname was? The one he used had been chosen at random in the civil registry years ago, when after finding him on the streets, Comonfort, Juárez's predecessor, arranged for him to receive an education and a roof over his head. However, without eliciting condescension, the young man always earned his sympathy.

"Modesto," said Juárez, "if you're going to do it, you have to be sure."

"Rest assured, Presidente, I have it all figured out. I already spoke to—"

"I don't want to know the details, or have anything to do with this," he cut in. "I'll fight my battle with Maximilian; he's the one I'm interested in."

"Yes, Presidente, but believe me: she's the linchpin without which Maximilian could not go on."

Juárez blew out his breath, uncomfortable.

"Do what you have to do."

"I promise I won't let you down."

"Don't promise, Modesto."

"Then wish me luck."

"I don't believe in luck. It has gone against us many times, Modesto. But while there are men like you anywhere in the republic taking up arms, the fatherland will exist."

Modesto smiled. He liked the president's grandiloquence. Hearing him speak about the fatherland, justice, and the law always lifted his heart.

"To die for the fatherland is to live forever," he replied, his emotions stirred. He left the presidential office feeling his mission was one of life and death, though it wasn't his life or his death that, at least for now, would turn the wheel of fortune.

Modesto arrived at La Chana's house dressed in civilian clothes, with no trace of his military uniform. He didn't want anybody to know that a Liberal was visiting a sorceress; it was an absurd precaution, for all manner of people turned to witchcraft and the dark arts to protect themselves from the inevitable: mothers asking for protection for their sons on the front, lovers praying for their men to be widowed so they could take their rightful place, politicians selling part of their soul to be able to gain power.

And La Chana said the same thing to all of them.

"There are no shortcuts."

But, foolishly, they insisted there were.

Modesto had known her for years, since, as a boy, he and his friends had gone to her to have their fortunes told. He laughed at the premonitions and then had to take back every word when by divine justice they all came true. Since then, he had visited the *curandera* from time to time so that she could run a raw egg over his back and cure his envy and curses. The egg always went rotten.

When he walked into her little room, the smoke made him cough.

"You've become delicate since the last time," she said as she slapped his back. "So, *muchacho*, what brings you here?"

"I need your help, Chana."

La Chana fixed her eyes on his.

"Love or money?"

"Neither."

"Oh, my! You need me to do a job for you?"

"Something like that. I need a poison."

La Chana took a drag of her cigar.

"Who for?"

"You know who for."

"I'm a witch, not telepathic."

Modesto smiled.

"For someone in court."

"I see," she said, sitting back in her chair.

"Something that's discreet, Chana."

"That's how old women kill. Men kill with metal."

The two of them fell silent. La Chana was trying to unsettle him, and it was working.

"I can pay you well."

"Blood debts can't be paid with money, *muchacho*."

"I don't understand."

"Death is paid for with death."

Modesto shifted in his seat.

"Well, I'm prepared to pay the price."

"Watch your words, *muchacho*. You're playing with fire."

He knew that already, but some hidden part of him suddenly made him have doubts. *Make her give you the poison, Modesto. Make her give it to you, then go.*

"Just give me the poison."

La Chana asked again.

"Who's it for? Him or her?"

Modesto took a deep breath.

"For whoever takes it, Chana."

"Quite the poisoner you've turned out to be, boy." La Chana crossed him with some branches dipped in black water and said, "I'll give you the plants. But the blame's all yours."

"Done."

So La Chana gave him a little package containing some tolguacha herb.

"In small doses it causes madness. But if you overdo it, it can kill."

"I owe you one, Chana."

"It's not me you owe, *muchacho*. Not me."

He left La Chana's house with a bag hanging from his belt and a debt on his conscience. He hurried off in search of his contact.

The spy network had been woven with complete secrecy, and often they didn't even know the names of their informants; that way, if they were captured or tortured by the Conservatives, they could die without betraying anyone. If they were going to be shot, it would be with their eyes open, as befits the brave. But the time had come to make contact with Salvador. He knew there were people who had infiltrated the palace and could carry out the task he needed. It was time to take the risk.

The Liberales usually met in secret at a house that wouldn't arouse suspicion. They played cards and drank aguardiente, and between hands and drinks they filled one another in on what was happening at the palace or the progress that Juárez was making. Modesto remembered his shock when he discovered that Salvador Murrieta, of Conservative stock through and through, was on their side. He'd heard about the Murrietas, but never dared establish any kind of relationship with them, in part because he'd have broken out in hives around such a Conservative family, and in part because the opportunity had never arisen. How would it ever arise, with Modesto inhabiting such different circles? In Mexico, the separation between social classes was like water and oil in a pot, making it possible to live one's entire life without mixing. And yet, by some twist of fate, the person he had to contact to carry out the mission that Juárez had authorized was Salvador Murrieta. He struggled to accept it at first; he had his reservations and even requested some proof of loyalty. Salvador proved himself above and beyond one day when he saved Modesto from the French bullets by dragging him wounded from a pool of other men's blood and hiding him in a brothel. For a month, Salvador visited him each day to check on his condition.

Modesto waited for instructions for their next meeting. Salvador always arranged to meet him in public places—parks, banks—but this time he was surprised to be told that the meeting would be at Chapultepec Castle. Salvador, using who knows what devices, had managed to obtain an invitation for Modesto García one Empress's Monday.

It must be a joke, thought Modesto; just thinking about going to the castle and kissing the hands of that bunch of traitors made his stomach turn.

Seeing him arrive, Salvador Murrieta welcomed him courteously with a military salute. Modesto was surprised by the coolness with which he handled himself, the same quality that had brought him to Miramare a few years before.

"Are you out of your mind? If they discover us, we'll be shot," Modesto whispered to him.

"Relax, Modesto," Salvador said. "The best disguise is in plain sight, where everyone can see us. Act natural and nobody will suspect a thing."

Modesto glanced at the men in the room: they were dancing in circles, fulfilling the protocol of the European courts. The ladies tried not to faint in their tight corsets, and the soldiers and politicians boasted of their victories to the royal audience. For all intents and purposes, they were minding their own business. Only one man observed Modesto with curiosity: Joaquín, Salvador's elder brother, was trying to remember where he'd seen him before. Feeling watched, Modesto raised his glass in his direction. Joaquín, disconcerted, raised his, too, and then turned to speak to three gentlemen at the back of the room.

"Your brother suspects. I hope he doesn't recognize me . . ."

"Who would? Everyone here is close to Maximilian. To be here, you need an imperial invitation. They'll never suspect."

Modesto felt extremely uncomfortable; he was unaccustomed to pretending to be someone else. When he disliked somebody, he declared war on them to their face, giving them the reasons for his hostility in no uncertain terms; he wasn't a spy or a diplomat like Salvador. This was senseless torture. It would be best to leave the castle before it was too late. He was prepared to be arrested, for someone to yell *Liberal!* in the middle of the room, he was even prepared to be shot from behind, but he wasn't prepared, after an eternity, to encounter *her* there.

"Brother dear, would you do me the honor of the next dance?" said Constanza, who'd rushed over from the other side of the room after seeing him.

"I didn't think women could choose their partner," he said jokingly.

She hit him gently on the shoulder. They laughed. Salvador knew that, had they been alone, she would have pinched him, for his sister only asked him to dance to pass on information. They suddenly seemed to notice Modesto's presence.

"Where are my manners . . . ," said Salvador, noticing that Modesto was watching his sister closely. "Captain Modesto García, this is my sister, Constanza Murrieta, lady of the court of our empress, Carlota of Belgium."

"Pleased to meet you," she said.

But before Constanza had raised herself upright after curtsying, it was as if a pitcher of cold water had been thrown over her.

"Constanza, at last we meet again."

"Have we met?"

"I could swear we have, though it was many years ago."

Constanza was sure the captain's face wasn't among the many she'd memorized since she'd been at court. Still, she remembered it: there weren't many like his. Dark, strong, perhaps too strong to be considered attractive, but undoubtedly there was something about him that brought back a memory of another age. Then he smiled, certain he knew who she was, and that she recognized him. How could she forget? He was a man now and not a child, but that wicked smile had featured in her dreams more than a few times.

"Modesto? Modesto from the civil registry?" she whispered.

Perplexed, Salvador watched them. How could Constanza know Modesto?

"That's me," he said, bending forward in a bow.

Constanza looked at her brother in horror: she knew at that moment that Modesto was an infiltrator in the court. A supporter of Comonfort, a spy; a man so close to Juárez that she could see him in his eyes. There, in Chapultepec! Her brother had gone too far.

"Salvador," she said. "We must speak."

Salvador took his sister's hand and placed it in Modesto's.

"It's him you must speak to. Why don't you dance with my sister, Modesto? I'm sure it will be a most worthwhile dance," he said, winking.

It was crystal clear. She was one of them.

The music began to play; Constanza felt her heart race. He took her in his arms. He wasn't well versed in formal dances, but it wasn't his lack of practice that made them tense when he rested one of his large hands on her waist.

"You've grown," he finally said.

"It was to be expected," she replied, ill at ease.

"And look at what you've turned into. Quite the little lady."

Constanza remained serious, as if dancing with an enemy.

"How's your mother?"

"You can ask Salvador."

He smiled, showing a row of extremely white teeth contrasting with the bronze of his skin.

"What're you doing in the palace?" she asked.

"Searching for you. Without knowing it, of course. Since when have you been the empress's lady?"

"From the beginning. I'm a Murrieta, remember?"

They turned and turned in a waltz; Constanza was beginning to feel dizzy.

"Poor Don Vicente: two Murrietas turning against him . . . Three, if we count your mother."

Constanza made eye contact. They spoke without opening their mouths.

"So?" she asked. "Why're you here?"

He didn't hesitate.

"We need you to give the empress something to drink."

Hearing the *we*, Constanza knew Modesto wasn't referring to a handful of people, but to all Mexico. Everyone. It was a heavy burden. The music continued to spin.

"What kind of something?"

"Something that will send her back to Europe, or farther."

"A poison?" *Please,* she thought, *don't let it be a poison.*

"Yes," he declared. "Someone close to her has to administer it, Constanza. It has to be you."

The music suddenly stopped, in time with her senses. Constanza turned pale. She didn't know what had made her so dizzy, the waltz, running into Modesto again—the Modesto of her childhood night-mares, now a man—or hearing that she had to poison Carlota.

"I need some air."

And slowly, holding Modesto's arm, Constanza headed to one of the grand floor-to-ceiling doors.

"I don't know if I can do it."

"Why not?"

"I'm not an assassin."

Modesto looked at her.

"We're at war, Constanza. In war, you kill or you die."

"But you're asking me to do something, something that isn't . . . I can't do it."

"You must do it for Mexico. Don't you see how they've dressed you up? You look Prussian. Where's the girl I knew? What happened to that girl who accompanied her mother to the civil registry against her father's wishes, Constanza? You know that's the real Mexico, not an empire. Even Iturbide was only emperor for eleven months, and he was Mexican. And this isn't an empire; it's a farce . . . It's just another intervention by a foreign army."

"But she's a good woman. You have to believe me. I've seen it. She wants to do things for Mexico."

"She's as guilty as he is. We have to put an end to what they represent."

"Lower your voice; you're going to get us killed," she ordered, realizing they were just a few yards from the monarchs.

He seemed to suddenly realize that he wasn't in Juárez's office, but in the middle of an imperial ceremony. It all seemed ridiculous, absurd, illogical. Discreetly, Modesto handed her a pouch of herbs.

"Give it to her gradually and she won't even notice. Do it for your country."

Constanza was petrified.

Modesto, clicking his heels together in a military salute, kissed her hand and said goodbye, leaving her in a state of utter confusion.

46

María Ana Leguizamo never liked her name. Whenever her mother called her from the other side of the field to come help with household chores, María Ana always, always thought she'd been given the ugliest name in the world. With all the beautiful names she could've had! She would've liked to have been called Xóchitl or Jazmín, the mere mention of which evoked the smell of flowers. As she washed clothes at the river, she recited a string of names, threading them together as if listing the Aztec princes. *Albertana.* She soaked a shirt. *Aurelia.* She wrung out the water. *Adelaida.* She scrubbed it with soap. *Abigaíl.* She rubbed its elbows and neck against a stone. *Alfonsina.* She soaked it in the water again. And that was how she spent the hours, imagining infinite possibilities. She usually introduced herself using a false name whenever she had the chance: when she went to buy tortillas, she was Petunia; when she delivered clean clothes to the boss's house, Azucena; another day she was Solsticio. As if with each name she had the opportunity to be reborn and to reinvent herself. As if each name had the ability to give her part of the life she dreamed of, far from the world of poverty in which she was growing up.

Though they lived in Cuernavaca, she'd been born in Pachuca, where her mother was from. Even before she was born, her mother decided to change the course of destiny and emigrate, fleeing a cholera epidemic that was killing everyone: babies, children, and adults. When

María Ana was only one week old, she wrapped her up, stowed the small amount of money she'd earned by washing clothes in a wafer box, and left the village before dawn, hoping that, if death was to find them, they would be on the road and not in a bed with no mattress.

It seemed incredible that two such fragile creatures could have survived the disease and the dangers of the road, but Doña Eulalia was as strong as a tree, and where others gave in, she only grew stronger. She had the greatest motivation: her little María Ana, whom she loved from the day she saw her emerge from between her legs, squatting in the middle of a coffee plantation. She hadn't known she was pregnant until the moment she bore her; she'd felt some discomfort over the months, but her round matron's body had hardly changed shape with the child growing inside. In her ignorance, she'd thought she must be hungry all the time because of the long treks; eating tortillas with frijoles at all hours, she grew fatter and fatter, and the more she ate, the more hungry she was, because life was a never-ending vicious circle of eating, sleeping, working the land, and more eating. Until, one day, there was a cramp in her belly, and squatting behind some bushes, to her surprise and good fortune, she pushed out a beautiful little girl. It took her a while to recover from the shock and the pain, and a bit longer for the happiness and uncertainty to set in. But then, with ancestral wisdom, she found strength in her weakness, cut the cord with a sharp stone, and held the babe to her breast so that she could drink her milk. Being without a husband, she knew immediately that the Juarista who'd taken her one night without consent must be the girl's father. She accepted this truth as the Blessed Virgin Mary must have: with joy and without giving it much thought. She never told her daughter who her father was, nor did the girl ask, accustomed like all the women and girls of her community to living alone and obeying orders. In her village, men weren't heads of the family but studs that inseminated them and left without looking back. That's how it had always been; that's how the animals did it. She'd seen it since she could remember with the livestock, the roosters, the horses. At any rate, why worry about the direction of the wind? The important thing was that her daughter was perfect, healthy, complete. And she was pretty.

María Ana grew like a wildflower: as dirty or as disheveled as she was, her beauty always stood out among the greenery of the country-side. The sun caressed her every day without burning her skin. Her almond-shaped eyes had a girl's sweetness and were caramel-colored at the edges, as if an eclipse was about to take place behind the iris. Her hair was so black it seemed to have a blue tint, and her plump mouth was like a summer peach. The years couldn't have made her more beau-tiful, but they did make her more voluptuous: when she reached the age of development, her body became a figure eight, and to control the imbalance caused by the development of all her curves, she began to sway with each step. Between her breasts there emerged a little channel down which the sweat ran. When she walked, though she barely noticed it, her breasts quivered, reminding the men who watched her make her way through the market crowd—lustfully—of two full pitchers of water about to spill over.

One of these men ventured to speak to her one day. He was twice her age, dark, tubby, with a black moustache that allowed no sunlight through, and long eyelashes, but his voice was serene, and he loved his job more than his own mother. His name was Ignacio, and he was a gardener at a house on the outskirts of the village, but on Sundays, his day off, he ran a small flower stall in a street market.

He'd been observing María Ana for some time. Each Sunday, he hoped to see her appear among the crowd of native women who arrived with baskets on their backs and their hands scabby from spending the day cooking tortillas on a comal. He courted the one with the huaraches and the one with the fried bananas, but was beginning to tire. He might not be an Adonis, but at least he knew how to talk to plants, and had not lost his gift for caressing. He saw the girl inspecting fruit, talking to the merchants. He saw her laugh. And that day, blessed be the Virgin of Guadalupe, María Ana approached to see the Mexican marigolds.

"How much?"

"Are they for you?"

"It depends on the price."

"If they're for you, they're free."

"And why would you do that?"

"Because you're so pretty."

"Just for that?"

"Yeah, just that."

María Ana appeared to weigh the offer.

"And you're not going to ask me for anything in return?"

"Well, what do you want me to ask you for?"

"I'm just asking."

They both fell silent for a moment.

"What's your name?"

Used to making up names all the time, she had no trouble lying.

"Concepción," she said, showing her teeth with a smile.

The gardener tied up a bunch of fifteen flowers with a ribbon and gave it to her.

"Here. A flower for each of your years."

"How did you know?"

"I know everything, kid."

María Ana smiled.

"If you come back another day, I'll give you more flowers."

María Ana took the bunch and left, but after a few steps she was unable to resist the urge to turn around. The gardener was watching her. She set off again. She could feel the man's eyes on her backside, sensing him concentrate so he would not miss a single detail of her gentle sway. She quickened her pace; she was used to attracting attention, but there was something about this man, a certain something, that made her think that, yes, perhaps she would come back for more flowers.

The next Sunday, María Ana returned for more flowers. And the next Sunday, and the next. By the fourth Sunday, Ignacio Sedano, as the gardener was called, had persuaded her to go live with him on a hacienda near Cuernavaca. Doña Eulalia flew into a rage. She cried, she begged her daughter by all that was sacred not to go with that old cradle snatcher, but María Ana, with the insolence of her fifteen years, paid no attention to her. They argued, they fought, and the mother even shook her daughter to try to snap her out of her tantrum. It was all to no avail. After a great deal of yelling and screaming, afraid that her child would run away in the middle of the night, Doña Eulalia let her go toward the destiny that was circling her.

Despite the pain and disappointment, she found the strength to say, "I wish you the best, my girl. But if, God forbid, something goes wrong, wherever your mother is, you'll have a home. Do you hear me?" And after kissing her and crossing her forehead and chest, Eulalia said, "God be with you."

And as they hugged, María Ana replied, "Goodbye, *mamita*."

With that goodbye, María Ana parted company not only with her mother but also with her childhood, her virginity, and her name. From that day on, she made everyone call her Concepción, and she never turned back.

Concepción Sedano, like María Ana, knew nothing about life, but the new woman she believed she'd become was in a hurry to live it, as if a giant clock inside her were setting the pace. She was in a hurry to do everything, to grow, to eat, to reach a future that seemed to always be just out of reach.

All because of the garden. The house where Ignacio worked—though it was an ancestral home that to Concepción seemed like a castle—was old, ill tended, and riddled with damp. It had been built by a Spaniard with a French father who, busy exploiting the silver mines of Taxco, left it in the hands of other owners, and from those it passed on to others, and others still, until the beautiful property started to fall to pieces. From time to time a carriage arrived at the house carrying distinguished people who didn't speak Spanish or any language Concepción had ever heard. They came to see the property because they were interested in spending the weekend there. That was how Concepción discovered that there was an entire world that had been hidden from her. She learned that, in spite of everything she knew, she knew nothing at all about anything. Living with Nacho Sedano was a window through which she saw a Mexico she hadn't known existed, and that was enough to make her endure more than she would've otherwise borne. Concepción was fascinated by the gentlemen with yellow or red hair and white skin, accompanied by ladies who walked carefully to avoid getting earth on the hems of their dresses. She didn't know how to lift a skirt to keep it clean; she only did so to carry mangos or lemons in her lap. She didn't know what it was to be afraid of dust or mud, and she spent hours watching these women who covered their heads with hats in an absurd attempt to escape the sun. They received several foreigners each week. Due to the poor state of the house, many of them left to stay somewhere else, but some remained just for the garden. Because, oh! The garden was something else altogether. With care, affection, and an immense knowledge of botany, Nacho Sedano had made this plot of land his little Eden. The trees and plants competed with one another, each in their own way, in size and exuberance. He tended the grass like a jockey tends his horse, and he knew every plant by its first name. Nacho spoke to the flowers softly, unhurriedly, with an affection that Concepción had never known in him. With her, after the first few months of cohabitation, he became terse. He could spend the day in silence and only break it to ask her for things. *Concepción, I feel like some lemon water,* and so Concepción went to gather lemons to make the water. *Concepción, I feel like some guava jelly,* and off the girl went in search of guavas with which to make the dessert. *Concepción, I'm hungry. Concepción, draw me a bath. Concepción, I'm cold, make me some hot chocolate.* A long list of orders preceded by her made-up name.

But as soon as he went out into the garden, Nacho was transformed into sweetness personified. *Look how big and pretty you are,* he said to the arums. And if a freak storm threatened to damage his buds, he ran to cover them with a protective cloth. Seeing him like this, anyone would say he was the most caring man they'd known.

Encouraged, perhaps, by this affection he professed for his flowers, or surprised at the tenderness he was able to show toward nature while to her he barely said a word, Concepción opened two buttons on her blouse and, letting him see more flesh than the neckline normally allowed, said to him jealously, "You say nicer things to those plants than to me."

"But I do things to you I don't do to the plants . . ." And thereupon he turned her around, lifted the skirt of her dress, and raised her onto the kitchen table; he grabbed her braid to ram into her from behind. Concepción allowed him to do it with her arms crossed, face down on the table, clutching the edges of the tabletop that shook like everything in her.

"I don't do *this* to the plants, do I? *Do I?*"

Ow, Concepción kept saying, and *Slowly,* and *It hurts,* but that only excited Nacho more, and he kept going until he finished with a slow, dull groan that indicated to her it was finally over. As he withdrew, without looking her in the face, the man bit her ear and gave her a slap on the bottom. Her buttock barely moved; the red mark on the skin remained a little longer. The pain in her soul remained forever.

Concepción took a few minutes to recover from the goring. She readjusted her dress, and then, with difficulty, she walked slowly to the stream to wash away the trickle of semen and blood running down between her thighs.

Part Three

47

Marie Henriette was an unhappy queen. The kindness her dark eyes carried in her youth had faded so gradually that someone who hadn't seen it would think they had always been that way, but they were like embers that had burned for too long. She was tall, solid, and some thought her stature was a reflection of her character, for nobody could persuade her to do anything against her will.

Her strength of character was of little use when she married Leopold II. He crushed it slowly, her barely noticing, until she was under his control. She found it easier to accept his infidelities than his tyranny. There were many things the Belgian king could be loathed for, but in her mind, he was a much worse husband than monarch; by dint of disappointments, something in her withered. So when she started hearing about her sister-in-law Carlota—she was out of her mind, she was having paranoid delusions, and she'd given birth to a child she couldn't see because she was being held hostage at Miramare—she knew it would be up to her to help the poor woman. In a way she suffered from the same ills without the refuge of mental instability. She'd always believed madness was an escape like any other, and sometimes she'd been tempted to lock herself in her room until the world stopped revolving, but she was made of sterner stuff. Some women escaped when they were convicted as witches or lunatics. The rest were left feigning devotion to endure destinies that were more a burden than boredom. With her madness, Carlota had chosen the abysmal middle ground of false indolence.

"I'm going to fetch Charlotte," she told her husband one day.

Leopold looked up from his papers without moving his head. Marie Henriette held her breath for a moment, waiting for Leopold to say something. Receiving no answer, she continued.

"I'll leave tomorrow."

Leopold stood, and, leaning on his knuckles on his desk as if he'd been waiting for this for some time, he said, "You've already decided, I see."

Marie Henriette replied with a concise "Yes."

"You're making a mistake. Charlotte is better off where she is."

Marie Henriette thought about her husband's bad blood; he was a man capable of selling his mother to the devil if necessary. He preferred to leave his sister in the hands of strangers, in a castle built on a rock. He would leave her to rot there just to remove an obstacle. He would do the same with Marie Henriette if he could. Would he dare? She felt a stab of uncertainty. And when she was about to protest, Leopold spoke before she did.

"All right, go. But not alone. Baron Auguste Goffinet and Dr. Bolkens will accompany you."

"Dr. Bolkens from the village of Geel?"

"That's right."

"We don't need a doctor, Leopold. Much less a lymphatic, tiresome Flemish one."

Leopold took a deep breath before saying, "Henriette, sometimes I don't know if you're stupid or just pretending to be. Dr. Bolkens goes or there will be no journey."

Marie Henriette, long accustomed to the offensive remarks his royal mouth directed at her, said nothing; she simply turned around and walked out.

In addition to the company, the queen left with twenty thousand gold francs and an unlimited letter of credit for the House of Rothschild in Vienna. It was July 5, 1867, just one year since Carlota left Mexico, and yet a slow, torturous road into darkness.

Upon arriving in Augsburg, there was a telegram at the hotel reception from Maximilian's brother the emperor Franz Joseph. Marie Henriette read it with a look of disgust.

"Is something wrong, Your Majesty?" a countess who was accompanying her asked.

Marie Henriette thought about screwing the telegram up into a ball. Instead, she held it out to the countess with an ironic "Franz Joseph *authorizes* me to allow Dr. Bolkens to attend to Charlotte in Vienna." And then, to herself, she added, "As if we needed his blessing."

In reality Marie Henriette was closer to the Habsburgs than to the Belgians, for she was an Austrian archduchess by birth. However, since her marriage to Leopold II, Vienna had felt very distant; she was the queen of the Belgians and that was that.

With the wisdom she'd acquired during her years living with Leopold II, she said to her entourage, "Prepare yourselves . . . we're about to fight a little battle. Something tells me they're not going to let us take my august sister-in-law so easily."

And she couldn't have been more right. They were received in Salzburg by Dr. Riedel; the administrator of Miramare, prefect Edouard Radonetz; and the person in charge of all of them: Charles de Bombelles. Seeing Bombelles, Marie Henriette's stomach tightened. She was used to grappling with warts, but this man especially made her feel more than just repulsion or suspicion. There was something in him she couldn't describe, something in his gaze, perhaps. Something. She couldn't tell exactly what, and that disturbed her. For a long time, she'd thought she had learned to read people, and she considered Bombelles to be affected, but above all, false; next to him, Judas was a holy man. He looked at people with his head tilted, narrowing his already small eyes, and when he spoke, he kept a forefinger over his mouth, like children do when they lie. After the appropriate introductions, Marie Henriette proceeded to inquire about her sister-in-law. The first person to respond, as was to be expected, was Bombelles.

"The empress is in good hands at Miramare, Your Highness. You shouldn't have troubled yourself to come."

"You understand that the king and I are exceedingly worried about the news that reaches us, Charles."

Bombelles was no fool. He could smell the queen's distrust like a bloodhound. He already knew of her determination to take Carlota away; that was why she was there, to take her, but he couldn't allow it. For him, Carlota embodied a castle by the sea, life insurance in perpetuity. He'd gone to too much trouble to give up now.

"The empress is suffering from dementia praecox."

"That's why Dr. Bolkens is here. He's an outstanding specialist in illnesses of the mind, as you know. I'd like to hear a diagnosis from his mouth."

Dr. Bolkens stepped forward and nodded. Charles fixed his eyes on him; for a second, he wondered whether he was the venal type. Probably he was. *What will your price be?* he thought.

Charles de Bombelles glanced at Dr. Riedel, who for the first time in a long while had fallen silent, not daring to say anything in the queen's presence. Because it was true, there was a stony confidence in her. Her eyes were an unbreakable wall. Charles wished he could exude the same strength. She, on the other hand, didn't seem to care how steely she appeared. That was why she was queen. Suddenly, Charles remembered Carlota dealing with affairs of state at Chapultepec with the same regal demeanor, and he broke into a Machiavellian smile thinking of her now, small, wasted away to almost nothing in her room at Miramare. His thoughts were interrupted when he felt the weight of Marie Henriette's gaze. He immediately changed tactic: invoking the gods of the theater, he began to cry.

"Your Majesty, please, have mercy. I beg of you, do not appear before Charlotte; her condition is so fragile that your visit could kill her."

The queen opened her eyes wide. Not knowing what Bombelles was going to do next was precisely what surprised her.

"What are you saying?"

"I implore you, Majesty. My affection for the empress is great; I don't want anything to upset her. I fear for her. I'm afraid of the effect your visit could have on her."

Bombelles's eyes were quivering. Marie Henriette pulled herself together.

"Seeing as she is our sister, our affection for Charlotte is as great as yours, Charles. The empress will come with us whether you like it or not, and there's nothing you can do to stop us."

They continued the journey toward Miramare. With each hour, Marie Henriette found it harder to put up with Bombelles's sniveling. Sick of his nonsense, she headed straight to Carlota's accommodation as soon as they arrived, followed by the three men speaking over one another: *Wait, stop, for the love of God* and a string of profanities that the queen couldn't hear. She reached Carlota's room and slammed the door behind her.

Her spirit faded when she saw the woman lying in the bed and didn't recognize her. The room was poorly lit, and there was a nauseating smell floating among the curtains. She forced herself to take a couple of steps forward and when she reached the bed sat near the headboard, like a loving mother.

"Charlotte, dear, I came to fetch you."

Carlota lifted herself onto her elbows when she recognized a different voice.

"Who is it?"

"It's your sister, Marie Henriette."

Carlota blinked several times, forcing her eyes to look. She seemed to recognize her and made an attempt to smile, but she was suddenly overcome with shame: she was in an appalling state and was frightened. She held her hands to her chest in an imploring gesture, and Marie Henriette took them in hers.

"There, there, little one, everything will be fine now," she said.

Carlota sighed for the first time in months at the touch of hands that weren't there to threaten her.

"I'm afraid," Carlota said to her with horror in her eyes.

"What of, dear?"

"That they'll come to tie down my hands and feet again."

Marie Henriette tried to hide her astonishment. It couldn't be true. Had they done this to the empress? As if she were a common criminal? As if she were a lunatic?

Carlota pleaded with her.

"Promise me no one will come, that nobody will come in, that they won't tie me to the bed again."

And after saying this she looked toward the door, where Bombelles, who'd entered quietly, was observing the scene breathlessly.

Marie Henriette tried to regain her composure. Nobody would confirm such a statement, but what if it had happened? *Damned Bombelles,* she thought, looking at him.

"Don't worry. Nobody will dare hurt you while you're with me."

She hugged her, and Marie Henriette silently swore to protect the poor creature from the scheming men around her. She knew very well what they were prepared to do for power and money. She would bring her back from the edge they were driving her toward. She would bring her back from the inaccessible and inhospitable land she'd inhabited for the last year.

Bombelles turned around and left. Goffinet went after him, but as if by magic the man had disappeared; Goffinet searched from room to room until he found him. He was hiding in a cupboard, from which he made a final attempt to retain the empress.

"You can't take her! She's insane!" he yelled.

"You're the one who's lost his mind."

Then he grabbed him and, holding him by the lapels, lifted him up, making sure that Bombelles was left where he should've always been: cornered against the wall.

Dr. Bolkens gave her a quick examination before leaving.

"Well?" asked Marie Henriette.

"In my opinion, the empress was poisoned before she left Mexico." Marie Henriette crossed herself.

"What kind of poison?"

"I can't be certain without a more exhaustive assessment, but it may have been some kind of jimsonweed."

"And what are its effects? Will she recover?"

"It's difficult to know. It depends on the dose and over what period she was given it. It seems it was administered to her in small doses. Had it been more, it would've killed her."

"Poor Charlotte," Marie Henriette let out from deep down. "Thank you, Doctor, you may leave."

Carlota left the house in which she'd been held for the last few months with her soul in tatters, but enveloped in her sister-in-law's kindness and strength. After the horrors to which she'd been subjected, she didn't care where she was taken, provided it was far from there. She never imagined that Miramare could cause her to suffer so. When Maximilian showed her the plans for the castle and where the various trees would be planted, she'd genuinely thought that she would be happy there. That they would be happy. She'd arrived there a virgin and was leaving after giving birth to a bastard son who she would never see. What had they done with the child? She preferred not to think about it because, sure enough, each time her mind dared touch on it, she could feel her sanity slipping. It hurt too much. She preferred to think she was an orphan. Alone. There was nobody left in the world who loved her: not her father, or her grandmother, or Mathilde. And Maximilian? What had become of him? No one could tell her anything of his fate. What could've happened to him? By now, Napoleon would have withdrawn his troops . . . Why hadn't he come for her? Although, on the other hand, why would he if even when they lived under the same roof they'd barely spoken? He'd left her at the mercy of his hound, Bombelles, who'd degraded her and tortured her as if there was some personal glory in it. Would she ever be able to trust anyone again? Carlota had all of these thoughts while staring out the window of the train from Trieste to Laeken. En route, Marie Henriette conversed with Carlota. Three-quarters of the time, she was as sane as anyone, then she seemed to be plunged into a silence in which only she could hear the voices. Then Marie Henriette could smell her fear. That's what it was: fear of being taken back to Miramare. No matter how much her sister-in-law assured her it wouldn't happen, Carlota was suspicious and chewed on a handkerchief. Then she would calm down and her usual intelligence would be restored to her eyes. In them, Marie Henriette could see all the torment the poor woman carried inside. Too much anguish for someone so young.

Carlota let out a melancholic sigh of relief when she arrived at Tervuren Castle. By order of Marie Henriette, all signs of mourning had been removed to avoid upsetting Carlota's delicate health, because what nobody had told her, nor did they intend to tell her, was that during her absence, Maximilian, her Max, her husband and archduke, had been shot by Juárez's troops in Querétaro.

48

Cuernavaca, with its exquisite views, was often described as a paradise on earth. When they arrived there for the first time, the emperor and empress thought it picturesque, delightful, the perfect place for a summer residence, accommodations where they could be far from the court and where they could relax their etiquette. It would be their Petit Trianon, as Maximilian liked to say.

Maximilian fell in love with a beautiful house in very poor condition, but whose garden captivated him at first sight. The trees growing there were tall and provided shade that the oldest gardens of Vienna would envy. The emperor thought of his garden at Miramare, no less beloved for being so far away, and he missed the woodland that he'd built inch by inch with so much care and so much of his wife's money. He promised himself that he would make this place the haven he needed in the powder keg of his empire. Two weeks of every month, he went to inspect the work that was being carried out to restore the house, taking the opportunity to cleanse his palate with French wine and aged port, sometimes in excess. And just as he had turned Chapultepec Castle from the seat of the military school into a palace worthy of an emperor, he managed to rescue the Casa Borda from neglect.

On the other side of the ocean, in a letter from Bazaine, Napoleon III received disheartening news about Mexico. Nothing was going as planned. The accumulation of bad news and social discontent was making him consider radical measures; he couldn't allow the uncertainty to continue, let alone permit the financial burden to fall on France. He picked up a pen and wrote to the marshal to ask him to focus on preparing the French navy to evacuate the country. *The Emperor Maximilian must understand that we can't remain in Mexico forever,* he wrote.

"What are you writing to Bazaine, dear?" Eugénie asked from the table where she was playing cards.

"Same as always. That a government that's done nothing to become self-sufficient will be easily abandoned."

For Carlota, Cuernavaca also became her city of eternal spring. She rested there, strolled in the garden, read, sang at the piano, and even planted flowers, manual work that was forbidden to the nobility and that, if they did it every so often, was quite pleasing. She could understand why Maximilian liked being in proximity with nature so much. There she could relax, rest, and gather her strength before returning to Mexico City, or at least that was what she supposed until she met her.

The gardener's wife—a mere girl—was like a butterfly that fluttered around the garden, and when not among the trees, she was doing household chores, preparing food, making beds, gathering the fruit that fell ripe from the trees to make drinks or dishes; some members of the court had even seen her cooking with rose petals. She was always wearing a cotton dress that revealed dark shoulders with pronounced collarbones, so smooth and shiny that they looked like polished mahogany. She swayed in a way that seemed affected to Carlota, because she knew very well that a woman didn't need to wiggle so much in order to walk. Princesses were taught to walk as straight as poles, without swaying their hips, but this young woman defied the norms of modesty in every way. She wore nothing on her feet, and when she thought nobody was looking, she inserted her toes into the earth to cool them, like trees with their roots. Carlota watched her discreetly with some suspicion, while also envying her freedom, but what she desired most was her smile. She wore it always, even when there was a trace of dissent in her eyes, though the difference between her submission and Carlota's was that the girl wasn't aware of hers. One day, Carlota decided to speak to her.

"What's your name, *muchacha*?" she asked in impeccable Spanish.

"Concepción Sedano, señora."

Saying this, Concepción realized how long it had been since she'd invented herself a new name.

"How old are you?"

"Sixteen, señora."

Just a child, Carlota thought, but then remembered that she'd only been a year older when she married Maximilian. *How young I was,* she thought.

"When you're in my presence, I want you in shoes and covered with a shawl."

Concepción lowered her head.

"Yes, señora."

"You may leave."

The girl glanced at the immensity around her. Where was she supposed to go? It was the first time someone had thrown her out of her garden, and her pride wobbled.

Concepción observed the emperor with the same interest with which he observed the hummingbirds. Compared with Nacho's coarseness, he seemed a fragile creature. Ignacio had a stiff black moustache as if made of wire, while the emperor had spongy red whiskers like a cloud. The only similarity between them was the way they spoke to the plants, though when the emperor did so, Concepción couldn't understand a single word; he spoke in a language that she'd never heard before, each word ending in *um* or *ea*, which she found funny. How could someone call those flowers *poinsettias* or *Bellis perennis*? In his expressions she sensed more admiration than affection, because he marveled at the colors of flowers and at the strange shapes of leaves that were as ordinary to her as a sunrise. But to the emperor, every specimen was a jewel worthy of study.

One day, Concepción discovered she liked following him with her gaze as he walked among the plants.

Maximilian had been wandering around the garden for a while, beyond the trees and exposed to the sun; the crown of his pale head soon began to turn so red that it hurt just to look at it. He called for servants, but nobody came; without realizing it, he'd traveled some distance from the house. Suffering from a headache and sweating in a wholly inappropriate manner, he decided to breach the rules of decorum and go to the kitchen himself to request a remedy. When he walked in, Concepción was alone, preparing nopales; she was so surprised to see him enter her domain that she almost sliced her finger with the knife. No foreigner ever came into the kitchen unless it was to check that everything was impeccable, and they always sent the ladies or footmen, certainly not the emperor in person! Worried, Concepción looked at her bare feet and then from side to side, hoping the empress wouldn't walk in after him, for she would earn a good scolding. Seeing that he was alone, she felt some relief, but only a little: this was very unusual.

"*Porr favorr . . . ,*" he said with a strong German accent. "Something for the burn."

And then, as embarrassed as he'd ever been, he indicated the red patch on his head.

Seeing the raw skin, Concepción pressed her lips together. It must have been very painful if he felt the need to speak to her in person. She'd burned herself before, though not from the sun—for her skin had always protected her from the onslaught of its rays—but from the stove; she knew what she had to do.

She took a cotton cloth, soaked it in vinegar, and unceremoniously placed it on his head. Maximilian, his regal dignity wounded—he'd expected her to give him an ointment or cream that he could apply in the privacy of his room—tried to take it off, but without opening her mouth she let out a reptilian noise through her teeth.

"*Chss!*"

And she replaced the damp cloth, exerting gentle pressure with her hands on the imperial head.

Like a small child whose mother was trying to make him take his medicine, the emperor surrendered, charmed by her interdental hissing sound. Because, even if the girl hadn't spoken, the noise betrayed a vibrant voice full of life. Maximilian imagined a newly tuned musical instrument. *A voice,* he thought, *full of exciting promises. The voice of a siren.*

They remained this way for a couple of seconds: him completely still, not daring to move, and her crowning him with a cloth. Maximilian tried to understand what had suddenly made him relax, and he couldn't decide whether the peace he felt came from the relief of the cloth drawing the heat from his body, or from contemplating a woman in such close proximity. Normally he felt uncomfortable among women. Ever since he'd seen a painting of the naked slaves of Smyrna, being near them had unsettled him. But this girl was different. She had none of the malice of ladies of the court, who displayed an insipid and absurd flirtatiousness. Though she was very pretty, she didn't seem to know it; Maximilian had never seen such black hair or such plump lips. A gust of wind carried past her to him, and Maximilian could smell her. She smelled different: she gave off different humors than European women. She didn't smell sour, or of fresh onion or garlic, but of slowly kneaded maize.

Concepción suspected that, if she touched the emperor, her fingers would sink into his white skin. The man seemed soft as masa, and she was tempted to pinch him to see if she could mold his flesh. She had never seen skin like his. She'd never seen a body unaccustomed to physical exercise and working the land. A body that had never known the pleasure of climbing a tree or crossing a river. A static body that longed to feel. She'd never seen a person who was almost transparent.

After a time without exchanging a word, Maximilian took the girl's hands in his and lowered them slowly, then he took the vinegary cloth and put it between their hands, pressing them together. They said nothing, but looked at each other. Not knowing the protocol and unsure what to do, Concepción quickly withdrew and left the room. Maximilian watched her walk away, and seeing her, he thought she moved like a butterfly. A butterfly that he didn't have in his precious collection.

49

Constanza knew Carlota was leaving for Yucatán because Philippe told her one afternoon while he was teaching her the *passé composé*. Between lessons, Philippe—who wasn't usually talkative—tried to strike up conversations with Constanza. It was subtle at first, asking her about her parents. While surprised, she replied without going into detail. Then she asked him about his childhood, and he told her of the cave and Mr. Walton. And eventually, having reached a tacit confidentiality agreement, they became accustomed to these moments of intimacy when they felt they could speak freely. Constanza did so with the full intention of obtaining information on the Belgian troops and the colonel, though she rarely managed to. Philippe liked to ask her about more mundane things, such as how she felt being a lady of the court; he asked her about her life outside Chapultepec, and seemed genuinely curious. She gradually gave in, like dough that has been allowed to stand for long enough; however, she had her reservations. She took care not to say too much or reveal her vulnerabilities, which in her mind were quite numerous. Nonetheless, she liked sharing herself with Philippe. After all, that was what she'd wanted from the day she laid eyes on him. She listened to him speak with his foreign accent, and her heart laughed. If he'd spoken to her on the day they met like he did now, she would've fallen at his feet; but just as water turns to ice, since she realized she was at court not to love a man but to defend her country, Constanza had turned cold at incredible speed. At night, she locked herself in her room on the first floor of Chapultepec and, instead of dreaming about how to seduce a lover, she invented codes to send hidden messages to her brother.

Philippe, on the other hand, arrived in bed and, when he closed his eyes, dreamed of an amalgam of women who, like witches or sorceresses, changed form with each kiss, from one woman to another. He kissed Constanza, he kissed Carlota, he kissed Famke, and he made love to them all with the same vigor.

"Yucatán? That will be a very long journey!" she said when Philippe asked her if she knew about the expedition the empress was about to embark on.

"It's for reconnaissance. You know, to explore her dominions."

"Will the emperor go?"

"No. He'll stay here, for a change."

They looked at each other, trying not to give anything away.

"I suppose I'll be accompanying her."

"I will, too."

"You will?"

"Colonel Van der Smissen will be going. And I don't think he'll go alone."

Eureka, thought Constanza.

"Why isn't the emperor going?"

"I believe he wants to take care of the finances. The coffers are not as full as they should be. From what I hear, he wants to speak to the new minister who just arrived from France."

"Ah, yes. Langlais."

"That's him."

"And how do you know all this?"

"Have you heard what they say about the walls having ears?"

"Yes," said Constanza with a half smile.

"Well, everyone here treats me like a wall."

They certainly do! thought Constanza.

Despite the fact that such a journey would be extremely dangerous as well as exhausting, she was delighted at the idea of traveling around the republic—as she secretly called it—if a man like Philippe was part of the expedition.

Philippe didn't realize that Constanza was feigning ignorance to encourage him to talk. She knew a lot more than the Belgian suspected: for instance, that Maximilian was delighted to send the empress away for at least fifty days. The emperor was beginning to hear comments about what a good governor she was, and he often came off worse in the comparisons. He was proud that, on his command, Carlota was no longer allowed to appear before the council of ministers without being summoned, nor could she enter Maximilian's office without his express invitation. The emperor was colder than ever toward her. Though Carlota pretended not to care, Constanza noticed that she now rode alone more than usual, as if deciding to distance herself from a court where, increasingly, she was hamstrung. She also knew—because Salvador had told her—that under the law, the Juarista government's tenure had ended in October 1865, and Benito Juárez, going against the constitution and with several Liberales opposing him, had been reelected. Maximilian saw a crack in President Juárez's questionable legitimacy, and he wasn't prepared to let such an opportunity pass by.

He certainly wouldn't leave the city in such a situation. He preferred to send the empress away and enjoy his solitude in more pleasant company.

Carlota and her entourage, made up of her closest ladies-in-waiting, Manuelita and Constanza; a couple of ministers; Van der Smissen and Philippe; and a detachment of Belgian soldiers; plus a few members of the court such as a chaplain and a physician, left for Yucatán early one November morning. Five carriages headed toward Veracruz through mud and calamities that made them fear the worst; some of them ran off the road and had to be rescued, fortunately without casualties. Constanza struggled with the temperatures and complained bitterly.

"I can't stand this heat with these dresses on, Manuelita. The embroidery's digging into my neck."

"Oh, be quiet, girl, and fan yourself. What I can't stand is the dust."

"Have you seen the empress? She's traveling in a closed carriage and even then she looks like a miller's wife!"

"Be quiet, girl!" Manuelita scolded her. And then, after looking at her again, she said, "Don't we all look like that."

Arriving in Orizaba, they were met with a gusty northerly wind that forced them to wait two days before continuing the journey. They stayed in the home of a Conservative family that had supported them from the moment the monarchs set foot in Mexico, the Bringases.

"Your Majesty! Welcome to our humble abode," Sra. Bringas said when she received them.

Constanza looked around: the *humble abode* was a hacienda where horses could gallop, and anything from maize to coffee could be grown. But above all, what caught her attention was the familiarity with which the señora spoke to Carlota, as if they had been friends all their lives; it infuriated Manuelita, who tried without success to compete for the empress's attention. But Carlota, much more relaxed than she had been in Chapultepec, barely noticed. She'd been wanting a change of scenery for a while, though she hadn't admitted it to anybody.

Philippe noticed with some displeasure that Colonel Van der Smissen spent a lot of time with Carlota. They walked in the garden for long periods, and on occasion, out of the corner of his eye, he thought he saw the colonel take the empress's hand; however, the movement was so fleeting that Philippe couldn't be sure if he'd imagined it.

Constanza, however, was in no doubt. She was very aware that there was a spark between them, masked by the formality of their roles, but nonetheless a spark. Deep down, she fervently hoped Carlota would dare to love, or at least allow herself to be loved, by someone, for it was clear that if she waited for the emperor, she would grow old without experiencing any pleasures beyond contemplating the archduke's portrait on the wall.

At Orizaba, they boarded a ship and began the crossing to the Yucatán Peninsula, which, in the words of the empress herself, proved to be the worst voyage of her life. And it must have been, because when she came out of her cabin, she looked like a poor sick bird. But with her feet on dry land, the sun on her face, and the innocence of the people she encountered, before long Carlota felt that it had been worth the journey. Compared to Mexico City, Mérida was beautiful, tranquil, peaceful. The people seemed so honest and kind that, moved, one afternoon she said to Constanza, "This place restores one's faith in humankind."

Carlota wasn't there just to discover the virtues of those lands. She had secret instructions from Maximilian, who was aware of the separatist movement that had existed in the state since 1839; Carlota was there to promote the laws with which they would be compensated should they express their full support for the empire. There was talk of establishing a viceroyalty under the supervision of Almonte; they wanted to keep him busy away from the court. The reception that the people of Yucatán offered the imperial delegation worried Constanza. It was clear they were happy with the visit; people unhitched their horses from their carriages to ride alongside Carlota's calash, greeting her with a shower of petals. They were grateful that a leader had finally come to them after being left so long on the margins. They threw flowers from the balconies, and the church bells rang as they passed.

Carlota was mesmerized. For the first time since she had arrived in Mexico, she felt like an empress. She visited churches, but when she saw the Mayan ruins of Uxmal, her wonder was such that she immediately gave instructions to create a museum there.

"I want part of the budget to be allotted to protect and preserve these ruins," she said to one of her ministers. "And see to it also that laws are enacted to prevent pre-Hispanic artifacts from being exported."

The reply to everything was "Yes, Your Majesty."

She attended presentations at schools, where the children showered her with gifts, covered in seashells, that they had made themselves or that local artisans had crafted. She toured the south with a smile on her lips; from Sacalum to Calkiní—where they gave her palm-fiber hats—and in the villages, instead of choosing grand accommodations, she stayed in humble places that helped her connect with the people. She wore simple clothes, her only embellishment the flowers she wore on her head. In the eyes of many, including Philippe, she didn't need anything else to look regal. She exuded a sense of peace, as if she were finally where she was meant to be.

"I've rarely seen enthusiasm as sincere as I have seen today," she would say in her speeches. "You've given me your hearts; now receive mine."

Despite that, people whispered behind her back. If Carlota had been able to hear, she would have shuddered with rage at some of the ladies whispering, *Poor girl, so young, so lovely, yet barren; God gives and God takes away, because as you can see, she has everything in life, but she can't have children; I wouldn't trade places with her for anything in the world, I'd rather have my family,* and endless other expressions of pity based on the rumors. And why wouldn't they believe it, if the emperor had been forced to adopt Iturbide's grandchildren to ensure heirs to the throne?

Carlota, unaware of the gossip, carried out her duties with the utmost diplomacy, not just because she was educated and trained to do so, but because the truth was, she hadn't been so happy in a long time. She felt useful again, of value. The wheels of her life were turning again, driving her forward. She didn't stop for a moment. She was in and out of the carriage, traveling with barely time to rest, but Carlota was grateful for the activity after months of the political immobility to which Maximilian had subjected her.

But there is a limit to everything.

And it was betrayal that drove her to that limit.

Constanza, always at her side, thought the time had come to take the bull by the horns. Seeing how Carlota had been received in Yucatán made her think the empire was gaining ground. She had to do something. For Mexico. For Juárez. Her brother, Modesto, her mother . . . they were right. The empire, however good its intentions were, was madness. It couldn't go on.

One day when Carlota's face was the picture of exhaustion, Constanza took the opportunity to sow some seeds.

"Your Majesty, you should rest a little."

"I can't, Constanza."

"Of course you can, Majesty—"

"I can't!" yelled Carlota. And then, realizing she'd lost her decorum, she tried to explain herself. As she did so, Constanza could see the same ghosts that haunted Chapultepec emerge. "I'm a childless woman. I have nothing else to do."

In a low voice, Constanza said, "Don't be so hard on yourself, Majesty, you will have a child one day. The emperor—"

"The emperor is busy in Cuernavaca," Carlota cut in. "He always succumbs there. He succumbed there yesterday, and he will succumb there tomorrow."

Constanza didn't understand.

"Pardon, Majesty?"

Carlota did not answer, she simply lowered her head, as humiliated as a fighting bull about to receive the coup de grâce.

"Max doesn't love me. He doesn't desire me. He prefers the flesh of a common servant woman to my regal hands. She's very pretty."

Constanza fell silent, incapable of saying anything. She knew the pain of deceit was like no other pain. She had noticed that the emperor was spending a great deal of time in Cuernavaca, where he often went to escape affairs of state. So the empress had good reason, she thought, to be taciturn, and to take long walks with Colonel Van der Smissen by the lake. Good reason, also, to cry.

After a pause, Carlota went on.

"So . . . how could *I* give the emperor children?"

They both knew exactly what she meant. How, if Carlota had never been with a man?

Then, with remorse in her throat, Constanza plucked up her courage and heard herself saying something unthinkable to an apostolic Roman Catholic empress.

"Your Majesty, in Mexico . . . in Mexico we have remedies for your problem."

"Remedies?"

"Unorthodox ones, Majesty."

Carlota opened her eyes wide.

"You mean witchcraft?"

"Some might call it that. I prefer to call it white magic."

"White magic?"

Constanza decided to see it through.

"Yes, Majesty. Don't look at me like that, nothing diabolical . . . Just herbalism with a little faith."

"Constanza," Carlota said very seriously, "I don't need herbs; what I need is a man to lift my skirts." Carlota's expression was very sad. She'd never felt so humiliated before. But she had opened up her heart, and now she didn't want to close it. "Is there a man who will love me one day, Constanza?"

And Constanza, sensing that Providence was serving her the opportunity on a silver plate, said, "The herbs I have help with that, too, Your Majesty."

And as they sat in silence trying to read each other's thoughts, Van der Smissen knocked on the door and asked to come in.

"What is it, Colonel?" Carlota asked with a frown.

"The carriage is ready to take us to the gala dinner, Your Majesty."

"Thank you. We'll be right there."

When Van der Smissen left, Constanza noticed a look of melancholy in Carlota's face.

"You know," she said to Constanza, "he reminds me of my father."

And then she stood and gave the order to set off.

They arrived in Mérida, where the city's dignitaries were hosting a dinner in their honor. Given how happy the journey had been and the countless expressions of affection from the people, Carlota thought it would be full of Yucatecan figures. But once again, as at La Scala in Milan, she found that the event was attended by not even half of those invited.

Van der Smissen sat to Carlota's right and could see displeasure and a certain nervousness in her, as if all her joy had suddenly vanished again.

"They probably didn't receive the invitation in time," Van der Smissen said in an attempt to comfort her.

In answer, Carlota gave him a sad look. She picked up her glass, but before putting it to her lips, she hesitated: terror struck her in the face.

"What is it, Majesty?"

For a fraction of a second, Van der Smissen thought he saw terror in her eyes, as if she'd just seen the devil.

"What's the matter, Carlota?" he said less formally.

And hearing her name, the crazed look faded.

"It's nothing, Alfred," she said. "I must be tired."

And she drank.

It was true, she was exhausted. They'd been traveling for weeks, and despite her youth, the journey was taking its toll. She slept poorly, and after tasting dishes she was unaccustomed to—such as *relleno negro* or *dulce de zapote*—she was beginning to suffer from stomach pains. In place of innards, she felt like she had snakes writhing inside her. To escape her worries, she distracted herself by saying extremely long prayers in which she asked for strength of spirit and body. But she was weak. She thought of Maximilian, of the fact that he also suffered from constant diarrhea and severe stomach cramps, and felt for him. *If he feels like this all the time,* she thought, *I don't know how he can take two steps forward.* But just as he found strength in his weakness, she would, too.

Van der Smissen started to worry about the empress's health. Though she never shirked her religious obligations, he'd never seen her behave so devoutly: now she prayed almost obsessively. She spoke a lot about God and about the devil. He thought Carlota needed to rest before she had a nervous breakdown. But every dawn the empress washed, dressed, and rushed out to begin her day. The most important thing was duty, just as her father had taught her.

It wasn't just Van der Smissen who worried about her. Philippe watched her from the shadows, silent. Despite how happy and excited she seemed when she attended the official ceremonies, he feared something bad was about to happen to her. He felt again the anguish he'd felt as a child, when his little brother, Noah, had begun to cough up blood in the cave. He had to do something. Carlota wasn't well. She seemed increasingly absent, as if the light in her eyes was suddenly going out and plunging her into darkness.

"You must get word to the emperor," a worried Philippe said to Constanza after the dinner.

"Are you insane?"

"The empress needs rest, Constanza, they're killing her with all this work. The pace has been frantic for weeks. She'll never let up of her own accord."

"And since when have you been so concerned about the empress's health?"

"Since always. It's my duty."

"Your duty . . ."

Philippe stopped himself from looking at the ground in an effort to hold her gaze, but it was too late. Constanza knew then that Philippe had feelings for the empress. He was an open book. What a fool! How had she not seen it before? Philippe had just bared himself in front of her without realizing it. Nonetheless, Constanza gave nothing away.

"And how do you expect me to reach the emperor?"

Philippe hesitated. Seeing how close Carlota was to her ladies, he'd presumed they also had direct access to Maximilian.

"I can't communicate with him," she said. "Someone more trusted has to tell him." And then Constanza tipped over the first domino. "Get the colonel to do it."

"Van der Smissen?"

"Who else? Haven't you noticed how he looks at her? And what's more . . . how she looks at him?"

Philippe felt a stab in his stomach.

"Yes, I've noticed," he said, swallowing his pride. "But you tell him."

"And why would he listen to me?"

"Because you always get what you want."

Constanza suppressed a smile.

"I'll see what I can do."

Philippe didn't have to try hard to persuade Constanza. It was the moment she'd been waiting for; at last, she'd found a way to approach the colonel. And that was a stroke of luck.

Nor did Constanza have to try hard to persuade the colonel. When she requested an audience with him, he'd already sent a letter to the capital to ask the emperor to catch up with the empress in San Martín Texmelucan. She entered a temporary office where the colonel had arranged an austere pecan desk, a small bookshelf, and a pair of chairs; when she sat, Constanza smelled damp earth in the air.

"Thank you for your information, Constance, but I notified the emperor a couple of days ago."

"Oh!" said Constanza. "So you agree it would be imprudent to subject the empress to more exertion."

"You'd have to be blind not to see it."

"Forgive me for being so bold as to trouble you with this, Colonel. You understand that I'm concerned about the empress. I presumed I could come to you."

"*Mais oui.* You did the right thing, mademoiselle."

"And if you will permit me an indiscreet question . . . Why will the emperor meet her in San Martín? Are we not returning to Mexico City?"

"Evidently not. We'll cross Lake Chalco and from there we'll travel to Xochimilco before heading to Cuernavaca."

"Cuernavaca?"

"The emperor has decided to rest there. There's a house with a beautiful garden. It's what the empress needs now, given the circumstances." And then, almost without being aware of it, he heard himself thinking out loud. "Poor Carlota," he murmured. He looked at Constanza, who observed cautiously with an expressionless face. But she thought the same.

Van der Smissen took two steps to the little table that functioned as a bar and poured himself a glass of port.

"*Voulez-vous?*" he said, offering her a glass.

"*Non, merci, monsieur,*" she replied.

Though she was the picture of discretion, Constanza hadn't missed anything. Her heart raced. She hadn't thought the conversation with the colonel would prove so fruitful; she decided to squeeze a little harder. She could tell when somebody wanted to talk, and the colonel was hopping like a pumpkin seed on a hot plate.

"What is most concerning, Colonel, the empress's health or the state of the country?"

Van der Smissen tugged on his moustache and took a sip of his port.

"All of it, mademoiselle, all of it. The French marshal says everything is going well, but Juárez remains at large."

Thank God, thought Constanza. "Then there's no reason to be alarmed."

"Nonsense!" he yelled. "The war seems to be indefinite, there are guerrilla attacks daily, but Bazaine claims he's pacifying the country . . ."

He looked at his half-empty glass. Constanza hurried to pour him more port.

"But the emperor is gaining more control over the situation," she suggested.

"What he has is more palaces and theaters," the colonel said with disdain. "If he can't survive by his own means, this empire won't survive. Some empire . . . sustained at bayonet point. This is suicide."

Constanza knew Van der Smissen would regret this conversation the next day. She decided to change the subject.

"The empress is a remarkable sovereign," she was bold enough to say.

He gave her a serious look. He knew she was referring not to the monarch but to the woman.

"Yes. Yes, she is," he said.

"And she feels very alone."

Van der Smissen's gaze turned so severe that Constanza blushed.

"You may leave now, mademoiselle."

Walking backward to avoid turning away from him, Constanza left the room.

50

It was Concepción who seduced the emperor, not the other way around. He wouldn't have known what to do, but she took it upon herself to be the nest where the poor bird could seek refuge. Not even Maximilian himself was aware of it until Concepción had lured him in. It wasn't that the emperor was virility on legs. He had many defects: he had bad teeth, his breath stank owing to various digestive problems, he had almost no hair on his head—which he tried to make up for with his copious beard—and he was old enough to be her father. But there was something about him that aroused Concepción's curiosity; for the first time in her life, she sensed she could be with a gentle man, a man who wouldn't hurt her when he penetrated her. She would be the one who set the rhythm, she would take the lead. And the idea of the soft love of a gentleman instead of the rough love of a crude gardener—a tender, nonviolent love—was a powerful aphrodisiac.

He must've seen it coming without resistance, because all of a sudden, visiting the Cuernavaca garden became a vice, and for the first time he didn't seem as interested in the plants. The fact was, Maximilian was going through a difficult time and—she believed—she could fill the void inside him.

Schertzenlechner, his beloved, the love of his life, had left an abyss of disillusionment in his heart.

It began when rumors of betrayal reached him. One of his closest men had passed on secret information to ministers about the family pact.

"We suspect Schertzenlechner," everyone said to him. And Maximilian, naturally, refused to believe it.

It couldn't be him. Anyone but him. But the evidence was irrefutable. One by one, they placed documents on his desk that proved his disloyalty. A friend, whom he not only paid as well as the best valet in Vienna, but who also received the priceless currency of his heart. After drinking almost an entire bottle of wine, he called him into his office.

"How could you betray me, Sebastian, when I gave you everything?"

"What're you talking about?" his valet replied. And then, after making sure they were alone, Sebastian reached to caress his beard. Maximilian gently pushed his hand away.

Schertzenlechner was surprised. Never in all the time they'd spent together, which was many years, had Maximilian rejected one of his caresses.

In response, Maximilian pushed the documents at him that proved he'd been leaking information about the secret letter of protest he'd written traveling to Mexico onboard the *Novara*.

"Max, you don't believe that I—"

"I want your resignation."

The men held each other's gaze. They knew one another well enough to tell when words weren't needed.

"So, that's it? This is how it ends?"

"You betrayed me, Sebastian. How could you?" A knot formed in his throat.

And then, as he expected Schertzenlechner to plead with him, to get on his knees and beg him for forgiveness, kiss him, remind him of all they'd been through and tell him to think carefully about it, that they had so much history together, Sebastian struck.

"If you dismiss me, I'll publish information about us."

Maximilian went pale, not because of the possibility of being outed, but because of the coldness with which his love had just threatened him.

Just then Charles de Bombelles, his friend and accomplice since childhood, burst into the office with better timing than Zeus himself pouring down on Danaë in the form of golden rain. Hearing Schertzenlechner's threat, his blood boiled.

"You must imprison him, Your Majesty," he suggested with fury and some pleasure.

"No. Not prison," said Max, whose heart was softer than cigarette paper. "Send him back to Europe."

"What are you talking about, Majesty?" Bombelles complained.

"You heard me. Send him back to Lokrum."

Schertzenlechner smiled as he left the office. He knew Maximilian wouldn't dare touch him, not for punishment, at any rate.

And while the decision to send him back with all expenses paid and a lifetime pension wasn't popular, everyone at court was relieved to be rid of not only a spy but also the emperor's lover.

Nonetheless, Maximilian found enough courage and love inside him to write him a farewell letter.

> *Dear Sebastian,*
> *Since you are not coming to Chapultepec, I must pick up a pen to wish you a safe journey and to tell you that, though nobody in this world, not in any of the diverse situations I have lived through, has ever tortured me as profoundly and as harshly as you, nor caused me so much pain, I nevertheless forgive you with all my heart and all my soul. May God reward you and give you the peace you were unable to find by my side. I will remember you in my daily prayers.*
> *Maximilian*

In the midst of this grief, Concepción entered the stage, fresh as moist clay, letting the earth cover her toes. While he wandered the garden, she approached him barefooted, and with sincere kindness she handed him a straw hat with which to cover his head; she smiled at him, and he thought he saw a world of tenderness in her eyes. Another day, while he was writing poems in the garden, she approached again and, like Mary Magdalene with Christ, knelt, took off his shoes, and washed his feet with a pitcher of cool water. And so each time she approached him she showed, without saying anything, an amorous demeanor that completely ignored all the rules of etiquette. He experienced something he'd never felt with anyone. It wasn't love, for he believed he knew what that was and didn't recognize it now. It was more like curiosity, mystery, taboo. He'd always been attracted to forbidden waters, and all at once the girl in the garden—the pretty Indian, as he called her in his thoughts—began to personify all of this. She was nothing like the ladies of the court. If he wanted, he could have any of them with a snap of his fingers. He'd never had the urge. Concepción went from being the gardener's wife to a window through which he gazed at the prohibited again. And when the time came, she knew how to welcome him into dark, sturdy arms, which he was unable to resist, while Ignacio, who knew about their love affair, gave himself over to drinking in his room, inconsolable. He understood that the owners of the house had *droit de seigneur*, and he wasn't about to confront the emperor of Mexico. He was well aware of the girl's charms, and as much as his pride was wounded, he had to learn to share her.

51

Carlota was supervising preparations to return to Chapultepec when Constanza brought her the letter containing the terrible news. She opened it, read it, and immediately fainted. Constanza had to hold her to keep her from falling flat on the stone floor.

"Majesty . . . help!" she yelled while she tried to support her in her arms. The rest of the ladies soon arrived.

"What is it?" asked an alarmed Manuelita.

"I don't know. She read the letter and fainted."

Manuelita del Barrio picked up the correspondence, reading to herself silently.

"Mary, Mother of God! Her father has died. King Leopold . . ."

The ladies all crossed themselves in unison.

Constanza rushed out of the room and said to Philippe, "Call for the emperor, quick."

Philippe ran off, worried.

King Leopold I, the empress's father, had died in Brussels a month earlier from complications with kidney stones. Though he'd suffered from stones for some time, Carlota had still expected him to live for many more years. He wasn't a man whom death stalked closely.

Three months of official mourning were proclaimed in Mexico City, where the emperor and empress went with grieving souls: her for her loss and him for his separation from Concepción. But it was Carlota's sorrow that resounded most loudly in the carriage. The empress secretly blamed herself for being so far away. She reproached herself for not being by his side to receive his final blessing, the blessing of the man she loved so much. She'd always considered him the most loving of fathers. Her only comfort was that she'd received his blessing in England before leaving. She looked at Maximilian, the prince who'd turned into a frog, and tried to justify her actions: he was the cause of her distance. She was far away to be with the man to whom he had given her—at her own insistence—to settle in a country whose throne her father had wanted them to accept. It consoled her to think that, finally, he would be reunited with her mother, but at the same time, the bereavement was crushing her whole.

Black ribbons were hung from windows all over the country, subjects sent heartfelt letters expressing universal sorrow, the imperial flag was flown at half-mast, and a protocol was established to receive the condolences of the diplomatic corps, government officials, and members of the French army. And while Carlota was grateful for the demonstrations of respect and affection, she didn't personally receive anyone. She shut herself in her room, and no matter how many times they asked her to receive those offering their sympathies, she replied, *Have them sign the book.* She was referring to the visitors' book, in which everyone who passed through Chapultepec to commiserate with the empress could leave their name.

Maximilian tried to show her affection in this painful time, but it was too late: between them there remained only camaraderie. By now, they knew they didn't love each other, and they didn't pretend not to know. They were colleagues, invested with rank and responsibilities to which they devoted themselves with stoicism, but neither of them pretended there was any sentimental bond between them. Curiously, once they understood this, their souls were freed. They accompanied each other, supported each other at difficult times, even asked each other for advice, each of them listening to the other. But beyond that, nothing. They became mother and son, brother and sister, and when it came to pleasure and love, it was better to say nothing; that way the disappointment hurt less.

The letters of condolence arrived by the sacksful. Some they read and others they didn't, depending on the sender. One of the letters that Carlota read was from her governess the Countess of Hulst, who lived in France. The empress had agreed to come out of her room for a few minutes, and she was playing a somber piece on the piano under the watchful eye of Constanza when Manuelita appeared, morose from having to dress all in black, to deliver the letter. Since Carlota had fainted at the news of her father's death, nobody gave letters to her alone anymore. Carlota saw who the sender was and seemed cheered.

"Oh! My beloved countess!"

Manuelita breathed more easily when she saw that the letter didn't seem to carry bad news. Carlota read in silence, and sighing now and again, leaned back in her armchair.

When she'd finished, she said, "What a pessimistic woman! I love her, but how could she be so negative? She always sees the glass half empty."

"Who, Your Majesty?" asked Constanza, pretending to embroider a handkerchief, silently glad that the empress had stopped playing the piano so melancholically.

"The Countess of Hulst, my old governess. She never lets up: she continues to insist that being here is suicide, that I should return to Miramare."

She'd always opposed the young princess embarking on her Mexican adventure. She'd tried to dissuade her a thousand times, and a thousand times Carlota argued with her in the hope she would see her error. The woman never ceased in her efforts and, even now, as she offered her condolences to the girl—now a woman—whom she'd helped raise after her mother had died, she came back with the same tedious refrain. That being there was madness, that she should return, that she would only find death and dishonor.

Constanza pretended to disagree, but deep down she was relieved to find that some people in France thought like the Mexican Liberales. *How foolish can a person be?*

"Get me paper and ink, Constanza. I'm going to reply."

Constanza stood and brought it to her.

"I'll retire to my rooms," Carlota said.

"But Majesty, it does you good to leave your bedchamber. Don't lock yourself away again like last week."

"What a fusspot you are, Manuelita. Pain likes seclusion," she answered.

As soon as she had left, Constanza threw her embroidery on the chair; if there was one thing she hated, it was sewing.

"I swear," Manuelita said to her. "Sometimes I feel like shaking that woman."

And though Constanza wanted to laugh at the comment, she pretended to be offended.

"Show some respect for the empress, Sra. Del Barrio."

And then she left to see what she could hear around the court.

The atmosphere was heated. People were saying that France was going to withdraw its troops, that the end was near. The situation was spiraling out of control. The Confederate general Robert E. Lee had surrendered in the United States, and Leopold I's death filled the monarchs with pain and sorrow, not just because they'd lost a great sponsor of the empire who did the impossible to ensure that his son-in-law's throne was recognized in Europe—he had even interceded with Queen Victoria to persuade her to send an ambassador to Mexico so that the empire had the diplomatic recognition of the British—but because when he died, the Belgian Crown passed to his son, Leopold II.

Leopold II never had any fondness for his sister. Ever since they were children, he'd enjoyed tormenting her, and he did all he could to enact laws to strip power from princesses. To him, women were good for very little and a hindrance, especially women with power. These had to be watched very closely. He'd always considered the Mexican adventure to be absurd, and he preferred not to embroil himself in it: he had no interest in entering into arguments with the United States or in having an empress sister on a French throne.

Even so, following the royal protocol, he sent an emissary to Mexico to make the news of Leopold I's death—and his ascension to the throne—official. But Maximilian had other plans.

"What do you mean you won't receive him?" said Bombelles. "Protocol requires that you do; he's a king's emissary to a foreign emperor married to his only sister."

"Well, he should've thought of that when he decided not to send any more Belgian volunteers."

"You can't insult him like this, Max."

"Of course I can. Leopold also wants to take control of Carlota's inheritance from her father. Not on any account. Say that I'm indisposed in Cuernavaca."

And however much his advisers insisted, Maximilian didn't give in; it was Carlota who received the emissary in Chapultepec, and it was she who bid him farewell when, his pride wounded and commiserating with the empress for her husband's lack of political refinement, he left for Europe without being received by the emperor.

The delegation set off in the direction of Puebla. From inside the carriage, now and again the emissary peered through the dust-covered window, trying to take in the snowcapped volcanoes rising above the green valley.

Frustrated because he couldn't see much through the small window, he asked the coachman, "Excuse me, sir, do you mind if I travel with you?"

A little surprised, he gestured with his head.

"Oh, I'm most grateful."

For the rest of the journey the two men talked, distracted by the trees, feeling the pure air beat against their faces, glad because the conversation made the ride less tedious. The coachman, however, looked from side to side warily.

"What is it?" the emissary asked.

"It's just that there should've been a French army escort, and it hasn't arrived."

"Shall we wait?"

"I don't know. It's not good to stay still for long before we reach the coast. This area's full of *bandidos*."

"In that case, we'd better continue, don't you think?"

The man hesitated. There wasn't a single soul near them.

"Yes, we'd better."

As they passed Río Frío, a band of outlaws attacked. The emissary was shot in the head, and the rest of the delegation were seriously injured.

"But who were they?" the survivors asked anxiously. "Thieves?"

"No, they must have been Juárez's troops, because they didn't steal anything."

Though Maximilian sent his personal physician to attend to the wounded, nothing could be done for Leopold II's emissary. He died on the spot.

When the king heard the news, he flew into a rage, not at the emissary's death—though undoubtedly that bothered him—but at his brother-in-law's lack of etiquette. So proper when it came to dancing waltzes and so foolish when it came to political dealings.

"Wretched good-for-nothing," he murmured when they told him they hadn't been received. "I'm not surprised he's banished from every land he sets foot on." Then he tore the letter in half and said to himself, "Maximilian just signed his death warrant. He won't be receiving any more help from Belgium, not for anything." And pounding the desk with his fist, he yelled, "Not for anything!"

In her room, the empress was thinking about her reply to the Countess of Hulst. She wanted to stay calm and avoid being impertinent with a kind woman of an advanced age who, though she often questioned Carlota's decisions, did so only out of the great affection she professed for her.

She sat down and, accustomed as she was to writing long letters, after thanking her for the letter she had received, her condolences, and her other courtesies, went straight to the heart of the matter:

Allow me to correct you on a few points, for I sense your despair at the matter at hand. Our task, which you judge so severely and that you consider almost impossible, is not so unattainable. Only the heavens know what will happen, but if we fail, it will be no fault of our own. Don't give too much credence to what you hear in our beloved France; I shall not try to understand the reasons for the recent stir about the Mexico expedition. The "kingdom's glory" has been quite suddenly upset by unexpected obstacles unknown there, at great cost in money and soldiers. It remains what it has always been: an audacious and difficult idea; but what merit can there be without risk?

Carlota smiled. She liked the tone she was achieving in the letter. She continued.

This expedition has founded an empire that is not just an illusion.

She was about to underline *empire*, but changed her mind and went on.

Perhaps all you see is ambition (of which the whole world accuses me), but it was not me who was the motive for our journey to Mexico. Nor will I be the motive for those who wish to reembark because there are a few clouds on the horizon or the coast is not clear.

Carlota dipped her pen in the ink. She took a deep breath. She was beginning to feel energy build inside her, as if with each line, with each word, she was reinforcing her oath as a sovereign, as if once again feeling the pride and dignity they invested in her on the day of her coronation in the city's cathedral. She felt like an empress again. She remembered how alone she'd felt at Miramare, how boring her life would have been had Mexico not presented itself as a font of opportunity; she remembered how much she'd sacrificed for a country that was not her own. She was so far away and yet so near; she had devoted herself body and soul to a common good greater than her own, out of duty. Thanks to Mexico she'd learned how to live.

And having filled her heart with this spirit, she wrote:

> *Put yourself in my place and ask yourself if life at Miramare was better than life in Mexico. No, a hundred times, no. I prefer a station that requires activity and duties, even difficulties, to contemplating the sea until the age of seventy . . .*

She slowly breathed out. At last, she'd said it. She had gotten it off her chest. She had wanted to shout it from the rooftops for so long. She felt freer, lighter. Her soul was a feather floating in the air. She paused for a few seconds before continuing.

> *This is what I have left behind and this is what I have acquired, and now draw a veil over it and do not be surprised that I love Mexico. Farewell, dear Countess.*
>   *With affection,*
>   *Carlota*

She reread the letter and folded it in half, then she lay on the bed, looking up at the ceiling with sadness in her soul. Without her knowing why, tears began to cascade down her face, until she slept.

52

In Maximilian's words, Cuernavaca was an earthly paradise, and he had no qualms about saying so in a letter to Carlota. He described the divine plain of a broad valley stretching in the distance like a mantle of gold, the mountains rising up one after the other in whimsical forms, tinged with the most marvelous colors, from pinks to purples and violets. Some were fragmented like the rocks on the Sicilian coast, others were covered in green like the Swiss mountains, and behind it all, standing out against the dark-blue sky, were the gigantic snow-covered volcanoes. All of the seasons of the year coexisted there because there were none, reminding him of Italy's forgiving May climate. *The city of eternal spring*, it was called. Such a landscape was worth fighting for. Carlota, no longer captivated by her husband's poetic spirit, replied without much interest.

> *I'm glad you are happy in your paradise. For me, there is no longer a paradise on earth.*

The empire's end was at their heels. Maximilian was receiving letters from Napoleon III telling him that, despite his promises to never abandon him, he would have no choice but to do so. The money was running out, and the troops couldn't be sustained. After many negotiations, Bazaine agreed to pay the Belgians and Austrians, but not the

Mexicans. There wasn't enough money even for uniforms. Maximilian sent emissaries to Paris to intercede with Napoleon III and Eugénie, but they grew increasingly disenchanted.

"Perhaps the idea to create the empire was not altogether good," Eugénie said, doing a volte-face. "It's sucking us dry! What do they expect? For France to pay for the soldiers' every last button? Tell them it's impossible. Our duty is to France."

Napoleon listened to his wife, wanting to wring her neck.

"So now the empire's a bad idea? At what moment did it go from being the most glorious page in modern history to being a bad idea, Eugénie?"

"The moment Maximilian became incapable of sustaining himself, of course."

And though his wife's shift of opinion annoyed him, he recognized that there was truth in what she was saying. Maximilian had spent a year and a half drafting utopian laws instead of governing, and time was bearing down on them and bringing with it the prospect of war with Prussia.

It wasn't just France whose loyalty was in doubt. Austria, under pressure from the United States, put off the embarkation of volunteers who were supposed to depart for Mexico.

"Faithless cowards!" complained Maximilian when he heard the news.

But when everything turned sour, he went to Cuernavaca, where even the shadows glowed with their own radiance. If they could have seen it in Europe, he would have been the envy of any Hungarian, with his wavy beard down to his chest and a red moustache that covered his bad teeth. If they could see how he drove wild horses like a ranchero and heard his good command of Spanish. He lived as if he'd never lived any other way, because when everyone else turned away, Concepción displayed a naïve and innocent affection, devoid of any political interest, that filled him with tenderness. Nobody had ever looked at him with such clear eyes. Nobody—not even Carlota or Schertzenlechner—had come to him in search of the man; they were always looking for the archduke, the emperor, but never Maximilian.

And for him, this was glorious.

Meanwhile, in Mexico City, Carlota felt emptier than ever. Melancholy and depression flattened her, and it seemed that nothing in the world brought her comfort. She had no desire to do anything. Her dreams had been fulfilled, and there was nothing left to imagine. They were all gone.

Sharing her husband with Schertzenlechner had been painful, but in her heart and in her head, she knew that she couldn't compete with that love. She could never give him what Sebastian gave him, and in a way that made her humiliation more tolerable. But Maximilian preferring another woman—that was an unbearable pain.

He was never there, neither governing nor facing up to the chaos that lay ahead, and Carlota knew that it was because of her. She knew it. That woman sucked his brains out and distracted him with God knows what indigenous tricks. Otherwise, how could it be that with the imperial coffers empty, instead of halting the renovation and provisioning at Casa Borda, these had accelerated? Maximilian, with the letter from Napoleon III informing him of the troops' withdrawal, spent his time making drawings of the work to be carried out. *Beauty,* Carlota thought contemptuously. *Always the beautiful and the vacuous before the practical.*

She was beginning to feel hostility toward everything Mexican. The country to which she'd given so much was suddenly taking it all away. Constanza was the only person she confided in.

"Mexico City rejects us. They don't want us, do they, Constanza?"

"Why do you say that, Majesty?"

"I see it. I feel it. They're false. They put up victory arches, but it's just adornment. Mexico's national pride has been wounded; a lot of dirt, a lot of corruption for centuries. I can't fight that."

Constanza froze. She responded in kind to the empress's sincerity.

"You're right, Majesty." The young woman changed the subject. "Have you been taking the herbs I gave you, Majesty?"

"Yes," she said, a little embarrassed.

"And have you noticed any improvement, Majesty?"

"Oh, Constanza, the emperor spends two weeks of each month in Cuernavaca! He's there more than he's here. I even had to set up a Mexico City–Cuernavaca telegraph so he could attend to the country from under that woman's skirts. It's a disgrace."

"Be patient. Keep taking them, and before you know it you'll see that everything will be different, Majesty."

Very different, she thought with a pang of remorse as she tidied papers on the desk. Turning around to face Carlota, she felt afraid: bewitched, Carlota was staring blankly. She was wandering while looking into the void, and yet her mouth broke into a smile. A madwoman was looking at her.

"Majesty," Constanza called to her nervously. "Are you all right?"

Carlota came around.

"Huh?" she said, coming out of her trance.

"Nothing, nothing, Majesty."

They pretended nothing had happened.

"Is there anything else I can do for you, Majesty?"

"No, you may leave. Thank you."

"With your permission," she said.

Outside, Constanza stopped behind the door and held her hands to her mouth to suppress a sob. She was certain, as she'd never been before in her life, that she would burn in hell for eternity for quietly poisoning a good woman.

53

Every evening, the sky over Laeken reverberated while, with a vacant stare, Carlota played the Mexican national anthem on the piano. People asked her why she played it, and Carlota, making their hair stand on end, answered, "Tell the emperor not to worry, Napoleon will never abandon us."

He'd already abandoned them. Mexico hadn't been among Napoleon's concerns for a long time, for better or for worse, but she clung to the green, white, and red with the same confidence she had years ago. For her, time had stopped. Stuck in a clock that didn't keep time, it didn't disturb her in the slightest.

The appalling state in which Carlota arrived shocked even her brother King Leopold, who had a heart of ice. Seeing her, he didn't know how to react. He'd heard stories about her condition but thought they were the usual exaggerations of women, incapable of assimilating defeats and misfortunes with a soldier's fortitude. But once he saw her before him, he felt pity for her: his poor sister had been reduced to skin and bone. The anguish of her abandonment had consumed her, giving her the appearance of a thin, pallid ghost, her freshness gone. Whatever beauty she'd possessed had evaporated, leaving a sediment of fear. She had the expression of a dog that had been brutally abused and feared everything. If somebody approached without making their presence known, Carlota jumped. In some kind of desperate attempt to swallow herself up, she hunched over like an armadillo in its armor; just as impenetrable, just as coarse.

Arriving in Laeken seemed to revive her lucidity. She recognized the corridors and rooms where she'd played as a child, the portraits on the walls were familiar to her, and she grew fond of her late father's little dog, which she sat with on her lap for hours, stroking it. She was home. Reluctantly, she allowed her new ladies of honor to dress her and brush her hair, looking at them with suspicion as they held their hands to the sky, imploring her to trust them.

"Nobody is going to hurt you, Archduchess," they said.

But the memory of Constanza lashed at her like a thunderbolt. Every face was a face of betrayal, of gradual poisoning. Constanza giving her herbs to drink to attract a man's love: *Drink, Majesty, drink.* Constanza, the lapdog that wags its tail, licks, and then bites. She shook her head to cast Constanza Murrieta's face from her mind, wanting to be able to suspend her disbelief, her stupidity.

Her suspicion wasn't entirely unwarranted, since it was Leopold II who chose the ladies. Her eldest brother's sinister look terrified her. For now he only growled, but Carlota knew that he was also a rabid dog waiting to bite.

Even so, Leopold went for walks with her, though Carlota sensed that it wasn't for the pleasure of her company but to see how mad she was. Her instincts weren't deceiving her: Leopold's motivation was not kindness but to test how far he could stretch the cord without it breaking, and at times Carlota's sense and good memory disconcerted him. She remembered each name, each street, each look from the politicians, ambassadors, and ministers she'd met in the last two years, even if she had spent only minutes in their company. Not even the Goffinets demonstrated such lucidity, and they had to rely on each other to put two and two together. Why did they say, then, that his sister was mad?

She spoke coherently, which was doubtlessly an inconvenience: the more deranged she was, he thought, the better for Belgium, because it would mean the return of the Belgian state's hundred thousand florins from Austria. Leopold felt his stomach clench when he thought of the Habsburgs basking in his sister's wealth, his poor, stupid, foolish sister. With the Goffinets' help, he'd already managed to render void her joint ownership of Miramare and Lokrum—half of which belonged to her through her marriage to Maximilian—and the debts with the Habsburgs had been annulled. Not a single centime from the Belgian coffers would be paid to the Austrians. And all thanks to two things: the fact that Maximilian had never consummated the marriage, and because his sister, as everyone knew, had lost her sanity. Leopold hoped that nothing would change. Carlota's madness couldn't have been more profitable. So whenever Marie Henriette told him, with joy, how she'd visibly improved, that she was becoming more beautiful and had put on weight, instead of smiling, Leopold's expression turned as stern as a cook boiling cauliflower.

Marie Henriette also noticed Carlota's distrust of her ladies. She could see how uncomfortable she felt among unknown women; she'd never seen so much fear in her eyes, as if the ladies, far from helping her and assisting her in her tasks, were spiders weaving a web on which to wait to devour her.

One day, trying not to upset her, she asked, "Did the ladies in Mexico treat you well?"

Carlota dropped the frame in which she was embroidering a handkerchief. Marie Henriette, feigning ignorance, picked it up and gave it back to Carlota. She pretended to count the stitches on her embroidery and persisted:

"What were they like?"

Carlota stared at her.

"Sinister."

"What makes you say that?"

"They were bad to me. They made me believe they loved me, that they respected me, and then they bit off my hand. Especially . . ."

Carlota broke off.

"Especially what?"

"Especially her. Constanza. She was the worst."

"Did she hurt you?"

"She went all the way."

And then, leaving the embroidery on her lap, she sank into silence again.

Marie Henriette didn't need to know any more. She knew betrayal like the back of her hand. And Dr. Bolkens had said it was likely that Carlota had been poisoned in small doses for a long time. Straightaway, she set about trying to find a lady-in-waiting who was loyal, honest, incorruptible, and, if possible, with more patience than Job.

After several interviews and drawing on her instinct, she knew who among all the castle's inhabitants was right for the position. Her name was Marie Moreau; she'd been born in Friesland the daughter of a general. Alongside her chambermaid, Julie Doyen, she would be responsible for looking after the empress. They'd been in Marie Henriette's service for years, and she knew them well. They were quiet, caring, and with iron stomachs. They would be the queen's eyes and ears and would report back to her.

Like the breeze cooling summer evenings, Carlota felt as if life was worth living again. She reemerged like a bud forcing its way through dry earth. Marie Henriette devoted herself to her with the same dedication she'd shown her daughters long ago. She oversaw every detail, from her clothes to her food. They walked in the gardens arm in arm, they embroidered together, and Marie Henriette soothed Carlota when she woke in the night soaked in sweat, seized by panic and the final tremor of her paranoia. Her fear of being poisoned gradually subsided. She ate meals twice a day, snacked once, and stopped drinking from fountains. Sometimes she even laughed, though it was a laughter devoid of happiness.

On their evening strolls, Carlota looked at the mountains and, at a slow pace, her memories flooding back to her, she often spoke to Marie Henriette of how beautiful Mexico was.

"If only you had seen it," she said. "There are few places so lovely on the face of the earth. The snow paints silhouettes on the mountains; the sun doesn't shine but burns insolently; the trees dance . . ."

Each time this happened, Marie Henriette put herself on guard and commended herself to the angels so that, by the grace of God, she didn't ask her about Maximilian. She knew one day she would have to tell her that her good, beloved emperor, who as it turned out was neither good nor beloved, had been executed by firing squad. That before dying he'd ordered his locket ring containing his first love Princess Maria Amélia of Braganza's hair, which he wore every day, to be delivered to his mother, Princess Sophie. Marie Henriette's legs shook when she thought of Maximilian's greenish body, twice badly embalmed in an attempt to preserve it on its journey to Vienna, before being placed in three coffins: one lined with velvet, another of wood, and a final one of zinc, made to measure because his long, noble figure didn't fit in the caskets of commoners. But days went by, leaves yellowed on the trees and fell to the ground, covering the earth in an ochre mantle, the icy winter arrived, and Carlota still hadn't asked. Marie Henriette sensed that Carlota knew the emperor was dead, because she never asked after him. Her indifference could only mean an unequivocal desire to remain in blissful ignorance, and Marie Henriette wasn't going to be the one to destroy it for her. But there was only so long that reality could be ignored. Carlota would have to be told that Maximilian was dead, because with her condition improved, she could read the newspapers. Every day she was brought a copy of *L'Étoile belge*, but first they checked that it didn't contain news about Mexico.

Carlota knew they were hiding something, because sometimes she asked sarcastically, "Will I be allowed to read the paper today?"

And they all gave false smiles.

They decided that it would be Father Deschamps, who'd married them and from whom she had received her First Communion, who would give her the news. On January 12, 1868, almost seven months after the execution, the priest said to her, "The emperor is dead, the Mexicans executed him. He was shot like Iturbide."

"Then it's all over now," said Carlota.

Tout est fini. The idea struck her head-on, stunning her.

"So, we no longer have a throne?"

"I'm afraid not, child."

And just when he was about to tell her they should pray for Maximilian's eternal peace, Carlota clapped her hands and, leaving Deschamps openmouthed, said, "We must petition Napoleon for the Spanish or Italian throne!"

"What do you mean, child?"

Had he been close enough to Carlota, he would've been able to hear a little click. Suddenly Carlota seemed to understand with complete clarity what she'd just heard. She could see the images she'd feared, that she had suspected for so long. Doubt gave way to understanding. Fear washed into a sea of calm. Madness yielded to reason. Maximilian was no more.

"Dead," she remarked. "Executed by Juárez."

"Yes, child."

"At least he had a glorious death," said Carlota, trying to cushion the blow of the news.

And then, after letting out a groan, she broke down into tears. She cried from grief. From pity. From loneliness. From anguish. From abandonment. From rage. From impotence. From lost faith.

Marie Henriette ran to embrace her.

"It's all right, little one, it's all right."

"Oh! If only I could make my peace with the heavens and confess!"

Marie Henriette was crying, too, but from happiness. Carlota had rediscovered her devotion. There was hope. There was a remedy. Surely she was nearer to recovery than she was to insanity.

"Of course, dear, of course. Confess, nothing would please God more. You can do so tomorrow morning. I'll arrange everything so that you can."

But in the middle of the night, gripped by a panic attack, she sent for Marie Henriette.

"I can't do it; I don't have the courage to confess."

"Don't worry, dear, whenever you're ready," the queen replied, trying to hide her disappointment.

After the sad news, Carlota wrote letters to her former governess and to Mexico's former ministers in Paris, and in all these letters, there was no trace of incoherence. It was as if Maximilian's death, far from disturbing her, had brought her back to the world of the living. She embraced the sacraments again, and both her reading and her conversation became fluent. With the exception of Leopold, who wasn't pleased with the turn of events, everyone was delighted that it seemed as if all Carlota needed to return to sanity was to continue to live in peace with Marie Henriette caring for her.

And with the tranquility of the moon rising each night, changing its phase but not its essence, the days passed until misfortune, tired of chasing her in circles, decided to steal the sanity to which Carlota, after losing her father, her grandmother, Maximilian, her son, and the empire, had clung tooth and nail.

It was on January 22, 1869, three years after the house of cards collapsed.

From the depths of Marie Henriette's soul came a scream of terror that shook Laeken like an earthquake, cracking the foundations of the royal marriage. Her only son, heir to the throne, was dying in her arms at the age of just nine. Two days before, the child had been skating on a frozen pond; the ice hadn't been thick enough, he fell into the water, and the cold engulfed him. He didn't drown, but after falling in and out of fever several times, pneumonia ended up killing him.

Leopold screamed, too, but his scream was more rage than pain. With his son's death, the Belgian throne was left without a successor; he couldn't countenance the possibility of any of his other descendants, all of them women, acceding to it. Power was conferred upon men and only men. There was crying. Reproaches. The rabid dog was about to bite. And even with her heart flooded with sorrow, Marie Henriette became pregnant again.

Carlota sensed that she was tired, apathetic, and seeing her with child reawakened old ghosts that she tried in vain to silence: of the devil, of the Church, of the army. These specters became more present when, nine months later, the queen gave birth to another girl.

Shouting. Complaints. The insults were endless. Marie Henriette cried.

"I'm not the one to blame!"

"Who else, if you were carrying the baby in your belly?"

"How could I know it would be a girl?"

"You have bad blood! You're only capable of producing women! Even Charlotte was able to have a male!"

"And what good did it do her, when they snatched him from her as if she were a dog?"

"I disown you, woman! Get out of my sight."

Marie Henriette fell into a silence in which only Carlota managed to reach her. They shared the same pain: the pain of being born women. They laid their heads in one another's laps and stroked each other's hair, plunged into the silence of their mutual sorrow. Though their malaise was not madness, Marie Henriette thought she was close to losing her mind, and sometimes she wished she could escape like Carlota to a world where she couldn't feel her immense sadness. The sun did not warm them. The cold turned them to stone. Laughter made them cry, and rolls of thunder exploded in their heads. Life had no meaning, they told each other without speaking.

But unlike her sister-in-law, one morning, Marie Henriette rose, wiped away her tears, and found the strength of spirit to dress, pack her bags, and leave for the town of Spa. To hell with Leopold, Laeken, and everything that inhabited it. Only Carlota weighed on her conscience. She knew that, without her, the poor woman would be defenseless. What would become of Carlota if she left? She couldn't leave her at the mercy of her husband. Perhaps, she thought, she should take her with her, away from that filthy, fatuous court, but Leopold, once again displaying his despotism, wouldn't allow it.

"Take your horses, your parakeets, and your llama, but Charlotte stays here."

"You only want to make her suffer. You won't rest until you've seen her lose her mind, isn't that so?"

"Out of my sight, woman."

Marie Henriette gathered the dignity she still had and turned away.

When she said goodbye to her sister-in-law, they embraced so hard that their corsets dug into their ribs. She held her face in her hands, touched her lips with a kiss, and said, "Forgive me, but I can't bury myself alive."

"I will write to you," Carlota said.

And Marie Henriette, unable to bear it any longer, left without looking back. She spent the whole journey trying not to think too much about the future that awaited poor Carlota.

May she find a way to the light, she thought to herself.

It wasn't light but more darkness that her brother brought her. After Marie Henriette's departure, he couldn't wait to remove her from the palace: he sent her to Tervuren Castle, near enough so that the slight wasn't too obvious, and far enough that he didn't have to see her.

Though she had an entourage entirely at her service, and nobody deprived her of her freedom, Carlota felt as if the spirit of Miramare was flitting around the rooms of that castle. Fear and loneliness seeped into her bones again. Was she condemned to a life in which everyone she cared about would disappear? Without exception, all the people she'd been able to feel the warmth of humanity with had vanished like clouds dragged by the wind. Or they died: she was a plague, she made everything she touched rot. Everything. Everyone. No one.

And Carlota—as her brother had hoped—relapsed.

She locked herself in her room where, feverishly, she wrote twenty letters a day: letters asking to be rescued from her confinement, to be freed from her prison. She became aggressive and, whenever the doctors tried to give her medicine, she kicked and fought, crying, *They're trying to kill me!* and spitting whatever it was in the face of whoever was there. She spent her days devising plans to escape, to flee, to shake off the yoke of her imprisonment.

Until, one day, in a state of complete calm, she handed a letter to Marie Moreau.

"It's for Queen Marie Henriette. Deliver it to her and only her."

When she was far enough away, with a puzzled expression, the lady opened the letter; she did so without remorse, for on the doctors' instructions, they had to know what the empress's intentions were at all times.

Madame Moreau turned pale as she read:

> *I invite you to kill yourself with me, for I wish to escape*
> *the captivity to which you so unjustly condemned me.*

It wasn't the first letter with suicidal overtones. Nor would it be the last.

54

Colonel Van der Smissen had secretly loved Carlota for a long time, though he would sooner shoot himself in the head with his own pistol than confess it. King Leopold I had placed him at the head of the Belgian legion sent to guard the empress, and in so doing he appointed him more as his daughter's protector than as a soldier. He accepted the position with resignation and under the weight of the discipline that prevented him from questioning an order, but in his heart he knew it would be a secondary mission in his military career. However, upon meeting her, he realized he'd been too quick to judge. It wasn't her appearance, for she seemed to be uncomfortable in her body and reluctant to show enthusiasm about any of her attributes. She had an unusual, almost fragile beauty, attractive black hair, and a very pale complexion. No, it wasn't her looks that struck him but her extraordinary sense of duty. Despite her young age, the empress was an old soul—proper, humble, and devoted—but above all, she had a gratitude toward the Belgian troops that Van der Smissen could only describe as moving. It wasn't a feeling that exploded like cannon fire. It was much more subtle; it set slowly like cement, and once dry it became hard and unbreakable.

Soon after he entered into her service, it became clear to the colonel how much the empress was suffering. He'd seen it before and knew it firsthand. Rejection was a red-hot iron that marked the face and the soul, with no escape no matter how much one tried to hide. That the emperor preferred the company of others was an open secret. And the colonel could see that, while Maximilian kept himself busy with other bodies, other bones, other bloods, she remained alone, firm, as severe and as inscrutable as a Greek goddess. And it wasn't that the opportunity didn't present itself—a few of the nobles courted her—but that she never succumbed to wooing or niceties. She had a strong sense of state, an indestructible moral bond to the power that had been invested in her.

Van der Smissen watched her closely but always maintained a cautious distance. Little by little, the empress earned his respect and—even more important—his loyalty. Until one day he surprised himself by putting obstacles in the way of men requesting an audience with the empress, lest any of them be a rival. *Are you stupid?* he rebuked himself. *As if you have any chance.* But he couldn't help feeling jealous. Nothing escaped his attention. He had a particular dislike for Philippe Petit, one of his men; anyone could see from a mile away that he preferred to be near Carlota rather than fighting in Tacámbaro, where much of the Belgian legion had been massacred owing to their inexperience and carelessness in combat. And though the lad had shown no signs of making an inappropriate move, the colonel kept his eyes on him just in case.

Thus, he became accustomed to seeing her without touching her. Smelling her without becoming intoxicated. Listening to her without rushing into anything. He had no choice. He was a colonel of the Belgian army, and she . . . she was the empress of Mexico, the queen of England's cousin, daughter of King Leopold I of Belgium, sister-in-law of Emperor Franz Joseph, daughter-in-law of Sophie of Bavaria, daughter of Louise of Orléans, granddaughter of Maria Amalia of Naples and Sicily, great-granddaughter of Ferdinand I of the Two Sicilies, and sister of the Duke of Brabant and of the Count of Flanders. Who could aspire to her? He—Alfred Louis Adolphe Graves, Baron Van der Smissen—could only dream of such a utopia.

Nonetheless, he loved her. He loved her even knowing he could never consummate his love for her. He loved from a distance, from the darkness, from the shadows. Each time she asked him to accompany her to stroll in the gardens, their peaceful pace and unhurried conversation more than satisfied him. Each time she exploded with helpless rage at Maximilian and walked straight into him at the door to the office, he contained the urge to kiss her forehead and say, *Don't cry, my princess.* And he felt the same urge each time she spoke to him in French at a table in the tea room, telling stories about Belgium, remembering the streets they used to walk down. Each time they were struck with nostalgia, and without needing to say it they both knew they missed the flavor, the color, the smell of their country; each time melancholy snatched a sigh from their lungs; each time Van der Smissen believed he would forever be cursed, because having known her, once he had shared the air with such a woman, he could no longer live without her.

He swallowed all of this.

If Carlota had looked more closely, she would have discovered it in his eyes.

And then Leopold I died.

Important figures lined up at Chapultepec Castle to offer their sympathies to the sovereigns. People came from all over to sign the book of condolences for fear of committing the imprudence of failing to appear on one of its pages when, after the period of mourning, the empress ran her eyes over them. It was an absurd fear, for when her grief was at its height, the only arms in which she sought comfort were those of a man who reminded her of her father, a man who spoke the same language as her and with whom she could recall anecdotes intensified by the romance of their shared remoteness.

"Do you remember, Alfred, that my father had a dimple under his left eye when he smiled?" Carlota would ask him.

"*Oui, je me souviens, Altesse.*"

"Do you remember, Alfred, that my father ordered a twenty-one-gun salute to celebrate my birth? He adored me so!"

"*Oui, je me souviens, Altesse.*"

"Oh, Alfred! I miss him! How I would've liked to say goodbye, to kiss him, to thank him for all the blessings and affection. But I am so far away!"

And the colonel, accustomed to fighting duels, certain that he could run his sword through an enemy's throat if he ran out of ammunition, didn't know what to do when his greatest enemy was himself.

Without saying it, they knew that the other's presence was a comfort. The list of problems that afflicted them was endless. The Mexican adventure was proving to be a failure; though Juárez remained in retreat from the city, he said that, wherever he was, there would be the presidency. Maximilian hadn't managed to unify the empire. He hadn't even been able to visit it beyond the roads guarded by the intervention forces. And on top of all that, he'd named Iturbide's grandsons as his heirs: the eldest he'd sent to Europe, and the youngest was hanging around in the palace waiting to inherit the crown, while their mother fought to have them returned. One foolish act after another. There were some good decisions, but while Carlota was aware of them, they were offset by the string of political miscalculations that the archduke had committed lately. Of all of them, the affair with the pretty Indian, if not the most grievous, was the one that hurt most.

She would go out riding escorted by Van der Smissen, and when they arrived back at Chapultepec, he dismounted beside her to help her down. It was a rare moment when he could hold her around the waist, and for a brief, almost ethereal instant they looked each other in the eyes.

Carlota, who'd never shown any interest in the men of the court, began to notice how well the colonel's uniform suited him, how sturdy his arms were, how manly his demeanor was. Dark-haired, with a beard as thick as the warp of a Persian rug, he was the diametric opposite of Maximilian. His small, blue eyes scrutinized everything with intelligence, questioning, analyzing. Eyes that didn't allow themselves to be deceived by appearances, or distracted by the flutter of butterflies. Nor had Carlota noticed how tall he was until, one day, she saw him coming out of the emperor's office with Maximilian, who suddenly seemed insignificant, tiny, pale, and soft alongside the battle-hardened colonel, who could knock a man down with his chin. Or his voice. She was captivated by the voice at a short distance, when their conversations didn't warrant grand words or displays of eloquence. She liked listening to him say *Chapultepec*, *cake*, or *saddle*. That was when Carlota noticed that his tone was deep and gravelly—it reminded her of the sound of hooves being rasped—but more importantly that it was devoid of any poetry.

When the emperor went to Cuernavaca, they went out for walks in the Alameda park, and if the sun grew strong, Van der Smissen would ask for permission to roll up his sleeves; in his veins, Carlota could then see the tension of arms accustomed to physical labor. But what she liked most of all was the way he dragged out her name in something between a groan and a caress. *Charlotte*, he would say.

Almost without realizing it, the afternoons and walks they enjoyed together became their reason to wake up each morning. After carrying out their respective duties, they went out to walk without the presence of chamberlains or ladies, just the two of them; however, they could feel everyone's eyes on the backs of their heads, from the ladies to Philippe and Constanza, from the housemaids to the cooks, from the footmen to the stable hands.

And then, one day, Carlota said to him, "Let's go away, Alfred. I need air."

Van der Smissen prepared everything, and they left for Lake Chalco. Nobody watched them there. There they were no more than two people in search of anonymity. Two people in search of silence for their words. They went there often at dusk. The sun would set, and they would return to the castle hoping that it would take longer to sink below the horizon the next day, because with each sunset they felt a part of their soul die. Until, on a barge one evening, the twilight came down on them with particular haste.

"We must go, Charlotte. It's not safe being here alone."

"No, wait, Alfred, let's stay another minute. It's so pleasant here."

"But, Charlotte . . ."

"Please," she begged. "Let's watch the sunset."

"All right," he agreed.

Together, side by side, they contemplated the sun setting too fast.

"Is this what death's like?" asked Carlota.

After thinking for a moment, Alfred replied, "Let's hope so."

"Do you fear death, Alfred?"

"No," he said. "I'm more afraid of an empty life."

An empty life, she thought. She felt the same way when she lived at Miramare. Now she was beginning to ask herself what an empty life was. Everything was relative.

"I'm more afraid of a long life," she said.

"Why do you say that, Charlotte?"

"I don't know. The thought of living too long scares me."

"How long's too long?"

She blew out a breath.

"I don't know. When it weighs too heavily, I suppose. Life should be lighter, don't you think?"

And she looked at him with such sadness that Van der Smissen had to make an immense effort not to kiss her.

To the colonel's complete astonishment, she took his hand, and they sat with their palms together as if looking into a mirror, and then she entwined her fingers with his.

She didn't say anything to him. No sound, no plea, no request came from her mouth. But they were both flooded with desire.

"Charlotte . . ."

"Alfred."

They asked for permission without words.

They consented with their eyes.

And at that, Carlota began to feel.

The hands accustomed to brandishing a sword glided over her back. Her whole body was a bristling cat. She trembled. And yet she knew that this barge, this lake, was the only place in the world. That was all he did: he brushed his fingers against her. No more and no less. But Carlota could anticipate the surge from the wave that was approaching. He touched her slowly, as if afraid he might break her. But he knew what he was doing. He had done it many times, albeit with less smooth flesh. Less noble. Carlota's breathing was hurried. Her energy pulsed in places unknown before now. She moistened. She felt the urge to open her legs but didn't. She controlled herself with supernatural force. She was afraid, but she wanted it. She wanted to feel. At last. At last, she felt. Her skin spoke to her, begged her to keep feeling. To let the hands keep going, let them search. Let them find her. She tilted her head back and then Alfred, her colonel, kissed her. He kissed her neck. Contrary to what Van der Smissen had expected, her skin tasted not of nobility but of woman. It was just Carlota, simply Carlota. With one hand he held the small of her back, and with the other he stroked her collarbone. His mouth. That mouth, which had spoken to her so many times in the closeness of silence, began to explore her. Under her ears. The center of her neck. And she couldn't hold back any longer and searched for his lips. He responded. She felt a strong, firm, fleshy tongue against hers. She moved urgently and then he said, "Slowly, relax, let me." Embarrassed, she stopped. But he looked at her. He looked at her with those blue eyes that told her there was no other moment, there was no present other than the one they were experiencing, loving each other, touching each other, feeling each other. They were two people for the first time. With no surnames or names. A man and a woman. Nothing more. Then she opened her lips and let him in. She needed to prolong the moment. She let him discover her. Carlota felt that she was going to explode. But no, not yet. She couldn't even remotely imagine what was to come. He picked her up as if she were a feather and laid her on the boat. He kept kissing her as he undressed her. She trembled and covered her face with her hands. She didn't want to see. She did not want to. Though the night covered them in darkness and they had to feel their way, she feared his nudity. She didn't want to see him. But then he positioned himself over her, whispering words into her ear that she did not understand, and she felt him slide inside her. She received him full of grace. She wanted to let out a moan but contained herself. That part of her that had been missing was now complete. The lake's water accompanied their rocking. She started to say something, but he covered her mouth.

"Quiet," he ordered her gently, and he looked at her. She obeyed.

"Kiss me, Alfred," she pleaded.

And he kissed her as they rocked together, disintegrating with pleasure.

55

Carlota's room in Tervuren couldn't have been gloomier or bleaker. She had decorated it with her wedding dress, a bouquet of withered flowers, a pre-Hispanic idol, and, to the horror of anyone permitted to enter, a life-size model of Maximilian: a ghost with whom she had long conversations in which only she could hear the answers. Queen and lady of the dominions of her parallel universe that didn't reek of death or betrayal. She liked watering the flowers on the rug, and the servants had to be at the ready to rush in and mop up the puddles.

Like an overfilled waterskin, she burst. She split open. She exploded. She came apart. Too many detonators for a mind wounded by misfortune and depression, a depression as deep as the lakes between the mountains of the Valley of Mexico, her valley of tears. Too much pain, and the will to bear it exhausted. Mexico. The coup de grâce that condemned her from the moment she entered the ring, boarded the *Novara*, for the best fight of her life. The ears and the tail. White handkerchiefs for the empress. She was just nearing thirty. That was all. Three decades of light. After that came the shadows, if not total darkness.

She locked herself in her room for hours. Madame Moreau took care of her with loving patience and with sorrow in her heart. Every day, when she woke her, she tried to find the woman from Laeken, the devout empress who must still inhabit this body somewhere, but she found only a void.

Carlota wrote compulsively. Ten, fifteen, twenty letters a day. Mutilated letters that never reached their addressees, though they were read by physicians, ladies-in-waiting, and people close to her to learn the hidden desires and intentions of her little royal head lost in limbo.

At first, Marie didn't understand what she was reading. She needed time and counsel before she could decipher the encrypted messages that Carlota wrote with great care in impeccable handwriting. Marie shuddered when she saw the truth hidden behind these confessions of a mad-woman, for there was nothing on the surface that revealed the ravings of her mind. But she'd lost her senses, there was no doubt about that. Or was she feigning? Seized by this doubt, while Carlota wrote at her desk she watched from a corner of the room where she pretended to be reading (and sometimes she was). Carlota didn't write in a trance. She seemed at peace, enjoying the tranquility of dipping the pen in ink and shaping letters on the page. From the corner, Marie listened to the murmur of the nib on the paper; it was relaxing, which was why, seeing her so serene, in silence, not talking to the model of her dead husband or gamboling on the rugs as if in a meadow, she let her write. But all she had to do was read what she had written, and her heart was crushed like a grape being turned into wine. Carlota had always been an exceptional letter writer, and even in her madness she still was. She wrote letters to Napoleon III full of hatred and love. Sometimes the French monarch embodied the devil himself; sometimes, the most absolute generosity of the Almighty. Then she wrote to an idealized version of Maximilian. Her letters conveyed hopes and dreams of a life that hadn't been theirs. A life in which they'd been happy, a life of love and complicity. But, more than anyone, she wrote to a living Maximilian. A Maximilian who hadn't so much as brushed near death. And finally, the recipient who most disconcerted Madame Marie Moreau was a complete stranger to her: a

Belgian soldier, apparently, whose name she'd never heard mentioned. A soldier called Philippe Petit.

"Who is this Philippe?" Marie asked, intrigued.

"He was a soldier in the Belgian legion," they told her.

Madame Moreau's mind raced like a steam engine. Why, in the whole universe of men that Carlota addressed, was this rankless soldier worthy of her deranged letters? Was he the father of Carlota's child? She had to find out.

In the letters she thanked this Philippe for saving the emperor from his personal Calvary on Las Campanas Hill; Maximilian and Christ, victims of the same executioner. Marie crossed herself at the irreverence, unable to take her eyes from these lines. In secret, and with a certain timidity, Carlota sometimes said to her, *If I were a man, I'd rather be on a battlefield than suffer the prison of these torments.*

If I were a man, thought Marie, and she crossed herself again.

The letters only grew worse. From one to the next, the violence increased. Death seemed like the only escape; offering herself up for sacrifice seemed like the most logical and satisfactory way out. And given that there was no way to end her existence by the sword, she would do so by the only means possible: starvation. But then they brought her lunch, and she ate normally, as if the universe of the letters existed parallel to the real one, never intersecting. In one she killed herself. In the other she lived. In one, Maximilian had been saved from the rifle fire; in the other he lay buried in the Habsburgs' royal crypt in Vienna. But from one encrypted message to another, Marie looked in horror at the clues that Carlota was leaving for the little bird that dared eat the bread crumbs on the path, entire paragraphs of a madwoman telling the truth. Marie, bewildered, read as Carlota, in her madness, confessed things that she would never have dared to if she were sane:

> *The marriage I had left me as I was before, though I never refused Emperor Maximilian children . . . My marriage*

was only outwardly consecrated. The emperor made me
believe it was, but it wasn't, and not by any fault of my
own, since I always obeyed him, but it's not possible that
it was, or I wouldn't have ended up as I am.

So there it was, in her handwriting. Maximilian's marriage had not been consummated. Poor Carlota had been left a virgin. Or at least, Marie silently thought, she hadn't been deflowered by the emperor. Because she had given birth, and to a bastard; that was a fact.

What could have become of that boy born in the Gartenhaus? She could only hope that Charles de Bombelles had found a trace of goodness in his inhumane heart and given him to some good people. Otherwise—Marie prickled like a sea urchin—it was likely that the boy was as dead as Maximilian.

56

1865, Mexico

The gossip said that Carlota had a lover, and many eyes were turned indiscreetly to Van der Smissen. Their walks together at Lake Chalco, and the glow that Carlota suddenly had, didn't go unnoticed. She couldn't help blushing whenever someone looked at her, as if she wore a sign that said *adulteress* on her forehead. Though she enormously enjoyed her Alfred's company and the pleasures he afforded her, guilt tormented her. There was only one person whom she trusted enough to open up like a mussel parting its valves from the steam, and that person, as enthusiastic as if she'd waited her whole life for the emperor to be cuckolded, was Constanza.

Amused and even proud of the empress's infidelity, she covered for her. And when Carlota felt the recriminating gaze of her late father, seeming to say, *Oh, my child, what have you done? Lying with a soldier on a barge on Lake Chalco like a commoner,* Constanza gave a rousing speech in defense of lovers on a par with Alexander the Great at Gaugamela.

"No, no, and no, Majesty. Do you think the emperor doesn't lie with that girl in Cuernavaca?"

"Yes, but—"

"But nothing. Kings and queens have always had lovers. You're not reinventing the wheel, Majesty."

"Yes, I know, but—"

"You have nothing to be sorry for, my lady. Hasn't the emperor been traveling Mexico for years with that Sebastian, the one with the unpronounceable surname?"

"Schertzenlechner . . ."

Carlota grew feeble just uttering his name.

"That's the one."

"Yes, but—"

"Majesty, forgive me, but I don't understand why you feel guilty."

"I'm being very weak."

"Weak? You, weak, Majesty? Allow me to tell you that I have never met anyone in my entire life as brave and as strong as you."

"I've succumbed, just like the emperor, Constanza. We've both succumbed."

"One swallow does not a summer make, Your Majesty."

And as she said that, for the first time, the beginnings of a smile appeared on Carlota's face.

"One swallow does not a summer make," she repeated.

The two women were silent for a moment.

"If only the emperor had loved me like Alfred does," Carlota murmured.

And then, Constanza, with her usual complicity, lied to silence the ghosts of regret.

"And the emperor loves you in his own way, Majesty."

Carlota gave her a puzzled look.

"And what way is that, Constanza?"

The young woman swallowed dryly and remained silent, unsure how to answer.

Then in a low voice, the words almost pouring out, she said, "At some time he must have loved you. He still must love you, my lady."

"Perhaps if I'd had wings or branches for arms . . . ," said Carlota.

"But in his letters he shows affection, Majesty."

"Those are just words, Constanza, and the wind takes them. Formalities, protocol. What good is it if he calls me *flower of my heart* or *angel of my life* if he then prefers to sleep on a mat rather than share my bed?"

Instead of answering her question, Constanza decided to stoke the fire.

"You have a man in your bed now, Majesty."

Carlota looked at her gravely.

"Yes," she said. "But how do I hide from God's eyes?"

"God will forgive you, my lady."

"God has already condemned me, Constanza."

A shiver ran down Constanza's back when she recognized that this was the glaring truth. *Poor woman,* she thought. Nobody did the right thing by her. Not even her: after learning to appreciate her, she was doing nothing to help her, quite the opposite. While he was at it, God would condemn her, too.

"Majesty, don't punish yourself," Constanza was bold enough to say. "We're not in the Middle Ages."

"How curious you should say that, because life here seems like the Middle Ages; one moment we're happy, comfortable, and serene, only to realize that a band of guerrillas could attack us at any time."

"Why do you say that, Majesty? Because of the cannons set up here, on the castle roof?"

"And from the signal system we use to communicate with the city, Constanza. Like in medieval times. It's a constant *Who goes there?*"

Constanza could only nod.

"The night before last, I jumped out of bed when I heard the artillery fire."

"Two nights ago, Majesty?" asked Constanza, surprised; she didn't remember there being an incident. Seeing the empress nod, it dawned on her. "Oh! That! It wasn't artillery! It was fireworks for Candlemas!"

And she explained that saints and patron saints were commemorated by launching enough fireworks into the air to split the earth in two the whole night long. Carlota, annoyed, retorted, "As if God would've chosen four in the morning for the Annunciation!"

They both laughed.

"Constanza . . ."

"Yes, Majesty."

"Do you think we should keep the French in Mexico?"

Constanza opened her eyes wide, trying to hide her astonishment at the change of subject. For a very short moment, she thought she could act as diplomat.

"Your Majesty, without the French, the empire won't stand."

"But they offer their fraternal support in exchange for our money. We're paying them."

"Are you saying that if you don't pay them, they'll leave, Majesty?"

"The French do nothing by halves. Either we have them fully on our side, or there's no sense in keeping them here."

"In that case, Majesty, best let them go."

"Thank you, Constanza."

And leaving Constanza with ideas fluttering around her head, Carlota gave her permission to go.

Constanza couldn't bear the remorse: sometimes she thought it would be better to kill her than to continue poisoning her. Although, in secret—so that only her conscience could hear her—she told herself that perhaps Modesto's herbs would only have a light effect, since she was administering them in such small doses. Constanza wished Juárez would hurry up and win the war and throw the monarchs out. She wanted Carlota to leave, to flee, to run away from Mexico and return to Belgium to die in peace, freeing Constanza from the enormous burden she bore on her shoulders. But she knew that the evil was already done. Her wounded conscience would never recover from the onslaught. Her soul would drag its chains of guilt and punishment for eternity. That was why she was so supportive of Carlota's prohibited love: to forgive herself. To give the empress back a little of the life she was stealing from her one sigh at a time.

57

A man's spite can be as dangerous as a sword. Though Carlota was no more attainable than a star, when Philippe confirmed his suspicions about her and the colonel, something inside him turned to ice. It wasn't rage; that was a familiar feeling. Nor was it impotence, or sadness, but suddenly the insecurities of his childhood flooded back and drowned him. Philippe, disarmed, was left choking. Constanza was the first to feel his resentment.

"What's the matter?" she asked him, interrupting their lesson on third-group verbs.

"Nothing."

"Well, it doesn't seem like nothing." She fixed her eyes on him, waiting.

"It's just that I don't trust the colonel."

Constanza exhaled sharply.

So that was what it was. Jealousy. Corrosive jealousy, forcing him underwater when his entire body was made of metal. His face held a strange severity.

And suddenly, Constanza felt as if time had stopped. There was silence. The world's sounds disappeared. Philippe's face remained impassive, though to Constanza it seemed as fickle as a candle's flame. She couldn't think of anything he could ask of her that she would refuse.

"Philippe," she said to him then. "You know Carlota will never notice you."

He felt horror like a red-hot iron being driven into the back of his neck.

"She'll never look at you with the eyes I look at you with."

Philippe observed her. A five-letter thought was left suspended in the air: F-A-M-K-E. He recognized her gaze. He'd been looked at like that once, with that desire to ravish him. He wanted to feel it, too. But he couldn't understand why the empress always got in the way, as if any other woman was a consolation prize. He could have whomever he wanted. He knew it. No woman had ever escaped the draw of his virility. So why didn't he give himself permission to love? He was an idiot, he recriminated himself. And he was pondering these and other mysteries of love and the absence thereof when Constanza, slowly but nonetheless taking him by surprise, stood, took him by the hand, and led him to her bedroom. There, Philippe, who despite his surprise had known very well the direction in which they'd been heading, gazed at Constanza as she lay on the bed.

Then she said, "Imagine I'm her."

Constanza, with perfectly orchestrated choreography, grabbed her skirt by the hem and began lifting it slowly until she was completely covered. She disappeared beneath it. What was left uncovered was a pair of open legs that made way for him with all the benevolence that the Red Sea showed to Moses. A woman's body without a face. Philippe looked at her, feeling his stiff member fighting to burst out of his trousers. He couldn't see her face, but noticed the frantic beating of her heart: her chest rose and fell under all the fabric. Despite his immense desire to throw himself on top of her, Philippe approached slowly. Still dressed, he lay next to her and his fingers slid like snakes up her thighs until they separated the lips of her vulva; without seeing her, he could feel Constanza shudder. The tips of his fingers began to stroke her, circling her genitals, and then, without warning, he pinched the clitoris.

What're you doing? Stop, stop . . . , said Constanza while lifting her knees more to make space for her lover. *Stop, stop right now . . .* , she stammered as she opened her legs wider. Philippe was moving his fingers with greater relish. Constanza's moans were muffled under the fabric, but her moaning was growing louder. *Oh, oh, oh, what is this? Oh my God, what is this?* she said. *Touch me. Touch me more.* Then Philippe inserted his fingers; he felt the flesh open with a crackle, and Constanza secreted something like semen. The sheets were soaked.

And to his astonishment Philippe heard Constanza, her voice faltering, order him, "Call me . . . Carlota, Philippe . . . Call me Carlota."

Without stopping, Philippe obeyed.

"Carlota, oh, my Carlota. Car . . . lo . . . ta . . ."

Philippe felt his hard organ emerge like the serpent from a snake charmer's basket. He felt for one of her hands and held it to his groin. Blindly, Constanza began to rub. She did it with difficulty, struggling to both give and receive attention at the same time. Her skirts were beginning to suffocate her, and in a fit of passion she forgot her supposed anonymity and allowed Philippe to see her flushed face. For the first time, Constanza saw the expression of a man on fire, and infected by his lust, she pulled down her tight bodice, allowing breasts with rosy nipples to escape. Philippe, still conducting the concert, set his baton aside to lap at them with a pup's gluttony. Constanza was burning, about to explode, and then Philippe left the nipples and headed south, to that red, moist, and fleshy vulva, and he sucked at it. In a trance of pleasure, Constanza rolled her eyes back. She supported herself on her elbows, letting out a scream, and Philippe knew he'd finished.

He lay on his back beside her. Constanza took a few seconds to reemerge like a snail after a storm, not daring to speak. She looked at Philippe's still-erect member; she wasn't sure what she should do now. They lay in silence, trying to gather their thoughts. Stunned, Constanza wondered whether she remained a virgin, since there had been no penetration, but the fact was she felt as deflowered as she could have been.

Philippe, on the other hand, was wondering who the woman he'd just discovered was.

"So this is what drives people crazy?" said Constanza in an attempt to rescue her innocence, and as she said the words she felt a fierce attack of conscience.

Philippe did not respond.

Suddenly they were overcome with shame. Constanza covered her legs. She was still moist, as was the bed. The moans would've been heard clearly in broad daylight: Constanza, shut away in her bedchamber with one of the empress's soldiers. The palace would know about it sooner or later.

Philippe waited for everything to be back in its place before leaving the room. For the rest of the day, he remained pensive. He was experiencing something new. Perhaps, he told himself, he could love this woman. Perhaps Mexico would be his children's homeland. A new world, cocooned by the complicity of a woman who allowed him to have his fantasies. Her allowing him to think about Carlota while he made love to her had been the most exciting and erotic moment of his life. Despite their best attempts, no Belgian whore had managed to make him feel like he was with another woman. And Philippe knew that Constanza, unlike the others, hadn't pretended.

58

When Constanza opened the door to Philippe, she knew a torrent of pleasure would enter with him. He loved her with such patience and virility that she wondered if all men were like him. He never stopped until he'd satisfied her fully, making every pore of her skin vibrate until she begged through tears for him to stop because so much pleasure was unbearable. Hidden away, they loved each other as day broke or when night fell, whichever happened first. After so long without a woman, Philippe allowed his self-imposed abstinence to burst, and for the first few weeks, his lovemaking capacity seemed endless. Carlota and Van der Smissen didn't love each other like this; their love was more serene. Constanza and Philippe, on the other hand, aroused the envy of Eros himself. They didn't speak with words. Constanza knew that words were deceptive, sharpened swords that could cut with both sides. They preferred to speak with their eyes, with their hands, with their ears, with their noses. They preferred to allow their senses to perceive breath, to decipher silence, feeling the sheets on their skin, savoring the salt of their sweat. They cherished each other without words; they weren't needed to dream that life thereafter would be long and full. Constanza, however, knew that if she spoke, she would turn everything to mud, like a field after a flood. She struggled to see a future with Philippe in which there was no empire. He spoke of future glories in which the sovereigns would gain control of Mexico. There would be no more wars or spilled blood. They would bring peace. Mexico would become the great country it could be. A paradise between America and Europe.

"Then we'll marry and make a family."

Constanza would give a half smile, swallowing. But sometimes, just sometimes, betrayed by her feelings, she believed it could be true. Deep down she knew her happiness with Philippe would be fleeting if he discovered what she'd been doing in recent months. And however much her conscience writhed like a worm in vinegar; however much she wanted to confess to him, huddled under his arms as she sought the words to apologize, before giving up when she heard her lover's gentle snores; however hard she tried to open her heart, she wasn't prepared to douse her newfound passion. So she stayed silent. As silent as the dead. She would sooner hang herself than reveal her secret. *All women have secrets,* her mother had told her, and from the moment she made the decision to poison the empress, she'd condemned herself to silence. To the grave.

One day, finally, their bodies quieted. No longer able to shield themselves behind the enchantment of their imaginations, for they each knew the flavor of the other very well, other more bodily ghosts materialized.

The burden of guilt tormented Constanza every day. The empress was sinking into lapses of the mind that were put down to exhaustion, but she knew it was her fault; she could see it in her absent gaze. Sometimes she felt as if the empress was looking at her aghast, realizing what she was doing, and Constanza would turn in the other direction, overcome with doubt. Carlota appeared in her dreams and yelled, *How could you do this to me?* She asked herself the same thing. Why hadn't they asked her to poison the emperor? That would've caused her less conflict. And when these thoughts assailed her, she saw Maximilian with his greenish, taciturn face, forever afflicted with diarrhea from dysentery that was slowly killing him, and she wondered whether there was someone else in the court, camouflaged like her, giving him another type of poison. When the guilt felt too heavy to bear it alone, she turned to her brother.

She and Salvador walked in the gardens together, always under the watchful eye of Philippe, who, without being a spy, could've played the part perfectly if he'd wanted to. He observed them from a distance like a predator, scanning the horizon, trying to read the movement of their lips. He wondered how they had so much to talk about, no matter how close their family bond. He squeezed his eyes shut, because his brother's face appeared, saying, *I'll come back for you,* and his heart clenched with envy. He saw anguish in Constanza's face, distress, and his head told him there was something she was hiding from him, but his heart couldn't accept it.

He started to have strange thoughts about her. He asked himself why her attitude had never seemed strange to him before. That aura of constant service she had, like a soldier on the front lines. The many meetings with Salvador, who often introduced her to people he never saw again, even though, one afternoon, they talked until the sun went down. Constanza was always alert, but in a different way from the others, as if she'd sold her soul to the devil and was waiting for him to collect. How, he thought, had he not realized? Or was it all a product of his imagination? Was it jealousy slowly eating away at him? He shook his head and made himself think about something else.

Philippe watched Salvador kiss her cheek and say goodbye. The conversation with her brother was over. She stayed alone as he walked off, leaving her immersed in some kind of void. For a moment, Philippe thought he was looking at a fisherman's wife watching the boat sail off under a stormy sky. There was sadness in her gaze. Philippe turned away before she headed in a different direction.

Constanza wandered the garden for a few more minutes. She didn't want to see anybody. Her brother had just given her news that had left her ice-cold. She sat on a bench and held both hands to her head. It felt very heavy. She let it drop forward. It must be true, there was no doubt.

"The emperor's expecting a child," she whispered to herself.

It can't be, she thought. But Salvador had been clear. The girl in the Cuernavaca garden was pregnant and all indications were that it was Maximilian's child. The emperor was as proud as a huntsman posing next to his slain quarry. At last his virility was proven. He was going to have a child. Salvador had shown her an intercepted letter from a French officer to his family, in which he wrote:

> *What is certain is that the emperor and the empire are most unpopular here, and everyone is waiting to see both disappear. But Maximilian isn't very upset. His main concern is going to Cuernavaca to see a Mexican girl expecting his child, which pleases him beyond all measure; he's very proud to have discovered his flair for fatherhood, an attribute that was often questioned.*

So that was it. All the trips to the Casa Borda garden had ended in this. With a *mestizo* heir.

This will finish Carlota, Constanza thought.

Then she remembered her brother's words, the ones still boring into her conscience. *That child must be killed.* Remembering them, she trembled like a leaf in the autumn wind.

"We're not murderers, Salvador. Or is that what we've become?"

"Don't you see? There can't be any heirs to this absurd throne. That child must be killed."

"I won't carry that on my conscience, Salvador. If you want to kill it, find someone else. I can't do it."

"Don't worry, it's already been arranged."

Constanza cursed the moment her father decided to bring a European prince here to govern. Now she would have blood on her hands, even if it was only by omission. The blood of an infant. The blood of an empress. She might not be driving a dagger through Carlota's heart, but she was bleeding her drop by drop, emptying her mind of sanity. *Mea culpa, mea culpa, mea maxima culpa,* she said to herself, recalling the catechism that had seeped into her bones through repetition. And then, in punishment, she dealt herself a blow to the chest.

She stood up and smoothed her skirt with her hands, before heading to perform her palace duties. The sooner she completed her mission, the better. She wanted to leave Chapultepec and never return.

Philippe sensed that something wasn't right. Constanza seemed on edge, disoriented. He tried to read her thoughts, and it infuriated him that he couldn't. Constanza was many things, but she was not a transparent woman. She was as prickly as a hedgehog. He wanted to know what was going through her mind when she looked at him with those eyes like a hungry cat's. When he slept, he had nightmares in which, while he made love to her, he squeezed her head until the skull cracked, and then Philippe woke, pale. He didn't know how Constanza aroused such violent urges in him. It frightened him; this woman would make him lose his mind. Just when he was beginning to believe that loving her was a mistake, fate interceded to prevent him from going mad for her.

Chapultepec awoke one morning caressed by wind that bent the crowns of the trees. The air howled and brought with it the stench of decadence, as if the atmosphere were marred with betrayals and bad omens. The news of Carlota's nocturnal outings with Van der Smissen in the Chalco Valley had reached Maximilian: Charles de Bombelles passed on detailed reports that his spies supplied him with. The emperor, in an act of feigned outrage at his wife's honor being tainted, decided to send the colonel as far away as possible. And he wouldn't go alone. The empress's entire Belgian retinue was ordered to leave. Not satisfied with that, a new humiliation was added: Maximilian instructed that General Ramón Méndez, a native, would guide them. When Van der Smissen found out, he burned with rage. He knew that Maximilian was doing it out of pure spite, to make him pay for having the temerity to touch his wife, even though the emperor himself had condemned her to a fallow existence. An emperor was superior to a commander and, if it wasn't clear already, he made it evident where it most hurt: rank.

"This is a humiliation! He places the Belgians on a par with the natives, clearly inferior to the other European troops!" Van der Smissen complained.

The colonel's indignation infected the entire regiment. In the corridors, they demanded the defense of their honor. The commotion was such that Maximilian summoned him behind closed doors. As soon as he was in Maximilian's presence, the emperor went for the jugular in a much more subtle way than Bombelles would have liked.

"You understand that I can't allow you to stay at Chapultepec, Colonel."

"My presence didn't trouble you before, Your Majesty."

They looked at each other. Maximilian knew the colonel well enough to know he wasn't an easy man to get the better of.

"You will comply with my orders. Whether you like it or not."

"My soldiers are not willing to follow a man who not long ago was a tailor into battle when they should be led by a man with the Legion of Honor, lord."

"Are you referring to yourself?"

"Who else, Your Majesty?"

Maximilian had the impression that Van der Smissen was being haughtier than usual. He found it attractive.

"Then you will have to tell them it is a direct order from the emperor."

"If you want to humiliate me, you don't have to punish the entire Belgian delegation. Those men came of their own accord to take care of the empress."

"As you have taken care of her?"

There was silence. Had he not been the emperor, Van der Smissen would have challenged him to a duel right there.

"I've taken better care of her than you, Your Majesty."

"No doubt, Colonel. That's what they've told me."

There was another silence.

Maximilian looked at the man in front of him, scrutinizing him. How curious that Carlota, of all possible men, fell into his arms.

"As a sign of my generosity," the emperor suddenly said, "you will leave in the company of the French general Felix Douay for San Luis Potosí, and then you will cross the desert to Monterrey."

Van der Smissen turned pale.

"Cross the desert?"

Maximilian nodded.

"Many won't survive such a journey," said the colonel.

"Why not, if they will have a man with the Legion of Honor leading them?" Maximilian said with a sarcastic smile.

Van der Smissen said nothing. If crossing the desert was the price to pay for having loved the empress, he would pay happily. He left with his dignity intact.

Not far away, the rest of Carlota's Belgians received the news. Philippe felt as if he were being pushed into another cold cave. This time, he couldn't escape: the whole Belgian regiment had to leave. The Juaristas were gaining ground. In the northeast, the imperialists were confined to Monterrey, Matamoros, Parras, and Saltillo. General Mariano Escobedo was planning incursions into Monterrey from Nuevo Laredo, and reinforcements were needed.

But Philippe wanted to make love, not war. He'd avoided the massacre at Tacámbaro, in which the majority of the Belgians had encountered death. Where was Albert, his traveling companion? Where were the rest of the volunteers who headed to the battlefield filled with excitement? Perhaps their remains now rested in the cemetery known as the Panteón Francés de la Piedad in the south of the city. Philippe had enrolled to protect the empress; he would die for her if necessary, but not leagues away from her. His romantic idea of protecting her involved hand-to-hand combat. Or taking a bullet for her. Being able to look at her before dying. Instead, it seemed his path was going in a different direction, away from her and from Constanza. Because, of all the ghosts that swirled around him, Constanza was the only one of flesh and bone. At least, he thought, she would give him a reason to return.

The news of their imminent parting made Constanza's heart stop. How could she endure Chapultepec without him? The castle would bear down on her with the empire's suffocating weight. She realized then that, since she'd arrived there as a servant of the empress, her driving force had always been him. Afternoons learning French, secret conversations, the anguish of not being able to tell him that she was an informant for the Juaristas, knowing Carlota through his eyes, the sex. Could she learn to be alone again? Sometimes she chided herself for allowing herself to love him. Everything would be much easier if she didn't now have a love to miss. She wanted to feel as she had before, when she didn't know him. She wanted to feel innocent again, to return to the refuge of her mother's lap, retreat to the pleasure of prohibited books. But it was impossible. How could she drink this glass of sour milk? She would have to go back to being with herself. She berated herself for being so weak, for allowing herself to be seduced by forbidden fruit, for allowing the serpent to enter her. But all her self-recrimination was in vain. What was done was done. Constanza, for the first time since she arrived at the palace, cried inconsolably.

Carlota pretended to learn the news from Alfred himself, when in reality she'd been expecting the moment from the first day she loved him. She was unaccustomed to happiness lasting long. In fact, she was unaccustomed to happiness at all. Crowns were always made of thorns.

"The emperor's sending us to the northwest, Charlotte," he said to her, gritting his teeth.

"For how long?"

"Indefinitely."

She fixed her eyes on his, reading him like a book.

"Maximilian knows, doesn't he."

Alfred nodded.

The shame. Her honor felt stained. Here it was: the horror she had feared for so long. It was not the sin that diminished her, but the penitence.

"Will we see each other again?"

"It's unlikely, Charlotte."

Carlota held her hands to her chest, trying to shield herself from the pain inflicted by an invisible sword.

She gathered all her strength in order to recover the dignity and pride that she'd once had. That she'd always had. She forced herself to think. Alfred recognized a look in her eyes that opened up an abyss between them so wide that no amount of pleading, no expression of regret, would enable him to cross it. Carlota knew that duty came before pain. What was more, too many limits had already been crossed.

"Then we say goodbye here, Alfred."

Van der Smissen felt as if the world were narrow and his agony immense.

"Charlotte, I . . ."

"You don't need to say anything, Alfred."

He wanted to remain stoic, but he took a step forward to be closer to her. She could feel his breath and contained the urge to throw her arms around him. In Chalco she was a woman; at Chapultepec, an empress. She couldn't allow herself the luxury of confusing the two. He knew it, too. He took her hands and kissed them with all the tenderness he could muster. They remained like this until they believed they'd found the courage to say goodbye forever.

Van der Smissen loved her in silence for the rest of his days. He never admitted it to anyone, though they slandered him for it, and when drinking with the soldiers on a few occasions they tried to wheedle it out of him. For him, Carlota was sacred, and he never allowed the memory of their time together to be sullied by telling someone about it. That would be like sharing her. He respected her to the point of adoration. And for the time he had left to live, he thought that being in her service had been the most bitter privilege of his existence.

Many years later, back in Belgium, he devoted himself for a long time to writing his memoirs. *Memories of Mexico*, he called them. Everyone believed he did so to leave a record of an era, an important time of his life. But in truth, it was his way to return to her. To be with her again. Mexico and Carlota, Carlota and Mexico: they were the same thing. He didn't allow himself to betray her by mentioning what they had. It wasn't necessary. Carlota was on every page. He wrote for as long as he could, for with each word he felt closer to her, until one day he had no option but to bring the memoirs to an end. That was when he felt the horror of her absence bear down upon his solitude. He woke and, once again, she wasn't there, and every day for the next three years he lost her over again. But this time with the certainty of a forever that was too painful, for there were no more words with which to remember her.

Tired, dejected, and alone at the age of seventy-two he took his lieutenant general's pistol, drank a glass of cognac, closed his eyes, thought of his Charlotte, and shot himself in the temple.

59

In the eyes of the world, Carlota lost her mind suddenly. But God knows she'd gone mad as slowly as a turtle making its way to the sea as gulls circled above threateningly. By all appearances she maintained the finery of her rank. They dressed her, did her hair, and tended to her with great care. She no longer suffered the mistreatment to which Bombelles had subjected her during her stay at Miramare, which she barely remembered now. However, while she had no lack of care, her letters revealed the anguish she experienced being trapped in the body of a madwoman, in a castle with no way out, a woman in a man's world. A world that resembled a mousehole. *If I had been a man,* she wrote in her letters over and over again, yearning for another sex, another life, a body that was allowed to be in harmony with her mind. *If I had been a man, Querétaro would have been avoided,* Madame Moreau read with horror and also a little tenderness.

But of all the letters, the ones that most disturbed her lady-in-waiting were those she wrote frantically to a certain Philippe. In them, danger always reigned. Everyone wanted to kill her, to make her sick. Poison her. And her only way out was to escape. She devised escape plans with extreme care and impeccable handwriting, gave precise instructions and other details that amused everyone except Madame

Moreau, to whom they seemed so full of sadness and desperation that when she read the letters in secret she always ended up in tears. They all mentioned names from the Mexican adventure that Madame Moreau had never heard before. But she was struck by the lucidity with which Carlota recalled events in the midst of the ravings of her disturbed mind.

With nothing better to talk about, the forty or so court servants found it extremely entertaining to try to stitch together the loose threads of the empress's madness. Between them all—chambermaids, gardeners, coach house cleaners, chefs, cooks, kitchen hands, stable hands, grooms, pages, porters, guards, and footmen—they gradually built up a picture of what could have happened to make such a young woman lose her mind, and for them, the letters were the main source of information. Carlota gave them scraps every day. Her writing communicated clearly how her brother Leopold had stripped her of her inheritance: *Leopold has become the treasurer of my patrimony,* she said. *Another outrage in the long list of violations that I've suffered.*

Poor woman, they all thought, though not out of pity. It was more an amalgam of respect and helplessness, aware that they were looking at a woman whose adversaries had tried to fold her like a piece of paper, but who'd proved to be harder than a tree trunk.

Her ladies observed her with some affection when she bowed to the trees in the garden and, adopting the most exquisite protocol, struck up long conversations with them. If only her madness were always as innocent as this, Madame Moreau thought. Because when Carlota was at her worst she'd seen her violate the rules of decorum, making the hair of anyone witnessing these breakdowns stand on end. When it happened, the empress cursed with a vocabulary so crude it made everyone around her want to cross themselves. But the worst came at night. At night, she could be heard moaning as if the devil had taken possession of her, entering through her vagina and emerging through her mouth. By the time the horror-stricken Madame Moreau arrived to help her, she would find Carlota naked on the bed touching herself while she streamed tears, in the clutches of a memory, perhaps. A terrible spectacle.

Madame Moreau tried to soothe her by holding her hands away from her thighs, and then, once she was calm, covering her with the sheets and holding her. There they remained, until she sensed her modesty returning. *If I had been a man,* she repeated, as she did in her letters. And later, in her own room, her lady-in-waiting prayed, saying a rosary forward and backward for the salvation of Carlota's tormented soul.

The torment grew worse in the letters. Each time she saw Carlota writing, the lady-in-waiting prayed to ease the sinful load that the writing no doubt carried. Indeed, after reading them, one had to wash one's eyes with holy water. Carlota asked the person named Philippe to come and pull down her drawers and beat her.

> *Come here, straight to my bedroom, without touching,*
> *with a rod, a whip, and a stick; hit me all over my body*
> *until my thighs bleed, from behind, from the front, on my*
> *arms, on my legs, on my shoulders. I will undress myself;*
> *I will endure everything as if it were nothing. Only cow-*
> *ards die from these things, and I am not that.*

Madame Moreau, a little excited despite her horror, held her hands to her mouth as she kept reading.

> *Of course, then you shall undress and I will do to your*
> *body what you did to mine.*

"Mary, Mother of God!" said Madame Moreau, and fanned her flushed cheeks with the letter.

Marie Henriette came to visit her each week, and sometimes Carlota seemed so lucid that it frightened her. She still remembered the episode at Miramare, where the empress was kept for so long, and she asked the heavens to make sure she wasn't making the same mistake.

They spoke of Maximilian's death, of his body's greenish color from being embalmed twice and poorly each time.

"Those Mexicans are savages," said Marie Henriette. "They didn't even have a coffin of his size ready."

"The Mexicans," Carlota replied with restraint, "did what they could."

Carlota, in clear demonstration of her sanity, had commemorative tokens of the emperor's death printed, showing Maximilian wrapped in a Mexican flag on a sinking boat.

Marie Henriette sometimes doubted the severity of her sister-in-law's condition and thought she was close to a recovery. But she was also tormented by the idea that they were treating Carlota as if she were deranged, when she was just sad and disappointed. So she was grateful when she showed signs of dementia, because then she forgave herself and the doubt in her faded, and then she felt as cruel as Leopold.

But Madame Moreau had no doubts. She knew from the letters that Carlota had lost her mind, despite the periods of peace that manifested themselves from time to time. Her impure thoughts about the soldier Philippe continued, and Madame Moreau imagined him as a wonder of a man. What had he had with Carlota so that she wrote to him in such a sinful way? The gossip had always mentioned the Belgian colonel, Van der Smissen, and some had even said he was the father of an alleged child, yet the letters weren't addressed to him, but to some unknown soldier. There was no doubt, Moreau thought, that he was not so unknown to Carlota. She imagined the empress being whipped by this lover and she broke into a sweat. Reading the lascivious letters awakened parts of her body that had been dormant for years. But Carlota was the madwoman, not her. She just read the frenzied writing of a disturbed mind and then confessed. There was no madness in that, she told herself. She did it to help her. To know how to calm her when she was struck by fits of insanity in the darkness of night.

> *I flog myself all over, as if I were a horse, harder on my bare thighs. This gives me the most extreme pleasure, a gratification I've never felt before. My thighs swell red, blood and life rising.*

The lady wondered whether she should hand the letters over to the priest. Perhaps, she thought, she would show them to Pierre, the handsome thick-bearded cook, to help decide how to proceed. Yes, that's what she would do. She continued reading just to make sure it didn't mention a suicide attempt, as the letters sometimes did. The temperature in the room was rising by the minute.

> *I whip myself in the very middle of my backside; I give myself a generous spanking, and the pleasure is so great that I forget that it is me doing it. On one occasion, I thought it was you, Philippe, flogging me. And so it begins: I am overcome with a furious need to be whipped. I take off my drawers and put them in a wardrobe. I lie on the sofa with my backside, the round part, in the air. I hold the whip in my right hand and flog myself in such a way that it hurts and blisters me.*

Madame Moreau stopped reading. Was there a worse hell on earth than that of wanting to inflict pain on oneself? And yet, why did the image of Carlota groaning with pain give her a tingling in her crotch? The devil was using the empress to torment her. She had to stop, but she couldn't. Curiosity compelled her to keep reading.

> *It would be more gratifying if we whipped each other.*

Madame Moreau stuffed the letter down her corset and ran to the kitchen. Hopefully, she thought, Monsieur Pierre would be alone.

The years passed as quickly as the periods of sanity: they grew ever shorter. The mental breakdowns reoccurred with increasing frequency. So much so that there came a point when it frightened Madame Moreau more when she appeared sane. One way or another, out of sheer habit, she'd learned to handle her madness. Besides, Carlota wasn't a violent madwoman. She allowed herself to be read to, she played the piano. And she always had an aristocratic aura that could soften the hardest of temperaments.

But just when everyone had settled into a routine, Tervuren burst into flames.

The fire started without warning, without revealing its source. The inferno took the form of tongues of fire that consumed the castle at a fierce speed. Some said it had started in the pressing room on the first floor, but confusion reigned. The flames devoured everything in their way. A lady took the empress out into the garden, where everyone, some with more courage than others, watched powerlessly as a vengeful fire swallowed every object and living being in its path.

"This is serious," said Carlota, "but beautiful."

Those who heard looked at her with horror, fearing she had started the fire for the simple pleasure of watching it.

"You couldn't have . . . ," sobbed Marie Henriette.

"No, no. It is forbidden," Carlota replied.

They looked back at the flames, which, according to Carlota, were dancing.

"But now," she said with a smile, "at long last, we shall go to another castle."

Though nobody dared say it, everyone was filled with reasonable suspicion. Everyone made the same assumption about who had caused the tragedy. The castle was reduced to black ash as volatile as Carlota's mind, which never found its way back.

She didn't smile when they moved her to a medieval fortress surrounded by a moat. Bouchout Castle would be her new residence, her entire universe, the place she wouldn't ever leave in the forty-eight years she had left to live.

60

When Modesto arrived at the Casa Borda garden with a group of Juárez's soldiers to kidnap the emperor's lover and kill her and her five-month-old son, Concepción was no longer there. She'd run home, to her mother, when she discovered she was pregnant. Her youth didn't stop her from understanding that she couldn't bring up a fair-haired child under Ignacio's guardianship. He'd put up with her infidelities because they weren't with just anyone; they were with the owner of the house, and for as long as he could remember, Ignacio had known about the *droit de seigneur*. As if that weren't enough, the owner was also the emperor of Mexico. But the outlook was ever gloomier. Things were being said. There were whispers. The empire had foundations of clay. The money was running out, and there was nothing to pay the troops with. The French were visibly withdrawing. And Concepción, frightened, decided it was time to return to the fold and recover her true identity. She would take up her real name again, the one she'd renounced so many times, the one she'd tried to forget. It was inevitable. It was the only way she could disappear and become invisible to everybody, whether Juaristas or Conservatives. She had to disappear, in part because of common sense, and in part because, before leaving, Maximilian had asked her to do so.

"If they arrest me or execute me, the child's life will be in danger," he told her.

Concepción hugged herself, scared to death.

"I have some friends, the Bringas family, in Jalapilla, who'll take care of the child. You must get the baby to Sr. Karl Schaffer, the husband of the family's eldest daughter. He'll know what to do."

"You're going to take my child away?"

"It's not your child; it's the legitimate heir to the empire. You must understand: if it remains with you, it will be killed."

Concepción didn't understand the full implications of these words. For her, the empire had never been bigger than the garden; still, she obeyed. Following orders without complaint had become part of her temperament. Her mother welcomed her with open arms and remained with her throughout the pregnancy. A long, mysterious pregnancy full of foreboding, because Concepción suspected that the baby would never be allowed to live in peace. And she was right. He wasn't yet six months old when a tall, bearded Austrian appeared to take him to Paris.

On Mexico's big day, the Day of Our Lady of Guadalupe, Maximilian set off for the capital. There, a court of distinguished men awaited to try to persuade him to abdicate or to remain on the throne, such was their indecision and confusion. Terror floated in the corridors. The sound of a plate being dropped in the kitchen made people jump, and they wandered the palace with looks of distress. All of their thoughts were sad. And an urgency to leave the country began to spread like a virulent disease. Finding themselves in water up to their necks, some decided to make their move before the emperor did, like rats abandoning a sinking ship. The staunch monarchists passed through the Murrieta house; having predicted that the vessel was going under, they packed their belongings in a chest and set sail for Europe. They tried to hide their feeling of being uprooted, and masked their farewells behind a veneer of good humor.

"You know Mexico's best city is Veracruz?" one compatriot said to another.

"Veracruz?"

"Yes, because it's where you leave from!"

They said goodbye to one another with warm embraces and set off on their self-imposed exile; it was that or the gallows. And many of them, without the courage to face the latter, chose the former.

Juárez had returned from the United States and was advancing, reconquering land like the Catholic monarchs on their way to Granada. The idea of abdicating tormented Maximilian. He missed having his adviser and loyal friend by his side, but Bombelles had gone with Carlota to Europe to intercede with Napoleon III and the Holy Father. He felt alone. Everyone had abandoned or betrayed him. Only Carlota remained steadfast. *Poor Charlotte,* he repeated to himself. He'd been unfair with her. The letter she'd written before leaving for Europe still resounded in his ears. He envied the woman's strength of mind. Perhaps that was what he yearned for when he married her: to be infected with the confidence and fortitude he so badly needed. Before leaving, Carlota had written to him:

> *To abdicate is to condemn yourself. Granting oneself a certificate of incapacity is unthinkable except in the elderly or the weak of mind. It is certainly not the act of a thirty-four-year-old prince, full of life and with his future ahead of him. Sovereignty is the most sacred property in the world; a throne is not abandoned as if fleeing a gathering dispersed by the police.*

The letter went on for several pages with passionate eloquence. Maximilian knew Carlota was trying to persuade his weak mind. Strength. How he envied her.

He would have to write to her and ask her what she thought. He would also write to his mother. His beloved empire had butterfly wings. He'd tried to put down roots in arid soil. Another chimera to add to the list. He waited, staying at the residence of a Swiss immigrant, where he spent the days playing cricket with friends. And at night, though the cold seeped in through the hacienda's uncovered windows, he looked at his abandoned castle on Chapultepec Hill.

The French withdrew from Chihuahua, while in France, Napoleon III gave a speech to the National Assembly declaring his final decision to abandon the Mexican adventure. The blame, he said, lay with, among others, Marshal Bazaine, who at over seventy years old had fallen in love with a Mexican woman thirty years younger, and since then led his men from the comfort of a desk while his new wife pampered him.

Just as, a couple of years before, he'd granted them an audience to decide whether to become emperor, Maximilian decided to submit the decision on whether to abdicate to his notables. Of thirty-five, only seven, including Marshal Bazaine, voted in favor of abdication. Despite the differences they may have had, the marshal didn't want to see Maximilian dead, something which—he was certain—would happen if he was left without an army. The empire, as he had said on so many occasions, was sustained at bayonet point.

In his desperation, Maximilian told the marshal, "You must declare a state of emergency in the whole country."

Bazaine opened his eyes wide, shocked by Maximilian's foolishness. He explained that not only was his suggestion unviable, but it was also madness.

"I do not believe it advisable, as we withdraw, to subject the French army to the irreparable rigors of a state of emergency."

Much to his regret, Maximilian knew he was right.

The Austrians and Belgians were also beginning to leave the country. Van der Smissen had led his men's withdrawal. Even so, there was still a glimmer of hope for Maximilian. God willing, he thought,

Carlota's endeavors in Europe would have the positive result he hoped for. Where others had failed, she would succeed, he told himself. All his optimism was dragged down a fierce river when he received a telegram from the empress. *Todo es inútil.* It's all useless. Three words that sent him to the gallows. But her news wasn't the worst. Other telegrams arrived later from Bombelles. They informed him that the empress had lost her mind. Frightened, Maximilian headed slowly with the imperial army toward Orizaba, the city he loved and where—it should also be said—he was welcomed. From there, he sent a letter to Marshal Bazaine. Swallowing a knot in his throat, with stomach cramps that could have been from nerves or from the diarrhea that never left him in peace, he wrote a few lines that wounded his pride more than anything in the world. On the verge of tears, he wrote:

> *Tomorrow I intend to place in your hands the necessary documents to bring to an end the violent situation in which I find myself, and not just me but also Mexico.*

He had to go back. Back to Carlota or to what remained of her. Go back with his tail between his legs, but go back. Deep down, he suspected his return would be welcomed, for some Austrians had told him that, after Franz Joseph's terrible defeat in the Battle of Königgrätz, there was widespread discontent. It wasn't just Mexico that was calling for an abdication. The Austrian people, disheartened, were also calling for his brother's. Throughout the Austro-Hungarian Empire, cries of *Long live Maximilian!* could be heard, and Venice, where he had been branded a good-for-nothing, was now requesting the return of its governor. Reading this, Maximilian's wounded pride was soothed.

Franz Joseph complained bitterly to their mother, Princess Sophie.

"If Maximilian tries to come back to Austria, I'll bar him from entering, Mother. And I'll remind him: we have a family pact; there's nothing for him to return to."

"Your brother won't dare return, Franz."

"But Mother, Napoleon III has him in a stranglehold, and my informants tell me he's in Orizaba preparing for his return. That Maximilian, he's a fool and a coward."

"Ridiculous!" exclaimed the princess. "Don't talk about your brother like that. Maximilian would sooner bury himself under Mexico City's walls than allow himself to be degraded by French politics."

And when the conversation with her firstborn was over, she went to her office, dipped a pen in ink, and with the same words, and other more grandiose ones, she communicated as much to Maximilian. Dying for the sovereignty of a nation was a worthy death for any Habsburg.

Just a few weeks after deciding to leave, Maximilian changed his mind. From Orizaba, he started sending letters to dissolve regiments so that soldiers could be repatriated, or if they preferred, undergo voluntary absorption into the national army that he would command. His only experience of combat had been at sea, but that wouldn't deter him. His mother and Carlota were right. Without the French, he would finally be free. He would command his own army, without Bazaine, without Van der Smissen, without France. He was the Austrian Pulque, and the time had come to show them what he was. If he had to die in Mexico, it would be with the dignity and pride that he'd lacked in life. He turned back and set off for Querétaro.

61

Philippe didn't return to Belgium. Like the emperor, he changed his mind at the last minute. He didn't know exactly why he was turning back. News reached him that the empress had returned to Europe, and the Republican army's chant could be heard all over the country, a folk song that alluded to the belly that the empress was taking away from Mexico. *Goodbye, Carlota, and goodbye to your bump, the people rejoice to see you so plump*, they sang, making fun of her. At last, someone had done the empress a favor, they said. There were few things the rank and file liked more than kicking someone when they were already down. Philippe lowered his head like Saint Peter denying Christ three times. He tried to keep as low a profile as his foreignness allowed. When they crossed the desert to Monterrey, he'd almost died of thirst. Each soldier had just two liters of water to boil their food, drink, and wash. They passed through Agua Nueva, Saltillo, and Santa Catarina. He'd managed to master Spanish almost without accent, but his blue eyes and blond hair gave him away as soon as he left the northern cities that the Belgian delegation had reached with great difficulty. Nonetheless, being alone made traveling easier, since nobody expected to see a member of the Army of Intervention by himself, heading in the opposite direction of the sea.

Staying in monarchists' houses—recognizing them by their anxious faces—where he was given food and provisions, he gradually made his way back toward the capital. But sometimes, when luck wasn't smiling on him, he spent nights exposed to the elements. He remembered everything that Van der Smissen's troops had been forced to go through. At first, he'd looked at his superior with some disdain, for he couldn't drop the idea that the colonel had defiled something sacred. However, before long, he saw in him such great misery that he began to take pity on him. Van der Smissen had lost the will to do anything: to live, to fight. When there was an opportunity to abandon his post and embark on a ship, he didn't hesitate for a second. The tirades he'd always directed at his troops vanished like clouds in the wind. There wasn't much left of him. And Philippe began to see just another man fighting to survive in his own cave. A man who, despite his rough edges, had been wounded like him. Without ever saying a word to Van der Smissen, he forgave him. He forgave him for affronts that not even the colonel himself knew he had committed. Perhaps, Philippe thought, Van der Smissen had given the empress a little happiness, and that was enough.

He remembered the day a native boy gave the colonel a cigar; stunned, he took the gift and the child ran off. When he looked carefully, he saw that it wasn't a cigar but a rolled-up message. It contained instructions to leave Tulancingo, where they were awaiting orders. Maximilian had dissolved the Austro-Belgian troops, including Philippe's unit. The colonel contacted a Republican general to tell him they were leaving, to prevent the many bandits that surrounded them like *zopilotes* from pillaging the town; the Republicans and the French had for some time communicated to hand over garrisons.

C'est fini, Van der Smissen thought. And it was true.

Philippe didn't embark with them. One night, he grabbed his bedroll and, once again, decided to be the master of his own destiny. Mexico had been a new beginning for which he hadn't yet found an ending. He had to know. Leaving would be the most logical solution, but also the one that meant failure. He had gone in search of adventure, and to return rich, with land and a military rank. Philippe sighed. Who was he trying to fool? He'd never intended to go back. But if everyone was scattering, what was left in Mexico for him? He had to stay and find out. Whatever hell he chose, he wanted to look it in the eyes first.

He returned to Chapultepec to find it empty. There were no ladies or footmen, no chambermaids or members of the court. It looked like a ruin, not from material but from spiritual decline. Nothing of the empire remained there. So he left in search of a monarchist, someone who could tell him the whereabouts of the nobles, but they'd all sought refuge in their homes, windows closed and curtains drawn tight. And then he remembered the names Constanza had said to him, of her brothers, of her father, Sr. Murrieta, of the house they had. Where had she said it was? He tried to remember, but couldn't remember the name of the district. If only he'd paid more attention! He spent days trying to recall, before finally giving up. When he stopped trying, as if by magic, as if the universe were telling him which path to take, the name of the street, the district, the area all came back to him as if Constanza herself were whispering it in his ear. *Santa María la Ribera,* the whisper said. And Philippe clapped his hands.

After making a few inquiries here and there, he found the Murrieta residence. He arrived at Constanza's house praying—for the first time in years—for the family to still be living there. Or for anyone to be living there who could tell him their whereabouts. It wasn't unusual to see abandoned residences: the owners covered paintings and furniture with sheets, hoping the light material would be enough to protect them from bandits that pillaged the treasures of families that had left with only the clothes on their backs. His prayers must have been heard, because a serving girl answered his knock timidly; however, she was under instructions not to let anyone in or to give anything away.

"Does Constanza Murrieta live here?"

"Who's asking?"

"Philippe Petit."

"What's it about?"

339

"It's personal."

"Where have you come from?"

"I'm from the empress's personal guard," he said in a whisper.

The girl narrowed her eyes, suspicious.

"I'm sorry, I can't take your word for it."

Philippe was beginning to grow anxious. As he began insisting, the girl threatened to slam the door in his face.

And just when Philippe was about to beg, he heard a voice very like Constanza's ask, "Who is it, Petra?"

Philippe's heart stopped.

"A young man's asking for Señorita Constanza, señorita."

Philippe stretched his neck.

The woman tried to see him through a small crack in the door, because Philippe had had the nerve to stick his foot in the doorjamb.

"Let him in."

"But, Señorita Clotilde . . ."

"I'll take care of this, Petra. Thank you."

The girl opened the door, and the pressure eased on Philippe's foot.

The girl suddenly changed her attitude and smiled.

"Come in, señor."

He went in. But he was no longer paying any attention to her. His focus was on the woman who'd allowed him in. Tall, thin, wearing a dress that covered her from the ankles to the lace-edged neck without fully disguising her figure underneath, hair gathered in a bun that allowed a pair of locks to escape to one side of her ears. She didn't look like Constanza, yet Philippe knew immediately that she was her sister, the fragile, sickly girl that she'd sometimes mentioned. In her hand, Clotilde held a handkerchief that she used to cover her mouth when she coughed.

"Are you looking for Constanza?"

"That's right, if you could tell me where I could find her, I'd be extremely grateful."

340

"She's not here," she said plainly. She could see the disappointment in his eyes.

"Oh!" he replied. Then he said, "Allow me to introduce myself, I'm—"

"I know who you are," she interrupted, looking from side to side to be sure nobody had seen him. And to Philippe's surprise, Clotilde approached, took him by the arm, and said to him, "You're not safe in this house. Please, follow me."

Philippe obeyed, astonished. The woman, despite her slight build, guided him firmly toward a little study; they stepped into the semidarkness of the room and she closed the door.

"I know who you are, Philippe. Constanza told me everything."

"She did?"

Philippe feared that Constanza's brothers also knew about their relationship and that was the reason for the secrecy. Just when he was about to ask, Clotilde spoke.

"My sister and I don't talk much, but we communicate a little."

"I see."

"I've heard terrible things, Philippe, things I haven't wanted to tell anybody."

"Señorita, if I've offended your sister in any way . . ."

Clotilde raised her hand and Philippe could have sworn she let out a *shh*.

"What the two of you did or have stopped doing is none of my business."

Philippe was baffled. *What a strange woman,* he thought.

And then Clotilde said something that left him stunned.

"Let me give you a piece of advice: trust nobody, Philippe. Nobody."

He frowned. Clotilde persisted.

"Trust nobody." And then, moving closer to his ear she added, "Especially not a Murrieta."

"I'm afraid I don't understand."

"The Murrietas are not what they seem, señor. If they discover you're here asking for Constanza, they'll put you on the blacklist."

"Who will?" he asked, perplexed.

"The Republicans, monsieur."

"But you're Conservatives here . . ."

"That's what they'd have you believe, but they're not. Everyone has two faces."

Philippe turned pale.

"What do you mean, 'everyone'? Constanza's the empress's lady, and her brothers . . ."

As he said this, he noticed Clotilde roll her eyes.

"Don't you understand? Trust nobody. Go back to Belgium before it's too late. And, please, don't make me say more. I've already said too much."

"Please, I beg you, explain."

They were speaking in low voices, almost in whispers, and Clotilde kept looking at the door nervously.

"Salvador and Constanza are informants for Juárez," she said point-blank. "They think I don't know, but I hear things."

"That's impossible."

"Believe me. I know."

"It can't be," Philippe repeated.

"Yes, it can."

Constanza, a traitor? It couldn't be true. It had to be some kind of misunderstanding. He knew her. He'd sat with her for a couple of hours every afternoon for the last two years; they'd traveled to Yucatán together, lived in the palace together, slept together. No. It couldn't be true. There had to be an explanation. Constanza had told him about Clotilde, a sickly girl with a somewhat simple intellect. Her poisoned testimony wasn't reliable. But suddenly, the image of Constanza meeting people he never saw again, the walks with her brother in the garden with her head bowed, the silences, the anguished looks . . . suddenly it all fit together so perfectly that Philippe felt like the stupidest man on earth.

"Go, Philippe," said Clotilde, interrupting his thoughts. "They mustn't know you've been here."

"But I need to speak to her. Please, I beg you, tell me where she is."

"If I see her, I'll tell her you're looking for her. But she doesn't come here often."

"I'll come back every day at this time until I speak to her."

"Don't punish yourself, Philippe. Constanza doesn't want to see anyone. Like I said, she rarely comes, she grabs a couple of things and leaves again. We don't know where she is or who she's with. My mother's devastated and my father . . . never mind my father. If he sees her here, he might kill her for refusing to accompany the empress on her journey to Europe."

"I'll be back," said Philippe.

He left the house more bewildered than when he'd arrived. And more convinced than ever that he wouldn't leave until he knew the truth.

62

Constanza didn't accompany Carlota to Europe because, when she discovered what half the empire suspected, she didn't have the courage to finish the job that had been given to her. How could she continue to poison her when she was expecting a child? She couldn't. She wouldn't. She would have needed colder blood and a lesser conscience to do that.

She heard it straight from Juana, the young girl responsible for collecting the empress's chamber pot and who was instructed to report on the imperial menstruation each month.

"Are you sure?"

"Completely."

Her blood froze. From that moment, a coldness entered Constanza's body that made her age at once. She wrapped a shawl around her shoulders and felt the urge to warm her hands with her own breath. She trembled. She cursed the moment when she'd stoked the fire of Carlota's affair with Van der Smissen. A pregnancy wasn't something she had even considered. Somehow, she'd believed the stories about the empress being infertile, because even if she never slept with the emperor, she assumed that there was no smoke without fire. It was too late for regret. Perhaps the baby wouldn't survive, Constanza thought. And each time this idea crossed her mind, she prayed that it would be so. As far as she was concerned, this was a thousand times better than the baby being born disabled by her actions.

She avoided Carlota like the plague. She was terrified. She was afraid to look her in the eyes, and Carlota, like a dog sensing fear, smelled her, searched for her, pursued her. Constanza couldn't escape or evade her. She had to face her demons.

It was Carlota who confirmed what she already knew.

"Your herbs worked, but not in the way I'd hoped."

Constanza felt her heart race.

"I'm pregnant, Constanza."

"Congratulations, Majesty . . ."

"Don't congratulate me, for the love of God. You know this child has come at the worst possible time. It's a bastard."

"But Majesty, no one has to know. Dynasties are full of bastards."

Saying this, Maximilian's rumored illegitimacy slid across the room like a cloud's shadow. Though it was never discussed, there had been murmurs about Sophie of Bavaria's closeness to L'Aiglon—the Eaglet—as Napoleon Bonaparte's legitimate son was known. And in fact, Carlota always suspected that Franz Joseph's distrust of his brother came from the possibility of Maximilian claiming the French throne one day.

But Carlota shook her head, and in a low voice to scare away the devils that tempted her she said, "Nonsense." And then she repeated, "No one must know."

"Of course, Majesty; I'm incapable of sullying your honor."

"I'm not referring to the identity of the child's father, Constanza. I mean no one must know I'm expecting."

"But, Your Majesty, with all due respect, and seeing as there is confidence between us, allow me to tell you that there are already rumors."

Constanza was rambling. Carlota looked at her with complete seriousness.

"Rumors?"

"Yes, Majesty," she said, lowering her head. "People suspect."

"I see."

There was silence.

"Well, not a word must come from our mouths. Let them talk. They can whisper all they want. We won't give them the pleasure of confirming the rumors. Above all, we must safeguard the future of the empire. That's our only concern. We'll leave for Europe in a few days to speak to Napoleon III."

Constanza opened her eyes wide.

"But it's the rainy season, Majesty. It's imprudent to travel in these conditions. The roads are dangerous, they're rivers of mud . . ."

"I know. It will be the greatest sacrifice I make for my new homeland."

"But it's the worst time for yellow fever, Majesty. You'll have to go through the infected area. And in your condition!"

"Duty makes this sacrifice necessary, Constanza. That is precisely why I must leave now. I don't want anyone to notice my condition. It would make me weak in the eyes of men. Men are like that; when they see a pregnant woman, they see a sick woman. I have no time to lose."

"But going does not guarantee that the troops will remain, Majesty. Ambassadors have had audiences with Napoleon and failed to make him change his mind."

"Precisely. He needs to speak to an empress. Where others failed, I shall succeed. There is nobody on the face of this earth who can say no to me."

"And will the emperor go, too?"

"He's the head of the empire; he must remain here." And then, reasserting herself with pride, she added, "But I am the neck of this empire, and I will turn it in the direction I choose!"

Constanza looked up, struck by Carlota's spirit. She could see fire in her eyes. Ambition. Power. And suddenly, her attitude changed completely. The light vanished, as if the force of the argument had sucked out all of her energy.

"I feel weak . . . ," she said.

Constanza brought her a chair.

"Sit down, Majesty."

"No, it's not that; it's as if I suddenly feel I'm going to lose my mind." Carlota fixed her eyes on Constanza. "I'm afraid," she said.

Constanza tried to act natural, but couldn't. She took her by the hands, squeezed them hard, and said, "Majesty, I'm sorry. I'm so sorry."

"What is it, Constanza? What have you to be sorry for?"

"For everything. I didn't want to hurt you, my lady."

"With the herbs? We didn't know that not even the herbs would arouse the emperor's passion for me, Constanza. That's not your fault."

Constanza felt the world bear down on her. She didn't have the courage to confess.

"Stop taking them, Majesty. Stop taking them."

"Why would I keep taking them? The deed has been done."

The deed has been done, Constanza repeated silently.

It was true. Her work was done. The empress's blood had been poisoned, but she wouldn't allow it to continue until she was dead. God have mercy on her soul.

"Get ready to leave with me, Constanza. I'll need you by my side."

"Yes, Majesty."

She didn't obey her. The next day, she decided to disappear. She told no one she was leaving. She was filled with uncertainty and doubt, but completely certain of one thing: she couldn't do anything more to betray the empress. She was tempted to tell Philippe, but she knew that mail was intercepted and feared being exposed. Leaving the court under those circumstances would spell trouble for her family and for her, so she preferred to hide. That way, if they were asked, they could say in all honesty that they knew nothing of her whereabouts.

By the time Constanza left, Carlota was beginning to lose herself in the passageways of paranoia. She believed she was being followed, that they were poisoning her. Everywhere she looked, she saw Napoleon's spies, and kidnap and assassination attempts. Horrified, she recognized her own delirium and tried to regain her composure. She began to feel that she couldn't withstand so many blows to her heart. All her loved ones were abandoning her. But Constanza's desertion broke her heart. She ordered a search of the whole castle, and when she wasn't found, fear gripped her spine. *They've murdered her and gotten rid of the body,* she thought. She begged them to find her most favored lady. She couldn't have vanished. She asked Manuelita del Barrio over and over again if she knew anything, but nobody could say. Constanza had gone to her room as she did every night, and no one had seen her come out. Only a pair of shoes were missing; everything else was hanging in her closet. An idea took hold in Carlota's mind, an idea that tormented her from that day until her last. Everyone who was dear to her had been erased and no longer existed. She would be the last to die.

More alone than ever. Like the living dead: that was how she felt. And the one thing that could have become a reason for joy became a secret she wouldn't be able to hide. She was pregnant. She was expecting a bastard. And however much she wanted to pass the child off as the emperor's, she knew that no one would believe it. She'd barely seen Maximilian in recent months.

It was better to remain silent. She didn't want to distract herself with these thoughts now. The priority was to save what remained of the empire, which was crumbling like a sandcastle.

Any movement in Chapultepec aroused suspicion of abdication. There were whispers. Conservative society lived with its heart in its mouth. Everything would change if the emperor abdicated. Everyone's fate was hanging by a thread. The Republicans were advancing, regaining territory as quickly as the Army of Intervention was retreating. And Carlota knew the emperor well enough to be aware that, under pressure, the thought of abdicating would pass through his mind every five minutes. She couldn't go to fight for the survival of the empire only for news to reach her in Europe that Maximilian had caved in. So, before leaving, she sat at her desk, took a deep breath, and knowing that what she was about to write would decide Maximilian's fate, with full use of her faculties and a great sense of duty, she drafted a letter.

One does not abdicate, the first line said.

For the next few days, Carlota broke cover. Wearing diamonds, she went on her own to a thanksgiving service at the cathedral; she did it to quell the rumors that, facing defeat, she'd sent all of her jewels back to Europe. After the ceremony, some women in her court said goodbye to her with tear-soaked faces. Though the empress hadn't announced her plan to leave, Chapultepec was abuzz with speculation. Preparations were already underway and it was just a matter of time before it was public knowledge. The empress would leave, and the emperor would probably follow her.

In early July, Carlota left with a small retinue to save the unsavable.

In Constanza's absence, Manuelita del Barrio took her place, pleased to be able to go to Europe and relieved to escape the uncertainty of Mexico.

Meanwhile, somewhere, Constanza was trying to forgive herself. What a mistake it had been to take sides without first being sure. So many preconceived ideas. She felt dirty, treacherous. Not toward the country but toward herself. She needed to atone for her guilt but didn't know how. She needed to speak to her brothers. She needed to face her mother.

When Constanza appeared at the family home with red eyes, she never imagined she would run straight into a much thinner, grubbier Philippe, who had been waiting for her hopelessly every afternoon. Seeing each other, they were unable to recognize the Constanza and Philippe from before. It had been so long, and at the same time not so long. But by then, Carlota was drinking water from every fountain in Europe.

63

Philippe didn't have to be a psychic to see that Constanza was being crushed under the weight of her conscience.

"What're you doing here?" she asked as soon as she saw him.

"Nice way to greet someone who could have been dead."

"Go away, Philippe."

"Why, Constanza? What's going on? What did you do?"

Constanza's eyes trembled like water drops.

"I can't tell you."

"Please, Constanza. Why aren't you with the empress?" He looked around; they were exposed. They had to go inside the house; they were in danger: her for being a deserter, him for being an imperialist. Nobody was safe.

"All right," she said. "Come with me."

Constanza knocked on the door and Petra peered out. Seeing her, she let out a cry.

"Mary, Mother of God! Señorita Constanza!"

And she opened the door. They went into the parlor feeling like intruders. Philippe could see that Constanza was nervous and hoping not to encounter any members of the family, at least not for now.

"Petra, don't tell anyone I'm here."

"But, señorita . . . your mother will be pleased to see you. You have them all very worried."

"Please, Petra."

The girl, incapable of going against the wishes of the children of the house, agreed.

Constanza took Philippe by the hand and led him to the library. She closed the door so that they were in semidarkness and there, in silence, she held him. And then, in a fit of maternal concern, she scolded him.

"Have you lost your mind, Philippe? What're you doing here? I heard that Van der Smissen's regiment had embarked for Belgium. If anyone sees you here . . . Why didn't you leave?"

"I didn't want to go without you."

Constanza narrowed her eyes.

"You stayed for me?"

"Did I do the right thing?" he replied with another question.

"You're mad."

For a brief moment, the complicity that they'd had took hold of their hearts again, and Constanza felt how much she had missed Philippe. She wanted to bury herself in his chest and stay there forever. She wanted to start over, to go to a place where there were no wars or imperialists or Republicans. A place where they could just be two people discovering each other, without flags or colors.

Then suddenly, the spell was broken. Philippe adopted a tone unfamiliar to her and even to himself until then.

"Clotilde told me you can't be trusted. That I shouldn't trust you. Why did she say that, Constanza?"

"I don't know what you're talking about."

"You know very well. Please, don't make me beg. I've been waiting for weeks for you. No one knows anything about you. The empress left for France without you. The Republicans are hard on our heels. Who are you hiding from? Who's looking for you?"

Constanza knew she was escaping from herself.

"Nobody's pursuing me. The Juaristas wouldn't dare lay a hand on me."

"Don't be naïve, Constanza."

"I'm not," she said.

Philippe sharpened his words, fearing the worst.

"And why would you not be a target for the Juaristas?"

"Because I . . . because I'm . . . a Murrieta."

"All the more reason!"

"Philippe, you don't know anything!"

"Expliquez-moi!"

Constanza paced in circles. All of a sudden, she looked at him with a strange expression, as if he were a horse injured in battle and she had to put him down. She was about to deal the final blow.

"Philippe, I . . ."

He had the severe expression of a Romanesque Christ.

"I . . ."

"Yes?"

"I did something bad. Very bad. To the empress."

"What did you do, Constanza?" he asked, unsure whether he wanted to know the answer.

"I . . . I . . ."

"What?" he said impatiently.

"I poisoned the empress!"

There it was; she'd said it.

Constanza blew out, letting the air out like a pricked balloon. She felt lighter. Meanwhile, a ton of truth fell on Philippe.

"No. You wouldn't be capable . . ."

"I did it. In cold blood. For months. Every night, I gave her an herb tea to poison her. In time, I no longer had to give it to her, she made it for herself. She thought it would help her win the emperor's heart."

Philippe slumped into an armchair.

"I didn't want to kill her, I swear, Philippe . . . I never let her take large quantities. Sometimes, when I saw it was too much, I watered it down. I didn't want to kill her, I swear," she repeated.

"But why?" Philippe asked in an attempt to organize his thoughts.

"I'm a spy for Juárez." Hearing herself, Constanza felt like a fake. A Judas kissing the empress before handing her over. "My father doesn't know," she then said in a childlike way, as if Philippe cared.

He looked at her with disdain.

"Who else knows?"

"A few people. I can't tell you who."

Constanza went to Philippe to grab his hand, but he shook her off. He didn't want to see her, let alone feel her. She disgusted him. He could've strangled her. How had she been able to fool everyone? How could he have been drawn to her? And what about the empress? Thank the heavens, the poison hadn't worked.

"What herb was it?"

"A poisonous one. You don't know it."

"I want to know its name."

Constanza hesitated.

"Tolguacha," she answered.

"What's that?"

"A plant. Similar to jimsonweed."

Philippe turned pale. Constanza's nightmare became all too real.

"Constanza, in low doses jimsonweed doesn't kill, but it makes you go mad; it causes hallucinations, it affects the mind."

"I know," she said, and she felt her voice crack in her throat.

"May God forgive you for what you've done, because I can't," he said, standing up.

"Where are you going?"

"Far away from here."

"Take me with you," she begged. "Don't leave me."

Philippe stopped at the door. Slowly, he turned around until he was facing her.

"Constanza," he said, "be grateful I'm not dragging you in front of the emperor, but that will be the only consideration I have for you. From now on, I'll hate you for as long as I live."

Constanza didn't know where the torrent of fury came from deep inside her, but she raised a hand and slapped him. The rage disappeared as soon as she saw Philippe's reddened face looking at her with contempt.

The memory of Philippe's slapped face would remain with her until she died.

And Philippe left with his soul as poisoned as his beloved empress's.

Part Four

64

One afternoon when the wind polished the sky, a new lady-in-waiting arrived at Bouchout Castle. She was younger than the empress, but her sad expression made her look older than she was. Madame Moreau interviewed her, her advanced age now requiring her to be cared for instead of being the caregiver. Julie Doyen, the chambermaid, was also glad to see reinforcements arrive to help with Carlota's care. Though she was docile, she needed to be watched over day and night. And as the empress herself said before she lost her sanity, nobody she cared about would outlive her. Carlota, like the Angel of Death, buried everyone. Madame Moreau and Julie Doyen often feared they would be next, but the years went by and, though they had aged, they still lived. They had sympathy for the girls who entered into Carlota's service, for they couldn't help but think that their lives would end in the coming years; Carlota had a terrible gift for sucking the energy from them.

But when Madame Moreau interviewed this new lady, she sensed a different aura about her. She'd interviewed enough women to be able to identify a true commitment to service when she saw it: caring for a noble required the devotion of a cloistered nun. And for some reason, Madame Moreau felt that a force greater than duty had brought this woman here.

"So, mademoiselle, you say—"

"Constance, madame."

"Yes, yes, Constance, of course. You say you knew the august Empress Carlota in Mexico?"

"That's right, madame."

"And what was your role at the palace?"

"I was a lady of the court, madame."

"And what brings you to Bouchout Castle?"

"Duty, madame."

"Are you not a long way from home to be fulfilling your duty?"

And the woman, in impeccable French with echoes of another language, said, "Well, madame, I was with the empress when she was still of sound mind, and I have never in my life encountered a more brilliant spirit or a braver woman. I want to accompany her in her illness as I accompanied her in health."

"I see."

And then she added, "I fear I didn't do everything I could at that time. I hope to be able to remedy this and find some peace. The empress suffered a great deal, you know." The woman seemed to remember something that caused her anxiety. "May I ask you a favor?"

Madame Moreau raised an eyebrow.

"Oh?"

"Please don't mention to the empress that we once knew each other. I don't want to upset her."

Moreau's sleuth's nose put her on guard.

"I hope," she said, "that you're able to atone for your guilt, Mademoiselle Constance."

The lady pressed her lips together.

And then Madame Moreau declared, "You can start tomorrow."

Constance was the Belgian identity she gave herself without the need for a baptismal font; behind her, buried in some part of Mexico, she left Constanza.

The next morning, she arrived at Bouchout Castle wondering whether Carlota would recognize her. She didn't know whether she would have the strength to look her in the eyes, whether she could hold her gaze. Madame Moreau led her to see the empress.

"Majesty, may I introduce your new lady-in-waiting, Mademoiselle Constance."

An owl could not have opened its eyes wider. Constanza trembled. Had it not been for Madame Moreau's presence, she would have gone down on her knees to beg for forgiveness that instant.

The empress seemed to have a sudden breakdown. She started destroying everything she could lay hands on: books, prints, drawings, paintings. She broke everything except the pictures of Maximilian, as if in some kind of trance. It was her own quixotic burning of the novels of chivalry. Madame Moreau moved to restrain her by the arms and shouted to Constanza for help.

Constanza approached, and looking her directly in the eyes, she said, "Your Majesty, of all the empresses I know, you're the only one who does this."

With Madame Moreau looking on in astonishment, Carlota was instantly calmer.

They looked at each other. Constanza spoke to her without needing to say a word.

After a few seconds of silence that brought with it the sound of a calm sea, she said, "Don't be afraid."

"Who are you?"

"Constance, Majesty."

Waves broke on the coast. The tide was going out.

"Don't be afraid, Majesty," she repeated. "I'm going to take care of you until my final breath, you hear?"

Carlota nodded. And then, to the surprise of Madame Moreau—who was ready to die and rest now—Carlota embraced Constance, breaking down in tears on her shoulder.

As if life were giving them a second chance, they became insepa-rable again. Constanza wasn't sure whether she'd recognized her, though she thought not. Nor was she sure whether Carlota would know that she'd been the cause of her insanity. After that violent outburst, she showed no more signs of distress. Madame Moreau didn't link the fit of rage to Constanza, for similar outbreaks had happened in front of other people.

Constanza washed the empress, changed her morning outfits for indoor dresses fit for a princess, and did her hair, though it saddened her enormously to see that Carlota no longer had her long black locks because, for hygiene, they'd been cut short. Constanza dressed her in colored hats to match her dresses, and went to great pains to lace her shoes with the same fabrics. Though Carlota had never been particularly concerned about how she looked, she was sensitive to compliments made to her about her appearance. She liked to sit with Constanza at the piano and play *à quatre mains*, and sometimes, when the rain fell in the gardens, they stayed inside playing cards.

Always during the first few days of the month, Constanza took her to the jetty on the castle's moat, took off her shoes, and said, "Let's dip our feet in the water, Majesty."

With this childish game, Carlota was able to keep count, perhaps not of the years, but of the days. They rode together in a carriage along the park's paths while Constanza read to her. Sometimes, she thought the empress had fallen asleep as she read, because for chapters she didn't speak at all, but she soon discovered that she simply liked silence. Then, facing the sun, she allowed the rays to wash over her face with her eyes closed. Constanza was intrigued and dismayed, watching her have lengthy conversations with imaginary people in many different lan-guages. She spoke easily in French, Spanish, English, German, and Italian, and Constanza remembered the woman she'd once known with fondness. But, if she paid attention, she could tell that the conversations were disjointed, meaningless, interrupted by laughs that would make the devil himself shudder.

Mexico always featured. Sometimes it was in a more veiled way than others, but it always came out like snails after rain. In the middle of playing a song on the piano, Carlota would begin to play the opening bars of the national anthem, "Mexicanos, al grito de guerra." Constanza felt her stomach wrench. On other occasions, she asked Constanza to bring her tortillas. And when they strolled among the trees in spring, and the triumphant flowers opened their petals after the winter, Carlota held her hands to her chest, marveled at the plants' resurrection, and exclaimed, "And Maximilian isn't here to see this!"

Constanza knew that, in the passageways of her memory, Mexico was present, clinging to the cortex: a green, white, and red rust of ambiguous and confused recollections.

Her blood froze again one afternoon when, for no apparent reason, Carlota said to her, "I was happy in Mexico."

Constanza stopped her embroidery with the needle in the air. It wasn't just a random sentence. It wasn't a vague memory of her experience. It was as if the empress knew that Constanza knew, too. And it was true. Despite it all, in Mexico, Carlota had been happy.

Caring for her in the last years of her life was the penitence Constanza imposed upon herself. Taking care of her until the end. Watching over her. Loving her as if she were a sick mother, accompanying her in her madness as a silent witness to her misery, was the way she found to apologize for burying her alive.

65

1866, Mexico

When Philippe left the Murrieta house never to return, whatever dignity Constanza had left went with him. He knew her secret. Perhaps he would keep it, perhaps not. But she'd just committed the worst indiscretion an informant—a spy—could commit. Who was she trying to fool? She had been neither. She was a minion. Everyone had manipulated her at will, at their convenience. She left the library in search of Petra, finding her in the kitchen preparing nopales.

"Petra, will you tell my mother I'm home?"

The girl immediately dropped her machete-sized knife to go in search of Doña Refugio.

A few minutes later, she arrived to greet her daughter with astonishment.

"Constanza!" she cried, and she ran to hug her.

Constanza watched her mother come down the stairs with her usual expression, but something was different, because Constanza didn't run to embrace her. She wasn't sure whether the change was in her mother or herself. As a child, she'd thought of her mother as all-powerful, all-forgiving, the place she could go after rolling in the mud with the pigs. Why couldn't she feel that now? Suddenly, she understood. Her mother would always be a mirror, the model to copy as she grew older. And at that moment, she felt an enormous sense of loss: she no longer wanted to be like Refugio de Murrieta.

"My dear child, are you all right?" she asked without waiting for a response. "Come, come, let's go to my room."

Alone, she spoke with great seriousness.

"Tell me, Constanza, what happened? Is the emperor going to abdicate?"

"I don't know, Mother. I haven't been at Chapultepec for some time."

"Where have you been living?"

"With Modesto. He hid me in his house."

"Modesto and you . . . ?"

"No, Mamá. Though he hopes, I suppose."

"But why did you go? You should be with the empress."

"I couldn't do it anymore, Mamá. I feel dirty. A murderer. Look at what I've become!"

"Murderers run people through with swords."

"You think? What is Salvador, then? And Joaquín? No, Mamá, no. You condemned us. You used us at your convenience."

"No. That's not what I did. I gave you the chance to do something for your country."

"And what country is that, Mother? Look at us. Hundreds dead, thousands . . . for nothing."

"Not for nothing: for everything. In war, you kill or be killed. There're losses on both sides. You complain for no reason, Constanza."

"I didn't want this, Mother. I can't sleep at night."

"But you will, dear. You will. Juárez is regaining our sovereignty. Soon, everything will be how it should be. Mexico will be ours. Were you happy seeing us governed in a foreign language? One day, you'll look back and realize you did the right thing."

"I killed a brilliant woman, Mother! Haven't you heard the stories? She's lost her mind, and . . ."

"And what?"

"She's pregnant, Mother."

Refugio crossed herself.

"It's better if the baby isn't born. If it is, they'll kill it anyway," she said.

"I don't know who you are anymore, Mother. How could you say that?"

"You're the one I don't know. Look at you! Accept the consequences of your actions with dignity. Even Carlota knew that duty requires sacrifice."

"You can't imagine how much," Constanza said, as if to herself. And then she stood. "One day you'll regret that you condemned me, Mother."

"I didn't condemn you, dear. I taught you to be free, to make your own decisions. If you've been condemned, it's your own doing. If blaming me eases your guilt, then so be it. But don't fool yourself."

Constanza left the house in a state of bewilderment. Sadness. Desperation. She wanted to run away. Forget about everything. Sometimes, she thought killing herself was the only way out. Yes, perhaps that was what she had to do. End her life after all the senselessness. But then she reconsidered: it couldn't end like this. There had to be another solution, another way. For the first time in ages, she felt the need to pray. A void in her soul was crying out for her to connect with her spiritual side again, to read the Song of Songs again and marvel at the poetry of the sacred scriptures, to say the rosary again with her sister, to look at the great void inside her again. To return.

When Constanza left, Refugio sat on her bed in the solitude of her room, sad and pensive. She wondered what she'd done wrong. She considered whether other decisions would have been wiser. Whether another life would have been possible on this earth, whether other paths could still be chosen once the paving on this one had crumbled to rubble. Constanza, her Constanza, was suffering. The last thing she'd wanted was for her daughter to be unhappy. She had so many plans for her girl. So much life to show her. She'd pushed her toward the best version of herself. Wasn't that what she'd been doing from day one? From the moment she saw her, she'd known her child was destined for greatness. And what had she achieved? Tears and bitterness. Had she made a mistake? Doubt made the hairs on her arms stand on end. A shiver of guilt ran down her like lightning cleaving through the sky before thunder. And what if Vicente was right and it would have been better to let the girl serve in the court, fall in love with an idea, work toward a utopia? Should she have left her to find her own way? Her head was spinning. *Look what you've turned me into.* The words echoed in her conscience. Advising an intelligent woman wasn't easy. That was the cost of having judgment. Refugio knew that every sin carries its own punishment. The truth was that it hadn't been hard to persuade Constanza, and sometimes she'd wondered whether the price for using her was too high to pay. Time would begin to put things in their place, and suddenly Refugio felt afraid.

66

As Karl Marx was publishing *Das Kapital*, Alfred Nobel was setting the world alight with dynamite, his new invention, and Maximilian was falling from grace—with a shipment about to reach Veracruz of two thousand nightingales he'd ordered to release among Chapultepec's trees.

The emperor had walked into a trap. As soon as informants reported to the Juaristas that the imperial command was in Querétaro, in no time, the city was besieged by twelve thousand men led by General Mariano Escobedo, another seven thousand under General Riva Palacio, and a further two thousand belonging to General Porfirio Díaz, men who'd managed to evade the clutches of Marshal Bazaine for years and had never stopped fighting, not then and not now. In total, the Republican army now numbered sixty thousand men. And Juárez had managed to negotiate a loan from the United States of America to fund the war against the empire.

Despite the chaos, disease, and shortages of water and provisions that ravaged the people of Querétaro, the artillery fire raining down on the walls, the broken windows, the deserted streets, and the looted stores, after two months of the Juarista siege, the emperor still made time for ceremony. He decorated his men on the anniversary of the committee of Mexicans who'd traveled to Miramare four years earlier to petition him to establish the empire, and despite the hunger, thirst, and death that circled them like *zopilotes*, his men were touched that their sovereign was ready to share their fate. *No monarch has ever descended from the throne to suffer the greatest dangers and hardships alongside his soldiers,* they said to him. And Maximilian felt that, for the first time, he was doing the right thing.

Querétaro was dying of starvation. Maximilian's messengers who went out in search of provisions wound up hanging from bridges with signs saying "The Emperor's Post." It was a matter of days before the town succumbed, for even in the imperial ranks there were discordant voices calling for the act of insanity to end. Orders were contradicted. Nobody was obeyed. Weariness. Exhaustion. Betrayal.

Meanwhile, on the other side of the ocean, Carlota was held at Miramare to hide her pregnancy, to make her give birth in isolation so that her child could be taken away from her. She was in a constant state of distress. She was afraid all the time. Through some kind of magical connection with Maximilian, she felt the emperor's terror at the turn of events. Or was it her own fear?

The empire fell at Querétaro.

At four o'clock in the morning on May 15, 1867, Juárez's troops stole through the Cruz neighborhood and occupied Plaza de la Santa Cruz without firing a shot.

"My emperor," his men said to him, "there are Juarista troops in the plaza."

Surprised but with resignation, Maximilian looked at Prince Salm-Salm, a loyal German friend, and said in his language, "Salm, it's time for a bullet to make me happy."

Horrified, the prince replied, "Escape, Majesty."

"No, I will do no such thing. Habsburgs do not run away."

He dressed, and at that early hour headed with his most trusted men to Las Campanas Hill. They were on foot: they had eaten their few remaining horses out of hunger and desperation. A Juarista colonel called Gallardo—who did justice to his name, which meant *gallant*—allowed them to pass.

"Let them through," he said. "They're fellow countrymen."

Just an hour later, General Mariano Escobedo sent a telegram to the governor of Michoacán:

> *I'm pleased to inform you that the Convento de la Cruz has been occupied by our troops. The staff officer in charge there handed over the battalions who surrendered at their order.*

On the little Las Campanas Hill, imperialists gathered after arriving on foot of their own accord to join the emperor, without knowing for certain whether it was the end or whether they were mounting a resistance. The bells rang out in the churches; in time with the ringing, there were cries of *Viva la libertad!* People in their houses did not know what to think, confusion reigned, and many just prayed to God for the siege of Querétaro to end, whoever won, before they starved to death.

Maximilian turned to one of his men.

"Is it possible to break the enemy siege?"

"I don't think so, Your Majesty, but if you ask it of us, we will try. We're prepared to die."

The emperor gave a slight smile. Die. A word he was becoming accustomed to. Betrayal. Another word that he was still not wholly accustomed to. Because Miguel López, the man who had baptized his son, had opened Querétaro's gates to the Juaristas with the benevolence with which Saint Peter opens the gates of heaven. But it didn't matter. He would lie buried under Mexico's walls, betrayed or not. It was what destiny had decided.

As a cloud of dust that had been raised on the hill dispersed, horses' hooves could be heard. A Republican general reached the hilltop on horseback. He dismounted, and after a slight—a very slight—bow, imperceptible to a fool's eyes, he addressed the emperor.

"Your Majesty, you are my prisoner."

While the men looked on in disbelief, and without resistance, the emperor accompanied him until he was in the presence of Mariano Escobedo. Once there, slowly, with the subtlety of a knife grinder, he drew his sword, mustered his Austrian humility, and handed it over.

General Escobedo took it like someone receiving the keys to a city.

"This sword belongs to the nation," he said with a hint of pride.

At eight o'clock in the morning, Maximilian of Habsburg, emperor of Mexico, surrendered.

From San Luis Potosí, Benito Juárez, smiling, jubilant, and so happy he could have drunk a glass of mezcal, ordered his telegrapher to send a message to Mexico City that read:

Viva México. Querétaro has fallen to us.

Maximilian had gone from being an emperor to a prisoner of war overnight. From being called to the throne like Moctezuma and Iturbide, to being subjected to ignominy because of Napoleon III's betrayal. If his blood were spilled, the monarchs of Europe, the heirs of Charlemagne, would call the one they named *the Little* to account, and not just for Maximilian, but also for the German, Belgian, and French blood that had been spilled because of his arrogance.

Querétaro did not celebrate. Death wailed in the streets, and some didn't even dare look out from their balconies. Their spirits were as broken by the siege as the empire was. Entire families were ruined because they had members on both sides. Infants died from gastrointestinal illnesses before they learned to run on the paving stones, youngsters were pumped full of lead on the battlefield, the elderly died with horror in their eyes. There were few reasons to make merry.

With Maximilian a prisoner, two days after the fall of Querétaro, *El Diario del Imperio*, to avoid alarming the population and following its editorial line, published a coded message:

Never sing until your food is digested. The great effort that singing requires could interrupt the stomach's work and disturb your circulation.

Maximilian did not want his circulation to be disturbed, either. His digestion was another song entirely. He was very sick. If the Juaristas didn't kill him, the dysentery would. But despite it all, he was a Habsburg: a Habsburg was never abandoned to his fate. Part of his soul still believed that Eugénie de Montijo would help him. She was the reason he ended up where he was; she would be responsible for his liberation. What Maximilian didn't know, being captive, was that the only son and heir to Napoleon III's throne had just fallen critically ill. Under such circumstances, the French rulers had no time for anything other than their child's health. They barely registered Maximilian's fate on the other side of the ocean.

Maximilian hoped that the European monarchic machinery would be set in motion. Queen Victoria, Carlota's cousin, would undoubtedly be a lifeline to grab hold of. Half the world was under her rule. But since the death of her beloved Prince Albert of Saxe-Coburg-Gotha six years ago, the august queen had been under a terrible depression, and nothing would bring her out. She governed out of habit, and she couldn't be bothered to resolve political matters that, ultimately, had nothing to do with her dominions. Not even the Austrians came to his rescue. His brother Franz Joseph and his wife, Sissi, were about to be crowned to further expand their power. The Austrian Empire would now also be Hungarian. All of his brother's attention was on Hungary and the fondness the virile Hungarian count Andrássy had been professing lately for his wife. From time to time, drawn by the call of his blood ties, he took his mind away from his commitments to the citizens of Buda and Pest to inquire about the health of his sister-in-law Carlota. Rumors reached him of her delicate state of mind, as well as the complex situation his brother was facing in Querétaro, but Sissi soon persuaded him to leave them to fight for themselves. Each to their own, she would say. They had too many reasons for joy in their lives to sully themselves with bad Belgian decisions.

"They made their bed, they can lie in it," said Sissi, showing him a row of white teeth.

To clear his conscience, and because he was in a good mood as his empire grew, Franz Joseph made a decision.

"I'm going to restore all the titles, honors, and rights I withdrew from Max when I had him sign the family pact, Sissi."

"Why would you do such a thing?"

"If he's captured, Benito Juárez can't execute an Austrian archduke, a royal prince of Hungary and of Bohemia, brother of the Austro-Hungarian emperor . . ."

"I like the sound of that: Austro-Hungarian emperor . . ."

"And brother-in-law of the king of Belgium, related to the queen of England."

"But how will you inform him, since you broke diplomatic relations with Mexico?"

"I'll write a telegram to the minister in Washington and ask him to pass on the message."

"When Maximilian hears the news, he'll come running back to Austria. You know that, don't you, my dear?"

Franz Joseph seemed to think for a second and then he said, "I know."

And after sending the telegram, he washed his hands in a basin of Hungarian water and never devoted another second of his attention to the matter.

The telegram didn't arrive in time.

67

Benito Juárez had made the decision to execute Maximilian on the day the emperor embarked on the *Novara*. He couldn't allow any European, whether imperialist or colonialist, to consider trying to occupy an American country again. Even if that meant a Habsburg's blood trickling down a hill.

He gave instructions to try Maximilian before a military court, because first and foremost he was a man of the law and not some vengeful heathen who shot every enemy he crossed paths with. He was tried along with Miramón and Mejía and, though the emperor didn't attend what he considered to be a pantomime, the three of them were sentenced to death. Letters begging for clemency began to arrive in droves. Distinguished individuals sent telegrams pleading with Juárez to show the generosity of the victor toward the defeated, of the people who win and who forgive; everyone from Garibaldi to Victor Hugo sent messages. Hugo's letter caught the president's attention. He remembered the letter the Frenchman had sent from exile to the people of Puebla, praising them for defeating the Army of Intervention on May 5. He remembered smiling when he received news that people were hanging copies of the writer's letter from their front doors. *That man's a true Liberal,* he thought. The Frenchman's opposition to Napoleon III was no secret: he was his bitter critic, and the Mexican adventure had always made him grind his teeth, not so much for Mexico as for the waste it meant for France. The republic's victory would make the French defeat more humiliating, which was why, of all the letters received, it was his Juárez read with the most interest. He sat at his desk, as he liked to do when he was about to perform an important task, and putting on his half-rim spectacles, he began to read:

Hauteville House, June 20, 1867

To the President of the Mexican Republic, Benito Juárez, You have equaled John Brown. Today's America has two heroes: John Brown, and you. John Brown, thanks to whom slavery has ended; you, thanks to whom liberty lives. Mexico has been saved by a principle and by a man. The principle is the Republic, the man is you. For the rest, the fate of all monarchic assaults is to end up aborting. Any usurpation begins with Puebla and ends with Querétaro. In 1863, Europe pounced on America. Two monarchies attacked its democracy; one with a prince, another with an army; the army carried the prince. Then the world saw this spectacle: on the one hand, an army, Europe's most battle-hardened, receiving support from a fleet as powerful at sea as the army was on land, funded with all of France's wealth, with constantly renewed recruits, a well-organized army, victorious in Africa, in Crimea, in Italy, in China, valiantly dedicated to its flag, owner of large quantities of formidable horses, artillery, and ammunition. And on the other side, Juárez.

And one day, after five years of smoke, dust, and blindness, the cloud cleared, and we saw the two empires fall; no more monarch, no more army, nothing but the enormity of the usurpation in ruins, and on this rubble, a man standing, and beside this man, liberty.

You did such a thing, Juárez, and it is great. What you have yet to do is greater still. Listen, citizen and president of the Mexican Republic. You have defeated monarchies with democracy; you showed them the power of democracy. Now show them its beauty. After the ray of sun, show them the dawn. Show the Republic that grants life to the dictatorship that massacres. Show the people who reign and control themselves to the monarchies that usurp and exterminate. Show civilization to the savages. Principles to the despots.

In front of the people, serve the monarchs the humiliation of being dazzled. Finish them off with mercy. Principles are reaffirmed, first and foremost, by offering protection to our enemies. The greatness of principles is in ignoring. Men have no name before principles; men are Mankind. Principles know only themselves. In their supreme stupidity, they know only this: human life is inviolable.

Oh, venerable impartiality of truth! Law without judgment, occupied only with being law. What beauty! When we renounce taking the law into our own hands, only those who legally deserve death must face it. The scaffold must come down before the guilty.

May the violator of principles be safeguarded by a principle!

May he have this good fortune and this shame! May the violator of law be protected by law. Stripping him of his false inviolability, you shall lay bare the true kind: human inviolability. May he be left speechless when he sees that the side for which he is sacred is the side of which he is not the emperor. May this prince, who didn't know himself as a man, learn that there is a misery in him, the prince, and a majesty in him, the man. Never has such a magnificent opportunity as this presented itself. Will they dare kill Berezowski in the presence of a Maximilian who is alive and well? One wanted to kill a king; the other, a nation. Juárez, make civilization take this giant leap. Juárez, abolish the death penalty everywhere on earth. Let the world see this prodigious thing: the Republic has its murderer in its power; when the time comes to crush him, it realizes that he is man, it releases him, and says to him: "You are of the people like everyone else. Go."

That, Juárez, will be your second victory. The first, defeating the usurpation, is great; the second, pardoning the usurper, will be sublime. Yes, to those monarchs whose prisons are full; to those kings who hunt, banish, imprison; to the king of Siberia; to the kings that possess Poland, Ireland, Havana, or Crete; to the princes who judges obey; to the judges who executioners obey; to the executioners who death obeys; to the emperors who order a beheading with such ease . . . show them how an emperor's head is saved!

Above all the monarchic codes that drip with blood, open the law of light, and in the middle of the holiest page of the supreme book, may the Republic's finger be seen resting on this commandment from God: Thou shalt not kill. *These four words contain your duty. You will fulfill this duty.*

Two years ago, on December 2, 1859, I spoke on behalf of democracy, and I asked the United States for John Brown's life. I did not obtain it. Today I ask Mexico for Maximilian's life. Will I obtain it? Yes. And perhaps,

*by now, my request has already been met. Maximilian
will owe his life to Juárez. And the punishment? they will
ask. Here is the punishment: Maximilian will live by the
grace of the Republic.*
  Victor Hugo

Juárez sat back in his seat. If there was anything in the world he
liked more than being right, it was the pleasure of reading a well-written
letter. He had to admit that Victor Hugo was a man he would've liked
to sit down and converse with. The things they could tell each other!
However, while he understood the Frenchman's arguments, he couldn't
allow himself to weaken.

After a long night in which the words of the author of *Les Misérables*
ricocheted in his head, Juárez climbed out of bed. Still wearing his paja-
mas, he went to his desk, picked up his favorite pen, the one he wrote
important decrees with, and addressing the letter to Monsieur Victor
Hugo, he wrote:

It is not the man I kill, but the idea.

68

The aroma of jasmine exploded into the night air. The smile-shaped moon was shining in the sky, and the fireflies were dancing aimlessly. Refugio decided to go for a walk to distract herself, or at least to think while in motion. She walked for a few minutes, questioning herself. She needed to sound out her sons. She'd been keeping an eye on Salvador, who from time to time had brought her news both of the Liberales and of Constanza's progress. But she barely spoke to Joaquín. She missed him. They'd drifted apart almost without realizing it. She couldn't remember the last time she'd had a conversation with her son in which they shared affection. One without demands or explanations. Her Joaquín. Her eldest son. She respected him because he was incorruptible and incapable of betraying a comrade. It wasn't thanks to his parents: all they'd done was fill the mold he'd had from birth. Refugio knew that, had he gone over to the Liberal side, he would have overshadowed General Díaz himself. On occasion she'd been tempted to try to bring him into the cause, but she knew for that precisely these reasons he would refuse. If there was one thing she loved him for, it was the strength of his convictions. Where was he now? The cold night air hit her chest. A slight breeze brought the cool of the mountain snow, and Refugio wrapped herself in her shawl like a tamale. She had to go back to the house. Her brain had seized; her left temple was throbbing with anxiety. Yes. She had to go back in. And, if she could, drink a glass of cognac with Vicente to try to relax. Vicente. In the last couple of years, Vicente seemed to have aged as fast as a jacaranda's flowers fall. It was as if life had suddenly borne down on him. He was tired. That the European prince had turned out to be of a liberal persuasion had been a bitter pill to swallow. Each time he heard the rumors about the indigenous boys that the emperor adopted, or that, for want of heirs to the throne, he'd named Iturbide's grandchildren as dauphins, his heart grieved. Both of their hearts did. Vicente's for having chosen the wrong candidate, and Refugio's because of the affinity of his ideas with those of the Liberales. Not even President Juárez—with Zapotec roots in his native Oaxaca—had afforded the natives the protection that the emperor had. But her Vicente couldn't recognize such achievements. His hair had turned white, and he went from being a respectable man admired by all to spending the afternoons playing poker and drinking whiskey. He spent all of his time fulminating about every political decision made or to be made. He ranted and raved, and eventually Refugio decided to stop listening, for with each word her husband said, she felt her soul shrivel a little more. On more than one occasion, bewildered by the grandiloquent words that led nowhere, she found herself wishing she'd married a man whose mind was only concerned with how many cards to take at the blackjack table. But then her heart missed him, and she searched his eyes for the idealist that had once resided there. The ambitious man capable of fighting for an ideal when his leg had just been blown off in combat, and, for an instant, she would think she'd found him. Perhaps tonight would be one of those nights, she thought. Tomorrow, she would look for Joaquín to sound him out. Yes. That's what she would do. She wanted to know how he was. They wouldn't talk about politics or war; she just wanted to know he was all right. To hold him in her arms again. To know what he was feeling now that the empire was on the verge of collapse. To feel that a part of his being belonged to her. And realizing her selfishness, she felt a pang in her conscience stronger than Adam and Eve felt when they learned they were naked.

Ashamed of herself, she went to bed without doing any of the things she'd planned. Vicente was sound asleep, and the cognac remained unserved in the sidebar. Unlike her husband, that night, Refugio didn't sleep a wink.

She couldn't find Joaquín the next day, or the day after that. It was as if the earth had swallowed him whole. Nobody knew anything. Desperate to know his whereabouts, she finally went to Salvador. As she feared, he had devastating news.

"Mother, Joaquín was taken prisoner in Querétaro."

Refugio's color drained, and she said, "You must go rescue him."

"It's too dangerous, Mother. I could be exposed."

"We can't abandon him, Salvador. They'll execute him. Do it for your mother. I trust you. You know how to keep yourself safe."

Salvador hesitated. The country was a powder keg. Juárez's generals were advancing and capturing towns. Prisoners of war were dropping like flies, and requests for reprieve were rarely heeded, no matter how much one begged. Traitors were punished with a firm hand. And while Salvador had been adept at playing a double game, he knew he couldn't afford the luxury of blowing his cover. Neither could he abandon Joaquín. For the first time in years, he struggled with his conscience.

After much thought, he decided.

"I'll go, Mamá. But you'd better say every prayer you know."

Then he gave her a kiss on the forehead that meant goodbye. Refugio, once again, was left alone.

Perhaps she hadn't been completely mistaken, she told herself. Being a sympathizer of the Liberales and giving two of her children to the cause might yet save Joaquín. She sat in a rocking chair in the living room, and for the first time in ages she commended her soul to the Virgin Mary, the Guadalupana, the Morenita, a mother like her.

Joaquín was awaiting his sentence at the Convento de las Capuchinas. In a more isolated cell, Maximilian, suffering from severe stomach pains, was also waiting. Salvador reached Querétaro after a grueling journey from Mexico City. The list of prisoners awaiting execution included senior Mexican and European officers. Salvador, aware that his brother would in all likelihood receive the maximum sentence, tried not to fall into despair. He climbed out of the Juarista stagecoach ready to negotiate his brother's release. After a couple of hours of hard bargaining, he sealed the deal with a handshake.

Joaquín's face fell when he learned that his brother negotiated with the other side: he was stunned, ashamed. He was prepared to see others betray the imperialist cause, but not Salvador, the man who not long ago had traveled to Miramare to ask Maximilian in person to come to Mexico.

"I knew it," he said when he saw him. "I knew our father was wrong to choose you."

Salvador remained impassive.

"Take this safe-conduct," Salvador said to him. "It gives you passage out of Querétaro and onboard a ship to leave the country. It's all I can do."

"I'd sooner be killed than flee my country."

"Don't be so proud, Joaquín. Save yourself and get out of Mexico."

Joaquín examined him with predatory eyes.

"If our father knew about this, he would die."

"Well, if you don't want his death on your conscience, don't say anything."

"He'll find out eventually. And you'll kill him."

"Nobody has to die, Joaquín. Not if you do as I say."

"I swore loyalty to the empire, Salvador."

"And I to Juárez."

A thick silence fell between them. Neither wanted to say anything he'd regret. They weighed the impact of their words.

After a few seconds, Salvador insisted, "Take the safe-conduct."

"No."

They looked at each other. They both knew what the other was thinking without saying anything.

"Take it," Salvador told him, "and one day you'll be able to hold me responsible for my sins. But don't let them execute you as a traitor to your country."

"There's only one traitor here, and it's not me."

"Take the safe-conduct, Joaquín. Do it for our mother."

"Mother will understand if I die for my principles. If a European prince can die for Mexico, so can I."

"You were always a fool."

"You're wrong," he said. "I was always courageous."

Before saying goodbye forever, Salvador held him by the lapels so that they were face-to-face. There were so many things he wanted to say, and yet, he couldn't say anything. He wanted to tell Joaquín that he envied his strength of mind, his fortitude in the face of death. The sense of peace with which he took responsibility for his actions. But he just gave him the most pitiful look he'd ever given him and stuffed the safe-conduct into Joaquín's breast pocket, then slapped him twice on the heart.

Salvador left the Convento de las Capuchinas heartbroken. He'd always known that his brother was as straight as an arrow. A man who could stare death in the face unruffled. A man unafraid of dying because he'd mastered the art of living. Salvador, on the other hand, felt that he still had a lot of life to live. A life of anguish and penitence, perhaps, but he wasn't yet ready to depart.

He returned to the city hoping his brother had come to his senses. Perhaps he hadn't been able to admit his fear to Salvador, but in the solitude of his cell he would reconsider. The Austrians who capitulated were allowed to leave without reprisals, and while his brother's imperialist history did not give cause for much hope, he had the safe-conduct. It would save his life.

After Salvador left, Joaquín noticed a fellow prisoner crying bitterly over a worn photograph of a little girl.

"My daughter," he said.

He explained that he'd never met her because he enrolled in the army before his wife gave birth. He kissed the photo as he prayed, preparing himself for death.

Joaquín approached and, resting a knee on the ground, he said, "With this, you'll be able to go home."

Then he gave him a pat on the shoulder and turned away.

The man, puzzled, examined the document. He couldn't believe it: a safe-conduct signed by General Escobedo himself! He looked up to thank his benefactor but didn't find him; he'd vanished as suddenly as he'd arrived. Thanking the heavens for the miracle, he stood and walked as quickly as he could in the opposite direction.

On July 8, 1867, a few hours after Salvador reached Mexico City to reassure his mother that his brother would soon be released, Joaquín was shot in the back in Plaza de Santo Domingo.

69

Constanza tried to go as far as she could from the stench of death and betrayal. But the farther she went, the more she felt her conscience pursuing her. However much she turned it over in her mind, she knew what she had to do. The entourage of Mexicans that left with the empress for Europe never saw her again after they arrived at Miramare. They heard terrible stories about her madness. Desperate to know the truth, Constanza searched everywhere until she learned the whereabouts of Manuelita del Barrio, who'd decided to remain in those parts with her husband when they saw that the empire had been lost. Her letter in reply left Constanza speechless:

> *They didn't let us see her again. The sinister Bombelles kept her in Miramare Castle, and though we were in Trieste, very nearby, they never allowed us to visit her. There were rumors that the empress was expecting. At our wits' end, we decided to go to Spain, anguished by the disheartening news that reached us of our beautiful homeland.*

There it was. That's what had happened. Constanza knew it was true, and it was easy to imagine that they would hold the empress hostage until she gave birth to the child. To the bastard. God protect it from misfortune and wickedness.

Constanza knew deep down what she had to do. She knew it was madness. But deep inside, close to the calm that she supposed was her heart, something told her she couldn't leave Carlota at the mercy of those men. If she wanted to be able to look in the mirror again without shame, there was no alternative. Her sacrifice would be her punishment. But she was afraid. She didn't know exactly of what, but she knew that going in search of the empress would be an arduous journey, all the more after what Manuelita had told her. In Mexico, she was at home, she knew where to go, who to turn to—and who not to—when she needed help. Europe, on the other hand, was a parallel universe that was too far away. Could she survive there alone, without a husband? How would she embark on this adventure overseas, however selfless it was, without a protector? Joaquín was dead. Clotilde was intent on forgetting everything that had happened in order to carry on with life as quickly as possible. And her mother . . . her mother and father gave a silent sob that, while imperceptible, would last forever. She missed Philippe, but Philippe had gone for good, with so much rancor and venom in his words that Constanza preferred never to look him in the eyes again.

She was alone, but determined. She had to go. It might take years to achieve what she was setting out to do, but she didn't care. She set herself a goal, and she would pursue it. Constanza never imagined that, while she sought her future, she would see everyone else's lives pass her by.

Despite her delicate state of health, Clotilde married a good man who spoiled her, told her he loved her, kept her, and—despite almost killing her with each birth—gave her many children. Salvador was appointed to government roles once Juárez returned to seize the National Palace, and Agustín, Monsi, never became a bishop because he decided to leave for the sierra as a missionary.

Fifteen years after the execution on Las Campanas Hill, fifteen years after Joaquín's death, Vicente died in his bed with sadness in his eyes, and Refugio learned to miss him.

The months passed this way, day by day, until years later, armed with a suitcase and equipped to become an excellent governess owing to her mastery of languages and finesse in the use of etiquette, having cut all of her ties, Constanza sailed from Veracruz in search of forgiveness.

When she arrived in Belgium, Constanza was in her late forties. The nineteenth century was nearly coming to an end, and the twentieth century would usher in a modernity that felt eccentric with its advances in science, technology, and medicine. The Lumière brothers were projecting their first movie, planes were furrowing the skies, and the modern era was about to celebrate its first Olympic Games. But when Constanza knocked on the Bouchout Castle door, she was thinking of only one thing: at last she would settle her debt with God.

70

At Bouchout, time moved slowly. Constanza aged alongside Carlota at a snail's pace, while outside the castle walls the world evolved by leaps and bounds. Airships flew overhead, families were seduced by the deafening sound of vacuum cleaners and washing machines that lightened the domestic burden, the telegraph was being supplanted by the telephone, and early internal combustion engines were powering Ford cars. And Carlota, who would have marveled at such inventions, was still watering flowers on her rug.

Marie Henriette continued to leave her self-imposed retirement in the town of Spa to visit her once a month, and together they allowed themselves to be swallowed in Bouchout's belly. She brushed her hair, she accompanied her on her walks, and when the empress rested, she took the chance to speak with Constanza and hear about Carlota's progress. Sometimes, she could see the lady's eyes well up when she told her about the episodes of psychosis in which the empress broke things, smashed plates on the floor, and tore any papers she found to shreds.

"Curiously, the only thing she leaves intact are the pictures of the emperor; goodness knows why," Constanza said in a low voice.

"Maximilian," Marie Henriette said. "Her eternal love will always be the archduke."

Constanza gave an involuntary look of distaste.

Marie Henriette sensed that Constanza knew more than she let on, but she could also see that Carlota was at peace with her, so she never dug deeper. If there was history between them, they could keep their secret.

Carlota, though fat and gray, aged like the evergreen trees. And, one day, Marie Henriette, the sister-in-law she'd loved and hated in equal measure—though she'd all but forgotten by then—died, unable to keep up with her.

Carlota never asked about her. Perhaps the pain of knowing she was gone was just more grief to carry, though by now she'd learned to keep her lost ones present in her delirium. One of the privileges of madness.

A phonograph livened up the empress's days with the records that, filled with enthusiasm, she carefully placed under the stylus again and again. Sometimes, the sound of airplanes cleaving through the sky drowned out the music. Carlota looked up in wonder: Maximilian would have been happy to see that mankind had managed to fly like the birds. He would have been happy flying over Miramare's woods, or Chapultepec Hill. But where she saw magic, Constanza saw horror. Whenever aircraft flew overhead, everyone in the palace hid underground. They were fleeing the bombings; the Great War had broken out.

To prevent the castle from being invaded by troops, one day Constanza had a wooden plaque made, which she positioned at the entrance. The sign said:

THIS CASTLE IS THE PROPERTY OF THE BELGIAN CROWN. IT IS THE RESIDENCE OF THE EMPRESS OF MEXICO, SISTER-IN-LAW OF OUR ALLY, THE EMPEROR OF AUSTRIA-HUNGARY. GERMAN SOLDIERS MUST REFRAIN FROM INTRUDING IN THIS DWELLING.

Once the notice had been put up, Constanza crossed herself and prayed it would work. She must have prayed with true faith, because no soldiers dared disturb the empress Carlota's rest, or, for that matter, any of the other inhabitants of the castle.

Oblivious to the world's convulsions, Carlota lived. She grew fat, she went quiet, and she isolated herself. Constanza read to her, sang to her, and her skin came out in goose bumps when the empress asked her to play the Mexican anthem.

"I was married to a great sovereign," she blurted out one day, point-blank.

Constanza made a futile effort to change the subject, but it was impossible. Hearing the anthem on the piano, the empress's mind had been set in motion: a spinning top that turned and turned and wouldn't stop. Mexico took hold of her, stoking the fire of her memories. She spoke of Napoleon III, of Maximilian, of Philippe. And when that happened, Constanza's soul writhed in pain; the memory of Philippe tormented her like no other. Then it was Constanza who remembered the nights she spent with him. They could've been happy. If only they could cross oceans of time . . .

Carlota pulled Constanza from her trance.

"I miss my dragoons."

"Your what?" asked Constanza.

"My Belgian dragoons. The Empress's Dragoons."

Silence.

Constanza never interrupted when Carlota spoke in this way, for she seemed saner than ever. The empress went on.

"Where's my Alfred? I was married to him, did you know? He was a great sovereign."

Constanza corrected her. "You must mean Maximilian, Majesty." And in a barely audible voice, fearing she would wake a monster, she said, "But Alfred was your child's father."

"Yes. My Alfred. Yes. I had a little boy, did you know?"

"And where is this boy?"

"I don't know. They stole him from me."

Constanza turned pale. Carlota remembered. Somewhere in the passageways of her memory, they were all alive, latent. Constanza saw a tear trickle slowly from the empress's eye.

And then she was plunged back into a silence that Constanza couldn't pull her from.

One Wednesday at seven in the morning, Constanza rose punctually, washed, and headed to the empress's rooms to help her dress. Carlota could barely see now because of the cataracts that covered her eyes, and the left side of her body was paralyzed.

When Constanza walked in, in a faltering voice, Carlota said, "Constance, could you do me the favor of closing the door a little so I may see my archduke?"

Constanza looked at the full-body portrait that hung in front of the empress's bed: Maximilian, in his admiral's uniform—the one he'd married her in—watched over her. The door half covered it. Constanza obeyed. As she did it, Carlota smiled.

"We could've been so happy, don't you think, Constanza?"

Constanza went as white as paper. In the over thirty years she'd spent beside her, the empress had never called her by her Spanish name. And she knew then, with the clear vision of an oracle, that Carlota had always known who she was.

"Yes, Majesty," she said. "You could've been happy."

Carlota seemed to be fading. Constanza feared the worst.

"Majesty, look at me."

But Carlota couldn't open her eyes.

"Majesty, say something."

But Carlota couldn't speak.

Then the empress turned her empty eyes toward Constanza and held out her hand to be kissed.

"At last," she said, "it's all over."

And then, Carlota, empress of Mexico, was no more.

Bouchout Castle opened its doors for the first time in decades so people could say goodbye to the empress. Some went out of curiosity, to see the madwoman who'd been shut away in the castle for half a century. Others went to pay tribute to the legend that this woman from another time was. Only one of them, just one, went with a grieving heart: an elderly man of some eighty years, with an elegant demeanor despite his age, whose face didn't hide the profound sorrow that his visit brought him.

The empress's body was dressed in lace, and she held a rosary in her hands. On her right wrist she wore a bracelet of green, white, and red stones, evoking other lands. The man approached the catafalque and took off his hat as a sign of respect.

Constanza, leaning against a pillar watching the people pass, recognized the head even from behind and despite the sparse gray hair. Slowly, as if fearing she would wake a ghost, she approached him. Her voice trembled when she said his name.

"Philippe?"

He turned around.

They recognized themselves as the people they had become: two sad, old souls, contemplating each other.

"Hello, Constanza."

She smiled.

"You've aged," she said out loud, releasing a thought that had been destined for silence.

Philippe shrugged. And then, as if time had eroded their resentment, they embraced in commiseration not only for Carlota's death but for an entire life wasted.

Constanza cried silent tears that she'd been holding in her throat for too long—many years—while he, with a trembling mouth, kissed her head of gray hair. They stayed like that for a long while. They talked for the rest of the wake, watching the faces of curious visitors pass in front of the empress's body. And like when they had spent the afternoons conversing between French lessons, little by little, as if their souls had recognized that the rancor had vanished and their mutual trust survived, they talked with the ease of times past. He told her that, after Mexico, he returned to Belgium, where he married and had two sons, now men. He told her that he never stopped thinking about the unfortunate Carlota, and that he'd tried to follow the trail of the son who was taken from her.

"He lived?"

"Yes. Bombelles didn't have the heart to kill him."

"So, where is he? Who is he?"

"He's a French soldier. General Weygand is his name. The accountant who raised him denied knowing the mother's name, which is hard to believe, and works for a financier who is a friend of King Leopold."

"It can't be."

"He's a great military commander. As far as I know, he served in the war, and he's the director of the Center for Higher Military Studies. All of his studies were funded by the Belgian Crown," Philippe said, winking.

"But . . . does he know he could be Carlota's son?"

"Only rumors. He heard a French officer—a certain De Gaulle—say something."

"De Gaulle?"

"Yes. Apparently in a conversation among officers someone said the intervention in Mexico had achieved nothing for France, and De Gaulle interrupted and said, 'It gave us Weygand.'"

"But in that case, he must know where he comes from."

"Probably, but he said nothing more. Weygand himself says that his birth is the only event in his life for which he is not responsible and that he has no significant memories from his childhood."

Constanza's eyes were wide open. If Carlota had known, she thought, perhaps she wouldn't have lost her mind. Perhaps she would have had a reason to stay sane and remain anchored to the world. It was too late now.

Philippe interlaced his fingers with Constanza's, held them to his lips, and kissed the wrinkled hand of his former lover.

"Let her go, Constanza. Let's let her go," he said.

Constanza nodded in silence, because an accumulation of tears stifled her voice.

A carriage with an enormous plume bore the empress's coffin away, escorted by lancers and grenadiers. That day there was heavy snowfall, and the tracks from the wheels were covered in a white veil as they passed. They were heading to Laeken, as Carlota had requested. At least, that's how Constanza had interpreted her wishes one day when she had said *I want to go to Laeken. You go up, and up, and then you disappear behind the towers.*

Constanza, after half a life alongside her, knew what the empress was trying to say.

She wouldn't be buried beside Maximilian, as would befit her as the consort of a Habsburg, since the marriage had been annulled. Instead, her remains would rest alongside her adored father, Leopold I; her mother, whom she barely knew; her brothers, who had gone ahead of her like the rest of her contemporaries; her beloved grandmother, and dear Marie Henriette. Finally, she would be with her loved ones after a long, long life of solitude.

Six old Belgian soldiers made the colossal effort to carry the empress's coffin on their shoulders. They were survivors of the Mexican expedition.

"The Empress's Dragoons," said Philippe.

Constanza could see the pride on the face of the man in front of her. She felt enormous respect then for the empress's deranged brain;

even in her madness she'd managed to preserve a space for fond memories. In her sad mind, there had always been a place for her unrequited loves. For Mexico, a land that never belonged to her but which she loved like the greatest of lovers. Because Carlota's sin was to always love in quantities that were too great: a husband unable to love her back, a son she never knew, a country snatched from her, an absent family, a lover lost.

Constanza, coming to the end of her days, was beginning to live in peace with the implacable silence of her conscience, because at last, having lived so long in penitence, she watched the empress's coffin descend. And she understood that, at some point, even if only for a brief moment, she had received Carlota's forgiveness.

Some Notes And Acknowledgments

I'd like to thank everyone who experienced the creation of this novel alongside me. Like any historical novel, while based on real historical events whose accuracy can be corroborated in various sources, it mixes fiction and reality. There is a legend that says that the empress lost her mind because she ingested herbs to conceive that in the long term proved to be poisonous. There's also the theory that she went mad because of a nervous breakdown from which she was never able to recover. In any case, I used fiction to tell a possible truth. The myths about Maximilian's homosexuality seem to have been proven. Schertzenlechner did exist and isn't a figment of my imagination. The letters that Carlota wrote to Philippe in her madness, asking to be whipped, also existed, but they were addressed not to him but to Charles Loysel, a French commander in Marshal Bazaine's general staff who barely appears in the literature on the empire. Whether these passionate and lustful letters were meant for him—and not Van der Smissen—remains a mystery; after all, madness sometimes takes us down passageways that are inaccessible to logic. For narrative purposes, I made Philippe the recipient of these letters: I have no difficulty imagining how fantasies with unconsummated loves can feature in delusions. These messages, which appear in a book by Laurence van Ypersele, are an interesting source for scholars of Carlota and of madness, and I highly recommend reading them.

Carlota and Maximilian's supposed children survived and led the most remarkable lives, deserving of novels of their own. One was General Maxime Weygand, whose resemblance to Van der Smissen is easy to see in their photographs, and the other was José Julio Sedano y Leguizamo, a secretary of Rubén Darío—who always openly boasted that he had a Habsburg as an employee, even if he was a bastard—who years later met the same fate as his supposed father when he was executed for espionage in France. The line between fiction and reality is sometimes very thin.

Thank you to everyone who has eaten, drunk, and breathed the Second Empire with me over these years. Thanks to my sons, Alonso and Borja, for the enthusiasm they show for my work even at their young age. From time to time they checked in to see what I was writing and suggested titles for the novel. To my husband, for believing in second chances and for being able to change course when the wind changes direction. To the students of the #MiércolesDeTaller, because they experienced this novel's creation from beginning to end: Juan, Vera, Érika, Eli, and Sara. I enjoyed every workshop with them. I hope I've taught them—as the firsthand witnesses that they were to the birth of this book—that a novel's magic doesn't come out of a hat. To Verónica Llaca, for giving me the impetus to start and the enthusiasm to finish. To my Mexican friends, who will forever be in my heart, in the distance, through madness and sanity. To Willie Schavelzon and Bárbara Graham, for their patience and encouragement in this long-distance race. And, of course, Martha Zamora, historian of the Second Mexican Empire, because without her exhaustive documentation, I couldn't have discovered these characters who passed so briefly through Mexican history and whose lives were so tragic. This woman's enthusiasm—devoting her life to researching the subject—moved me, and as if that weren't enough, she welcomed me into her home when she barely knew me, to talk about Carlota until I'd run out of questions. My heartfelt thanks for your generosity.

Bibliography

I am indebted to the following books:

Del Paso, Fernando. *Noticias del Imperio*. Mexico: Fondo de Cultura Económica, 2012.

Moyano Pahissa, Ángela. *Los belgas de Carlota. La expedición belga al Imperio de Maximiliano*. Mexico: Pearson Educación, 2011.

Reinach Foussemagne, Comtesse H. de. *Charlotte de Belgique, Impératrice du Mexique*. Paris: Plon-Nourrit et Cie., 1925.

Van Ypersele, Laurence. *Una emperatriz en la noche*. Mexico: Martha Zamora, 2010.

Zamora, Martha. *Maximiliano y Carlota. Memoria presente*. Mexico: Martha Zamora, 2012.

About the Author

Photo © 2014 Blanca Charolet

Born in Barcelona, Laura Martínez-Belli has lived in Mexico, Panama, and Madrid. Her debut novel, *Por si no te vuelvo a ver*, was a bestseller in Mexico. She is also the author of *El ladrón de cálices*; *Las dos vidas de Floria*, which was translated into Italian with great success; and *La última página*, which was shortlisted for the Premio Letras Nuevas de Novela in 2013. Martínez-Belli has taught creative writing in universities and cultural institutions and has been a columnist for several print media outlets in Latin America. Currently, she runs writing workshops at the School of Writers (Escuela de Escritores) in Madrid, where she resides. *The Empress* (*Carlota*, in the Spanish original) is her first novel to be published in English.

About the Translator

Photo © Colin Crewdson

Simon Bruni translates literary works from Spanish, a language he acquired through total immersion living in Alicante, Valencia, and Santander. He studied Spanish and linguistics at Queen Mary University of London and literary translation at the University of Exeter.

Simon's many published translations include novels, short stories, video games, and nonfiction publications. He is the winner of three John Dryden awards: in 2017 and 2015 for Paul Pen's short stories "Cinnamon" and "The Porcelain Boy," and in 2011 for Francisco Pérez Gandul's novel *Cell 211*. His translations of Paul Pen's *The Light of the Fireflies* and Sofía Segovia's *The Murmur of Bees* have both become international bestsellers.